In a time of fear, the One Who I Promised will come to the raka, bearing glory in her train and justice in her hand. She will restore the god to his proper temple and his children to her right hand. She will be twice royal, wise and beloved, a living emblem of truth to her people. She will be attended by a wise one, the cunning one, the strong one, the warrior, and the crows. She will give a home to all, and the kudarung will fly in her honor.

—From the Kyprish Prophecy, written in the year 200 H.E.

Tortall Books
By Tamora Pierce

The Song of the Lioness Quartet

Alanna: The First Adventure
In the Hand of the Goddess
The Woman Who Rides Like a Man
Lioness Rampant

THE IMMORTALS QUARTET

Wild Magic
Wolf-Speaker
Emperor Mage
The Realms of the Gods

Protector of the Small

First Test
Page
Squire
Lady Knight

TRICKSTER'S CHOICE

TAMORA PIERCE

Random House New York

To Phyllis Westberg,
for knowing the best time to fire me and
for giving me the best rewrite advice
I've ever gotten:
read aloud

Copyright © 2003 by Tamora Pierce
Jacket art copyright © 2000 by Joyce Tenneson
All rights reserved under International and Pan-American Copyright Conventions.
Published in the United States by Random House Children's Books, a division of
Random House, Inc., New York, and simultaneously in Canada by Random House of
Canada Limited, Toronto.

www.randomhouse.com/teens

Library of Congress Cataloging-in-Publication Data
Pierce, Tamora.
Trickster's choice / Tamora Pierce
p. cm. — (Daughter of the Lioness)
SUMMARY: Alianne must call forth her mother's courage and her father's
wit in order to survive on the Copper Isles in a royal court rife with
political intrigue and murderous conspiracy.
ISBN 0-375-81466-3 (trade) — ISBN 0-375-91466-8 (lib. bdg.)
— ISBN 0-375-82879-6 (pbk.)
[1. Fantasy.] I. Title. II. Series: Pierce, Tamora. Daughter of the Lioness.
PZ7.P61464Tp 2003 [Fic]—dc21 2003005202

Printed in the United States of America
10 9 8 7 6
RANDOM HOUSE and colophon are registered trademarks of Random House, Inc.

Contents

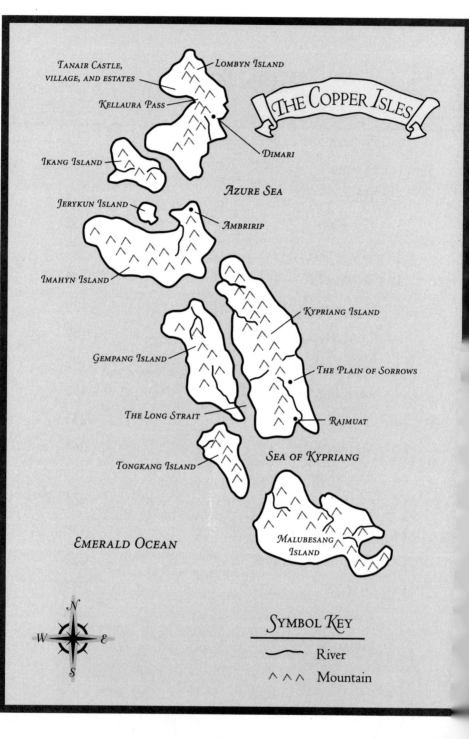

Tanair Castle, village, and estates

Lombyn Island

Kellaura Pass

Ikang Island

Dimari

The Copper Isles

Azure Sea

Jerykun Island

Ambririp

Imahyn Island

Kypriang Island

Gempang Island

The Plain of Sorrows

The Long Strait

Rajmuat

Tongkang Island

Sea of Kypriang

Emerald Ocean

Malubesang Island

N
W   E
S

Symbol Key

—— River

^ ^ ^ Mountain

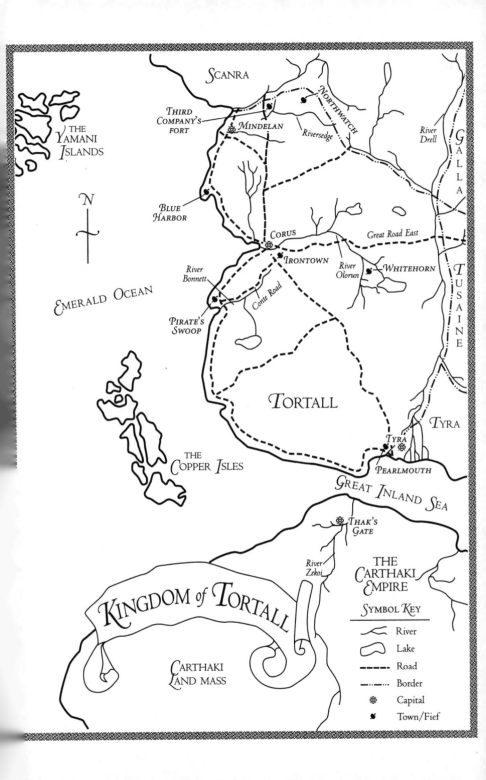

from *The Luarin Conquest:*
New Rulers in the Copper Isles
by Michabur Durse of Queenscove,
published in 312 H.E.

In the bloody decades before the year 174 of the Human Era, the Kyprish Isles were locked in strife. Rival branches of the royal house traded the throne on a number of occasions. In turn the crown had lost control over the warring houses of the *raka,* or native, nobility. Scholars said of those years that only the jungles prospered, for the trees and vines fed on the blood of the raka. During this time the Isles exported more slaves than imported them: victors sold their enemies into the Eastern and Southern Lands, only to enter slavery in their own turn when they lost the next battle.

Queen Imiary VI of the house of Haiming made repeated attempts to negotiate peace among the raka. Her efforts failed. She was overthrown after twelve years of rule. Her successor and murderer, Queen Dilsubai, also a Haiming, favored those nobles who supported her shaky claim to the throne, and imprisoned their rivals. The glorious days of the copper-skinned warrior queens of the Isles were over.

On the mainland, the pale-skinned easterners called

luarin by the Kyprish people saw the disorder, and the wealth, of the Isles. Rittevon of Lenman, younger son of a lesser noble house in Maren, found opportunity in the Isles' disorder. He raised funds and allies among the realms of Tusaine, Galla, Tortall, Maren, Sarain, and Tortall's southern neighbor Barzun.* For an army he summoned younger sons, adventurers, and mercenaries, all bought by the promise of the Isles' wealth. With them came battle mages trained in the arts of war at the university in Carthak. Rittevon and his chief ally, Ludas Jimajen, son of a Tyran merchant clan, placed their souls in pawn for the gold that bought the services of their battle mages. They bought all the raka nobles they could in advance, promising them status when Rittevon sat the throne.

The first assault came in stealth on April 5, 174 H.E. The invaders struck not the capital at Rajmuat, where rival Haiming cousins fought over the crown, but the stronghold of the noble house Malubesai, on the southern island that bears their name. This most powerful clan was taken completely by surprise. Their homes were left in ruins, their warriors in mass graves, and their descendants in chains, all at the hands of the luarin mages.

For the next seven years, luarin ships and armies ranged the islands from Malubesang to Lombyn, from Imahyn to Tongkang. Lesser raka nobles and various clans, seeing how the wind blew, offered their allegiance to the conquerors. These became the lesser nobility of the Isles, allowed to retain lands, freedom, and lives, but taxed into poverty after their strongholds were destroyed. For the greatest raka nobles and the royal house of Haiming, the luarin offered only slavery or death. On Midsummer's Day 181 H.E., the first Rittevon king was crowned as ruler of the newly renamed Copper Isles.

---

*Barzun was conquered by Tortall in the year 378 H.E., giving Jasson III of Tortall control of the eastern coastline from Scanra to the southern delta of the River Drell.

The domination of the raka people continued. The luarin nobles—once tailor's sons and blacksmiths, landless younger sons and mercenaries—took for their new houses and fiefdoms the names of the land and the old noble houses. More luarin arrived to settle and do business. Marriage among the raka was encouraged for the luarin lower classes, producing a multitude of part-raka servants and slaves. The luarin were there to stay.

Like most who lose such struggles, the raka declared that only war in the Divine Realms explained the failure of their patron god, Kyprioth, to defeat the luarin. The luarin priests taught, and the raka people believed, that Kyprioth's divine brother and sister, the war god Mithros and the Great Mother Goddess, had overthrown him. It was these gods, the priests of both races said, who took the right to govern the islands, while they gave Kyprioth lordship only over the local seas, to keep him occupied under their eyes.

Soon after the last battle of the luarin conquest, an ancient priestess gave voice not to her own prayers, but to the banished god Kyprioth. His promise was passed from raka slave to raka freeman, from raka mothers or fathers to their part-luarin children. Kyprioth told his people that the efforts of the luarin kings to erase the Haiming line had failed. One branch of the old royalty yet survived. The Queen's prophecy is his promise that, from that surviving branch, the One Who Is Promised would come. She would be the Queen with two crowns, chosen by the god to lead the Isles and those who love them to freedom once more.

1

PARENTS

March 27–April 21, 462 H.E.
Pirate's Swoop, Tortall, on the coast of the Emerald Ocean
George Cooper, Baron of Pirate's Swoop, second in command of his realm's spies, put his documents aside and surveyed his only daughter as she paused by his study door. Alianne—known as Aly to her family and friends—posed there, arms raised in a Player's dramatic flourish. It seemed that she had enjoyed her month's stay with her Corus relatives.

"Dear Father, I rejoice to return from a sojourn in our gracious capital," she proclaimed in an overly elegant voice. "I yearn to be clasped to your bosom again."

For the most part she looked like his Aly. She wore a neat green wool gown, looser than fashion required because, like her da, she carried weapons on her person. A gold chain belt supported her knife and purse. Her hazel eyes contained more green than George's own, and they were set wide under straight brown brows. Her nose was small and delicate, more like her mother's than his. She'd put a touch of color on her mouth to accent its width and full lower lip. But her hair . . .

George blinked. For some reason, his child wore an old-fashioned wimple and veil. The plain white linen covered her neck and hair completely.

He raised an eyebrow. "Do you plan to join the Players, then?" he asked mildly. "Take up dancing, or some such thing?"

Aly dropped her pretense and removed her veil, the embroidered cloth band that held it in place, and her wimple. Her hair, once revealed, was not its normal shade of reddish blond, but a deep, pure sapphire hue.

George looked at her. His mouth twitched.

"I know," she said, shamefaced. "Forest green and blue go ill together." She smoothed her gown.

George couldn't help it. He roared with laughter. Aly struggled with herself, and lost, to grin in reply.

"What, Da?" she asked. "Apart from the colors, aren't I in the very latest fashion?"

George wiped his eyes on his sleeve. After a few gasps he managed to say, "*What* have you done to yourself, girl?"

Aly touched the gleaming falls of her hair. "But Da," she said, voice and lower lip quivering in mock hurt, "it's all the style at the university!" She resumed her lofty manner. "I proclaim the shallowness of the world and of fashion. I scorn those who sway before each breeze of taste that dictates what is stylish in one's dress, or face, or hair. I scoff at the hollowness of life."

George still chuckled, shaking his head.

"Well, Da, that's what the students say." She plopped herself into a chair and stretched her legs out to show off her shoes, brown leather stamped with gold vines. "*These* look nice."

"They're lovely," he told her with a smile. "Which 'they'

is it that proclaim the hollowness of the world?"

Aly flapped a hand in dismissal. "University students. Da, it's the silliest thing. One of the student mages brewed up a hair treatment. It's supposed to make your hair shiny and easy to comb, except it has a wee side effect. And of course the students all decided that blue hair makes a grand statement." She lifted up a sapphire lock and admired it.

"So I see." George thought of his oldest son, one of those very university students. "Don't tell me our Thom's gone blue."

Now it was Aly's turn to raise a mocking eyebrow at her father. "Do you think he even notices blue-haired people are about? Since they started bringing in the magical devices from Scanra, he's done nothing but take notes for the mages who study how they're made. The only reaction I got from *him* was 'Ma better not see you like that.' I had to remind him Mother's safely in the north, waiting for the snows to melt so she can chop up more Scanrans." Aly had left a pair of saddlebags by the door. Now she fetched them and put them on a long table beside George's desk. "The latest documents from Grandda. He says to tell you no, you can't go north, you're still needed to watch the coast. Raiding season will begin soon."

"He read my mind," George said crossly. "That cursed war's going into its second year, your mother's in the middle of it, or will be once the fighting warms up, and I stay here, buried under paper." He indicated his heaped desktop with a wave of a big hand and glared at the saddlebags. "I've not seen her in a year, for pity's sake."

"Grandda says he's got an assistant trained for you," Aly replied. "She'll be here in a month or so. He *is* right. It's no good holding Scanra off in the north if Carthak or Tusaine or the Copper Isles try nipping up bits of the south."

"Don't teach your gran to make butter," George advised her drily. "I learned that lesson before you were born." He knew Aly was right; he even knew that what he did was necessary. He just missed his wife. They hadn't been separated for such a long stretch in their twenty-three years of marriage. "And an assistant in a month does me no good now."

Aly gave him her most charming smile. "Oh, but Da, now you've got me," she said as she gathered a wad of documents. "Grandda wanted me to take the job as it was."

"I thought he might," George murmured, watching as she leafed through the papers she held.

"I told him the same thing I did you," replied Aly, setting documents in stacks on the long table. "I love code breaking and knowing all the tittle-tattle, but I'd go half mad having to do it all the time. I asked him if I could spy instead. . . ."

"I said no," George said flatly, hiding his alarm. The thought of his only daughter living in the maze of dangers that was ordinary spy work, with torture and death to endure if she were caught, made his hair stand on end.

"So did Grandda," Aly informed him. "I *can* take care of myself."

"It's not the life we want for our only girl," George replied. "My agents are used to living crooked—you're not. And whilst I know, none better, that you can look after yourself, it's those other folk who worry me, the ones whose business it is to sniff out spies." To change the subject he asked, "What of young what's-his-name? The one you wrote was squiring you about Corus?"

Aly rolled her eyes as she sorted documents into stacks. "He bored me, Da. They all do, in time. None of them ever measures up to you, or Grandda, or Uncle Numy"—her childhood nickname for her adoptive uncle, Numair, the realm's most powerful mage—"or Uncle Raoul, or Uncle Gary." She shrugged. "It's as if all the interesting men were born in your generation." She scooped up another pile of documents from the desk. Soon she had the various reports, letters, messages, and coded coils of knotted string in four heaps: decode, important, not as important, and file. "So you can forget what's-his-name. Marriage is for noblewomen with nothing else to do."

"Marriage gives a woman plenty to do, particularly the noble ones," George said. "Keeping your lands in order, supervising the servants, using your men-at-arms to defend the place when your lord's away, working up your stock of medicines, making sure your folk are fed and clothed—it's important work, and it's hard."

"Well, that lets *that* straight out," she told him, her eyes dancing wickedly. "I've decided that my work is having fun. Somebody needs to do it."

George sighed. He knew this mood. Aly would never listen to anyone now. He would have to have a serious conversation at another time. She was sixteen, a woman grown, and she had yet to find her place in the world.

Aly rested her hip on George's desk. "Be reasonable, Da," she advised, smiling. "Just think. My da and grandda are spymasters, my mother the King's Champion. Then I've an adopted aunt who's a mage *and* half a goddess, and an adopted uncle who's a mage as powerful as she is. My godfathers are the king and his youngest advisor, my godmothers are the queen and the lady who governs her affairs. You've got Thom for your mage, Alan for your knight"—she named her oldest brother and her twin, who had entered page training three years before—"and me for fun. I'm *surrounded* by bustling folk. You need me to do the relaxing for you."

Despite her claim to studying the art of relaxation, Aly had sorted all of the documents on her father's desk. She set the important pile in front of him and carried messages to be decoded to the desk that she used when she helped George. There she set to work on reports coded in the form of assorted knots in wads of string. Her long, skilled fingers sorted out groups and positions of knots in each message web. They were maps of particular territories and areas where trouble of some kind unfolded. The complexity of the knot told Aly just how bad the problem was. The knots' colors matched the sources of the trouble: Tortallans, foreigners, or immortals—the creatures of myth and legend who lived among them, free of disease and old age. Most immortals were peaceful neighbors who didn't seek fights, since they could be killed by accident, magic, and weapons, but some were none too friendly.

George watched Aly with pride. She'd had an aptitude for codes and translations since she was small, regarding them as games she wanted to win. She had treated the arts of the lock pick, the investigator, the pickpocket, the lip reader, the tracker, and the knife wielder in the same way, stubbornly working until she knew them as well as George himself. She was just as determined a student of the languages and history of the realm's neighbors. How could someone who liked to win as much as she did lack ambition? His own ambition had driven him to become the king of the capital's thieves at the age of seventeen. Her mother's will had made her the first female knight in over one hundred years, as well as the King's Champion, who wielded the Crown's authority when neither king nor queen was present.

And yet Aly drifted, seeing this boy and that, helping her father, and arguing with her mother, who wanted her daughter to make something of her life. Aly seemed not to care a whit that girls her age were having babies, keeping shops, fighting in the war, and protecting the realm.

Perhaps I *should* let her work, George thought, then hurriedly dismissed the idea. She was his only daughter. He would never let her risk her neck alone in the field. It was bad enough that he'd taken her to some deadly meetings in earlier years, meetings where they'd had to fight their way out. If she'd asked to try the warrior life as a knight, one of the Queen's Riders, or one of the battle-ready ladies-in-waiting who served Queen Thayet, he would have found it impossible to refuse. His wife and Aly's adoptive aunts would have had many things to say to him then, and none would be a blessing. But she wanted to be a spy in the field. That he could and did refuse. He'd lost too many agents over the years. He was determined that none of them be his Aly.

He looked up, realizing that she had given him a weapon in her pursuit of fun. "What would you have done, mistress," he asked sternly, "if you *were* a spy and I needed you to go out in the field, with that head of hair acting as a beacon?"

Aly propped her chin on her hand. "It comes out in three washings, first of all," she informed him. "Second, if I was in Corus or Port Caynn, it would make no never mind. The apprentices and shopkeepers' young there pick up university fashions straightaway. Any other big city, I could just say it's the newest style in Corus. Or I'd say that they'd remember the hair and never the face under it, just like *you* taught me." George winced. Aly pressed on, "If none of that eased your flutterings, Da, I'd say that's what razors and wigs are for." She brightened. "I'll wash it out right now if you've a field assignment for me."

George got to his feet. "Never mind. Leave your poor hair alone. It's near suppertime."

When Aly stood, he came over to put an arm around her shoulders. At five feet six inches, she fitted just under her tall father's chin. George kissed the top of her very blue head. "I'm glad you're home, Aly."

She smiled up at him, all artifice and playacting set aside. "It's always good to see you, Da."

That night they ate with Maude, the Swoop's aging house-keeper and Aly's former nursemaid. Maude clucked over her hair, as Aly had known she would. She loved to make Maude cluck. Then she could remind the old woman how much she had changed from the Maude who had once disguised her young mistress Alanna as a boy and sent her off to become a lady knight. Maude always got flustered by that. Alanna was now a legend and a great lady of the realm. Maude could say it was fate that had made her open-minded back then, but she knew she was being inconsistent when she said it.

Aly liked to tease her nursemaid, not to mention every-one else. Her father knew her tricks and enjoyed catching her at them, which was fine. She knew most of his, too, because he'd taught them to her himself. She disconcerted most peo-ple, from the many boys who came calling once they'd no-ticed her mischievous eyes, ruddy gold hair, and neat figure to the hardened brigands and criminals who carried infor-mation to her father. She could even make her brothers yelp like puppies if she worked at it. Her twin, Alan, was partic-ularly vulnerable, since she knew his mind nearly as well as her own.

The only person she left alone was her mother. Lady Alanna of Pirate's Swoop and Olau, King's Champion and lady knight, known throughout the Eastern and Southern Lands as the Lioness, did not startle well. She had a temper and her own particular way of doing things. Alanna showed a sense of humor only around her husband. Aly knew her mother loved her two sons and lone daughter, but she was seldom home. She was forever being summoned to some crisis or other, leaving her children to be raised by her husband and Maude.

Not that her children required any more raising. Aly was sixteen, almost an adult and ready for adult work, as people were forever reminding her. Aly sometimes felt that everyone in her world had more exciting things to do than she did. She hadn't seen her mother, Aunt Daine, or Uncle Numair since the Scanran war began a year before. In the last month, while Aly had been in the capital, her grandparents were constantly advising the king and queen, so much so that she couldn't impose on their hospitality any longer. Her brother Thom, two years older, thought mostly of his studies. Her twin, Alan, who'd begun his page training three years late, was kept busy by the training master. She had seen him twice during her visit, and only for brief periods of time. She had felt left out, even as she had understood that for the time being, Alan belonged to his training master more than he did even to his twin sister. Rather than distract him from his training, she left him alone. Alan was like a cat: he would return to her when he was ready, and not one moment sooner.

All of the young men she had not flirted with and discarded were as busy as her brothers were. They prepared to march north when the mountain passes opened, as they would any day, or else they had left to guard the realm's other

borders. None of her family would allow Aly within cough-
ing distance of the war. So back home Aly had gone, feeling
restless and in the way. At least Da would use her for paperwork, which was *something*.

Sometimes she thought she might scream with boredom. If only Da would let her spy! As she decoded reports
and summed them up for him, she tried to work out a plan
to change his mind.

On Aly's third day home more reports arrived. One of
them was sealed in crimson, for immediate review. She deciphered it: the code was one of many she had memorized, so
she required no book to translate it. Once done, she read
what she had written and whistled.

George looked up. He sat at his desk, reading letters
from Tyra. "Somebody would tell you that's unladylike,"
he pointed out. "Not your dear old common-born Da, for
certain."

"No, not my dear old common-born Da," she replied,
smiling at him. "But this is worth whistling over. Somehow
our man Landfall's made it to Port Caynn. He's hiding out
there, with important messages for you."

George's brows snapped together. "Landfall's supposed
to be in Hamrkeng, keeping an eye on King Maggot," he
replied slowly, using the Tortallan nickname for Scanra's
King Maggur.

Aly reread the message, noting the apparently insignificant marks that marked it as coming from one of their
agents, not a forgery. "It's Landfall, Da," she said. "I taught
him this code myself, before we got him into Maggur's
capital four years back. He kept saying it was a hard day for
the realm when a little girl was teaching code."

George thought it over, rubbing his head. "Landfall.
Either he was found out and escaped in time, or . . ."

Aly finished the sentence for him. "Or what he has is so important he could only carry it himself. Maybe both. He must have come down by ship."

George got to his feet. "Well, I'd best see what it's about." Landfall was one of a handful of agents smuggled into Scanra in the years before the war. He was vital enough that he reported only to Aly's grandfather Myles or to George. "Be a good lass and handle these papers for me? I shouldn't be gone more than a day or two—I'll fetch him back here. Have Maude get one of the hidden bedchambers ready."

Aly nodded. "You'll get muddy, riding to Port Caynn now," she pointed out.

George kissed her forehead. "It'll do me good to get out in the field, even if it means getting some of the field on me. I'm that restless."

Aly waved goodbye from the castle walls as her father rode out of Pirate's Swoop, two men-at-arms at his back. The ride *would* do him good. She only wished he could go all the way to her mother's post at Frasrlund in the far north, where he clearly longed to be.

Aly returned to his office in a gloomy mood. Would she ever find someone to love as much as her parents loved each other? She would miss such a partner dreadfully if they were separated, she supposed, just as her parents did. At least she would have someone to talk to, someone clever who didn't gawp at her and ask her what she meant or, worse, be shocked by her. It wasn't much fun when the only people who could keep up with her were either related or at least ten years older than she was.

The day after her father's departure Aly heard the horn calls that signaled the arrival of a friendly ship in the cove. Normally she would have run to the castle's observation platform to see who the new arrivals were, but she was in the middle of a particularly difficult bit of translation: code entered as pinholes in a bound book. If she was not careful, she would flatten the delicate marks, ending up with gibberish instead of a message. She stayed at her task until she heard hooves in the inner courtyard. Gently she set the book aside and went into the main hall, then out through the open front door.

Whatever she had expected, the scene in the inner courtyard was not it. Hostlers gently led her mother's warhorse, Darkmoon, toward the stable. The big gelding limped, favoring his left hind leg. Aly eyed the rest of the arrivals. Ten Swoop armsmen who had gone north with her mother the year before helped the servants to unload their packhorses before taking them to the stable. The horses looked thin and salt-flecked, as if they'd been at sea. The men-at-arms looked much the same. So did Aly's mother.

Alanna of Pirate's Swoop and Barony Olau, King's Champion, watched Darkmoon as he was led away. The Lioness wore loose, salt-stained buckskin. There was salt in her copper hair, and she had lost more weight than the men. Aly knew her mother hated ships. She would have been sick throughout the voyage.

Aly trotted down the steps and kissed her mother's thin cheek. "What brings you here so unexpectedly?" asked Aly. "Is Darkmoon all right?"

Her mother looked up at her: even wearing boots, she was slightly shorter than her daughter. Fine lines framed the Lioness's famous purple eyes and her mouth, marks of long weeks in the open air, summer and winter. There were a few white strands in her mother's shoulder-length copper hair that Aly could not remember seeing before.

"He pulled a tendon," Alanna replied wearily. "Our

horse healers did their best with him, but he needs rest. His Majesty gave us a month's leave. Where's your father?"

"Off," replied Aly. It was the family's code phrase that meant her father was on spymaster's business. "He should be back soon—it was just a quick trip to Port Caynn."

Her mother nodded, understanding, and gave Aly a brief hug.

"Why didn't Aunt Daine heal Darkmoon?" Aly demanded. Daine, the Wildmage, spoke with and healed animals as easily as she took their shapes.

"Your aunt is having a baby shape-shifter within the month," replied her mother as the men carried her packs into the castle. "If she doesn't change below the waist whenever the child does, it might kick its way out of her womb." Alanna shuddered. "It wasn't even worth asking her, not to mention it made me queasy to see her go from bear to donkey to fish every now and then, while her upper half remains the same. Darkmoon will be fine with rest." She walked toward the castle steps, limping slightly.

"What happened to you?" Aly demanded, keeping pace. "You're hobbling like . . ." She'd been about to say, "You're old," but her throat closed up. That wasn't so. Forty-two was not old, or at least not *that* old.

"I took a wound to the thigh last autumn," Alanna said tersely. "It troubles me some yet."

"But you're up to your ears in healers!" Aly protested. "You're one yourself!"

Alanna scowled. "When you've been healed as much as I have, you develop a certain resistance. You know that, or you should. *What* have you done to your hair?"

Aly tossed her head. "It's the latest fashion in Corus," she informed her mother. "It's the height of sophistication."

"It's as sophisticated as a blueberry," retorted Alanna.

"Aren't you a little old for this kind of thing?"

"Why? It's fun, and it washes out. It's not like the world revolves around my hair, Mother," Aly said sharply. Why did this always happen? Home not even half a day, and her mother had already found something to criticize about her.

"Fun," Alanna said, her voice very dry. "There ought to be more to your life than fun at sixteen."

Aly rolled her eyes. "*Someone* has to enjoy themselves around here," she pointed out. "It certainly isn't you, forever riding here and there for *serious* work. You're always so grim!"

"You're *sixteen*," retorted Alanna. "When I was your age, I was two years from earning my shield. I knew what I wanted from my life, I knew the work I wanted to do—"

"Mother, please!" cried Aly. They hadn't seen each other for a year, but already they had returned to the last conversation they'd had before Alanna left. "Must you be so *obsessed*? I know all of this already. When you were my age you'd killed ten giants, armed only with a stick and a handful of pebbles. Then you went on to fly through the air on a winged steed, to return with the Dominion Jewel in your pocket and the most beautiful princess in all the world for your king to marry. I'm not you. If you were here more, you might have seen that much for yourself." She wished she hadn't made the accusation, but if anyone could make Aly lose control over her tongue, it was her mother.

Guilt pinched the girl as Alanna's shoulders slumped. "That's not what I meant," Alanna said. "That's not what I want. At least, it would have been nice, to have you do as I did, as far as getting your shield is concerned, anyway. But the whole point to doing as I did was so you could do something else, if you wanted to. It's just that you don't seem to want to do anything." She massaged one of her shoulders, watching her daughter. "Look, hair is, is hair, I suppose. If you want it blue, or green, or leopard-spotted . . . Who am I to say what's fit for a girl?"

She walked into the castle. Aly turned to see the hostlers and men-at-arms regarding her with reproach. "She's not *your* mother," she told them. "You try being the daughter of a legend. It's a great deal like work."

Aly didn't expect to see Alanna at the supper table that night, but the servants did. A second place had been laid, and Alanna was already seated when Aly entered the smaller family dining room.

"My first solid meal in days," Alanna informed her daughter as Aly took her seat. "I threw up all the way here on that cursed ship."

"It's still too wintry to ride?" asked Aly, accepting a bowl of oysters in stew from a maid.

Her mother had already begun to eat. Once she'd emptied her mouth she replied, "Not if I didn't mind getting here by the time I'm supposed to be back at Frasrlund." She ate with quick, efficient movements. "Seasick or no, the boat was faster. It's going to be a long summer. I admit, I will be the better for some time here."

"Then King Maggur means to fight on, despite losing his killing devices?" Aly inquired.

Alanna mopped out her bowl with a crust of bread. "He's still got his armies and his ship captains. If all there was to Maggur was that disgusting mage of his, we'd have beaten him like a drum last year. Could we not talk about the war? I've done nothing else for months."

Aly stifled a sigh. There were so few subjects she could safely discuss with her mother. Unless . . .

It had been over a year since their last talk. In that time she'd honestly tried to find something to do that would please her father, without success. Perhaps she had gone at it the wrong way. It had never occurred to her before to enlist her mother's help.

"You know what you were saying before, Mother?" she asked as the maid set a roasted duck between them.

Alanna carved it briskly, serving herself and Aly while Aly dished up the fried onion pickle that went with the duck. "I barely remember my own name at the moment," Alanna replied. "What did I say before?"

"That I needed to find work." Aly arranged her onions in a design on her plate. "As it happens, there is work I like, work I'm good at. And it's as important as warrior's work; I think you'd be the first to say as much."

Alanna looked up from her plate, her purple eyes glinting with suspicion. "Out with it, Aly," she ordered. "You know I have little patience for dancing around a thing. What's as important as a warrior's work?"

Aly put down her knife and folded her hands in her lap, where her mother couldn't see them. Making sure the proper casual spirit was in her voice and face, she said, "I would like to serve the realm as a field agent. With the war making a hash of things, I bet I could make my way into Scanra. We need more agents there. Or Galla, or Tusaine. We're about to lose one of our Tusaine folk—well, not lose, gods willing"—she made the star-shaped sign against evil on her chest—"but we have to pull him out of Tusaine, and we'll have to replace him—"

Alanna set down her knife so hard that it clacked as it struck her plate. "Absolutely not," she snapped. Her face was dead white. Her eyes burned as brightly as the magical ember-like stone she always wore around her neck.

Aly leaned back in her chair, startled by Alanna's vehemence. "I beg your pardon?" she asked politely, buying time until she figured out what she'd said wrong *this* time.

"No daughter of mine will be a spy." Alanna's tone made the word *spy* into a curse.

"But Da's a spy," Aly pointed out, shocked.

Her mother fingered the glowing stone at her throat and replied slowly, "Your father is a unique man, with unique talents. They are put to better use in the service of the realm than in his old way of life. I am grateful for that. He also has people of like mind, training, and background to help him in what he does. People better suited than his daughter."

"You're trying to say Da's no noble, no blueblood of Trebond," Aly said, finding the point that her mother tiptoed around. "You're trying to say spying is not a noble's work. But Grandda is a spy, too—what about him?"

"Your grandfather distills the information your agents gather. He serves as the visible spymaster so your father may work undisturbed," said Alanna. "That's different."

"You wanted me to have work that means something to me," protested Aly.

"Not *this* work, Alianne. I have to endure it when your father does it. I don't have to accept it from you." Alanna sighed and leaned back in her chair. "Spying is not fun, Aly. It's mean, nasty work. One misstep will get you killed. If you were hoping I'd talk your father around, you were mistaken."

"But that's what I want!" cried Aly, frustrated. "You're always after me to do something with my life. You tell me, make a decision, and I have! I help Da with it all the time and nobody objects!"

"Then I should have done so," Alanna said. "And I should have done it years ago. You're right—I was never around for your growing up." She pushed her chair back from the table. "While I'm here, I'll try to make up for it a little. We'll use our wits, see what we can do." Wincing, she got to her feet and walked past Aly. She stopped, hesitated, then rested a hand on Aly's shoulder. "I've been a bad mother to you, Aly. But perhaps I can help you find your way, at least." She took away her hand and walked stiffly out of the room. The maid pursued her, after giving Aly an annoyed stare, to remind Alanna that she'd barely had anything to eat.

Aly stared at the goblet beyond her plate. She knew that tone in her mother's voice, the one that had crept in as Alanna spoke of Aly "finding her way." Aly was to be her current project. Every time she was at home, Alanna seemed to require a task, something to keep her hands busy until her next summons to kill a giant, round up outlaws, fight a noble who challenged the Crown's judgment, or take part in a war. During her last stay she had gone over every inch of the Swoop's walls with masons, remortaring stones and building the walls higher by a full yard. The household had spent weeks cleaning out stone dust after she left.

Aly had no interest in being a project, liking herself as she was. Frowning, she considered her choices as she drummed her fingers lightly on the table. She could stay and have her mother talk at her until Da returned. Then she could sit about decoding reports by herself, feeling underfoot and alone, until her parents remembered there were other people in the world. It had happened before. The prospect was not enticing.

Her parents needed time to themselves. As it was, George would probably have to visit the spy Landfall, especially if the man was tucked away in a secret room for safety. It also occurred to Aly that she might not like the result when Da learned she had tried to enlist her mother's help. It was very hard to make Da angry, but that might just do it.

They deserve time alone, together, Aly told herself virtuously. I will give it to them.

She got up from the table and went to her father's office. If she applied herself, she could finish the rest of the correspondence that evening and leave her father with nothing to distract him when he returned. In the morning, she would sail her boat, the *Cub,* down the coast to Port Legann. She would even leave a note so that her parents wouldn't worry. She often sailed alone, and winter in the south had been fairly mild. The sea might be a little rough, but she could handle it. If the weather turned bad, she would take shelter with the dozens of families she knew along the coast. And it was early enough in the year that pirates wouldn't have started their raids yet.

She would sail to Port Legann, visit Lord Imrah and his tiny, vivid wife, and give her parents the time alone that they deserved. She would also avoid being turned into her mother's project. Alanna's energy was a fearsome thing. A few days before her mother left for the north, Aly would return to bid her farewell. If a tiny voice whispered at the back of her brain that she was running away, Aly ignored it. Her plan really was for everyone's good.

She finished the decoding and paperwork, leaving her summaries in a neat stack on her father's desk. That night she packed a small trunk. As the sun first drew a silver line along the horizon, she carried it down to the *Cub.* By the time the sun was clear of coastal hills, Aly was plowing through the waves, shivering a little in her coat. She imagined the result when her mother found her note on the dining room table. If her mother's past reactions were any indication, she would curse the air blue that Aly had dodged her plans. Then Da would return, Aly's parents would bill and coo like turtledoves for three weeks, and by the time Aly returned from Port Legann, both of them would be in a better frame of mind, ready to welcome their only girl-child. Aly liked it. This was a *good* plan.

For two days she enjoyed her sail and the solitude. Shortly after dawn on her third day out she rounded Griffin Point and found she had miscalculated. A clutch of pirate ships, their captains not aware that the raiding season had yet to begin, had destroyed the town that lined Griffin Cove. Aly tried to turn the *Cub*, but the wind was against her. They surrounded her before she could get her ship out of the cove.

By midmorning a mage was stitching a leather slave collar around her neck. It would tighten mercilessly if she tried to escape beyond the range of the mage who held its magical key. The captain of the ship that had sunk her beloved *Cub* watched as the mage finished the collar. "I want her head shaved," he snapped. "Nobody's going to buy a blue-haired slave."

Three weeks later, Rajmuat on the island of Kypriang, capital of the Copper Isles
Aly huddled in the corner of the slave pen farthest from the door, knees drawn up to her chest, arms wrapped around her knees, forehead on her arms. She was barefoot. Her hair was now only the finest red-gold stubble. She was dressed in a rough, sleeveless, undyed tunic, with a rag that served her for a loincloth. The pirates' leather collar had been exchanged for one that would keep her in the Rajmuat slave market until she'd been sold.

After three weeks, two of them on a filthy, smelly ship, her body was skinnier and striped with bruises. There was also a purple knot on the back of her head. That was a gift from one of the pirates, who had not expected her to know so many tender spots where her nails could inflict serious pain. To anyone inside or outside the pen, she looked as cowed as any slave about to be sold for the dozenth time.

Aly's brain, however, ticked steadily, working through what was likely to happen and what she could do about it. Tomorrow the slaves in her pen were to be sold. Escape from the pen was not impossible, but it would have required more time than she had, and there was the nuisance of her leather collar to consider. Her best bet was to be sold. She could then leave her new masters, acquire money and clothes, and take ship for home.

It was the selling part that most concerned her. At her age, she would be considered ripe for a career as a master's toy. This was not acceptable. She wasn't sure what she wanted to do about her virginity yet, but she did know that she wanted to give it up when *she* chose.

To that end she had eaten little until now. The other slaves had thought her mad for giving away half of the pittance they were fed, but Aly did not want to be as shapely as she had looked at home. The head shaving had been a blessing, though the pirates hadn't meant it to be. Anything that made her look odd and troublesome would help her to avoid masters who might buy her for pleasure.

Aly watched her companions over her arms. They clustered around the gate, knowing supper was on its way. When it came, she would get a last chance to make herself as undesirable as possible without actually cutting off important body parts.

The slaves stirred. Keys rattled. The gate groaned as it was pushed open from outside. The slaves shrank from the guards armed with padded batons who entered first, to hold them back. Cooks tossed a number of small bread loaves onto the floor. Next they set down pots of weak porridge. The slaves surged forward with the wooden bowls they'd been issued on their arrival.

The strongest captives kept things orderly at first. They held off the rest as they helped themselves and their friends. Only when they retreated did the others descend like starving animals to seize what remained.

Aly deliberately flung herself into the flailing mass of limbs, offering herself as a target for any elbow, fist, knee, or foot that might help to make her look ugly. She fended off the worst blows with tricks of hand-to-hand combat taught to her by her parents. The rest, accidental or weak, sharp or soft, Aly endured. Her skin would have few white patches left when she was done. The rest would be bruised, cut, and scratched, the signs of a fighter.

A white starburst of pain opened over her right eye. An elbow rammed her lower lip on her left, splitting it. She didn't see the fist that struck her nose, but through the bones in her head she heard it break.

Blood rolled down the back of her throat. Heaving, Aly struggled out of the crowd. She stumbled back to her corner, her face blood-streaked and her lip swollen to the size of a small mouse. Once she had the pen's wooden walls at her back and side, she clenched her teeth and molded the broken cartilage of her nose so that it wouldn't heal entirely crooked. The pain made her eyes water and her head spin. Still, she was pleased with herself and with the slaves who had unknowingly helped to mark her.

A while later someone's foot nudged her—it belonged to the big woman who'd been thrown into the pen two days before. Aly blinked up at her with eyes swollen nearly shut.

"That was stupid," the woman informed her as she crouched beside Aly. In one hand she offered a crust of bread soaked in thin porridge. In the other she held a bowl of water and a rag. Aly examined the bread with the magic that was her parents' legacy. It seemed unlikely that anyone would try to poison her, but checking was a reflex. She saw none of the green glow of poison in her magic, and accepted the food. As Aly maneuvered a scrap of soggy bread through her swollen lips, the woman gently wiped dry blood from her face.

"You'll have a nice fighter's scar on the brow, little girl," she remarked. She spoke Common, the language used throughout their part of the world, with a rough accent that Aly couldn't place. It was Tyran, maybe, but there something of Carthak in the way she treated her *r*'s. "And a broke nose—they'll brand you as quarrelsome," the woman continued, cleaning Aly's many cuts. "No one will buy you for a bed warmer now, unless they're the ones that like women in pain."

"For them I'll look like trouble. I'd be a dreadful bed warmer," Aly told her with an attempt at a grin. The effort made her wince. She sighed and popped another piece of bread into her mouth, although it was hard to chew and breathe at the same time.

The big woman rocked back on her heels. "You *planned* this? Be you a fool? A bed warmer gets fed, and clothed, and sleeps warm."

"With a good owner," Aly replied. "Not with a bad one. My aunt Rispah used to be a flower seller in Corus. She told all manner of tales about masters and servants. I'll wager it's worse when you're a slave with a choke collar." She fingered the leather band around her neck. "I'd as soon not find out. Better to be ugly and troublesome."

The woman got back to work on washing the blood away. "So were you always mad, or did it come on you when you was took?"

Aly smiled. "I'm told it runs in the family."

* * *

Think of this as a sort of divine present from me to you. It could almost be letters from home. I don't want you thinking that all kinds of dreadful events are taking place in your absence. I hope you appreciate it. I wouldn't do this for just anyone. The man who spoke in Aly's dream had a light, crisp, precise voice, the sort of voice of one who could annoy or entertain in equal measure. That voice didn't mumble, or speak in dream nonsense. Aly was completely and utterly convinced that it was a god who spoke to her. Now she knew why her mother had once answered a question about how she knew when a god was a god: "Trust me, Aly, you know." Aly knew.

Darkness cleared from her dream vision to show her Pirate's Swoop. It was the clearest thing she had ever seen in her sleep. She felt as if she had become a ghost who watched her mother. Alanna sat on a merlon atop the observation deck on their largest tower. Out on the Emerald Ocean, the sun was just kissing the horizon. Shadows already lay over the hills east of the Swoop.

Alanna rested a mirror on her thigh: an old, worn mirror that Aly recognized. Thom had given it to their mother when he was small, when he'd thought her the kind of mother who liked mirrors with roses painted on the back. Ever since, Alanna had used the mirror to magically see the things she wanted to find. Aly felt a hand squeeze her heart seeing her mother still using Thom's childish gift.

Alanna picked up a spyglass and trained it on the southern coast, despite the poor light of the fading day. After watching through the glass for a time, she set it down and grasped the mirror. Violet fire, the color of Alanna's magical Gift, bloomed around the glass. On the mirror's surface Aly saw only gray clouds.

Her mother cursed and raised the mirror as if to smash

it against the stone of the merlon. Then, gently, she lowered it back onto her lap and returned to the spyglass.

Footsteps. Ghost Aly turned to see her father walk right through her. He rested a big hand on the back of his wife's neck and kissed her under the ear before he asked, "Nothing yet?"

Alanna lowered the spyglass and shook her head. "I thought she'd come home in time to say goodbye," she said, shaking her head. "I have to sail tomorrow, George, I can't wait."

Aly looked down at the cove, where three ships flying the flag of the Tortallan navy lay at anchor. All were courier ships, built for speed. The king wanted his Champion in the north as soon as he could get her there.

Poor Mother, thought Aly. She'll throw up for the whole voyage. But she's going anyway, to get back to her duty. And she put up with it coming south, to give herself as much time with Da and me as she could. Now she thinks I don't care enough to see her and tell her goodbye.

"What of the mirror?" asked George.

Alanna turned vexed eyes up to him. "I'm getting nothing from the mirror, but there are a hundred reasons for something like that."

"Like you being exhausted?" George inquired gently.

Alanna rolled her eyes. "Don't start with that again, George."

"And why not, when it's true?" he demanded. "If you won't speak to the king, perhaps I should."

Tired? Aly thought, startled. Alanna the Lioness *tired?* Impossible.

She looked at her mother's face and saw lines she hadn't noticed before, at the corner of those famed purple eyes, at the corners of the Lioness's mouth. Aly remembered that her mother was almost forty-three.

"Field duty is a lot less tiring than serving as Champion during peacetime," Alanna told him. "And I won't have you saying anything to anyone." She sighed. "But it could be the reason I can't find her when I scry. I was never that good at it to begin with."

"If she's not home by the time you sail, I'll see to it she visits you in the north, to apologize for worrying you."

"I'm not *worried* worried. Aly can take care of herself. I just—bah." Alanna leaned back against her husband. "Thank all the gods the war is winding down. Will you write to me when she comes home?"

"I'll send her with the letter." George kissed the top of his wife's head. "Don't forget, Alan would have told us if there was anything to worry about. He can always tell if Aly's in trouble. Remember the time the horse threw her and she broke her head. Alan knew of it before Aly got conscious."

Alanna smiled reluctantly. "I'd forgotten that." She reached for her mirror. "Maybe I should give it one more try."

"And tire yourself more? I think not." George took the mirror from her hand and tucked it into the pocket of his breeches. "Why don't you go get ready for supper? Maude had them cook all your favorites."

"All my favorites? They'll have to roll me north, I'll be so fat." Alanna collapsed her spyglass.

"Ah, but you'll puke it all up on the trip, so eat away," George said in a falsely comforting voice.

"That's disgusting," said his wife drily. She turned and left him alone on the observation deck.

Only when she was gone did George pull a rolled scrap of paper from his pocket. When he read the message, the lines of his craggy face deepened and his broad mouth went tight. Ghost Aly read over his shoulder. It was a brief message in code from Lord Imrah of Legann: *She's not here.*

George crumpled the paper in his hand and stuffed it into his pocket just as Aly sensed her ghost self fade.

When Aly woke in the morning, she felt beaten all over—and so she had been, she remembered, by slaves fighting for supper. Her eyes were watering. She swiped at them with her hand and winced as she touched the sensitive bruising that ringed them, the legacy of her broken nose.

Had she really heard a god in her dream? Why would any god show her visions of home? She hadn't understood that comment about "letters," or the one about her absence. She wished she had tried to tell her parents that she was fine and would be home as soon as she could get away. It hadn't even occurred to her, she'd been so caught up in what her parents said. She did know that she *would* sail north as soon as she got back, to mend bridges with her mother.

Get sold, learn my way about, get free, get home, she thought, grunting as she struggled to her feet. That's simple enough. I'll make it up to her.

Please, Goddess, she prayed to her mother's patron deity, let me get sold to people I can escape from in one piece.

You asked me about slaves. They mean different things to different countries. There are slaveholders throughout the Eastern Lands, though slaveholding is an uneasy subject from Tortall to Maren, for one reason or another. Slaves are expensive, that's the thing to remember. You need vast lands to make slavery pay. They're a sign of wealth in the Copper Isles. Owning slaves there says that the master is as rich as any Carthaki lord. In Scanra, slaves are a sign of your skill in combat. It's the big farms like those in Maren, and in the Carthaki Empire, that need slaves all the time, to work their huge fields. And there's little their majesties can do about it. We buy back Tortallans taken captive if they can find them, but pirates strike and flee, selling some of their load here and some of it there. They're careful. They have to be. If they're caught, their punishment is painful and fatal.

—From a letter to Aly when she was twelve, from her father

2

TRICKSTER

May 4–6, 462 H.E.
The house of Duke Mequen Balitang, Rajmuat, Kypriang Island, the Copper Isles
Dressed in a light cotton tunic and leggings in the Balitang house colors of red trimmed with blue, Aly sat on a bench in the front foyer of the Balitang family's rambling town house. She was there to answer the door in case anyone came during the night. In a chest across the entryway was the pallet and blanket she would lay out for herself later. At the moment she was wide awake and planning.

Her hands were as busy as her mind. Deftly she used pliers and wire filched from the house blacksmith to shape a lock pick. It was part of a new set to replace those that had been taken by her pirate captors. She would be whipped if she was caught with pliers or lock picks, but she didn't intend to be caught. They were the next element in her plan to return home. With them she could open the smith's locked cupboard where he kept the special saw that would cut the metal ring off a slave's neck. The saw would break both the ring and its magic, a spell that would choke her if she attempted to leave the city.

With one ear cocked for the sound of anyone's approach, Aly reviewed her plans. Once free of the collar, she would disappear into the depths of the city. Already she was armed with a sharp knife she had stolen from the kitchen on her second day in the house. The law forbade all slaves to carry weapons, but Aly didn't care. She would always prefer the risk of getting caught with a forbidden weapon to the risk of getting caught without one at a moment when she would need it. With a knife and lock picks a girl of her talents could easily find decent clothes and a cloth to cover her stubbly head. Properly dressed, she could make her way through the marketplaces and help herself to enough coin to buy her passage on one of the many ships that sailed out of Rajmuat harbor every day. Her father had trained her well; she meant to prove it to him. Maybe when she returned he would be convinced that she could take care of herself as a field spy.

Her plan to discourage buyers who wanted a girl for their bedchambers had worked so well it was a little eerie. She had shown the market a sullen, scowling face that added to the impression made by her cuts and bruises. They marked her as a fighter, and trouble. Still, she had expected to get *some* bids. None had been offered—none at all. Even those who might like to break a troublesome slave had not blinked when they saw her. After two days of no offers, and the puzzled looks of both her fellow slaves and her sellers, Aly's owners decided to get rid of her. When Ulasim, the head footman to Balitang House, and Chenaol, the cook, purchased an expensive pastry chef, the slave sellers had thrown Aly in for free, to thank them for their custom.

To Aly's surprise, Ulasim and Chenaol kept her. It seemed they needed a slave-of-all-work, someone to obey the orders of everyone in the house. She stayed busy, but Mequen and his wife, Duchess Winnamine, believed that a well-fed slave was a harder worker. Their policy of kindness extended to clothes and even to healers. Aly could now breathe through her nose, although it would show the sign of the break all her days. The scar in her eyebrow was also hers for life.

Aly almost regretted the need to leave this interesting household. Its sheer size had not impressed her, despite the fact that the Balitangs hired or owned over a hundred servants and slaves in this great residence alone, not counting the family men-at-arms. Her adoptive aunts and uncles in the Naxen and Goldenlake households boasted as many servants, and the Tortallan palace had four times that many people to keep it in order. It was the makeup of the Balitang household and the family that intrigued Aly. If she hadn't known her parents would be worrying, she might have stayed on for a while to see what kind of people the Balitangs were. After years of lessons in the Isles' history, detailing the thorough job of conquest done by the luarin, or white, ruling class, she had expected to find all luarin in service and all the brown, or raka, folk as slaves. She had also expected that, as a luarin and a slave, she would need to prove over and over her ability to find tender spots on a raka tormentor's body before he or she decided to leave her alone.

Instead the pure-raka cook, Chenaol, had taken Aly under her wing and introduced her to a household that contained a majority of part- and full-raka servants and slaves, in addition to pure-luarin slaves like Aly, purchased as they came into the Isles' markets. As head cook, the wickedly humorous raka woman ran the kitchens with a firm brown hand and a sharp brown eye, supervising luarin, part-raka, and full-raka servants and slaves. She made it clear to all who came through her door that Aly was to be left alone.

"They gave her away, poor lass," Chenaol had told the household. "She's got enough on her plate without you lot tormenting her." It seemed Chenaol's word was law, regardless of her ancestry. Aly admired the woman. Chenaol was in her mid-fifties, a tart-tongued woman with sharp eyes. There were a few gray streaks in the coarse black hair she wore in a braid down her plump back. Her skin was the coppery brown shade of a full-blood raka, creased with light wrinkles about the eyes and mouth. Busy as she was, she still found time to show Aly the ropes in the rambling mansion.

The strangeness of this household didn't end with Chenaol. Ulasim, the brawny head footman, was also a full-blood raka. Of the Balitang's chief servants, the housekeeper, the steward, the coachman, and the healer were pure luarin and free, as was Veron, the commander of the men-at-arms. The chief hostler, the elderly Lokeij, was a full-blood raka slave who didn't seem to notice the collar around his neck, and half the hostlers who served under his eye were free and of mixed parentage. If the raka of the Isles were oppressed by their luarin masters, it was a thin, watery oppression in the Balitang household.

Already Aly had learned that the duke, the master of this house, had taken one of the raka nobility as his first wife and married her best luarin friend for his second. His choices might not have been worthy of note in another man, but Mequen was a descendant of the luarin ruling house, the Rittevons. Did this mean the luarin attitude was softening toward the enslaved raka, or did it simply mean that Mequen Balitang was far enough from the throne that no one cared whom he married? Sadly, Aly wouldn't get the chance to find out. Her parents would be fretting. She was going home, even if she had to manage all the arrangements herself.

Her escape would have been easier if she could just visit one of Da's Rajmuat spies, but Aly didn't dare. Spies were not to be trusted. Her identity was a vital secret in this new, hostile world. Tortall's enemies would pay any sum for her in order to use Aly against her family. They might even suspect that Aly knew something of her father's work. If that happened, they would squeeze her like a lemon. With those stakes, an agent might give in to the temptation to sell her for a profit. Even a faithful agent's communications to George might be intercepted. Aly had to get out of this one on her own.

There was a chance that her family might locate her first. Mother couldn't find her, if Aly's dream had been true, and the god had made her believe it was. It had been too vivid, too clear, and too convincing for her to deny it. So Mother couldn't scry her. Her father or Uncle Numair might track her down. Normally she would have expected Aunt Daine to have animals out to search, but Aunt Daine was in the process of having a child. Even the Wildmage couldn't attend to things while carrying a baby that changed shape constantly.

Still, Aly wasn't going to wait for rescue. She would free herself. If that didn't convince her father she would be a good spy, nothing would.

Sudden hammering on the house door made her jump. She hid her tools and went to see who was outside. A big white man and two men-at-arms, all soaked to the skin from the warm, pouring rain, strode into the hall. Aly greeted the first man with the deep bow of a slave to someone who was clearly a luarin noble, her palms together before her chest. His men had brown and reddish brown skins, marking them as warriors from either the lesser raka nobility or the bulk of the regular population of the Isles.

"I know it's late and doubtless they've retired for the night," the luarin nobleman said gravely, "but I'm afraid you must rouse the duke and duchess. Tell them Prince Bronau Jimajen has come with news of great import for them. *Royal news.*"

Aly took the prince's sopping cloak and went to rouse Ulasim. The likes of her didn't visit Duke Mequen and Duchess Winnamine in their personal quarters. When she gave Ulasim Bronau's message, the big raka went pale. "See the prince to the azure sitting room," he ordered as he struggled into his tunic. "Show his men to the kitchen to be looked after. Ask Chenaol for refreshments for His Highness. Hurry!"

Aly spread Bronau's cloak before the kitchen hearth to dry as she passed on her orders to Chenaol. The cook sniffed. "Remember, you have the right to refuse if he invites you to his bed, girl," she advised as she set out a tray and a bottle of wine. "His Grace will back you. He lets no one force his slaves. Not that many turn the prince down, though. When he visits the summer residences, he goes through maids like grease, a different one in his bed every night."

Aly nodded and ran to show Bronau to the sitting room. He took a chair with a sigh as Aly hurriedly lit candles, then the braziers that gave these city homes their warmth. As she worked, she reviewed what she knew of this man from the reports. Bronau was not of King Oron's immediate family, but he was the brother-in-law of Princess Imajane, the king's sole daughter. His older brother, Rubinyan, had married the princess. Everyone who knew him said that Bronau was a good man in a fight, a commander who had the respect of his men and the affection of the king and his family.

Aly glanced at him as she got the braziers going. He looked taller than he actually was, being only three inches taller than Aly. He had a warrior's build, with broad shoulders and heavily muscled thighs, fierce gray eyes, and winged brows over a nose that had been broken once. He wore his reddish brown hair in waves to his shoulders but kept his beard closely trimmed. His big hands carried an assortment of weapon scars. The main flaw in his comeliness lay in the mouth framed by his beard. His lips were thin almost to the point of invisibility.

Like most luarin nobles, he wore the fashions of the Eastern Lands, remade for a jungle city: elegant blue silk hose and a blue linen tunic over a semi-sheer shirt of white lawn. The tunic was embroidered in the raka style along the collar and hems in a silver design of coiling dragons. He was dressed for an elegant spring party. His blue leather shoes were not meant for walking or riding in the rain, and he wore jeweled rings on every finger, a gold earring with a diamond bauble in one ear, and several gold chains on his chest.

He caught Aly's eye and smiled, his face lighting with humor and tremendous charm. "I know. I'm scarcely attired for the weather."

Aly gave him a sidelong glance, that of a woman who likes what she sees. He probably saw that look all the time and surely expected it. He smirked at her.

"It's not for me to say, my lord prince," Aly murmured. The relationship between Tortall and the Isles had always been unsteady. She would get a measure of this man now so that she could add to her father's notes about him when she returned. Their people seldom got the chance to talk to one of the most powerful men in the Copper Isles.

Bronau's eyebrows came together with an almost audible snap. "Come here, girl," he said, beckoning.

Aly obeyed. There was little danger that he might try anything improper. Under slave etiquette, another man's slaves were to be left alone, unless the master or the slave involved indicated otherwise.

The prince gripped Aly's chin with his hand and inspected her face. "Not a drop of raka blood in you, is there?" he asked, curious.

"No, my lord prince," murmured Aly, keeping her eyes down.

Bronau released her. "I don't like the precedent, keeping luarin slaves. It gives the raka ideas. See here—if these raka dogs bother you, don't hesitate to tell Duke Mequen," he told Aly sternly. "He looks out for the slave women, and you can't trust the raka to behave themselves unless they know there's a whip close to hand."

"My lord prince is too kind," Aly said, bowing once again. Bronau obviously didn't know that Chenaol, who could juggle razor-sharp cleavers with ease, had discouraged most problems of that sort. "If you will excuse me, I will bring some refreshment to you," she murmured.

Bronau nodded and settled into his chair, watching the embers in the nearest brazier. Aly fetched the pitcher of wine and the tray of fruit, cakes, and cheese the cook had put together to the sitting room. As she set the tray where Bronau could reach it, then poured him a glass of wine, she made sure that nothing in her manner told him that she was interested in giving him more than food and drink. It wouldn't take more than the right look and the right smile with this man. She would be in his lap with his hand under her tunic before she could sneeze. Chenaol was right: Bronau had a flirt's air. When Aly got home, she'd suggest to Da that they try one of their female agents with him. Bronau might tell far more than was prudent to a pretty, listening ear.

Once he was served, she left him. She fetched a mop and set to work cleaning up the water the guests had tracked onto the marble floor of the hall. She was nearly finished when Ulasim raced down the steps from the family quarters. He slowed when he approached the azure sitting room, straightened his tunic, then went in to the prince. Both men emerged a moment later, to climb upstairs.

Aly watched them go. She'd give much to know what Bronau told the Balitangs. He'd said "royal business"—was that code for problems with the king? It could be. Oron was insane. Most of Rittevon House was these days. Aly's own mother had been forced to kill a Rittevon princess years before, when that lady started to kill people with an axe. The present Isles king was her uncle, a fearful and unstable man who turned on favored courtiers overnight.

Eavesdropping was not an option. If she were observed anywhere but at her post by the door, she would be questioned. Instead she finished mopping the floor. Later she would see what she could learn to take home to her da.

The next day the duke and duchess summoned the household to the hall where they held parties. It was the first time that Aly had seen any of the Balitang family but her master and mistress. Chenaol named them for Aly. The proud, brown-skinned girls, imperious sixteen-year-old Saraiyu and small, intense, twelve-year-old Dovasary, were the daughters of the duke's first marriage, to a raka noblewoman. His two full-luarin children, a four-year-old girl, Petranne, and three-year-old Elsren who was still awkward on his short, rounded legs, were by Duchess Winnamine. Other relatives who lived in the house were present, cousins who served Winnamine as ladies-in-waiting, a great-aunt, and the duke's uncle.

Duchess Winnamine sat on the dais, her elegant hands neatly clasped in her bronze velvet lap. Her brown eyes were only slightly accented with kohl, her brown hair dressed in curls that were tied up, then threaded through a velvet net on her head. Her sharp, straight nose and neatly curved mouth gave evidence of a strong will. She wore pearl drops in her ears, a gold chain around her neck, and only three rings, which was restraint in jewelry for an Islander. Many wore rings on every finger and several earrings, men and women alike.

Duke Mequen rose to his feet as the last to enter closed the doors behind them. He was about five feet ten inches tall, with the solid build of a man who rode a great deal but spent little time practicing weapons skills. His dark eyes were set under perfectly curved brows and framed by laugh lines. His nose was broad and straight, his mouth wide, his chin square. He wore his dark hair clipped short to draw attention away from the fact that it was retreating from his forehead. He was somberly dressed luarin-fashion in a black linen tunic over a silvery shirt and gray hose, with a ruby-hilted dagger at his waist, a signet ring on the index finger of his left hand, and a gold hoop ring in one ear. Aly liked the look of him. She already knew from his servants that he was a fair man, if unconventional in the way he ran his home and chose his wives. Now she could also see that he was well mannered and thoughtful, always nice traits to find in a noble.

Slowly his people quieted. Mequen looked them over, hands clasped behind his back. "I'm sure you've heard rumors," he said, his deep voice clear throughout the room. "His Majesty is no longer confident about my loyalty. He has invited me to prove it with expensive presents. While he evaluates these presents, my family and I are invited to visit our estates on Lombyn Island, where we must stay until he feels better about us."

Shock raced through the people like a physical thing. Some of their families, free and slave, had worked for the

Balitangs for generations. Because the duke was uninterested in court intrigues, they had believed the king would never turn on him.

"This breaks our hearts," Mequen said, his sorrow plain on his face and in his voice. "We are forced to sell lands and slaves to give the king the reassurances he requires. And those we can take with us are dreadfully few. Our Lombyn holdings, the inheritance of Duchess Sarugani"—the mother of his older daughters—"are small." He glanced at his steward. "Our chief sources of income are not gold and gems but sheep, goats, and rabbits. We cannot live there as we are accustomed to do. We cannot feed you all."

By now some of the women were crying. Husbands wrapped their arms around their wives. Children clung to their parents.

The duchess rose. "We will do our best to see you are cared for," she said, her calm voice flowing over them. "Our friends have asked to hire or purchase many of you. We will separate no families. We will sell you to no one known to treat his people badly. As soon as provision has been made, you will be told. It will be soon. We must be on our way in just a week."

The duke took up the explanation. "Should no one we trust offer for your service, we have sent for a matcher, one with connections and the magical Gift to see what your aptitudes may be. He will examine you and obtain new places for you. That begins today." Mequen let out a deep sigh. "Some of you will come with us. Many of you already know who you are. For the rest, tell the steward if you desire to stay with us. But remember, we go to a rougher way of life, far from any town. We will have few amenities, less food. The highlands are colder than our jungles, the land inhospitable. Think it over." He paused, then nodded. "May the gods bless you. May they grant us all voyages to safe harbors."

Chenaol shook her head, her mouth in a tight line. "It's back to the slave brokers for you, Aly girl, unless the matcher sees you have special skills."

"And you?" Aly asked, not worried in the least. She needed just two more nights to complete her picks. Once she was rid of her metal collar, she could bid farewell to the Balitangs and the Isles alike.

"I stay with Lady Sarai and Lady Dove," Chenaol replied. "Forever." She left the room with the other departing servants, a short, round raka woman dressed luarin-fashion in an orange gown.

A curious way to put it, Aly thought as she mingled with the servants. Not "with the duke" or "with the family," only with the two daughters of the first duchess. The raka duchess.

The longer Aly stayed here, the more she saw how frayed the relations between the full-blooded luarin and the full-blooded raka were. A push from the right people might throw the entire country into civil war. That was news worth taking home. Too often in the past the Copper Isles had meddled in Tortallan affairs. Perhaps its rulers needed something to keep them busy.

The next morning the slave matcher summoned all those who had not found other homes as yet. Most were the less skilled workers—hostlers, lower-ranking footmen and maids, slaves whom the carpenter and the smith would not need in the north, and Aly. After the family's friends and well-wishers had made their selections, over forty slaves remained.

"How does this work?" Aly whispered to the boy who carried messages for the house as they lined up before the matcher. "I never heard of it before."

The boy wasn't surprised. Everyone knew Aly was fresh-caught out of Tortall. They never thought to wonder how she spoke Kyprish, the language of the islands, so well. "He looks at ya," he whispered. "He's got the magical Gift and all. He's looked at the owners that hire through 'im, too, so he can match folks that go good together. Not that we'll have much luck, us not having skills. 'Less he sees a talent. Sometimes they can, the Gifted matchers, anyways."

Ulasim led them into the grand hall. People had come and gone over the last day to remove paintings, tapestries, and candelabra for sale. All that remained were the tables and chairs. They would be carried off in the morning.

Ulasim lined the slaves against the wall, his brown eyes alert for any sign of misbehavior. The matcher stood next to chairs occupied by Duke Mequen and Duchess Winnamine, waiting. He was a plump black man in typical raka garb: a wraparound jacket and sarong, both made of serviceable tan linen. He shaved his head but grew a tuft of beard, which he stroked as he talked to the Balitangs. Now Mequen nodded to him. The slave matcher started at the far end of the line.

Aly watched from under her lashes. After he had bathed each slave in the pale orange fire of his magical Gift, the matcher conferred with Mequen and Winnamine. Slowly he worked his way through the slaves until he was closer to Aly. She measured his Gift. He was powerful enough to notice her magical Sight. Doubtless he would try to do something with her because of it.

She had the Sight from her father, but its force was her mother's legacy; magic ran strong in Alanna's family. George used his Sight to tell when he was being lied to or when someone held out on him. Sometimes he could also recognize one who would be his friend or his enemy. It was different for Aly. Her sight enabled her to see immediately whether the person she looked at had magic or godhood; whether that person was ill, pregnant, or lying. It also revealed the presence of poison in water or food. All she had to do was concentrate on how she wished to see something. Her power made it possible for her to clearly discern the tiniest of details, things invisible to the normal eye, or to see far into the distance. A new master might value it for as long as she stayed with him or her. Aly was unimpressed by her skill. She would have preferred to have the all-purpose Gift wielded by her mother and her brother Thom.

The matcher had come to Aly's neighbor. She closed her eyes against the glare of his Gift as the man weighed the young slave. Finished, he addressed Mequen and Winnamine. "I'll keep him with the others, see if he can be trained. I'll send your percentage of his final sale when it's made."

"Very well," Winnamine said. "We've heard good things about your training school."

"It's to my advantage to treat them well," the matcher replied. "It always pays off." The messenger left. Finally the matcher came to Aly. "Look up into my eyes, girl," he said, his melodic voice kind. "This won't hurt."

Aly met his gaze. The slightest hint of orange fire grew around his hands. Then the matcher hiccuped. "What?" he began to say.

Something changed. Inside his round frame Aly saw another body, compact, lean, wiry. Under his face lay another: square, the strong chin covered in a short beard, a brief nose broad at the tip, sparkling dark eyes, and short hair. This was *not* an internal aspect of the matcher; this was something else.

Well, well, Aly thought, amazed. I have a god.

Gold light spread from the matcher's body, flaring out

around him like a sun. The Balitangs stepped back, shielding their eyes against the light with their hands. Vast, bell-like tones that sounded vaguely like speech rang out, the effect so powerful that Mequen and Winnamine dropped to their knees.

Aly felt no urge to kneel, nor did that light hurt her eyes as it did those of her owners. She gazed at the being who had come to occupy the matcher's body and leaned back against the wall, crossing her arms over her chest.

"Hello, there." A crisp, light voice, not the matcher's, came from the man's lips. "I apologize that we weren't able to meet earlier. I hope your journey here wasn't too harrowing."

"It was delightful," Aly said with her best nice-girl smile. "All lovely and serene, like sleeping on lilies, only without the bees in my nose. You spoke to me in my dream."

"I did," the god said, averting his eyes in a falsely modest way. "You'll get more. I don't want you to get homesick."

"But that's so *thoughtful*," Aly said innocently. "I'd thank you, but I just don't have the words. Until I find some, you might tell me just who you are supposed to be. Won't that be lovely?"

"Dear, you're being deliberately obtuse," the god inside the matcher teased. "You know a god when you see one. You may call me Kyprioth."

Aly thought swiftly. She didn't recognize the god's name, which didn't necessarily mean anything. Gods' names and importance varied from country to country. "Why would I want to call you anything, sir?" she asked, still in her character of a sweet young girl.

"Because I might be of use to you. In fact, I already have been." Kyprioth reached into the matcher's jacket and pulled out a tiny ball of light. "You sent a prayer to my sister, the

Great Goddess, in the matter of who would purchase you. I intercepted it, since I took care of that little matter myself. You may have the prayer back."

Aly frowned at him, forgetting her impersonation. She looked at the strong, wiry hand inside the matcher's well-padded one. "You did what?"

Kyprioth smiled. It looked extremely odd under the matcher's unmoving features. "I made certain that you would go to the Balitangs and no one else. I fixed your seeming so that no one else would bid on you."

Aly scowled at him. "Do you mean I got my nose broken, my eyebrow scarred, and the rest of me all battered for *nothing?*"

"The eyebrow scar is quite dashing," Kyprioth told her earnestly. "I'll fix your nose if you like."

Aly covered her nose with a protective hand. "No. I got this nose the hard way, and I'm keeping it."

"Well, keep this, too," the god said, thrusting the light-ball at her. "Use it to appeal to the Goddess another time."

Aly reached out and took the ball. It oozed into her skin like water into sand and vanished. She rubbed the spot, looking the god over. "What have you done to them?" she asked curiously, nodding to the kneeling duke and duchess.

"They're talking to a Great God," Kyprioth assured her. "Not me—they wouldn't listen to me—but to my brother. They can't see or hear us, if that's what you're worried about. He's telling them that they are beloved of destiny and are meant for great things in this world. They are to be wise and accept their banishment, for their time of greatness will come."

Aly raised an eyebrow at him as she mentally listed the other Great Gods that this one might be. "Won't Mithros mind that you borrowed his seeming?" she wanted to know.

"All the legends *I've* ever heard say he objects to it. Strenuously."

"What he doesn't know won't hurt him," Kyprioth said blithely. "I happen to know he's dealing with the start of a war on the other side of the world just now. Both sides are invoking him, of course—silly mortals. Don't you want to know what his seeming is telling them about you?"

"Not interested," Aly replied, smiling at the god with easy good humor. "I have plans."

"Very like your father, manner and all," Kyprioth informed her with a pleased smile. "I can't believe he hasn't the wit to put you to some proper work."

"You talk like you know him," Aly remarked. This was starting to get interesting.

"He and I have done quite a bit of business together."

"He never mentioned you," Aly said. "At our house, we usually share what gods are monkeying about with us today."

"Of course he never mentioned *me*," Kyprioth answered. "What sane man wants the people around him to know he's favored of a trickster? They might suspect that my favor causes certain interesting events in their lives, don't you think? Your father knows there's no point in mentioning something he can't change."

"I'll tell him you said so," replied Aly, her mind in a whirl. Her father would definitely have to explain *this* to her. She couldn't wait.

"Actually, you won't," said Kyprioth. His speech was clear, crisp, and fast, a promise of amusement in every inflection. It was the kind of voice that talked people into doing mad stunts. It made Aly very wary of him. "At least, not right away," he amended. "I have a small wager for you first. Play this out for me, and I'll deposit you at the cove at Pirate's Swoop. I'm the local sea god, among other things."

Aly raised an eyebrow. "Why should I dance to some trickster's tune?"

Kyprioth chuckled, a rich, warm sound. "Oh, my dear, I'm not *some* trickster," he informed her. "I'm *the* Trickster. Kyprioth is the name I have here in the Copper Isles, in addition to rule over our seas. Don't you even want to hear my wager?" He leaned close to Aly and whispered, "It's made to order for a girl with your skills."

Aly shrugged, hiding her sudden interest behind a mask of boredom. "I suppose I won't be rid of you until you tell me, so talk away."

"It's simple," he assured her. "Keep the children of this family alive through the end of summer. Do that, and I'll send you home as the gods travel. You'll be here one moment and there the next."

"And if I can't? If I lose?" Aly wanted to know.

"You'll serve me for an entire year," Kyprioth replied. "If you're still alive. I can't make any promises. If things go really badly, you might be killed by accident."

Aly twiddled her thumbs, pretending to ignore him. She wanted him to raise the stakes.

Kyprioth sighed. "I'll convince your father to let you be a field agent. I'm a god—I can do that."

"You can't force him," Aly said. She spoke from long experience with her father.

"No. But he'll pay attention if I tell him how good you are on your own," he explained. "I have a feeling you have a real knack for this. And I'll grant him a boon as well."

"I'm a slave," Aly reminded him. "These people won't listen to me."

"They will now." Kyprioth beamed at Aly. "That's why I needed my brother's seeming. He's telling the duke and duchess that he's chosen you, someone their enemies will

overlook, as his messenger. That they will come to no harm
if they listen to your advice. Sooner or later, of course, you'll
have to prove to them you're worth listening to, but I'm sure
you'll have plenty of chances for that. Have we a wager?"

Aly considered it, rubbing her hand over her short-
cropped hair. From her true dream she knew Mother had
already gone north for the summer's fighting, and making
things right with her had been the only reason Aly was prepared to rush home. On one hand, the wager meant she
would have to follow the Balitangs into exile. On the other
hand, what better way to prove to Da that she could manage
the work? Even if he wouldn't let her spy, he might attach
her to the king or queen as a sort of bodyguard, to keep an
eye on things. He'd know her ability if Aly showed him that
she was able to keep a family in one piece when they were
out of favor with a notoriously unstable king.

She might never get another chance like this. Her
father would be hard put to argue with a god's assessment,
especially if that god was the Trickster. Aly grinned. Even Da
couldn't refuse her if she did it. He was very good about
admitting when he was wrong. "We have a wager, then,
under those terms," she told Kyprioth. "But I'll need help."

The god grabbed her stubbly head in both hands and
kissed her forehead. Aly yelped: the kiss sent something like
a shock through her. "You'll get it," Kyprioth said. "On
Lombyn." With that he was gone.

If you've a story, make sure it's a whole one, with details close to hand. It's the difference between a successful lie and getting caught.

—*From* A Workbook for a Young Spy, *written and illustrated by Aly's father and given to her on her sixth birthday*

3

THE RAKA

The Long Strait and the Azure Sea

People out of favor with King Oron did not waste time in farewells. The king had slaughtered entire households, down to the last dog, once he decided he could not live with his fears. Two days after Aly entered into her wager with Kyprioth, the Balitangs loaded their belongings onto several cargo ships and prepared to set sail.

Only Prince Bronau came to see them off that humid morning. He kissed the duchess on both cheeks, embraced the duke, and kissed Lady Saraiyu's hand. Aly barely glimpsed this. Her new charges, Petranne and Elsren, did not care for ships, or the early hour, or Aly herself. Their governess and nursemaids had gone to other households along with seventy-four other servants and slaves. Winnamine assigned their care to Aly as the reason they had kept her with them. Neither the duke nor the duchess had summoned her to discuss the visitation from the god they believed to be Mithros. Instead they hid their thoughts behind polite, distant faces and told Ulasim that Aly would mind the little ones.

Aly hung on to Petranne and Elsren as they jerked and shrieked in her grip. At last she gave up trying to hear. She read the adults' lips, as she'd been taught by her father.

"I'll try to get word of events to you as often as possible," Bronau assured the older Balitangs. "The king's none too healthy. Things could change suddenly if he passes on. If Hazarin takes the throne, for instance."

"Don't speak of such things," Mequen told Bronau. "It could be taken for treason."

Winnamine rested a hand on the prince's arm. "*Try* to be careful, Bronau."

The prince grinned, then walked down the gangplank as the crew prepared to cast off. The Balitangs waved farewell. Bronau stood on the edge of the dock, watching as the ship weighed anchor.

"Come on, you raka dogs, put your backs into it!" yelled the luarin captain to his sailors. "'Less you want a touch of the whip to smarten you!" It was how many luarin in Rajmuat who were not part of the Balitangs' circle addressed their raka slaves and servants. Aly thought it was a foolish way to talk to someone who might be inspired to throw one over the rail into a shark-infested sea, but she would be the first to admit she did not have a conqueror's heart. She couldn't see who would profit by keeping the original owners of a country ground into the dirt.

Elsren broke out of Aly's hold and ran toward the rail. Still clinging to Petranne, Aly seized the boy by his shirt with her free hand and dragged him back. "I want Jafa!" wailed Elsren, tears running down his plump cheeks. Jafana had been his nursemaid. "I hate you!"

Aly sighed and wrapped an arm around him. "I know, and I'm sorry," she replied. "In your shoes, I'd hate me, too, but we're stuck with one another." She looked at Petranne.

Tears rolled down the little girl's cheeks. "Sometimes being a noble isn't much fun, is it?" she asked. Petranne shook her head.

Aly glanced at Mequen and Winnamine. They waited at the rail, none of their feelings on display as the ship drew out into the harbor. As Elsren calmed, Aly studied the city, not having seen it when she first arrived. Rajmuat was splendid, full of peaked gates and three-level temples, each with a spiked tower thrust into the sky. White or rose pink walls contrasted with the dark green of the trees that lined its streets. Homes also sported peaked roofs and intricately carved eaves, those on wealthy houses traced in gold or silver.

Something else reflected the sun, too, pricking Aly's eyes with swords of light. She looked up. High above the city Stormwings circled like vultures over a carcass. Aly shivered. These part-human, part-metal immortals feasted on the rage, fear, and death spawned by human combat. Their wings, each metal feather shaped precisely like a bird's, were the source of the bright flashes of sun on steel.

"They always know." Winnamine spoke quietly. "The Stormwings—they always know when unrest is starting. How can they tell?"

Mequen put an arm around her shoulders. "We don't know if they do, my dear," he replied. "Maybe they just know that it's a sure bet in Rajmuat. There *will* be fighting in the streets, if he doesn't appoint an heir soon, or if something happens to whomever he appoints. We're going to be well out of it."

"We *hope* we're well out of it now," replied the duchess.

Aly knew she had a point. Sometimes King Oron did recover from his fears. Sometimes he didn't. Sometimes he got worse. If Kyprioth was dragging Aly into the Isles' affairs, they might well be growing.

At least the Balitangs wouldn't miss life at court. They occupied themselves with charity work, fashions, books, and music, not politics, court, or trade. They kept their own accounts and oversaw the work of the household. Aly suspected that they would settle quietly into rural life, given half a chance. If she was to win her wager, she had to ensure that they would get that chance, at least until the summer was over.

She wondered why a Great God would take such a brief interest in the family. In her experience, once a god took an interest in a mortal, that mortal was stuck with that god for life. Still, that wasn't Aly's problem right now. Safeguarding this family, without calling notice to herself, was her problem. If anyone were to find out that the daughter of the Tortallan king's Champion and his assistant spymaster was summering in the Copper Isles, she wouldn't live long enough to collect on that wager. The thought made her grin as she turned her face into the fresh sea breeze. At long last she had a real challenge, and she meant to enjoy every moment of it.

The captain never made good on his threats to smarten his raka seamen with his whip. The ship glided up the Long Strait. The warm, damp winds drove them gently north along the long, slender neck of water that separated Kypriang, the capital island, from Gempang Isle in the west. Dolphins, always a sign of good luck, sped alongside the vessel, watching its occupants with mischievous eyes and what looked like mocking smiles.

The Long Strait was another world compared to Rajmuat's crowded streets and busy docks. Limestone cliffs rose high on either side, threaded with greenery and falling streams, capped with emerald jungles that steamed as the day warmed up. Brightly colored birds soared to and fro, indifferent to the ships that ploughed the blue waters. From the Gempang jungles came the long, drawn-out hoots of the howler monkeys.

"Tell me a story," demanded Elsren after his afternoon nap.

"Yes, a story," Petranne insisted, sitting up against the rail with her legs crossed. "A *new* story. Jafa only ever tells the same ones."

"Did not," retorted her brother. Petranne stuck her tongue out at him.

Aly listened to the howler monkeys and smiled. She sat cross-legged in front of the two children, keeping one hand in Elsren's belt. She had spent the morning dragging him from under the crew's feet. "Once the most beautiful queen in all the world had a menagerie," she began, thinking wickedly how Aunt Thayet would screech if she could hear this story again. "In it were those self-same monkeys you hear all around us, the howlers. Now, the queen was often out and about, and the only things she liked better than coming home were her reunions with her beloved king, and an unbroken night's sleep." Softly she told them about menagerie keepers who sold places in the palace gardens near the queen's balcony the nights after her return, then roused the howler monkeys to break the silence with their loud, penetrating calls. Woken from her sleep, the hot-tempered queen would race onto her balcony, bow and arrows in hand, in an attempt to shoot the beasts no matter how dark the night. Those who watched from below rejoiced in the fact that their queen slept without a nightgown.

"Of course, the king's spymaster put a stop to it, once he knew," Aly concluded seriously. "He made the keepers use the money they'd made to build another enclosure for the howlers, where they wouldn't disturb the queen. But there are still men who will swear by every god you know that they truly have the most beautiful queen in all the world."

Petranne and Elsren stared back at Aly soberly. Finally Elsren said, "That one was new. Tell another!"

"Yes, another!" pleaded his sister. "That was a good one!"

"You're from Tortall, aren't you?"

Aly turned to look for the source of the new voice. The older girls, Saraiyu and Dovasary, stood nearby, listening as Sarai fanned herself. There was no way for Aly to read what they thought in their level eyes or polite faces. It occurred to her that, being half-raka, these girls must have learned to hide their feelings well. They would have heard the people of Rajmuat and the rest of the Isles speak with careless cruelty of their mother's people. They may even have heard some of that cruelty from nobles of their own class.

Dovasary continued, "Your Kyprish is very good—you barely have an accent."

"Thank you, your ladyship," Aly replied meekly. She knew her accent was not Tortallan. Her teachers had come from Imahyn Isle and had pronounced her Kyprish as perfect. The Balitangs spoke with a Rajmuat accent.

"My sister asked you a question," Saraiyu said imperiously. "Are you from Tortall?"

Aly bowed her head, every inch of her the perfect servant. "Yes, your ladyship."

Dovasary plopped herself down beside Elsren and pulled him onto her lap. Aly disentangled her fingers from his belt. "Then you know stories of the King's Champion there, the one they call the Lioness!" she said eagerly. For the first time since Aly had seen her, the younger girl's eyes were alive with interest. "Tell us some!"

"Is she really ten feet tall?" asked Petranne.

Saraiyu settled neatly beside Aly, disposing her cotton

skirts perfectly. Waving her fan, she asked, "Is the Lioness as good with a sword as they say? The duchess made me stop my sword lessons." Her voice turned frosty as she spoke of her stepmother. "She said they were unladylike."

Aly scratched her head to cover her confusion. Can I talk of Mother as if I'd never seen her in my life? she wondered. No—as if I'd seen her once or twice, at a distance. They'll expect that. When Chenaol and Ulasim had first brought her to Balitang House, the steward had questioned her about her origins. Aly had claimed then that she'd been a merchant's daughter and a maid at Fief Tameran, south of Pirate's Swoop. The household there had been close to the Grand Progress several years ago. Everyone would have turned out to see the monarchs, the prince and princess, and the King's Champion ride by.

Now she folded her hands in her lap. "The Lioness is really that good with a sword, your ladyship," she replied to Sarai, this time acting the role of a polite servant. "King's Champion isn't a title for decoration. Every time a noble demands a challenge to settle a matter of law, the Champion must fight and win for the Crown."

"What happens when she loses?" asked Petranne.

Aly looked at the child, startled. "She doesn't."

"But everybody loses sometime," Sarai told Aly.

"Not the Lioness," Aly said, her mind scrambling. Mother lose? How could she? "Not since she's been Champion, that I know of." Remember, you only know the stories, she ordered herself.

"She must have lost sometimes, when she was training, maybe even when she first got her shield," Dovasary pointed out. "And Tortall's at war—she could be killed in that."

Aly's pulse raced. She fought to sound natural, to keep from showing her distress at the idea. "Oh, well, training and that, everyone loses," she said with a shrug when she was sure of her control. "But the war's a year old already, and the Lioness is hale enough. She visited her home just before I was taken." If Alanna was killed in the fighting this year, she would die without Aly having said goodbye.

"Tell us," begged Saraiyu, leaning forward, her dark eyes eager. "Tell us how she came to be the Champion. Tell us how she found the Dominion Jewel. Tell us *everything*."

Aly only had time to tell them the story of how the Lioness had brought the Dominion Jewel home to her king. Then Duchess Winnamine declared it was time for the children to study. Even Elsren had lessons in counting to do. Aly remained topside, relieved of her duties for the time being. She stood at the rail, enjoying the calls of colorful birds, the clear blue water under the ship's prow, and the sheer loveliness of the spring day.

She registered movement along the cliff tops on either side of the strait. Aly sharpened her Sight for a good look. Her fingers clenched on the rail as she realized that she saw hundreds of copper-skinned raka, men and women alike, dressed in the traditional wrapped jacket or round-collared tunic, and the tied skirtlike wrap called a sarong. Some wore garments that were richly decorated and jeweled, with more jewelry on their fingers and at their throats. Others wore plain colors with embroidery and strings of beads for ornament. The women drew their straight black hair away from their faces in a double-domed style, much like that of Yamani women, while the men wore headbands, turbans, or hats. The raka groups were of all ages, from the smallest infants to the oldest adults. They stood in silence, as far as Aly could tell, watching as the Balitang vessel passed by.

She turned to look back down the strait, to check whether the natives watched all shipping out here. Two vessels earlier had overtaken the three that carried the duke's household. No other ships followed in their wake, and nowhere did she see people on the cliffs behind them. The raka left as soon as the duke's ship drew out of easy view.

She tugged at a sailor's arm as he coiled rope on the deck. "Do they always do that?" she asked, pointing at their audience. "Come and see boats go by? They don't look like they mean to attack."

The half-raka man looked at her, then at the cliffs. "No," he said quietly, "they do not do that. They prefer to remain unseen when the luarin pass." He touched Aly's slave collar. "Do not draw attention to it," he said, nodding toward the duke and duchess, who sat at a small table in the bow playing chess. "The luarin get uneasy when the raka do things they don't understand."

I want to understand. Aly thought it, but she did not say it. She doubted that the sailor would confide in her. One thing seemed obvious: something about these ships drew the interest of many people on the two islands. The raka faces, when she used her magical Sight to better examine them, were expectant and eager. The sailor had told her the watchers were not typical. Something about the duke's party drew their attention.

His servants? Aly wondered, drumming her fingers on her thigh as she turned the matter over in her mind. Or his oldest daughters? Mequen was a Rittevon, a lesser one, but still of the line of the luarin conquerors.

Belowdecks she heard Elsren yell, "I want *up!*" Aly's rest time was over.

Before she fetched the child, Aly took one more look at the cliffs. The raka they had passed were leaving, returning to their jungle towns and their luarin masters' estates.

That night after supper the duke and duchess read to their younger children from a book of raka myths. Aly returned to the ship's rail to watch the cliffs around their anchorage, a small cove on Kypriang's lush western shore. The night, warm and damp, folded around her like a blanket. With her magical vision she didn't need light to see the raka, standing or seated on rocks that overlooked the cove. It seemed they required no light, either. Lamps burned only aboard the trio of ships that rocked on the gentle waters. The moon had just begun to show its rim over the mountains that formed Kypriang Isle's spine.

"They're our people, too." Twelve-year-old Dovasary rested her hands on the rail as she came to stand beside Aly. She spoke in Common, not Kyprish. "Our mother—Sarai's and mine—was a raka. Sarugani of Temaida. Her family was of the older nobility, from before the luarin came, but they don't have a title higher than baron now."

"They're lucky to have that much. None of our raka family talks about who they were or what they did before the invasion," Saraiyu remarked quietly. She came to lean on the rail on Aly's other side. "They must have seen their friends being slaughtered or sold. They would have beggared themselves with the conquest taxes rather than suffer the same fate."

"You're half luarin yourself," replied Aly, her voice idle, her attention apparently on the shoreline. "Begging your ladyship's pardon."

"That would be the half that cousin Oron seems determined to murder or disgrace," Sarai pointed out. "Even a madman should have more care for his own blood kin, particularly given the nest of vipers at court."

Aly smoothed a hand over the rail. "Forgive me for

saying it, but your ladyship comes close to treasonous talk," she murmured. "I'd as soon be with the part of the family that's exiled but alive."

"You won't betray us," Saraiyu replied casually. "I don't know about Tortall, but here the entire household is executed along with the suspected traitor. Then they sell the one who reported their masters, if they're known, to Carthak."

"Ouch," said Aly, meaning it. "That's not the way to create support among the lower classes."

"The thinking is that a servant of traitors who turns the traitors in is doubly treasonous, to her master as well as the king," Dovasary explained. "They like to nip that sort of thing in the bud."

Sarai turned to face east, watching the moon rise, leaning back on the rail with her elbows and rump. The torchlight slid along her long, barely hooked nose and over a full, sensual lower lip, then flickered along the curved lines shaped by her plain pink luarin-style gown. It lent sparkle to her brown eyes and caressed her perfectly arched brows and high cheekbones.

"Is it so hard, being half raka?" Aly wanted to know. "All Rajmuat—even a fresh-caught luarin slave like me—knows the lady Saraiyu is considered one of the beauties of the city."

Sarai's smile was crooked. "By men, and the raka nobility, and some of the luarin houses, yes, I suppose." She looked at her sister. "It's not vanity, Dove. I can count as well as the next person."

Dove shrugged. "I didn't utter a word."

Sarai made a noise that in a less attractive girl would have been labeled a snort. "And yet, when it comes to marriage, it's amazing how many luarin families discover marriages that were arranged when their sons were in the cradle. Marriages their young men had never *heard* of until then. Particularly the higher-ranking luarin nobles. I can't help but notice how many young men give way when they learn their mothers don't care for the color of the future bride's skin, however beautiful she may be."

Dove sighed. "And the raka nobles are wary around us because we've got Rittevon blood in our veins. They don't want to lose their sons the next time the king thinks his relatives are plotting against him."

"Dovasary!" whispered Sarai, shocked.

The younger girl leaned around Aly to look at her sister. "I have ears, Sarai, and people hardly ever notice me. I know what I hear. The raka don't want to risk the Rittevon insanity for their grandchildren."

Aly grimaced. She'd once overheard one of Tortall's young knights, a Bazhir, tell Grandfather Myles, "Oh, I'm considered wonderful when it comes to letting and losing blood for the Crown. But marriage? Even jumped-up merchants who weren't barons a generation ago won't let their daughters marry a Bazhir, whatever their wealth and standing."

I suppose I'd best remember what the Bazhir at home endure, she thought, before I go looking down my nose at the luarin. You really should have a clean house at home before you start picking at the way your neighbor does the dusting.

"What does a slave know of treason and kings anyway?" asked Dove. Her dark eyes were now intent on Aly's face.

Aly shrugged. "I was a maid in a nobleman's castle when I was taken," she replied. "*My* ears are as good as anyone's."

"I don't see how any Tortallan girl would want to be a maid, not with all the choices you have, compared to us," Sarai remarked. "If I lived there, I'd join the Queen's Riders, and learn to ride and use a sword and bow like they do. Or maybe even become a knight like the Lady Knight Keladry. The raka ladies of old knew how to fight. In the last great battle against the luarin, on the Plain of Sorrows, a third of the Kyprin warriors were female."

"And the whole army got thrashed," Dove reminded her sister mercilessly. "The conquerors had more battle mages, and more catapults, and ballistas, and liquid fire. It didn't matter how many women fought with the raka that day. They died just as easily as the men."

"You're so *prosaic*, Dove. Oh, look, the raka." Sarai pointed to the rocks about the cove. The moon was above the mountains now, a huge pearl in the indigo sky. By its light the people on the cliffs were clearly visible. "They've been doing that all day."

"Sarai?" called Winnamine. "Dove? It's time to sleep."

The two girls rolled their eyes at one another. "No late nights for us," Sarai remarked drily. They went below.

Aly turned back to watch the sea by moonlight. The older Balitang girls struck her as being much like falcons, always hooded and tethered, not able to hunt as their hearts desired. It was such a waste, keeping fiery girls like this in the background, not letting them forge their own path in the world. She'd like to see what these two would accomplish.

Two mornings later their ships emerged from the Long Strait into the Azure Sea, the body of water that lay between Imahyn and Lombyn Isles. Aly grinned as the captain jubilantly announced that the sea god Kyprioth was smiling on their voyage. Apparently this was the quickest, smoothest passage of the strait the captain had ever made. Duke Mequen finally stopped the man's recital of how unpredictable the passage could be, a tale of crosscurrents and wind gusts, with a reminder that he might annoy the god by too frequently mentioning his name.

Aly wasn't sure how easily annoyed Kyprioth was, but she was distracted from her thoughts as the Azure Sea emerged from its veil of morning fog. Its bright blue waters were clear. Vividly colored fish darted through its depths, circling a population of sea turtles, dolphins, and the occasional eel. The sun burnished the tops of the waves to the color of gold.

Elsren leaned precariously over the rail. "Gull boats!" he cried. Aly seized his luarin-style tunic, securing her adventurous charge. A multitude of boats was gliding toward them from Imahyn, Ikang, and Kypriang Isles. They were as colorful as the fish, with brightly colored sails, prows and sterns fashioned in long, pointed curves, and every inch of outer hull decorated and painted. Raka sailors, both men and women, dressed in no more than vivid sashes and sarongs, steered the graceful craft as they stared at the Balitang ships.

"Have you ever seen anything like this?" Mequen asked the captain.

"Never," the man replied, sweating. "*Never*. And I grew up on the Azure Sea."

"They're unarmed," Winnamine commented. She had a spyglass raised to her eye. "I don't see a weapon anywhere."

As the Balitang ships sailed north, the fleet of colorful boats parted before them. Elsren and Petranne clamored for a place in the bow. With Aly to keep them from falling overboard, they waved gleefully at the raka and loudly admired the rainbow bevy of ships. With the dignity suited to their more advanced years, Sarai and Dove came forward to stand with Petranne and Elsren, watching as their mother's people approached.

Aly sharpened her Sight until she could see the raka's faces. The sailors stiffened when the older girls showed themselves; some pointed to them. The raka flotilla swerved, its ships forming two polite lines. Then, one by one, the ships glided past the Balitang family's ship, one on either side of their bow. The raka merely glanced at the three luarin faces— Aly's, Petranne's, Elsren's—then fixed on Sarai's and Dove's light brown ones.

It's not us who brought the raka out, Aly thought. It's Sarai and Dove. The two half-raka girls. The two girls whose mother came from an old noble house—a *raka* noble house.

"If you are wise, you will say nothing of this to anyone," Winnamine said from behind them, her melodic voice soft. "Ever. Do you all understand? The king would not like to hear that we drew so much attention from the raka."

Sarai shrugged. "Nobody cares what the raka do," she replied, gazing at the people who sailed by. "Especially not the king."

"You never know who is watching," persisted Winnamine. "Don't encourage them. Go below."

"When Papa says." Dove didn't even look at her stepmother.

Aly knew Winnamine was right. It seemed that she could start to cover her part of Kyprioth's wager here and now.

"My ladies, my apologies, but this scares me," she whispered, the picture of an alarmed slave. "I've not been here long, but, well, back home there's stories of your king. This could get your house and those raka in trouble with him. We'd all pay for that, in blood, most like."

Sarai glanced at Aly, confused. Aly looked at her and shrugged, suggesting that it was just her opinion.

Dove sighed. She grabbed Sarai's hand and towed her older sister below.

"Well done," murmured the duchess.

Aly looked up three inches into the duchess's face. "The wisdom of what you said was just a little slow in reaching their brains," she offered.

"We both know it was the suggested threat to the raka that convinced them," replied Winnamine. She rubbed her temples. "They liked me well enough when I married their father, but now they're old enough to be difficult, just because I tell them things they don't wish to hear."

Aly thought of her own mother and winced inwardly. "It's hard, living in the shadow of a respected woman," she told the duchess.

Winnamine looked at her sharply. "Very wise, for a girl Sarai's age. Perhaps the One who appeared when the matcher looked you over chose well," she said, referring to the god's visit in terms that Petranne and Elsren wouldn't understand. "He said you were clear-sighted, and would see a way for us out of all this."

"I'm sure I won't need to do any such thing," Aly replied cheerfully. "You'll hardly know I'm here."

Winnamine shook her head with a rueful smile, then watched the raka craft that continued to sail by. After a moment she returned to Mequen. Tired of the spectacle, Petranne and Elsren followed her.

Aly remained in the bow, leaning on the rail. It was embarrassing to think that rather than truly expressing her independence, she had been difficult with her mother just for the sake of being difficult, because she was sixteen and stubborn.

That night they anchored in the harbor at Ambririp, off

the northeast point of Imahyn Isle. The family slept ashore at a proper inn. Mequen's and Winnamine's servants took care of the younger children. Aly remained with the rest of the household, the servants, slaves, and men-at-arms. They set up a communal supper on the beach near the dock where their ships were anchored.

Chenaol took command of the meal. True to what she'd told Aly about staying with Sarai and Dove, the raka woman had turned down other nobles' offers of higher pay and more leisure time. Now she sent Ulasim and two other men to the Ambririp market with a list. Three more servants dug a fire pit in the sand and hung a metal cookpot over it from an iron tripod. Once the men returned with Chenaol's ingredients, she set to work, shredding a chicken and cooking it in water, cutting up hard-boiled eggs as the meat simmered. One of the cookmaids chopped shallots, spring onions, garlic, and chilies. Another ground them into paste along with cut ginger, lemongrass, and lime juice. Once the broth was ready, everything went into it, including bean sprouts and bean-flour noodles.

Aly refused the hot sauce they offered her when her bowl was filled. She had tried it once in Rajmuat, at her first meal among the Balitang staff. They had roared with laughter as she gulped water to put out the fire in her nose and throat before finally showing her that yogurt or bread worked better to ease the bite. She'd laughed, too, once she doused the fire. Even now she grinned as they teased her about picking out the visible pieces of chili pepper. Finishing the contents of her bowl, Aly thought that perhaps she was getting used to Isles cooking. This dish made her eat only twice as much yogurt and bread as the raka, instead of her usual four times that amount.

Afterward some maids washed up. Everyone gathered

around the fire, luarin, part-raka, and raka alike. Back in Rajmuat the free servants and the men-at-arms each had their own hall. They didn't mingle with the slaves. Here, Aly saw, they felt too lonely and out of place to separate into their usual groups. A leather bottle was passed from one person to the next as each took a large drink of its contents. When it came to Aly, she sniffed, caught the unmistakable odor of liquor, smiled, and handed it on.

"That's arak, girl," Chenaol said comfortably, relaxing against a sack of rice next to Aly. "Distilled palm sap wine. It's good for you. Warm your belly, lighten your burdens."

Aly smiled. "But my belly's already far too warm from supper," she joked. "At this rate, I'll open my mouth one day and burn the trees down." That drew a laugh from the others.

Chenaol shrugged. "More for me, then," she said, and took a healthy gulp.

The skin made two more rounds of the household. The men and women from Rajmuat were homesick, though most agreed that life with the Balitangs was better than that with other noble households. Aly was startled to learn that many of the servants, including Ulasim, and a handful of men-at-arms were actually from the Tanair lands on Lombyn. This would be their first return home since the death of the first duchess, Sarugani.

At Balitang House the chores had been unending, and most of the staff had been too exhausted to talk at the end of the day. If they did talk, it wasn't to the new, junior slave. Here Aly was one of them. Now she got the worm's-eye view of the Rittevon court, told by those around her after they had gossiped with Rajmuat's other servants and slaves.

They were united in their belief that King Oron would die soon. The old man had been failing in health and mind over the last five years. Hazarin, the sole remaining child of

King Oron's first marriage, was the rakas' bet to inherit the throne. They thought Hazarin was as peculiar in his ways as his father, with an affection for huge meals and strange drugs. His next relative was his half sister, Princess Imajane, but under the luarin law no woman could succeed to the throne. Last of all there was Dunevon, born the same year as Elsren, child of the king's third wife.

"Oron's wives don't seem very lucky," Aly remarked. The people around her burst into laughter.

"You're right enough there," the head footman, Ulasim, replied with a grin. He was in his forties, a hard-muscled raka with direct brown eyes, black hair pulled back in a horsetail, a mustache, and a chin beard. His nose had met someone's fist, elbow, or knee far more often than Aly's had. He was a hard man, but fair, and the household respected him. He told Aly, "See, His Majesty starts to think his wives have lovers, and, well . . ." He drew his thumb across his throat.

"Maybe Lombyn's best for us," remarked one woman, her face shadowed.

"You haven't been there," Ulasim informed her. "It gets *cold* on the Tanair plateau. No jungle, the birds all drab little things . . ."

"There's condors," argued a hostler. "And crows."

"And *big* drab birds," retorted Ulasim. "It's in the middle of nowhere, not a town worthy of the name for miles. I was born on those lands. I know."

"Then why did you come?" demanded a maid. "You had plenty of offers to serve elsewhere."

Ulasim looked into the fire, his face somber. Finally he said quietly, "The duke's the best man I've ever served. I came to his house with Duchess Sarugani, and I never regretted it. These are good people. I won't turn my back on them." He looked around the circle, meeting everyone's eyes. He stopped at Aly. "Maybe you think we'll be left in peace out there. I don't. They'll need all the friends they can get." He took another drink of arak.

He'd be a good man to have on my side, Aly thought. If I can get him there without him thinking I'm up to something. That will be interesting.

She turned to Chenaol. "Did *you* know the first duchess?" she asked. Chenaol had the same Lombyn accent, dulled by years in Rajmuat, as Ulasim.

Chuckles sounded around the fire. "She was a handful," Chenaol admitted. "I worked for her relatives, House Temaida—that'd be the lesser nobility, the raka, Aly. Anyway, Sarugani came down from Lombyn and stayed with us when she was presented to the nobility. I was assistant cook for the Temaidas then. We got friendly because she liked my herb garden. I asked to go with her when she married, and the family agreed. She was spirited, always up to something. She had half the luarin nobles as well as the raka chasing her. And the present duchess, she and Sarugani were like sisters."

"You'd never know they were raka and luarin, they were that close," someone murmured. "Her Grace doesn't care what color your skin is."

"Now, Sarugani was fearless in the saddle." The head hostler, Lokeij, was present, a white-haired old raka slave everyone knew would never be sold. The family hadn't even suggested that he be put up for sale. "Ride anything in the stable, broken in or no. She made those luarin biddies cackle, riding in breeches like a proper woman of the raka."

"It was her riding that did her in," Ulasim went on. "Lady Dove was five, or a bit short of that, and Lady Sarai was nine. The duchess went hunting one day with friends. The horse failed in a jump—broke her neck and the beast's legs. My lord was nearly a ghost for long after. We looked after him and the young ladies till his aunt Nuritin moved in. *She* woke him up."

"Gave him an earful, told him he was a disgrace," said the raka healer Rihani with a grin. "Told him he was neglecting the girls and his house, he'd no male heir, and he'd let himself go to seed. Hounded him until he started to live again. Convinced him he'd best marry, since he wasn't getting any younger and he'd no son and all. That's when he realized what a treasure Lady Winnamine was."

"*Luarin*," said Lokeij, shaking his head. "Always getting themselves into this male heir mess. We raka know better. It isn't the equipment the clan chief's got, it's up here." He tapped his forehead. "The old king wouldn't be such a fool if he broke with luarin custom and made Lady Imajane his heir. *She'd* get the country in order."

"Hush!" someone whispered. Aly saw Lokeij jerk, as if he'd just taken an elbow in the ribs. "It's treason to talk so—a whipping at the very least!"

"So all those raka turned out to see Sarugani's girls." Aly used a tone that implied she didn't believe what she was saying. She wanted to steer the talk away from possible treason, as well as learn a little more about the family. "Is that it? Seems to me they were more interested in how beautiful Lady Sarai is. How important was her mother, anyway?"

The raka present exchanged glances. Finally Ulasim said quietly, "She was just from an old raka family, that's all. Personally, I think these raka knew of the duke's disgrace. How often will they see anyone who isn't raka being sent into exile? He is related to the king, after all."

Aly could have pointed out that other luarin nobles must have gone into exile, but her instincts told her it was time to shut up. It was always difficult to probe for information gently, without causing others to think she might know more than was safe.

Ulasim got to his feet as nimbly as if he'd never touched the arak. "I don't know about you, but we sail at dawn, and I'd like a proper sleep."

Aly sighed to herself. She would have to teach these people better ways to steer someone away from a dangerous line of thought. Ulasim might as well have shouted that she'd touched on a secret.

The footman's words signaled the other servants and slaves. They, too, rose and went to their hammocks aboard the different ships.

As Aly helped Chenaol carry the cooking tools back aboard ship, the cook told her, "Free raka—the ones who don't work for the luarin—keep their reasons to themselves. They don't trust us city folk, and we fear them. Every time they revolt, and they do, now and then, the luarin usually execute all the raka they can catch. That would include us. So people get jumpy when you ask too many questions."

"You don't keep any ties with your families?" Aly asked as she stowed the last of the herbs. She turned to look Chenaol in the face. The woman blinked. Liar's sign, thought Aly. That's what Da calls it when someone blinks during questioning.

"Seldom," Chenaol replied, blinking again. "Mostly we keep to our city family. Off to bed with you, then."

Aly obeyed, though it took some time for her to sleep. She was going through her memory, trying to see if she had ever known the proportion of Copper Isle raka to the luarin. And what secret was so important that even slaves and servants with drink in them wouldn't hint at it?

You do your bit, and then you get to pretend to be part of the scenery. You sit and you sweat and you hope that all those who are paid to go out and show their faces and do the bloody work don't foul everything up. The waiting for others to act on your information will give you the belly gripes, but that's what agents do. And I advise you not to pray as you wait. You don't know who will answer, times like that.

—*From* A Workbook for a Young Spy

4

THE ROAD

Lombyn Island, Tanair Castle and village

They set sail once more at dawn, baking quietly in a sudden burst of early summer. By midmorning Lombyn was in view, an island nearly as long and wide as Gempang, but far more mountainous, with a ribbon of green jungle at the mountains' feet, pine forest above, and then bare rock. Somewhere behind those granite barriers, Aly knew, was the Tanair estate, part of Sarugani's dowry and Sarai's inheritance. It was as safe as any of the Balitang holdings, since it belonged to Sarai and not Mequen, which made it less vulnerable to seizure by the king. As a refuge, it might just work, Aly thought.

Their ships were closing on Dimari's harbor when Aly noticed movement in the skies. Winged horses rode the columns of warm air that rose along the cliffs of Lombyn, their immense, batlike wings outstretched, their manes and tails fluttering as they climbed and descended. Aly adjusted her Sight. Above the jungles and mountains she saw even more of the great creatures, all colors of horse from solid black to solid white, roan, buckskin, bay, chestnut, piebald, odd-colored, flea-bitten, dapple, a universe of horsedom in the air of Lombyn. She gasped in awe, thrilled to see these great immortals playing in midair. Did Aunt Daine know there were so many in the Isles? Winged horses were rare in Tortall. Aly had seen a handful of the smallest kinds, no bigger than starlings, and only one of these big creatures. Hurroks, the predatory fanged and clawed variation of this breed of immortal, they had aplenty, but their milder cousins were scarce.

"In the old times, the *kudarung*, what you would call winged horses, nested in all of our Isles." Ulasim, dressed for the day in a sleeveless cotton tunic and breeches, had come to lean on the rail next to her. He squinted up at the fliers, a hint of a smile on his face. "They are sacred to the raka, the sign of our royal house, and its messengers. Then foreign mages banished the kudarung to the gods' home with the other immortals, without asking our thoughts on the matter. They left us only songs and paintings to remind us of their beauty. Kudarung are found in all sizes. Those are just the biggest of them."

"I'd heard they are different sizes," Aly murmured, entranced. "How prideful of those mages, to banish them without asking you." She remembered something she'd read in some of her father's reports. "But they're back now," she pointed out, her tone one of harmless interest. "So do they serve the Rittevon kings? I mean, you said they were royal messengers."

The smile Ulasim had brought to the rail vanished. His mouth flattened into a tight line. At last he leaned over the rail and spat into the water. "You speak lightly of serious things, Aly. Five of the kudarung were captured by Crown mages and forced to breed. So yes, the luarin king has kudarung as messengers, but they did not come freely to him, as they did to our queens." He turned to Aly, his brown eyes sharp as they rested on her face. "There will be more raka than luarin, in the Lombyn highlands," he said. "You should speak more carefully there. None of the raka are so tame as we let the luarin believe." He turned and went below, leaving Aly to consider what he had said.

They docked in Dimari, Lombyn's main port, around noon. Once again the family and a handful of body servants went to an inn to rest. The slaves and servants unloaded possessions from the ships, then packed them in wagons purchased by servants who had left for Dimari the day the Balitangs knew they were going into exile. Some wagons were already loaded with foodstuffs. Near them the servants had penned or cooped domestic animals. The duke had planned ahead, Chenaol told Veron, the luarin who commanded the household men-at-arms. Life was harder on the plateau where Tanair stood, the crops less plentiful. The duke had purchased supplies in advance, to keep the family and their attendants from placing a burden on the local folk. One of the island's merchant caravans had already been engaged to carry extra supplies in when they made their summer rounds. Not only would the family not create a burden for the people who had farmed Tanair for centuries, but they meant to expand what was grown and herded to the benefit of everyone.

"What *is* Tanair, exactly?" Aly asked the cook as she struggled to push a crate onto a wagon of kitchen supplies. "I mean, I know it's a fiefdom, but no one's said if there's a town anywhere near, or a river . . ."

"Tanair Castle is a tower with outbuildings," Chenaol replied with grim good humor. "Inner wall, outer wall. Then there's the village around it. Inti and Pohon are two other villages on the plateau. There's some luarin blood in the Tanair folk and some in Inti, which stands on the road leading to the western ocean. There's no luarin blood in Pohon. It used to be that any part-luarin who wandered into Pohon never wandered out, so the luarin stay away. Word gets around."

"How charming," Aly murmured.

Chenaol shrugged, her dark eyes twinkling in their folds of flesh. "Pohon folk are a righteous lot—or maybe *destructive*'s a better word. They're so cut off up there that they don't realize the luarin are here to stay, and breed. Maybe when they've had the chance to meet our ladies, they'll change their—Oh, curse it, those idiots will smash my peppers, mauling them about that way. You there!" she yelled to two dockhands as they slung baskets into a wagon. "Those aren't hay bales!"

Interesting, Aly thought as she continued to load the kitchen wagon. Chenaol had almost let something important slip. Why would the Pohon folk change their minds about luarin when they met "the ladies"? What about Sarai and Dove would change minds, and why did the cook want the Pohon minds changed?

Aly felt as if she was reading a book from which every second page was missing. She needed to learn more about the raka and their politics.

The next morning masters, servants, men-at-arms, slaves, and animals set out from Dimari, bound for the Turnshe Mountains, which formed Tanair's eastern border. On the first day they rode through lush, settled lands owned by luarin and farmed by raka. The people labored in the sun and heat, men and women alike wearing only a tied sarong tucked up to keep them out of the mud. This was one of the most fertile parts of the Isles. Everywhere that Ali looked she saw rice paddies, the plants covering the brown water in which they were planted in a green mist. They also passed coconut and bamboo plantations. Struggling to keep Elsren and Petranne from falling out of the covered, padded wagon where they would spend the rest of their trip, Aly did not envy the raka and part-raka who labored everywhere. When overseers descended on the slaves with whips raised, Aly had to look away. Without the Balitangs, she might have been one of those slaves, laboring in filth and being punished if she displeased a man with a whip.

This was the way most of the world lived, on slave labor. Tortall didn't encourage it, any more than Tusaine, Galla, and Tyra did, but some people in those countries did own slaves. Everyone ignored the working slave populations of the great farms of Maren. Aly just wasn't used to it. To her the slaves looked very like the convict gangs who labored on Tortall's roads and in its quarries and mines. At least those people had committed crimes to get a sentence of hard labor.

Overseers or no, when the Balitang wagons passed the farms, the raka straightened to watch them pass. Dark-skinned full-bloods or varying, light-skinned mixed-bloods, all shaded their eyes and looked on in silence as the wagons rattled by. Free raka, not wearing slave collars, dressed in colorful sarongs and light tops, stood by the road to see them. There they remained as the caravan, encircled by Veron's twenty men-at-arms, passed by in all its clatter. Others watched in the villages, from trees and upper-story windows of houses, on bridges and on rocks in the rivers. None of them said a word. All returned to their tasks as the last goat and man-at-arms went by.

Aly itched to question them but, trapped in the wagon with Elsren, Petranne, the duchess's maid, Pembery, and the house's mildly Gifted healer, Rihani, she had to accept it as an itch she couldn't scratch. That vexed her. Grandfather Myles always said it was impossible to have too much information. Aly agreed from the bottom of her heart as she watched those stony, copper-skinned faces. She would not sleep easily until she knew what was on the raka's minds.

They spent the night at a village inn and set out once more at dawn that day and the next. On their third day out of Dimari the road entered dense jungle. It was like being enfolded in a vast, warm, damp woolen cloak under the trees. The ground actually steamed in the early morning as the land gave up moisture under the warming sun. Here the raka appeared at the head of turnoffs that led to their villages. The deeper into the jungle they went, the fewer raka men wore sarongs or shirts in the heat. Many wore only a loincloth; they carried farm and woodland tools or hunting spears.

The men-at-arms rode closer to the wagons, but Aly saw no hostility on those raka faces. None of the onlookers so much as moved when they passed. What draws them to stare at Dove and Sarai? she wondered endlessly, until she wished she could just yank the questions out of her head and bury them under a rock. If the raka among the duke's people knew, they were not saying. She ought to know: she took every opportunity to drift near them when they weren't aware of her, listening in on their conversations. Many were as spooked by the local raka as Aly. None would speculate on what made them flock to view the Balitangs.

With the sun directly overhead they stopped on the road for a cold lunch of bread, dates, and sticky rice dumplings stuffed with beef and steamed in banana leaves. Aly expected Elsren and Petranne to complain at the rough fare, but they regarded the food and life in the wagons as an adventure. Elsren promised that as long as Aly produced new stories, he and his sister would behave.

"You have a happy nature," Aly told them as she cleaned Petranne up after lunch.

The four-year-old beamed at her. "I'm having fun," she informed Aly. "Aren't you having fun?"

Aly grinned at the girl. "Actually, now that you mention it, yes, I am. I've never seen jungle before."

"We have lots," Petranne explained as Aly scrubbed Elsren's upturned face. "There's hundreds and hundreds of islands, and they *all* have jungles on them."

"And have you seen them all?" Aly teased. She had spoken only half the truth to Petranne. The jungle, with its myriad flowers, trees, vines, and birds, was a gorgeous place, even if it was so humid it was hard to breathe. Aly could look at such beauty all day, except that she also knew the dangers of such thickly wooded ground. Jungles—any forest, for that matter—limited her field of vision. They offered outlaws too many opportunities for mischief. The fact that the raka could be so quiet in their movements, never giving away their presence until the Balitangs rounded a bend in the road and saw them, made Aly's nerves fizz with alertness. One of these times the raka around the bend might not be so friendly.

After lunch the raka witnesses vanished. Aly discovered she disliked that even more than she disliked having scores of raka silently watch the Balitangs. Their caravan passed a number of openings where roads and trails led away from their road, but they saw no one. As far as Aly knew, the jungle raka might be up to any unpleasant thing.

Their caravan traveled about ten miles before a horse on the lead wagon picked up a stone in her hoof. Mequen commanded their group to halt, which for Aly meant permission to climb out and look around. She stretched as she hobbled down the line of wagons and animals. Her entire body felt cramped. Not only had Petranne, Elsren, Pembery, and

Rihani decided to stretch out for a nap, but Dove and Sarai had joined them, filling the wagon bed as full as it could get.

The kinks worked from her back, Aly observed the jungle, thinking. Something wasn't right. This was more than the absence of raka watchers. What was it? She knelt, pretending to tie a sandal lace, as she examined their surroundings.

When in doubt, her mother had said during hunts and rides through bandit country, use your ears. Aly used hers. Leaf movement: some, in a slight breeze. Tree movement: no, the breeze wasn't strong enough. Moving water: the burble of the stream along the right side of the road. Feet in leaves: a couple of the men-at-arms crouched by the stream for a drink of water.

She heard no animals. Where were the calls of howler monkeys and the chatter of parrots? Where were the rustlings of mice and shrews in the leaf clutter? The jungle should have been alive with wildlife sounds. The hair at the back of her neck prickled. Something was very wrong. The raka who had vanished from the roadsides knew it, and now she did, too.

Aly looked up and down the length of the train. She didn't want to go shrieking to the duke and duchess. They would listen, but she would also draw the attention of the other servants and slaves, and she had been bred from the cradle not to draw attention. She needed to encourage someone else to voice concern at the silence.

At the back of the train, where the cows walked on tethers, five men-at-arms, some part raka, one full raka, had clustered to talk. There was tension in every line of their bodies. They would do.

Aly strolled up to them. "I know I'm new here," she began. The five men turned to stare at her. She smiled at them shyly. "It's just, you know, I'm a country girl at home, and my old dad taught me a few things."

The one named Fesgao, Veron's second-in-command and a pure-blood raka, raised angled brows. His ebony eyes were calm and level. His nose followed a straight line down from his forehead; he had high cheekbones and a square chin. Dressed in Balitang tunic and breeches, he was solidly muscled. His sword and dagger were plain but of good-quality steel. Aly guessed him to be thirty or so, younger than Ulasim and more reserved than the head footman. "And why should we be interested in what your father taught to you, little girl?" he inquired.

"Because Da taught me the same thing you have noticed," she said. It was a guess, but judging from the way two of the men looked up at the trees, it was a good guess. "Or do all your birds and mice and monkeys take a nap this time of day? Back home, we hear silence in the woods, and we arm up."

"And do you know woods?" asked Fesgao.

"I know the ones at home," she said. "I know them as well as Da."

The next moment Fesgao gripped Aly by the arm and drew her to the front of the line of wagons. Mequen and his sergeant, Veron, were idly talking while they watched a servant unharness the mare who had taken the stone in her shoe. The old hostler, Lokeij, waited with a fresh horse, his lined, monkey-like face worried as he looked at the lame mare. The other slaves liked to tease him that he thought of each and every Balitang horse as his own child.

"Fesgao, what's this?" demanded the sergeant. "And who's this wench?"

"A country girl who hears the same thing we do," said the raka, letting go of Aly.

"And what does she hear?" asked Mequen, his steady brown eyes on Aly's face.

She bobbed an awkward curtsey. "Nothing, Your Grace," she replied, keeping her eyes down as she acted the same country girl she had pretended to be for Fesgao. "Back home, in the woods, when the animals go silent, oft-times it's because robbers are waiting up the road."

"I'd like permission to scout ahead, sir," Fesgao said to Veron. "We five are country-bred like her. In the city streets you know I follow your lead without pause. Here . . ." He left the word hanging in the air as he met Veron's gaze.

The sergeant, a luarin, scratched his head and sighed. "Forgive me for saying it, Your Grace, but he's right. I'm not a raka jungle runner. Fesgao is."

Mequen looked at Aly. Now she returned his gaze in an un-slave-like manner, silently reminding him of a god whose voice had driven him and the duchess to their knees. After a moment Mequen focused his gaze on Fesgao. "What do you recommend?"

"If we may scout ahead?" asked Fesgao.

"Go," Mequen ordered.

Fesgao hand-signaled to three of his companions. They faded into the brush on the left of the road. Aly couldn't even hear them once they vanished from sight: these men were good.

Fesgao and the other part-raka guard started for the right side of the road. Suddenly Fesgao stopped and looked at Aly. "Do you wish to come and see for yourself?" he asked, an ironic twinkle in his eyes.

Aly shook her head. "*I'm* no warrior," she said, still the country girl.

Fesgao let the tiniest of smiles reach his lips. Then he

and the other man-at-arms skipped over the brook and vanished into the jungle.

Mequen looked around, his eyes assessing their company. "Sergeant, have your people on their horses, bows at the ready. Ulasim," he called cheerfully. "A word, if you please?"

The footman, who'd been talking to Chenaol, walked over to them. "Your Grace?"

Mequen lowered his voice. "Quietly—*quietly*—get the bows and spears out. Give them to any of the servants who can use them." He glanced at his wife by the wagon, and added, "Sarai and Dove as well. We may have a problem, but tell everyone to behave as if this were normal." As Winnamine sighed, Ulasim bowed. He ambled down the line of wagons, looking for all the world like a man taking a leisurely stroll, but he managed to speak to all of the free servants.

"It will take me days to undo the wildness that your putting weapons in the girls' hands will stir up," Winnamine told her husband softly.

"We may need that wildness out here," Mequen replied. "Winna, we aren't in Rajmuat now. We aren't living a round of parties and concerts and hunts. Perhaps the rules of Rajmuat no longer apply."

Aly started to ease back, keeping her head down, pretending to be invisible, since they seemed to have forgotten she was there. "Aly," said the duke.

She cringed and halted. After a moment she remembered who she was supposed to be, and bobbed a curtsy.

"Did the god warn you?" Mequen asked quietly. "Are these King Oron's assassins?" He and his wife watched her intently.

"Your Grace, I don't need the god for something as plain as this," Aly said, her voice just loud enough for them to hear.

"Frankly, I'd as soon not trouble him any more than I can help. Gods . . ." She chose her words carefully. "Gods complicate things." It was the understatement of her life, to judge by the havoc her mother's Goddess and her Aunt Daine's god relatives had wreaked.

"Here I'd hoped they would simplify them," Winnamine remarked with a sigh.

Aly grinned. "That wouldn't be very interesting," she said.

The duchess raised her eyebrows. "I do not like interesting things," she said, amusement in her eyes even though her tone was one of reproof. "They tend to bite painfully."

A thought caught Aly's attention. "You know, Your Grace, we might make some noise, to distract the robbers," she said. "Something to account for our still being here." She nodded toward the horses. Lokeij was almost finished hitching up the fresh cart horse.

Winnamine went over to the old man and whispered in his ear. Lokeij nodded and walked down the line with the limping mare. A moment later Aly saw two menservants go to work on one of the wheels of a supply wagon, cursing loudly. Lokeij stopped to confer briefly with Ulasim, who came trotting up to the duke and duchess, a worried look on his face.

"Your Grace, my lady," he said, puffing slightly as Veron rode up to see what was going on, "forgive me, but one of the men says we have trouble with one of the wagons."

"What do you mean, a wheel's coming off?" cried the duchess, the image of appalled nobility. "We can't loiter here! We'll never reach the inn by dark at this rate, and I simply cannot sleep in the open!"

Within moments the caravan was transformed, giving the appearance of an anthill that had been kicked. The men removed the wheel as others clustered around to see what the problem was. Veron's men-at-arms quietly armed themselves and mounted their horses, drawing in closer to the wagons. Ulasim and a couple of the servants moved down the length of the train. As they passed, Aly saw the gleam of weapons set within easy reach.

She started to head back to the children, but Winnamine called, "Stay, Aly. Pembery is exhausted—she never sleeps well when she travels. Help me to untangle these silks."

Aly returned to the lead wagon. Winnamine did indeed have a heap of embroidery silks on her lap where she now sat on the wagon seat. She also had a drawn crossbow at her feet, hidden from view by the horses and her skirt. Startled, Aly glanced at Winnamine, then accepted a tangle of threads. "I want the girls to have decent marriages among their peers, which they won't get if they act like raka highland savages," Winna told Aly quietly. "But I never said I expected all women to be helpless and unable to defend their families."

"Yes, Your Grace," Aly murmured as she made a mess of the thread.

The duchess smiled. "Of course. You come from the land of fighting ladies like Queen Thayet, the Lioness, and Keladry of Mindelan," she remarked, laying an emerald strand flat on the seat beside her. "Doubtless you feel naked without a weapon in your hand."

Aly frowned at the mass of silk in her lap. "Your Grace, you only hear about the fighting women because they make the most noise," she told the duchess. "Most of Tortall's women wouldn't touch a sword if you begged them to. We have all sorts of females among us, you know."

Winnamine raised perfectly plucked brown eyebrows. "And which sort are you, to be the god's chosen?" she asked, her voice a whisper.

Aly shrugged. "I'm the confused sort." That answer startled a chuckle out of Winnamine.

Fesgao and his men eased out of the jungle and over to the lead wagon. Mequen and Sergeant Veron came to stand with the duchess and Aly. Fesgao brought a stick with him. He used it to draw a rough map in the dirt of the road.

"There's fourteen of them, on either side of the road just before it crosses a bridge," he told them. "This creek joins a bigger stream there. It's maybe a mile ahead." The other four men-at-arms nodded their agreement.

Mequen asked the question that Aly wanted to ask: "Are they fighters, or local?"

"Poor men, Your Grace," said another scout. "And women—two of them, anyway. The weapons are either old or they're farm weapons. They're not royal killers, just renegade jungle raka."

Aly could feel the relief that rose from the duke and duchess.

"Well, if we go forward, now that we're warned, we can fight them off," said the duke. "Or we can fall back to town and send the local soldiers to clean them out."

"They'll vanish from the area if they think we know they were here, Your Grace," said Veron gruffly. "Then the raka dogs will go after the next prey to cross upwind of them."

Aly scratched her head. In for a calf, in for a bull, she thought, and said, "I don't know if this could work, Your Grace, and I hope you forgive my boldness, but what if you send men to come up on their backs?"

"We could strike from behind," Fesgao said. If he'd taken offense over Veron's remark about raka dogs, his face did not show it. "And you could attack from the road. They would be caught between us."

Veron looked at Aly and shook his head. "From the lips of infants shall the truth come unadorned," he said, quoting a proverb. "If we are willing to risk casualties, Your Grace, we could be sure this rabble won't harass our supply caravans in the future."

"Instruct your men, sergeant," Mequen said. "How long should we wait until we set out?"

Within moments Fesgao and the other scouts, along with two of Ulasim's footmen who could shoot, had vanished back into the jungle. Winnamine counted slowly to one hundred while orders traveled down the line of servants and wagons. The wheel was put back on its wagon; Aly was ordered to sit with the children and keep them calm. No one considered giving her a weapon. In every slaveholding country it was illegal to give weapons to slaves.

Instead, Aly got Petranne and Elsren to lie flat on the wagon floor as part of a brand-new game, seeing how long they could hold perfectly still no matter what they heard. As she waited she murmured stories to keep them calm, feeling the weight of the knife she had stolen in Rajmuat heavy under her waistband. Dove and Sarai, bows in hand, covered either side of the wagon, pushing up the canvas just enough so that they could see out and aim.

As the wagon rumbled forward, Aly remembered her father's long-ago advice not to pray. Now she wondered, Was that how it started with you and Kyprioth, Da? You praying, and him answering? I mean to ask you that, when I come home this autumn.

The bumpy ride seemed to last forever. Elsren and Petranne had just begun to complain that Aly wasn't making sense when the wagon jolted to a stop. They heard yells and the crackle of bodies in the brush. Two arrows punched through the canvas wagon cover. Aly pushed Elsren and Petranne tight against the base of the padded seats, where arrows couldn't reach them. Pembery and the healer, Rihani, huddled against the other bank of padded seats, keeping their heads down as the maid whimpered and Rihani mouthed prayers. Sarai, her lovely face grim, shot her crossbow and re-loaded it. Dove watched through her opening in the canvas, her small hands trembling on the stock of her bow. Someone outside screamed; others yelled. Aly heard the clang of metal on metal, and a crash in the woods.

The noise stopped for a moment. Then Veron and Mequen shouted orders. At last Ulasim opened the canvas door into the wagon. "It's clear," he told everyone inside. "Rihani, you are needed. My ladies, your father wishes you to attend him. Aly, also."

"I'll look after the little ones," Pembery said gratefully. She gathered Elsren and Petranne into trembling arms. Both children tried to wriggle free, clamoring to see the battlefield as the maid clung to them.

Aly followed Sarai and Dove to the head of the wagon train. They had halted just before the bridge. Some of the dead lay in the jungle on either side of the road. A few of the household staff and men-at-arms sported wounds, but none of the Balitang party lay among the bodies as far as Aly could see. Fesgao, Veron, and the rest of Fesgao's party of men-at-arms were forcing six bandits to their knees, binding them in ropes while other men-at-arms leveled weapons at the captives to prevent their escape.

Aly's temples began to throb. She had not considered this possibility, that robbers might be captured. The neatest solution would have been if they'd all been killed or if those left alive had fled. What would the duke say? He was a sensible man. He should realize there was no question of letting the captives go. They would only rob the next group to come up this road, or else they would get reinforcements and attack the Balitangs again.

Aly clasped her hands tightly behind her back so that no one would see them shake. The Balitangs could not turn back with captives in tow. They would never reach the safety of the village they had left that morning, with its royal fort and soldiers, by dark. The duke's people would be under constant attack along the way from would-be rescuers. At their present crawling speed, they would need two days to reach the next royal outpost. The local families would have plenty of time to steal their men back. If the Balitangs kept the captives until they reached Tanair, it would mean six more people who must be fed and guarded. The duke could spare neither guards nor food. If he enslaved the robbers, Aly wouldn't trust them, particularly not if the new slaves got word of their whereabouts to their families.

There's just one solution, Aly thought as the duke and duchess watched her sidelong to see what, if anything, the god would order her to say. She couldn't let them know that her particular burden of a god had given her a wager, not instructions. She also couldn't bear to tell them what they had to do, what her father, grandfather, and mother would have told them they *must* do. They had to execute six impoverished men.

"Let's kill these raka swine," Sergeant Veron said, inspecting one bandit's rusty sword. His eyes were gray ice.

"Make sure their kin think twice before they attack luarin."

Duchess Winnamine looked at her husband and nodded, her face an emotionless mask. "My dear, it's the only solution."

Mequen shook his head, troubled.

"No!" cried Sarai, who might one day be faced with such a choice. "We can't do murder, and that's what it is, murder!"

"It's survival," Ulasim said gently. He was there in his capacity as the head of the male servants and slaves.

"Forgive us!" cried one of the bandits, a haggard-looking man in his forties. "We would never harm the la—"

"*Silence,*" ordered Fesgao, his dark eyes flashing.

"We swore a vow, on the altar, that all we would take is food, when you have so much," babbled another bandit.

"None of the others would help or even stay to hear it done," the man next to him added. "They did not come to see you pass. They retreated into the jungle to hide their faces in shame, but they know how it is with our village. They know we are desperate."

"The lord took everything for the tax, *everything,*" explained the first man who had spoken, talking fast. "Our children cry, their bellies empty. So we swore the vow before three villages. Our people would have killed us otherwise, had we harmed the la—"

Fesgao stepped forward and slapped the man, rocking the bandit back on his heels. "Keep your mouth *shut,* you fool," he hissed.

Aly pretended to be concerned with one of her fingernails. Something besides the normal treatment of criminals was going on here. Fesgao had twice stopped these men from saying one particular word, one that began with "la." Ladies, again, she told herself. He stops them from saying "ladies" in front of the luarin nobles. And these ladies aren't just

important to the local raka. Fesgao also thinks the ladies are
important. She wrote these thoughts on the growing list in
her head of things to investigate.

"Their families will come to free them, unless they know
their men are dead. They will fear us, and stay well away, if
we do it," the duke said reluctantly.

"Make them slaves," suggested Dove. Everyone turned
to stare at her. "Then sell them at the next army post."

Aly whistled silently. Now there was a solution she
hadn't considered. She eyed the small, dark twelve-year-old
with new respect.

"You can't enslave them," Sarai argued. "Look at them.
They're poor, half starved. What is their village like, if the
men look this bad? Papa, we'd make their lives worse, not
better. Their families need them to hunt, and fish—"

"And rob, and kill?" Winnamine asked, cutting her off.

"Why do we even discuss this?" demanded Veron, his
voice hard. "These dogs attacked members of the royal family. By law they must die. If we had time, we ought to hunt
down and burn out their nest—in fact, we should report it at
the next royal fort. This sort of lawlessness only gets worse if
your first response is a soft one."

The adults debated it further. Aly thought the duke was
about to order Veron and his men to kill the captives when
Sarai interrupted again. "Give them a choice, Papa," she
begged. "Death, slavery, or free and *loyal* service to our family. If they pick service, we'll have six more fighters—"

"Who will kill us as we sleep, begging your ladyship's
pardon," Veron interrupted. "Your offer speaks well of your
heart, but you will put us in danger."

"Make them swear by Mithros," retorted Sarai. "Or one
of the raka gods."

"People have broken vows to gods before," Winnamine

reminded Sarai gently. "If the god is busy elsewhere, it might be too late for us when the god finally punishes the oath breaker."

"Make them swear in blood." The quiet suggestion was Dove's. "If that's what they choose. No one breaks a blood oath. We can trust them if they swear that way, and if they don't . . ." The girl shrugged.

Those who broke such an oath died as their own blood boiled in their veins. No mage, however powerful, had found a way to prevent that. The gods had decreed it, and so it remained, a promise no one would dare to break. Aly looked from Dove to Sarai, a peculiar emotion stirring in her heart. She wasn't sure what it was, beyond respect for both girls, but it was powerful and troubling. She put it aside for the moment and looked to Mequen for a decision. The duchess and Ulasim nodded. When the duke looked at Aly, she nodded and ignored Veron's confused look. He would be asking himself why she was even present, let alone why his master seemed to want her opinion.

Before anyone could stop him, the man who had first spoken had wriggled over to Sarai. Awkwardly he leaned forward to touch his forehead to Sarai's shoe. "You are as gracious as you are beautiful," he whispered.

Aly bit her tongue. It was Dove who had truly found a way to keep these men alive. She glanced at Dove, who met her eyes and shrugged. "She's prettier," the younger girl murmured as she passed Aly on her way back to the wagon. "Everyone always goes to her first."

The oaths were given, the bandits untied. When the wagons rolled on, they did so with six new men and a parchment that bore each former bandit's thumbprint in his own blood. If their families attacked, the men would tell them the bargain they had made, and invite them to live at Tanair.

They camped beside the road at sunset and moved out at sunrise. It took the better part of the day to reach the royal fortress at the foot of Kellaura Pass. Only as they approached the fort did the local raka emerge again to watch them go by.

Inside the fortress walls, the Balitangs spent a day bathing in hot springs, sleeping in clean beds, and eating meals that were not cooked in a single pot. Another day of plodding brought them through the pass, watched at different points by silent raka, and into the high plains country on the far side of the mountains. They stayed the night at a second royal fort, among soldiers eager for fresh faces and news from Dimari and the capital. The raka waited beside the road that led the Balitangs northwest, watching them without a sound. They made Aly's flesh creep. At home people waved, or called their greetings or insults. She wished the raka would say *something*.

Two days later they passed through a ring of high-thrust rocks and clefts onto a broad, grassy plateau. Here a log palisade encircled a hill: their new home, Tanair Castle and village. Aly complained of stiff muscles to Pembery, Rihani, and the younger children, then hopped out of the wagon. She walked alongside it as they approached Tanair, taking the chance to view what she thought of as her summer home. The twenty-foot-high palisade did not inspire her with confidence, though the fifteen-foot-deep trench that lay before it, with its flooring of jagged-edged rocks, had promise. The wooden bridge to the village gate was sturdy enough to take the weight of their wagons, but wooden bridges could be burned or destroyed in a hurry. That wasn't too bad.

Inside the palisade lay the village, built around the foot of a raised earthen table capped by a stone wall. Aly swept her eyes over the village as they walked through, her busy mind ticking off details that might be useful later. The streets

were clean and the houses sturdy, built half of wood and half
of stone. There was plenty of space for herd animals and
flocks if they had to be brought inside the palisade in an
attack. The place had two smithies, which meant Tanair had
a certain level of prosperity, and the people who lined the
main street to greet their caravan looked capable enough. The
colors ranged from pure luarin white to pure raka copper
brown. Unlike the people of the lowland jungles, these
villagers dressed for warmth in wraparound jackets and
leggings, many of them brightly colored and embroidered.
There was an inn with a proper stable, which meant that
travelers came and went, and that money fed the village cof-
fers. There were sheds and outbuildings, too, and temples for
the luarin gods and the raka gods on opposite sides of the
street. Aly liked it. People with a good life would defend it
more vigorously than people who were beaten down by their
masters and their fates.

The wagon train climbed up the earthen table and
through the gate in the stone wall, into Tanair Castle's outer
courtyard. It was on a direct line with the inner gate, which
revealed Tanair to be an ancient five-story tower with outbuildings. Aly had thought Pirate's Swoop was plain, but at
least they had three towers, connected by the castle's wings.
Lady Sarugani's family may have been ancient, but plainly
they were not wealthy. The soldiers who lined the stone wall
were old men and boys in their midteens.

Aly rubbed the back of her neck. Well, it's a challenge,
she thought. If I can keep these people safe here, I'll be able
to handle anything Da could throw at me later. And who
knows? Maybe King Oron will forget us. All I need is to keep
the children alive for the summer, after all. It might take him
that long to remember he sent the Balitangs away.

You promised me help! she thought to Kyprioth as she helped Elsren and Petranne out of the wagon. The sooner the better, if you please. I can't see everything at once!

There is no better spy than a slave. No one notices them. They may go anywhere, look into anything, if they are careful. They can ask questions that would be suspicious coming from others, because everyone believes a slave is stupid, even given evidence he is not.

—From a letter to Aly when she was ten from her grandfather, Myles of Olau

5

SETTLING IN

The realization that life as it had been lived in Rajmuat must now change struck the family, servants, and slaves as they looked over the grounds of Tanair Castle. In the outer courtyard lay stables, storage sheds, a carpentry workshop, a dovecote, a mews, and a small kennel. Within the inner courtyard the broad stone keep was supplied with a kitchen attached to it on the ground floor, a barracks for the men-at-arms, two wells, and a blacksmith's forge.

"But where do we sleep?" one of the Balitang servants asked.

"In the main hall, on pallets," Chenaol told them. "This castle was part of Duchess Sarugani's dowry when she married His Grace. When the family stayed here, servants and slaves slept together in the main hall, on the floor."

When some of the free servants protested that they would not sleep among slaves, Chenaol shrugged. "Before the family built the upper stories, my mother said *they* slept in the main hall, too," she said. "Their quarters are right overhead now, where the hearth fire warms the upper rooms."

A shriek from Elsren called Aly back to her charges. She calmly ended a hair-pulling dispute between the boy and his sister, Petranne, and gave both of them things to carry inside. Petranne tried to shove the box she held back into Aly's hands. "We're not *slaves*," the four-year-old said.

Aly looked at the thick gray clouds that raced over the sky, then shrugged and set the box in a cart. "All right, my lady, but don't come crying to me when the storm wets your dolls. That's the box they're in," she replied, slinging rolled blankets over one shoulder and a heavy pack over another. "Come on, my lord Elsren."

The boy turned, stuck his tongue out at his sister, and marched toward the castle door, manfully hauling a small basket. Petranne caught up with them as they entered the castle. In one hand she carried the box with her dolls in it; in the other she carried a basket with Elsren's wooden toys.

Everyone worked fast to get their belongings into shelter. After her last trip inside, Aly lingered on the steps to the keep's main door. Thunder growled in the distance. She gnawed her lip, trying to remember if she had found all of the children's things.

"So, Aly Bright Eyes," said Ulasim, coming to a halt beside her. The weight of the box he carried made the heavy muscles of his arms bulge, though he stood as if it weighed nothing at all. "Wishing they'd sent you back to the Rajmuat slave pens?"

Aly glanced along the line of his back. His tunic, pulled tight by the weight of the box, revealed extremely heavy muscles for someone who was a head footman. She raised an eyebrow. "Are you?" she asked, curious.

"I savor the delights of civilization," he informed her, his long mouth in a crooked line. In some ways he reminded her of Da. "I'm spoiled, that's all. I'll recover."

"But for you this is home, isn't it?" Aly wanted to know. "Aren't you glad to be home?"

Ulasim shook his head. "Tanair isn't my home. I'm from Pohon."

He'd startled her. She let him see it. "And you work for luarin? Chenaol says the people there hate luarin."

"They do. It's a long story. I will wager you a gigit that Elsren is now at the top of the stairs, ready to tumble down. He *is* three. They have a talent for such things at that age."

He was probably right. Aly raced inside, deliberately running with her knees together as she flung up her heels, the awkward run of a maidservant who hated it. There was no need for anyone here to see that Aly could be swift, that she normally ran with the wide-open stride of someone who had been trained to it. She meant to give the household as few reasons to ask questions about her as possible.

Elsren wasn't near the stairs on the second floor of the keep, but he had found and unsheathed one of his father's daggers, testing it on the wooden floor. Aly took the weapon, scolded Elsren, then threw the screaming child over one shoulder and climbed up to the third story. She plopped Elsren on the floor of the small chamber he would share with Petranne, next to a heap of his toys. As he started to play with them she got to work making the beds.

She was nearly finished unpacking when Pembery came for her. "His Grace and the duchess wish to speak to you in their rooms," she told Aly.

Aly curtsied to her and trotted downstairs, mentally listing all she had to do before she could sleep that night. Bathe the children tomorrow, she told herself. By the time Petranne and Elsren finish supper, they'll be so worn out they won't even be able to sit upright. Little monkeys. No wonder Mother spent so much time away, if Thom, Alan, and I were half as lively as these two. And I need to find that missing trunk of clothes. Ulasim might know what happened to it. . . .

She knocked on the closed door that was the entrance to the suite of rooms shared by the duke and duchess. "Come in," Mequen called.

"Close the door behind you," added Winnamine.

Aly bowed to her masters, wondering what was going on now. Their rooms—sitting room, bedroom, privy, solar— were only half unpacked. Lightning flashed through cracks in the closed wooden shutters, and rain thudded against them. The keep was so old-fashioned that none of the windows had glass, which was still too expensive for all but the greatest lords, let alone the raka nobility. Candles burned on branches set on tables; cressets of burning coals lit the main hall and stairs. Winnamine was kneeling beside a crate in the sitting room, taking out neatly folded clothes, while Mequen stood before the hearth.

"We're going to free you, Aly," Winnamine announced.

Aly held a finger to her lips to hush the duchess, then went to the door that opened onto the servants' stair. It gave way stiffly, and the landing and stairs were covered with dust and cobwebs. She closed it again, reassured that anyone who might have thought to eavesdrop from there would have left a mark. She couldn't depend on that reassurance in the future. The servants would be cleaning the back passages soon, for access to the rooms on the upper levels. She went to open the bedroom door. The bedchamber was undisturbed except for trunks and boxes piled by the door, to be unpacked as soon as the room was cleaned. She left that door open so that no one could sneak in and eavesdrop. She wanted to do the same with the servants' stair, but their conversation would echo through the stone corridor if she did.

"Forgive me, Your Graces," she said, bowing to her owners. "I'd prefer that no one overhear."

Winnamine raised her eyebrows, then continued, "My lord and I have discussed it. It's not right, keeping a slave collar on the god's messenger."

Aly rubbed her nose gently. This should have occurred to you, she scolded herself. True, she hated that metal ring. It was a constant annoyance, chafing her tender skin, pressing on her throat when she turned over in her sleep. The Balitangs had changed the radius of the magic on the collar for the greater spaces of Tanair, but even so, if she had to go farther than five miles from any member of the family, it would choke her until she returned to them or died.

And she needed the cursed thing.

"I thank you, Your Grace, but no," she told her mistress. "Truly, I don't require freedom just yet."

The duchess froze in the middle of lifting tunics from the chest. The duke turned slowly. Their brown eyes, his deep-set in folds of flesh, hers even under perfect brows, locked on Aly.

"This isn't our attempt to rid ourselves of you," Mequen told her. "You may masquerade as a servant, that's all, free to go wherever you like."

Aly sighed. "May I sit, Your Grace?" she asked. "I've been running up and down those stairs all afternoon. My feet are killing me."

Both of them stiffened momentarily, half offended that a slave would sit in their presence. It was Mequen who thawed first. "How thoughtless of us. Sit, please." He took one of the chairs for himself. Winnamine looked at her husband, raising her brows. He shrugged and flicked his eyes at Aly. Aly grinned, having read, "Are you mad?" and "She is the god's messenger" in their silent exchange. It was a good marriage when a couple could communicate easily without speaking.

The duchess carried the stack of clothes into the bed-chamber, then returned. Only when she sat down did Aly do so. It might have been too much to ask her to return to a room where the slave was already seated.

Aly took a deep breath and leaned forward, bracing her arms on her knees, a position her da favored when he needed to explain things. "Servants aren't free in a way that's useful, Your Grace. People expect servants to be loyal. Everyone knows that if a servant dislikes a master, he finds a better one. Nobody expects a slave to be loyal or clever. We hear things servants won't. And if slaves turn up somewhere they don't usually go, everyone assumes their masters ordered them to go there. I really am far more use to you as a slave."

Duke Mequen frowned at her. "But every slave wants to be free."

"Actually, some don't," Winnamine remarked in a thoughtful voice. "I've overheard them say that servants always risk finding themselves in the street with no money and no way to get proper work, while a slave is cared for all his days."

"If the slave has a good master," Mequen pointed out.

"There's another thing to consider," Aly told them. "I need answers to questions no one will answer for someone who's luarin, and free. Me being a slave solves that little prob-lem. Even free raka feel superior to a luarin slave."

"That's . . . very subtle," the duke remarked slowly. "Tell me, Aly, who were you in Tortall?"

"I was a maid at Fief Tameran," she said, gazing at him with wide, innocent eyes. She had chosen Tameran because it was a holding she knew as well as the Swoop. "I was vis-iting my sister at Bay Cove when the raiders got me."

"What sort of maid?" asked the duchess. "You seem rather more knowing than the usual run of servant."

"General," replied Aly, her voice casual. "Minding the other servants' children, helping in the kitchen when we had guests, sewing, gardening, the like. As for the knowingness, well, I've always been nosy, I suppose. We were schooled— by the queen's decree, all Tortallan children learn their letters and sums. I learned a bit more than that. As for the rest . . ." She shrugged. "It's just the way I am. Maybe the god made me smarter."

"You were free, but you wish to remain a slave," the duke said, as if he did not believe that he had heard correctly the first time.

"Once I have served the god, he's promised to send me home," Aly told him. It wasn't even a lie. "He won't need me forever, I'm sure."

Winnamine inspected her fingernails. "Then we'll reassign Pembery and give you her place," she said.

Aly winced. "You'll make her into an enemy I don't need, Your Grace," she replied. "And you'd be hobbling me. The god's told me what I must do. To keep you safe, I need to know this ground like I know my home. What I need for now is to range outside the walls. Can't I be given a herd to work? Goats would do best. They can graze anywhere. No one questions a goatherd clambering all over the land."

"You should have something to excuse your wanderings inside the wall as well," suggested Mequen. "What if at night, when everyone's indoors, you carry our messages for us? Thus we shall have reason to talk to you privately, when we give you notes to carry to the rest of the castle and the village."

Aly stared at him, startled. She hadn't thought the duke would have a talent for this kind of thing, but it seemed that he did. "Perfect, Your Grace, and thank you," she said, bowing in her chair. "I hadn't thought of that." The best secrets are those kept in full view, she thought to herself. *Everyone will see me running the Balitangs' errands, and no one will think twice about it.*

"But surely even looking after the little ones would be better than herd work," objected Winnamine.

"Not for my side of the god's bargain, begging Your Graces' pardon," explained Aly. "I need to learn how easy it would be for killers to strike the plateau. A herd will give me a reason to wander." She gnawed her lip and added, "If you wish to help me, I would be grateful if you would take the magic off my collar, so it won't choke me if I go more than five miles from one of you. A tablet of parchment would help, too, so I can make a map of things."

Silence fell for a moment as the couple considered what she had said. Mequen frowned in thought, then asked, "Why does the god take an interest in us? He didn't really say, except to tell us we have a great destiny."

Aly wanted to reply that the god had tricked them and that their children were his object. But then she would have to explain to these nice people that they were in the hands of a trickster, not Mithros. It would be far better for Aly if they didn't know about Kyprioth and his wager. "I don't believe gods are very forthcoming with things like answers, Your Grace," she replied. "I've yet to hear of one that was, anyway."

"Well," the duchess said, getting to her feet, "goats and messages it is. I'm afraid you must be demoted, Aly." She rummaged in a box that sat on a nearby table and produced a booklike tablet of parchment sheets stitched together. "Use this. What have you got to write with?"

"Charcoal's best, Your Grace, and easy for me to get.

Thank you," Aly said, fitting the tablet into the front of her tunic.

"Send the housekeeper to me, and I will arrange for your change in station," Winnamine said. "Report to His Grace or me here after supper for our messages. And let us know what we may do to help."

"Aly, come here." Aly obeyed, standing in front of the duke. He touched her metal collar with one finger and murmured a phrase in old Thak, the dead language favored by mages for spoken spells. The metal felt a little cooler on Aly's skin when Mequen dropped his hand. "There you are. You may go, then."

Aly bowed and left.

Worn out by settling in, the entire household made an early night of it after their arrival at Tanair. On her pallet in Elsren and Petranne's room, Aly dreamed of crows.

This dream felt real, but not in the same way as that dream of her parents. There she could not feel a thing. In this dream she sat in the fork of an immense tree, its bark rough on her skin. She heard the wind in the leaves overhead and smelled apple blossoms from somewhere. She was surrounded by crows who hopped from branch to branch above her, on either side, sharing her own branch. One flew at her, tugged her sleeve, and dropped back to the ground. Another struck her back with his claws, making Aly hang on to the tree trunk. The crow yanked her clothes, then fell away. Another darted up to pull at her leggings; one more took her right little finger in its beak and felt along its length. When its tongue tickled her, Aly pulled free. She sensed no harm in them, only great curiosity.

The one who had mouthed her finger now gripped her wrist gently with its beak, working its way up until it tasted cloth, then back down to her hand. It wandered over Aly's lap to her left side to repeat the procedure. Its fellows glided by to tug at Aly's clothes and hair. It seemed to be an inspection of some kind. The only one who did not touch her and jump back to the branches was the one who went from exploring her hands and arms to her ears, making her giggle.

"That *tickles,*" she said, lifting the bird down to her lap. Something had splashed or marked its back feathers with a white mark like a wave, a mark that sparkled faintly in Aly's Sight. "Vexed a mage, didn't you?" she asked the crow with a grin. "Were you tickling him, too?"

The mage was just crotchety, said a voice in Aly's head— Kyprioth's voice. *Our friend here has an excess of curiosity about humans even for a crow.* A new crow settled on the branch across from Aly. Unlike the other birds in the tree, this one wore sparkling rings on each talon and a necklace of sparkling gemstones. He blazed with godhood in Aly's Sight.

"Hello, Kyprioth," Aly said drily. "I take it all this is your idea?"

Most certainly, the bejeweled crow informed her in the god's crisp, kindly tones. *You asked for help, my dear. I have wagered that these crows will not be able to keep* you *safe from human predators until the autumn equinox. They will teach you their language, so they can spy for you.*

Aly scratched her head. Somehow, when she had dreamed of one day creating her own spy network, a flock of crows had not been part of her imaginings.

The crow who'd run afoul of a mage jumped from her lap to her shoulder. Gripping her flesh through her tunic with his powerful claws, he ran his beak through the inch-long brush that was her growing hair.

"That tickles, too, you know," she told him. The crow

continued to preen her. To Kyprioth she said, "If I have a wager with you, and the crows have a wager with you, where's the trick? Whenever there's a trickster about, there has to be a trick, everyone says so. What's yours?"

You don't have to worry, said Kyprioth, his tone entirely smug. *You're only here for the summer, remember? This is going to be my greatest trick ever, pulled off under the noses of mortals and gods alike, but it will take some time to put it in place. In the meantime, your new friends here will teach you useful crow sounds. You in turn will teach them to understand necessary human sounds.* He preened his chest feathers. *At least, I think the crows will teach you. Do you accept the wager, my cousins?* he asked the crows.

Will you keep your word about food? A crow's voice sounded in Aly's mind. It sounded like the speaker was a senior male. *There's barely enough in this high, flat place to keep two small flocks fed, let alone fifty more of us.*

I will ensure that you are all fed, Kyprioth reassured them. *You can't win the wager if you're starving.*

One female said, *I am not certain. You know how stupid two-leggers are.*

We are two-leggers ourselves. That voice was light, young, and male. It came from the crow on Aly's shoulder. *Or are you standing on your wings? We know they use counting words, just like us, and they have words for different kinds of predators. They are as much kin to us as Kyprioth there.*

You have always been too fond of those creatures, Nawat, said another female crow. *It isn't right.*

This seems like a lot of trouble to go to for a wager, added a new male crow.

If it's too much for you, I suppose I could take my wager to the ravens, Kyprioth remarked, cocking his head this way and that, as if he weighed up the crows. *Or the magpies. I thought you would find the stakes worth your while, but perhaps the ravens will like them better.*

We want the wager, snapped the female who had said she was uncertain. *Even if it takes forever to teach a stupid human.*

The crows shrugged their shoulders. *That means "very well,"* Nawat told Aly. *It means they agree.*

"What are your stakes?" Aly inquired, thinking they must be something special to cause the crows to jump when they saw their chance of winning slip away.

Nothing that concerns you, the stern female snapped. *So don't start thinking you can steal it for yourself. Now. We begin with numbers.*

Aly looked around for Kyprioth. He was gone. She shook her head and paid attention to her lessons.

Aly rose at dawn, her head buzzing with crow sounds. She scavenged a lunch from the yawning kitchen staff and went out to take charge of her goats. She had some experience at herding, from working with her friends who herded the Swoop's animals when she was younger. Time and education as her father's daughter and as a lady had put an end to the friendships, but at least she could manage fifteen goats.

The air was cool when she left Tanair, but she could tell the day would be warm, even hot. Except for puddles and damp grass, no traces of last night's thunderstorm remained. She led her charges up into the rocky ground just north of the point where the road entered the Tanair plateau. Grass sprouted everywhere between the granite boulders, which made the goats happy. Perched on the rocks, Aly could see the road and the palisade that enclosed castle and village, which made her happy. She could also see the two-man guard Veron had placed to watch the road and alert the castle if anyone came that way.

Once she was settled, Aly put aside her pack and walking stick. In all the stories of gods she had heard, she had learned that if a god wasn't somewhere else in the world, and the speaker was of interest to that god, all that person needed was to speak the god's name. "Kyprioth, I need to talk to you," she said quietly. "We are overdue for a private conversation."

"I'm touched," the familiar crisp voice remarked.

Aly turned. For the first time she saw the god standing on his own, not covered with someone else's form. She had seen the outlines of this shape in the matcher's body, so she guessed it was one he liked. He was only two inches taller than Aly, lean and wiry like a dancer, shoulders erect, bearded chin up. He had very short salt-and-pepper hair that was more salt than pepper. It extended all the way down to frame his mouth and face in that trim beard. His nose was short and broad, his eyebrows shaped in pointed arches. Leagues of mischief gleamed in his large brown eyes. He wore a Kyprin-style wrapped coat of green cloth. It was hung all over with charms, pins, brooches, and bits of jewelry. The native sarong covered his legs, the material made of intricate patterns woven in many-colored threads. The patterns shifted when Aly looked at them, making her dizzy. Even the knot over his left hip appeared to move in its many turns and folds. It seemed to be intertwined with fine silver, gold, and copper chains. His sandals were leather studded with copper. There were rings made of copper and studded with gems on all of his fingers and several of his toes. His lone earring was a copper hoop with beads on it made of colored stones.

"Well, here I am," he prodded. "Speak up. I can't do this

often. I don't want my divine siblings to learn I'm suddenly spending more time here in the last few weeks than I have in the last couple of centuries."

"I don't understand," Aly said, frowning.

"You don't need to," replied Kyprioth. "Too much information is bad for you mortals. Just look at your history if you want proof."

Aly made a note to ask the raka servants about Kyprioth and his relationship with the other Great Gods. She had a feeling it might be important. Changing the subject to keep him off balance, she said, "You're a god. Why not make yourself young and handsome?"

"I like myself this way," he informed her as the goats crowded around, sniffing him. "I look amiable and inoffensive, like an elder statesman, don't you think?"

"No elder statesmen *I* know," Aly retorted with a grin. "Ours all wear breeches or hose, like decent people." To the goats she said, "Get along with you! You'd think you'd never seen a god before."

"But they haven't," said Kyprioth, his voice smoothly reasonable. "And I like goats. They have so much talent for trouble. Aren't you happy with the crows?"

"The crows are delightful," Aly told him. "But they won't be enough. We need a mage, a real one, you know. Rihani's sweet, but mostly she knows healing. There's another healer in Tanair village. We've got a few who can shed light or start fires among the people who came up from Rajmuat, but if a real mage attacks, we are cooked cats. Unless you can make a mage out of me. A good one, of course."

"But you said it yourself, no one notices a slave," the god said reasonably. "You would be noticeable as a mage, particularly to other mages."

Aly scowled at him. "You were listening."

Kyprioth grinned at her. "Don't you wish you were a god? We can eavesdrop wherever we like and no one knows. Think how useful that skill would be for you. You don't need to be a mage, my dear. Your particular, *peculiar* array of talents is what interests me," he explained. "You really are quite exceptional, you know."

"Piffle," said Aly. "Da has dozens more skilled than me."

"Not necessarily, Alianne of Pirate's Swoop," Kyprioth replied. There was kindness in his voice. "You come of exceptional people, and you are a fitting heir to them."

"They don't think so," Aly pointed out. "And I agree. I'm the family layabout. Don't those four children deserve better?"

"Now you talk as if you believe all that nonsense you've been told about your unwillingness to work. We both know you aren't unwilling at all." The god lifted Aly's chin with a strong brown hand. "You were marked by fate from birth, just like your parents. Accept that, and see what you can accomplish here, on your own. It's going to be an interesting summer."

"Speaking of that, what am I here to protect them from?" Aly wanted to know. "You never said."

"All sorts of things." Kyprioth's voice was tart with exasperation as he released her chin. "Really, Aly, you have an imagination, *and* a sense of the real world. You shouldn't have to ask. Their family is out of favor with a monarch whose grip on sanity is loose, they've been sent to live in country far from any serious kind of defenses . . . would you like me to add a flock of hurroks or a herd of robber centaurs? Spidrens, perhaps? Rival nobles looking to gain favor with King Oron?"

Aly sighed. "No, thank you, the normal run of perils should be enough—"

He was gone, as if he'd never been there. Aly looked at the grass that had been under his feet: it wasn't even bent. "He'd be impossible to track," she told the kid that was leaning against her leg. "Aren't you supposed to be frolicking, or something?"

The kid butted her thigh.

"Shoo," Aly ordered. "I need to map this ground."

She was eating her lunch of bread and cheese when a crow flew down and lit a few feet away. Aly sat up as he stared at her. When he flicked his wings out in a settling-down gesture, she saw the white rippled streak on his feathers.

"Nawat?" she asked. "That's what they called you, isn't it?"

He replied with the wing shrug that was crow language for "yes."

Aly tossed him a chunk of the heavy brown bread. "So are you here to test me on what I learned?" she asked.

The crow gripped the bread in a talon and gulped down a piece. He answered with a rattling caw that startled the kids so much, they leaped over one another. Aly shook her head at the silly youngsters and searched her memory. "Five?" she guessed.

A wing shrug. She had gotten it right. Nawat voiced another sound.

"Hawks," Aly said with more confidence. "What's 'men'? Two-leggers, like me." She looked down at her chest. "Only flatter."

Nawat finished the bread and walked over to her. Gently he stretched his head forward and pecked her lightly on the bosom.

"Stop that!" Aly said, pushing him away. "I don't let males of my own kind do that, I'm not about to start with you!"

Nawat replied with a croak that Aly recognized.

"Men?" she asked.

The wing shrug. Nawat spoke two sounds that Aly correctly identified as "five men." *At least I'm learning a new language during my summer holiday,* she thought humorously. *So Mother won't be able to say I wasted my time completely.* She handed the crow some more bread.

That night she ate with the slaves and the six bandit men-at-arms in the castle courtyard: the soldiers refused to let the new recruits eat with them, blood oath or no. The servants ate in the kitchen, since they ranked higher than the slaves. The family and their attendants ate in the great hall.

Summoned to carry messages for the duke and duchess to people in the village, Aly slipped her first map to the duchess for recopying in ink. In return she took Mequen and Winnamine's messages and carried them down to Tanair village. Most were invitations to visit the Balitangs at the castle, written to the headman, the town's artisans and healers, and the priests of the different temples. It was nearly dark when Aly returned to the castle to take up a chore of her own.

As she passed through the castle gate, she saw that Sergeant Veron was in charge of the night guard. Tonight she waved to him as she trotted through the gate to the inner courtyard.

Veron frowned down at her, his gray eyes puzzled. "You are the slave Aly, are you not?" he called down to her.

"I am, Your Honor," Aly called back cheerfully. "Just taking messages about for Their Graces. Don't mind me."

She suspected that he was one of those people who was not happy until he could fit someone into a proper category, after which he could ignore them. He confirmed her suspicion by nodding and turning back to talk to one of his men.

Aly walked on through the open gate to the inner court-yard, where she stopped and bent to retie her sandal. As she did so she gave the courtyard ahead a quick glance. The slaves with no work to do lounged around a small fire, gossiping with a handful of off-duty men-at-arms who weren't too proud to be seen in their company. No one else was in that courtyard. A look through the gate to the outer courtyard showed no change since she had passed through. Soldiers paced the walkway on top of the wall, keeping their night's watch. Veron stood there, too, staring at the village below.

Straightening, Aly scratched her head, stuck her hands into her pockets, and strolled into the shadows at the base of the inner courtyard wall. No one had seen her. Moving noise-lessly but casually, as if she had every right to be there, she walked in the shadows to the guards' barracks.

The nice thing about sergeants in command was that they had ground-floor rooms, often with windows. Because it was warm for spring, Veron had left his shutters open for the cool evening air. Silently Aly pulled herself up onto the sill and swung her legs inward, waiting to make sure she wouldn't bump anything before she lowered herself to the floor. As she straightened, she did that inner twist of mind that let her Sight adjust. Now the room was as well lit to her gaze as it would be to a cat at night.

At first glance she found none of the safeguards that a wary man would set to alert him that someone had broken into his things, like a hair over the crack where the lid met the bottom of his chest, or a powdering of chalk or flour in front of it, or across the doorway. The lock on the chest was child's play. It required only three of the picks she'd stuck into her loincloth before the mechanism opened. Aly ran her hands gently through the folded clothes without disturbing them, checking for anything unusual. Da had taught her this trick, along with the art of picking pockets, using things with bells attached until she could search without ringing a bell. All she found were letters from Veron's home, neatly bundled and tied up with ribbon. Aly undid the ribbon to scan the letters. They were ordinary missives from parents and siblings, full of home news. Her Sight found no signs of code spells; none of the letters themselves was in code. She folded the papers as she'd found them, and retied them in the same way. Next she tested the depth of the chest against its height on the floor to check for hidden compartments. There was none.

She searched the room as she had the trunk, checking each possible hiding place on the bed before leaving it as she had found it, unwrinkled and straight. Quickly she moved on to the sergeant's shaving gear, chair, and table. She rapped the legs of the furniture to see if any held secret compartments. About to give up, Aly noticed a darker spot over the shadowed door.

With the hearth stool to stand on she could reach the area. She took down a slim, dark wood box that had been set on the door's thick frame. The lock was simple. Aly had it open in a trice. Inside were sheets of thin parchment, a reed pen, and ink that glowed with some kind of spell. With them she found a stick of clear blue sealing wax and a seal: a tiny eye over a spread-winged osprey, symbols for the intelligence service of the Copper Isles.

Gingerly Aly returned the box to its proper place. She placed the stool in the dents in the earthen floor where it had stood before the fireplace. Then she eased herself through the window and into the safety of the shadows outside.

Her suspicions about the sergeant were right. He was King Oron's spy in the Balitang household. He might not even be the only one. Should she let the duke and duchess know? Or should she keep that information to herself for now? They might insist on getting rid of Veron, and that wouldn't be practical. Aly knew from her upbringing that the spy you know is present is always preferable to the unidentified spy. Veron could be watched. He might lead her to other royal spies within the Balitang household, or even help her to locate spies sent by enemies other than the Crown.

It was the kind of thinking that always gave her mother headaches, a way of looking at several different possibilities for each situation. To Aly and her father it was a fine game, but Aly had learned early on that Mother hated it. That was a shame, because it was far more interesting that anything her mother might play at on horseback.

Still turning possibilities over in her mind, Aly drifted through the gate into the outer courtyard. A glance at the stables revealed that a lamp burned in the chief hostler's quarters. Why wasn't Lokeij out with his boys, among the group in the inner courtyard? The old raka was a sociable man, much given to telling fireside stories until moonrise.

Aly padded into the stables. They were empty but for the horses, who drowsed as she passed. Silently Aly walked into the one-story addition that housed the tack room, the stable boys' dormitory, and the chief hostler's quarters. She kept to the wall, where there was less chance she would step on a loose board. The murmur of voices from Lokeij's room was too low for her to make out what was said. Aly hesitated, then shrugged and opened the old man's door.

Lokeij, the cook Chenaol, the man-at-arms Fesgao, and the head footman Ulasim all sat inside. They had the look of old friends having a nice evening's chat, complete with drinks and a bowl of dried fruit and nuts to share. Aly blinked. All four were pure raka. She had known before that it was unusual to have so many pure-blood raka in the best positions in a luarin household. Only now, seeing them, did she realize that all four main servants here at Tanair were purebloods. Was that a nod to the older girls' heritage, or was it something more? Perhaps it was both, she thought.

"Good evening," she said with a smile. "This looks cozy."

Lokeij grinned at her, his dark eyes, framed by multiple wrinkles, twinkling with amusement. "Surely old friends may sit and talk when their work is done."

"Old friends who number two free servants, a slave, and a man-at-arms, all seated together?" Aly crouched by the door and wrapped her arms around her knees, curious to see what she might learn. "You're very relaxed in your standards for company."

"Why do I not think you are here for a drink?" Fesgao asked, pointing to the pitcher and a wooden cup.

Aly smiled crookedly. "I'd as soon gulp down a mouthful of fire," she replied.

Chenaol laughed and slapped her knee. "You won't get to like it if you won't drink it," she told Aly.

"But I'd like the use of my tongue until I die," retorted Aly. "I think it would eat away at the tongue of anyone who isn't raka."

"So then, curious Aly, why are you here?" Ulasim wanted to know.

Aly looked at each dark face, wondering if she was getting herself into trouble. She sighed. She needed some real answers, and she had to start somewhere. She had a feeling that these four people were more important to this household than their positions seemed to be. "Just who *was* Duchess Sarugani to the raka?"

"That is a question we will not answer," Fesgao replied. "Why do you ask?"

Then you just answered it, Aly thought. She was *very* important to you and yours. "I like gossip about my betters," she replied blithely. "And I was spooked by all those people watching us. Do they line the roads and sea lanes for every family that goes into exile?"

"Who knows why country raka act as they do?" asked Chenaol with a shrug. "Most of the time they laze, hunt, and fish. The household of an exiled duke—a Rittevon duke— was a show for them."

Ulasim leaned back and laced his hands behind his head. "Duchess Sarugani was of the lesser raka nobility," he told Aly, his eyes sharp on her face. "No raka ever married so high before. It stands to reason that people would take interest in her and her daughters."

Aly got to her feet, wincing as muscles she hadn't used in some time protested the change in position. Goat herding had not been so much work the last time she had tried it. "Oh. I didn't think of that," she said lightly. "It looked to me as if there was some big mystery about it all."

"Curiosity killed the cat," Fesgao remarked, his dark eyes unreadable.

Aly rolled her eyes. Why did everyone say that to her? "People always forget the *rest* of the saying," she complained. "'And satisfaction brought it back.'" She looked at the pitcher of arak. "Though if that's all you mean to drink, I doubt I'll come to be curious with you very often."

Their chuckles followed her out into the stable. Aly whistled a tune softly as she passed the sleeping horses. The raka had gracefully turned her questions aside, but they weren't good at facing down open queries. What they had said about the first duchess was true, but it was only part of a larger truth. From the way they had avoided her gaze, and from the stiffness of their movements, Aly was almost certain that Sarugani had not been minor raka nobility at all. Plans to do away with entire noble houses were usually flawed, as her readings of history had taught her. There were always second and third cousins tucked away in corners, waiting for the right time to announce they were of the supposedly dead house. Or those cousins neglected to wait and died as the result of a premature announcement. Had she money to wager, Aly would bet it all that Sarugani was the daughter of old, powerful raka nobility, probably even a very well hidden seed of the royal line. If that were so, then Sarai and Dove were doubly royal, raka as well as luarin. If *that* were true, if the mad king ever learned of it, no Balitang would be left alive.

The four raka whom she had just left seemed much friendlier since they'd left Rajmuat. During the long journey here she had overheard slaves and servants alike wonder why servants of Chenaol's and Ulasim's rank and qualifications had chosen the Balitangs' exile. Lokeij, of course, had been too old to sell, for all his skill as an hostler. And here they were, teamed with a real soldier who was also a pure-blood raka. Fesgao's quiet competence and leadership had impressed her during the bandit episode. Seeing these four together had crystallized things for Aly, giving her a working theory as to why these people had remained with Mequen and his family. They were guarding the hidden treasure that was Sarugani's daughters. If trouble came, Aly would have their help to protect two of the children, at least.

She stepped into the courtyard and frowned. She had forgotten another very important question. She would ask it at another time, though. Too many questions might make the four raka conspirators think Aly was an unhealthy person to keep around.

As she walked into the keep, she heard children crying,

"Aly, Aly!" Elsren and Petranne, who had been seated at the foot of the main stairway, hurled themselves at her. Dove and Sarai came in their wake, more sedate, but with the same eagerness in their eyes.

"A story!" clamored Elsren. "Mama said you might tell us a story if we were good and we were!"

"Please," begged Petranne.

"The duchess didn't actually *say* Aly would tell you a story," Sarai reminded her. "She said to ask Aly, *if* Aly wasn't too tired. Aly looks pretty tired to me." She turned her brown eyes on Aly, who saw wistfulness in them.

Petranne, who had hugged Aly enthusiastically, drew back, plucking coarse hairs from the front of her gown. "You smell of goats," she said, wrinkling her nose. She was very much the finicky young noblewoman.

"I don't care!" Elsren cried. *"Please,* a story?"

Aly looked at the four young Balitangs and told herself that if she was to keep them alive, she ought to get to know them. "Actually, I'd like a story of my own," she said, towing the younger children to a bench against the wall. "And then one for you."

"And then bedtime," Dove told Petranne and Elsren. "Aly rises very early now."

"What story did *you* want to hear?" asked Sarai. She settled on the floor gracefully, tucking her bronze-colored skirts around her long legs. Aly could see how Sarai would attract boys. Apart from her connection to the royal family, she was lovely in a sensual way, her nose long and curved, her upper lip a perfect arch over a full lower lip, her skin a creamy shade of golden brown. Her eyes were large with frivolously long lashes, tucked under delicate eyebrows. She wore her shining dark hair combed smoothly back and coiled into a knot of braids from which curled locks dangled. Hers was a face of passion and sensuality, one that promised a happy, if maddening, time for any male who took her interest.

Elsren and Petranne curled up on either side of the bench with Aly, leaning against her as they pleaded with their eyes. Dove found a stool and set it next to Sarai, folding her hands neatly in her lap once she was seated.

"Well, it doesn't really have to be a story," Aly said, putting an arm around each of the younger children. "I was just curious about a god somebody mentioned to me—Ky—Kyprioth. Do you know anything about him?"

The older girls traded wary looks. Finally Dove said, "I don't see how it could hurt. He's one of the old raka gods. He's the sea god here, except maybe to the luarin. The raka say he used to be the patron god of the Isles."

"Some people say that he played one trick too many on Mithros," Sarai added. "He is a trickster god. The Isles deserved one in those days, with all the clans fighting, and every island against its neighbors. You can see why people might think a trickster was running it all."

"The Mithran priests say that all the fighting among the raka weakened Kyprioth's power, so when the invaders came from the east, Mithros and the Great Goddess came with them, and threw Kyprioth from his throne," Dove told Aly. "The raka believe he'll regain his throne one day, and return the rulership of the Isles to the raka."

"Where did you hear that?" asked Sarai, curious. "I never heard anyone say anything about his return."

"That's because you attract attention," Dove informed her older sister. "I go out of my way *not* to attract it, so I hear more things. People forget I'm there."

"Oh." Sarai shrugged. "I hate being quiet. It's so very boring."

Aly, shaking her head at Sarai's indifference to what she

might learn this way, saw that Dove was shaking her head as well. For a moment their eyes met—hazel slave's and brown-black noble's—in perfect understanding.

Then Petranne yanked Aly's sleeve. "Now a story?" she asked, her voice teetering toward a whine.

The moment gone, Aly searched her memory for a tale. The information about Kyprioth she would consider later, in a quiet moment of her own.

"Once in a kingdom far away, a girl with a knack for handling horses came to a large fair held in the capital of Galla," she began.

"Will the Lioness be in this one?" asked Sarai eagerly. "Will there be battles?"

Dove kicked her sister gently. Petranne scowled and said, "Hush!"

Aly waited until Sarai was quiet again, then continued. "As I was saying, she came to the fair seeking work. . . ."

Frasrlund, on the Vassa River, Tortall's northwestern border
As soon as Aly's eyes closed, a vision presented itself, very different from those times when the crows taught her their language. This was one of Kyprioth's "letters from home" dreams, like the one in which she'd seen her father talk to her mother, with Lord Imrah's note in his pocket.

Now she rode high in the air, seeing the landscape below like a shadowy map. The place looked familiar. It was Frasr-lund, Tortall's northern harbor city, an island at the mouth of the powerful Vassa River. In more peaceful times she had visited it often, though never with such a good view of the place.

The skies were dark, but the night was lit with torches, their flames driven nearly flat by a hard wind out of the east. Cities of torches lighting thousands of tents lay over hilly land on both sides of the Vassa. Torches burned also on the ramparts of the city, isolated from the armies by the tumbling river.

Frasrlund had been under siege by King Maggur of Scanra since the previous year. Now the Tortallans had driven Maggur's army back across the Vassa. The flags on the southern side of the river were Tortallan, those on the northern side Scanran. So the city was yet to be freed completely. That would come when Maggur either no longer held the northern throne or else signed a treaty promising to leave Frasrlund to Tortall. Until then the Tortallan army could not retreat. The minute troops were moved away from Frasrlund, the Scanrans would swarm over the river again, to encircle the prize and try to starve its people into surrender.

Stalemate, Aly thought, shaking her head. They can't drive us off, and we can't leave the city to them. Splendid. Mother must be bored out of her mind.

Thinking of her mother, Aly suddenly found herself inside a large canvas tent, lit by oil lamps and warmed by charcoal braziers. Alanna the Lioness sat at a rude camp table, writing reports.

Men clamored outside. Alanna grabbed the longsword that rested on her table and swept the blade from its sheath. Aly clenched ghostly fists in worry. She couldn't see how an enemy might get so close to the tents that housed the army's commanders, but there was no sense in Mother taking chances. Immortals, mages, or spies might well get near enough to do real damage here.

Alanna reached for her shield, then spun to face the door. The flap burst open and a tall man with black hair and a black, trimmed beard entered in a swirl of wind and cold air. Aly recognized King Jonathan, as her mother did. Alanna dropped her shield and knelt, placing her sword at her side.

King Jonathan IV, co-ruler of Tortall with his queen,

Thayet, bent and scooped his old friend up into his arms. "Alanna, I'm so sorry," he said as he hugged her. "Is there any news yet?"

Alanna stepped back from him, confusion on her too-honest face. "News of what?"

"Myles hasn't been able to find a trace of her in Corus," the king said, pulling off his riding gloves. He investigated the contents of a steaming pitcher and poured its warm cider into a cup. "I've got the Bazhir looking around," the king added, "but we've had to be discreet." He drank and poured the cup full again. "Gods help us if our enemies find out she's missing."

Alanna turned her sword's hilt in her hands, her violet eyes on her king. "Thayet's missing?" When the king stared at her, blue eyes astonished, Alanna guessed, "One of the princesses? Really, Your Majesty—"

"Mithros," whispered Jonathan. "I thought you knew."

Alanna's hands tightened on her sword. She scowled at Jonathan. "Knew *what?*"

Jonathan rubbed his forehead and dropped into one of the empty chairs. "I thought George . . . Alanna, look, put the sword away."

Aly could see her mother was trembling. "Am I going to need it?" she asked, her voice tart. She went to her desk and picked up the sword's sheath, keeping her back to Jonathan. "Spit it out, Jon."

"It's Aly," the king began.

"She went to Port Legann . . ."

"Actually, it seems she never arrived there," Jonathan said, leaning forward on his chair. "She's missing."

Aly saw her mother's shoulders go stiff. She slid her sword into its sheath. "But George knows," she commented softly. "So *that's* why he hasn't written she's home. I thought maybe the letters went astray."

"He's looking for her. So have Myles and Gary and I. As soon as Numair settles Daine and the baby at the palace, he's going to search, too." He looked at her face and sighed. "I'm assuming George didn't want you upset—"

"Of course he didn't," Alanna said, putting her sword on its stand. "I hate it when he goes all chivalrous on me. I'm not some fragile blossom who can be distracted by—by bad news from home."

"He knows I need you here," said the king. "Not distracted. And everyone will notice if you go looking for her. You're too visible, remember. You don't want our enemies to realize your daughter, my godsdaughter, is missing."

"I'm not a fool, sire." Alanna fought to speak calmly: Aly could see it in her face. She tried to touch her mother's shoulder, even hug her, but her arms passed through Alanna's body. The Lioness rubbed her arms as if she felt a chill and told the king, "I know we have enemies. All of us whom Aly calls family. Has anyone besides me scried for her?"

"I have," said the king. "So has Numair. We've found nothing. Numair's tried crystal, flame, water . . . they turn gray or they vanish when he does. All I see is fog. Look for her if you wish, but I think something, or someone, is hiding her from us. You have to pretend nothing's wrong, understand? For Aly's sake."

"Yes, I *do* understand," Alanna said quietly. She lifted her sword and drew it half out of its sheath. The metal sparkled with purple fire. Aly hadn't realized why her mother had always insisted there be three inches of mirror-bright blade near the hilt of her swords. Now she knew the answer: her mother was using the blade as she would a mirror, as a tool to scry with, not just as a weapon. "And I'll be calm. I'll pretend everything's just lovely. I know Aly has the tools to survive. She can defend herself, she's cleverer than I ever was, and she has all those things George taught her. I have to believe she's alive, and she's doing her best to stay that way." She scowled at the gray fog that raced over the surface of her blade, and rammed it into its sheath. Turning, she glared at her king. "May I be alone now, sire?" she asked. "I need to write to my husband."

The king was getting to his feet as Aly's surroundings faded. Encased in a fog, the sight of her mother's quarters gone from view, Aly heard a familiar light voice in her head. *I believe you didn't think she'd be worried. I believe it never occurred to you that she knew what you could do, let alone that her hope would be that you could protect yourself.*

She always treated me as a feckless child, Kyprioth! Aly retorted silently.

An impression you encourage, as I recall, the god reminded her.

The fog vanished. Aly sat in the crows' tree, surrounded in the night by crows.

We could be sleeping, trickster, one of the crows informed him. *Instead of laboring to teach a two-legger.*

One crow, with a silvery streak on his back, walked over to Aly and sat in her lap. *She's learning,* Nawat told his brethren. *Listen to how well she does. Aly, what is the noise for twenty?*

6

OF GOATS AND CROWS

Aly woke in the morning with a headache. While the other slaves and servants who had shared the great hall floor roused, she put away her bedding, gathered her day's meals in the kitchen, and took the goats out. Today she led them to a spot in the hills north of her previous day's grazing site so that she could survey a new part of the ground she might have to defend.

Once the goats were settled, she ate bread and cheese. The food and the crisp morning air cleared her head. Feeling a bit less worn, Aly washed her face and cleaned her teeth at a spring tucked between two rocks. She marked it on her map. If the afternoon was as hot as it promised to be, she meant to take a proper bath. She regretted the absence of soap, but unless she was ready to plod back to Tanair, she would have to manage without. Besides, Aunt Daine disapproved of people who used soap in a water source.

For a while Aly simply lazed, warming up in the sun, watching the goats, and thinking of her visions and dreams. She was just as glad not to be going home for a couple of months. By the time she returned, her mother would have forgiven her father for not revealing that Aly was gone. When Alanna was in a temper, anyone with sense was happier someplace else. Her father would survive—he could always laugh away her mother's bad moods—and Aly would come home when the storm had blown over.

She wished that her mother or the king had said what kind of baby Aunt Daine had birthed. No one could even magically tell the child's sex while it was in the womb. It had shifted both sex and shape constantly, pummeling poor Daine with everything from elephant feet to ostrich claws.

"I'm glad *I'm* not a shape-shifter," she told the younger goats, who were grazing nearby. "Well, there are advantages, but having a baby doesn't seem to be one of them."

Aly was studying the map she had made the day before when a shadow momentarily blotted out the light on her tablet. She looked up, to see a lone crow gliding overhead. At last he landed on a rock nearby and stayed there, flicking his wingtips. It was the crow's way to say, "This is my territory." Aly saw the white streak that marked him as Nawat, by far the most encouraging of her crow teachers.

"Nawat, it's too nice a day for more lessons," she called to him. "Didn't we do enough last night?"

Nawat hopped down beside her, still flicking his wingtips. Overhead Aly heard the voices of nine more crows. They flew toward the cut where the road led east, naming the things they saw, starting with calling Aly and her herd of animals *possible food*. They also identified Nawat, a badger in the rocks, the human-made wide trail through the barrier edge of the plateau, a herd of deer retreating to the mountain forests, and a lack of humans on the deer's trail.

Aly was quite pleased with herself. She had understood every sound they made. "I must be the best student you ever had," she remarked. Looking from the sky to Nawat, she saw the marked crow had opened her pack and was eating some of her bread.

"Now see here," Aly began. Then she remembered that Kyprioth had promised the crows would be fed. "He better not have told you *I'd* supply food for all of you," she complained. She picked up the roll he had picked at and tore it into pieces. Slowly she sat next to him and offered a piece with her fingers.

Nawat accepted the offering, stuffing it and the remaining bread into his large beak into the pouch under his tongue. Once his beak was full, he flew off. Aly dusted off her hands. "You're welcome!" she shouted after the retreating bird. When he was gone from view she picked up the parchment tablet and got to work.

In the days that followed, crows flocked to Tanair in their family groups. Nawat led them to Aly so they would get a good look at her. Once they were all familiar with her, the crows spread out over the plateau, relaying what they saw back to Aly through messengers, or describing the land during her dream lessons. These came at night, when Aly learned their speech as the crows learned hers. In the morning Aly rushed to write down all the crows had told her, forming a rough picture of the plateau from their descriptions. Nawat was always there to help, day and night.

She was startled by the complexity of the crow language. She also enjoyed their company, both in her dreams and out in the fields. She had always liked the glossy black creatures. Like Kyprioth, they were tricksters, stealing laundry, causing dogs to chase them until the dogs were exhausted, and trying their luck by interfering with pigs at their meals. Now she found their wicked sense of humor extended to their dream conversations with her. Only Nawat would not tease Aly, by day or by night. She seemed to fascinate him.

While the sun was up, as the crows described what they saw in the distance, Aly familiarized herself with the nearby village and farms. She struck up conversations with bakers, smiths, mothers, and herders. She helped women to hang laundry and tugged stubborn clumps of weeds or large rocks from the paths of farmers' ploughs. She held straps for harness makers and chased thieving dogs. The people were suspicious and wary of her. She expected that and didn't force herself on them. The important thing was that they got used to seeing her around.

A week after her first encounter with Nawat, Aly was mapping the ground on the southwestern side of the road when he told her that people were coming. Aly thrust her tablet between two stones and grabbed the staff that was the only weapon she was permitted as a slave. A few moments later she heard the approach of horses.

It was Sarai and Dove, dressed for riding and flushed after a morning gallop. Behind them rode their bodyguards: Fesgao and another man-at-arms. The girls swung out of their saddles and shook the stiffness of a hard ride from their bodies.

"We thought you could use company," Sarai remarked, unhooking a canteen from her belt. She opened it and drank greedily, letting water spill over her cheeks. If she was aware of the two men watching her, she gave no sign of it.

Aly looked at the girls. "Not to say that I'm not honored, my ladies, because I am, but it's hardly fitting for you to come see the goatherd," she pointed out in her best good-servant manner.

Dove sighed. "We're desperate, Aly. If we have to work in the stillroom one more day, Sarai will bite someone's head off. Then Papa would be disappointed in her. We thought a gallop would air us out."

"I hate stillrooms," grumbled Sarai as she took the saddle from her mare. Dove unsaddled her own mount. It seemed the girls planned to stay awhile. "If I have to stew up any more smelly plants, I will *scream*." Sarai placed her horse's blanket on the grass and sat on it. Aly watched Fesgao and his companion as they dismounted at a distance to leave the girls and Aly in relative privacy.

"Sarai is happier on horseback," Dove explained. "I don't mind mixing up spices and medicines, but it's hard to concentrate when Sarai starts to mutter."

Sarai plucked out the jeweled pins that held her coiled and braided hair in place. She set them in a pile beside her and pulled her heavy black hair out of its style as she lay back on the blanket. Once down, she arranged it in an ebony fan around her head. It was still wet from a morning's wash. "You could take my place, Aly. I'm sure Rihani would be happy for you to work in the stillroom. I'll tend goats."

"My heart just stopped dead with anticipation," asked Aly. "But no, I cannot leave the goats. They would bleat for me. I would hear their cries with the ears of my heart."

"You weren't really a maid, were you?" asked Dove. She had settled on a rock that overlooked the valley and the guards' position. "You don't talk like you were a maid."

"I'm an educated one. Most of us Tortallan common-born are, these days." Aly kept her eyes on her map as mentally she kicked herself. She could not act like her old self here. Just because there was no age difference between her and Sarai, and only four years between her and Dove, she could not treat them as equals. It didn't matter that on her mother's side her blood was far bluer than that of descendants of a ruffian lot who had invaded the Copper Isles scarcely three hundred years ago. "They insist on it. All children attend school for five years to learn to read and write and figure. The priest said I was his most promising student," she added proudly, the country girl praised by an educated man.

"King Oron says that your king and queen will regret educating their people one day," mused Sarai. She turned her face up to the sun. "An educated populace makes trouble, that's what he thinks."

And he's as daft as a Stormwing, Aly thought. Aloud she said meekly, "It's not my place to say, my lady." Motion drew her attention as Nawat landed beside Sarai. He poked his beak through the shimmering heap of hairpins. "Lady Sarai, look out."

Sarai sat up and yelped to find a crow so close to her. The bird snatched two jeweled pins and bounced back, steadying himself with his wings as the girl scrambled to her feet. "Give those back, you!" she cried, reaching for him. He leaped away again and again, leading Sarai on a chase across the grassy meadow. Aly gathered up the other hairpins before he returned for those as well.

"He's not at all shy of humans," Dove remarked from the rock where she sat, her arms clasped around her drawn-up knees.

"He isn't a normal crow," Aly admitted. She hid a smile. The crow jumped higher and higher each time Sarai lunged, but he never actually took flight. Aly knew he was tormenting the girl on purpose. "Perhaps he's someone's runaway pet."

"Oh, no," Dove replied. "It's illegal to keep crows as pets. Well, not illegal as in a law written in books, but the raka get really upset by it. Even luarin won't defy the custom."

"Why not?" Aly wanted to know. She knew two people at home who kept pet crows.

"They're sacred to Kyprioth," replied Dove. "Since tricksters have to be free to create mischief, the raka say it's bad luck to the house to hold a crow against its will."

"Well, nobody's holding this fellow now," Aly pointed out. "He just seems to have adopted me."

"I give up," Sarai told them, panting, as she returned. "He can keep them." She collapsed on the blanket and fought to catch her breath. Aly wordlessly leaned over and poured the other pins into Sarai's lap.

"Kyprioth will be pleased," observed Dove. "He likes bright, shiny things, they say." She looked at Aly as Sarai began to braid her hair once more. "Do you have other stories about Alanna the Lioness?"

A jerk of her hand left a smear of charcoal on Aly's map. She painstakingly rubbed it off the parchment. Guilt flooded her veins as she remembered her mother's worry in the dream. "Why such interest?" she asked, glad she didn't blush easily. "I mean, forgive me, ladies, but I can see why the little ones are interested. All that fighting, and adventure. Children love heroic stories. You aren't children."

"It isn't just children who need heroes," Sarai replied, shocked. "Don't you see what she's done for women, for all women? The Lioness, your queen, Lady Knight Keladry, they're living proof that we have a warrior spirit, too, that it hasn't been bred out of the luarin blood. The Lioness is a true hero. She protected her country when no one else could, man or woman. Mithros, she found the Dominion Jewel, she's killed giants and monsters to defend those who can't fight them! That *proves* that we can do things men do. Not in the same way, perhaps, but we can still do them!"

"Everybody needs heroes, Aly," Dove added. "Everybody. Even grown women. Even slaves."

Aly looked at the younger girl. Dove's small, dark face was alive with enthusiasm. Keen intelligence shone in her dark eyes, and fire burned in her tawny cheeks. Something about her reminded Aly of the Lioness herself, though she would be hard put to name it. "Even the raka, my lady?" she asked.

"Especially the raka," Sarai told Aly.

Dove shrugged. "There's room enough in the Isles for both peoples, if only everyone could be brought to see as much."

Fesgao approached them and bowed. "My ladies, it is almost noon. Your father will be concerned."

Groaning, Sarai and Dove got to their feet, saddled their mounts, and rode away. Dove turned in the saddle just before they reached the road, and waved goodbye to Aly.

The dust had settled from their departure when Nawat returned. He walked over to Aly and dropped the two jeweled hairpins into Aly's lap. She grimaced and wiped crow saliva from the pins.

"Thank you, but slaves don't own jewels," she told him. "I would get in trouble if I'm caught with these. I'll give them back to Sarai. But it's sweet of you to want to give me a present, though," she said hurriedly. Without thinking, she reached out and ran a hand along the crow's glossy back. "I'm sorry," she said, pulling away. "I forgot you're wild. I didn't mean anything by it."

Nawat climbed onto her lap and gently ran his beak through Aly's growing hair. She closed her eyes, relaxing in the sun.

Hours passed. Gray clouds slid across the sky while Aly, Nawat and the goats prowled the countryside. By late afternoon rain began to fall. Aly wrapped her map book in oiled cloth, whistled the goats in, and led them home. Nawat flew overhead, perching under the roof of a village barn as Aly took her charges through the castle gate. She was soaked clean through. She wanted nothing more than dry clothes and a hot meal.

She put the goats in their outer courtyard pen. Entering the inner courtyard, she found the slaves and the six former bandits huddled under the eaves of the barracks and the kitchen. All stared miserably at the sky. The rain showed no sign of letting up. Unless they found room in the stable, they would have to eat in the wet, doing their best to keep rain out of their bowls.

The door to the keep opened to frame Duke Mequen, flanked by his duchess and Ulasim. "This is ridiculous," he said. "All of you, come into the hall. We'll manage for tonight, but I'll see to it that we get more tables and benches for the future. From now on, this household eats together."

"The servants won't like that," Lokeij murmured in Aly's ear.

She looked at the old hostler. "They'll learn to live with it, I suppose," she replied. "Somebody told me that's how it used to be done in older castles—the household ate and slept all together. It's only been the last two centuries that nobles took quarters of their own and the servants had a separate hall to sleep in."

Lokeij gripped the back of Aly's neck with a friendly hand. "A word of advice. Slaves aren't so knowledgeable about history," he murmured. "Not raka slaves, not luarin slaves, unless you've been specially educated and sold as a tutor. Are you a tutor?"

Aly smiled at him. "That's so sweet," she replied. "My da always said my brains were too big for my head."

Lokeij looked into her face, his rheumy dark eyes inspecting her almost pore by pore. "If I were you, little parrot, I'd rub dirt in my bright feathers and work harder to pass for a sparrow," he said.

Aly spread her tunic, streaked with grass and mud stains. "The goats have taken care of that, don't you think? I'm sparrowing already. Chirp. Tweet." She winked at him and entered the castle. She wanted to change to her spare set of dry clothes before supper and to return Sarai's hairpins.

That night, when she dreamed her crow lessons, Nawat was not there. Instead the senior female crow took over. In addition to teaching Aly new sounds and hearing Aly's explanation of sounds and behaviors made by humans, she introduced Aly to the new crows who had come to Tanair.

Aly saw no sign of her friend the next day, either. She heard and easily interpreted the calls of the crows, but Nawat had become company for her, out alone with the goats. She missed him as she took shelter under a tree from the daylong drizzle. With Nawat to talk to, she wouldn't have been so aware of the cold and damp. To warm up she tried some of the hand-to-hand combat exercises she had learned, but soon found that mud and wet grass made for tricky footing. More often than not she went sprawling, which amused both the goats and the crows.

When she returned to the castle at the end of the day, she found that long tables and benches had been placed in the main hall. There was an order to the seating. The duke and his family were on the dais, near the big hearth. The servants were arrayed at a long table set at right angles to the left of the dais. The men-at-arms who were not on duty took their seats at the first long table to the right. The slaves had lower tables—those with special skills like carpentry and smithcraft on the right, with the soldiers, general slaves like

Aly, and the slave maids on the table below the free servants.

The new arrangement did not sit well with everyone, particularly the free luarin servants and the men-at-arms who had come with the family from Rajmuat. Ulasim and the fifteen other full- and part-blood raka seemed perfectly comfortable. Aly was just happy to be warm, dry, and sitting down.

Once the weather cleared up the next day, Dove and Sarai began regular visits with Aly after they and their guards took a morning ramble through the country around their new home. Sometimes they brought Petranne and taught the four-year-old to ride her pony, as her guard guided it on a lead rein.

Aly welcomed their company, particularly since Nawat had not returned, neither in her dreams nor during the day. She soon saw that, on the older girls' part, her attraction lay in her stories of Tortall, those too bloody or full of bedroom gossip for Petranne and Elsren. In exchange, Aly extracted Isles gossip from her visitors. Sarai knew most of the luarin and raka nobility, as she had been presented at court. Her descriptions of life there were precise, cutting, and without illusions. Dove seemed to have spent her time in Rajmuat in different circles, among the capital's intellectuals and more worldly merchants, studying politics, trade, and the affairs of foreign nations.

The more time she spent with those girls, the more respect Aly had for them. They would have been at home in the circle of clever, observant women that were Aly's adoptive aunts. More than once Aly caught Dove eyeing her after she'd asked a question that a slave might not be expected to ask. She had to wonder if Dove, at least, did not suspect there was much more to Aly than a metal ring around her neck.

Sometimes the Balitangs stayed long enough to eat

lunch with Aly. More often they visited for a short time before they returned to the castle and the duties Winnamine
had set for them. With only a fifth of the servants who'd
worked at the Rajmuat house, every member of the family
was now required to help with chores. Mequen met with
villagers, supervised repairs to the walls, and oversaw the
building of new sheds and sleeping quarters within the castle walls. Sarai and Winnamine plied their needles, not on
ladylike embroidery and tapestry work, but on plain sewing
for the household. Dove, who loathed needlework, worked in
the stillroom and learned to spin. When the older girls described their labors to Aly, they spoke as if work were an adventure. Aly hoped they would feel the same when winter
made it impossible to leave the castle.

Twice a merchant caravan came to Tanair with supplies.
On both visits Aly saw the merchants reach the Balitang
lands through the road in the rocks. The crows warned her
ahead of time so that she could look over the merchants and
decide if they were a threat or not. They were always welcomed at village and castle, both for the items they carried
and for the news of the realm.

Two weeks after her arrival at Tanair, Aly was drowsing
in the late morning sun when the crows set up a racket that
made her jump to her feet and draw the stolen knife from
her waistband. She couldn't tell what they were saying—none
of their sounds were those she had been taught. Skeins of
shrieking birds flew by, bound for the southern road, where
they circled and dove at a man who walked there.

Aly sharpened her Sight until she saw the newcomer as
clearly as if he stood before her. A young man of her age, he
carried a sack over one shoulder, one not big enough to hold
what he might need for life on the road. His luarin-style
tunic and leggings were patched and darned, showing plenty

of wear. He was barefoot, and he walked in an awkward manner, as if he had not really mastered the use of feet. The strangest thing about him was the way his skin looked to her Sight: feather patterns showed under every inch of bare flesh.

Curious, Aly told the goats "Stay," and trotted down to the road. Something about that feathered pattern was very interesting.

"Hello, Aly," the newcomer said in a pleasant baritone as she approached. His skin was dark, but not raka brown— more like her da's coloring than a raka's. His eyes were brown, long-lashed, and deeply set on either side of a long, thin razor of a nose. His cheekbones were sharp, his chin square with a hint of a point. His mouth was long and slender, the lower lip fuller than the upper. He wore his short black hair tousled, as if he'd combed it back with his fingers. He was nearly six feet tall, with a wiry build. The way he moved, Aly half expected him to leap straight up into the air at any moment and not come down. The feather patterns under his skin were even clearer to her Sight up close than they'd been when she first looked at him. She thought that if she touched him, she might *feel* feathers, as if he'd pulled a human skin on for a disguise.

He'd called her by name. "Do we know each other?" she asked.

"I looked different before." The newcomer knelt and placed his sack in the roadway. "I am sorry I have been away so long," he added, undoing the knot and spreading out the cloth. "I had to practice this shape. It is not what I am used to. I am used to it now, though." He looked up at Aly. "I am here to serve you and the two-legger queen-to-be."

Aly peered into his face. If he wore another shape normally, one with feathers . . . "Nawat?" she whispered.

Nawat smiled at her, his entire face lighting up. "I did

not want you to see me fumble like a nestling," he explained. "This shape, and the talking, are hard. My friends say I am even sillier than a nestling." He waved up to the crows whirling over their heads.

"But . . . are you a mage?" Aly asked, tucking her knife back into her waistband. "A, a shape-shifter? A god?" But I would have seen those things in him, she thought, completely bewildered.

"I am Nawat Crow," Nawat replied. "*They* could do this, if they wished." He looked up at the crows again. "They do not wish."

Aly sat on a boulder at the side of the road. "Aunt Daine never said crows could make themselves into humans."

Nawat shrugged as birds did, thrusting his shoulder blades up from his back. "We do not give away all our secrets." He smiled. "I can help you better this way. I learned to make arrows for the two-leggers." He gestured to the contents of his open satchel. "They prize arrows, and no one makes them by the stone sticks where you live."

"Castle," Aly murmured, nibbling her lower lip as she tried to work this all out in her mind. She nearly had control of her thoughts when she made the mistake of truly looking at Nawat's satchel.

"Goddess save me," she whispered in awe, picking up a feather as long as her forearm, stippled in a pattern of gold and soft black. "This is a griffin feather! And this one, and this . . . How did you get these?" she asked. "They're worth a fortune. Everyone knows you hit what you shoot at with griffin fletching."

"They are sparkly," Nawat said. "The griffins shed them. I thought if I brought you a present that was made of discarded things, no one would punish you for having them."

Steel glinted through the heap of shimmering griffin

feathers. Carefully Aly pushed them aside. At the bottom of the pile she found strips of metal, shaped like bird feathers. She gulped. With a trembling hand she lifted a feather a handspan in length and drew its tip along the corner of the cloth satchel. The corner fell neatly away, as if sliced by a razor. "*Stormwing* feathers?" she whispered, meeting Nawat's deep-set gaze. "You're carrying *Stormwing* feathers?"

Again that shrug. "They molt," Nawat replied. "The feathers are shiny. I collected them and washed them," he added.

Aly was glad to be sitting down. Neither griffins nor Stormwings liked others to approach their nests or flocking grounds. Her own mother would rather face a company of hill bandits than a nesting griffin. "What did you mean, the two-legger queen-to-be?"

"She lives with you in the stone sti—the castle," Nawat corrected himself. "She flocks with you sometimes, when you sit with them." He pointed over Aly's shoulder. When she looked back, she saw that the goats had followed her and were grazing beside the road.

"So much for telling you to stay," Aly remarked, more to herself than to the goats. She turned to watch Nawat again. He means Sarai or Dove, I bet, she thought. That's why Kyprioth wagered me that I couldn't keep the children alive. He wants a half-raka queen, and he fears he won't have a contender after this summer.

"Are you not glad that I came?" Nawat asked, a worried look on his handsome face. "I will help you better this way, with arrows, with the crows. I will be your friend."

The word hit Aly's own heart with all the force of an arrow loosed from a bow. She had no real friends here. Spies don't have friends at all, she told herself, but Nawat's offer was impossible to resist. She was lonely. Nawat at least wouldn't penalize her for being luarin, Tortallan, a slave, or her parents' daughter.

"Put those away," she told him, pointing to the piles of feathers. "We'll go eat lunch and figure out what story you will tell the Balitangs, so they'll take you on as a fletcher."

"I cannot say I am a crow?" asked Nawat, tying his satchel up once more.

"You can, but they'll think you're mad," Aly said. "They won't let you near the family unless you have a story they will believe."

"You will tell a fine story," Nawat said cheerfully. "You do well with such things."

Aly grinned. "Thank you for the compliment," she replied.

"It is my first," replied Nawat. "I am glad my first compliment is a good one." Aly looked at him to find his eyes twinkling with mischief. Aly shook her head with a smile. It would be good to have a friend who was a crow. They knew how to have fun.

She worried about taking a stranger who was not raka home, but her worry turned out to be useless. The castle's part-raka bowyer, Falthin, was a single man whose son had drowned at sea two years before. Nawat reminded him of his lost child. Falthin took the young man into his village home eagerly, particularly when he had seen the treasure trove of feathers Nawat brought with him.

Hearing about the newcomer, Duke Mequen, Sergeant Veron, and Ulasim each went separately to Falthin's shop or to his home to meet Nawat. All returned with good things to say. Nawat's singularly innocent, friendly nature opened doors for him that the feathers did not.

Aly overheard Ulasim tell Lokeij, "The boy is a bit simple, but good-hearted—no threat to us as far as I can tell."

At some point during the summer she would find out what precisely Ulasim meant by "us," but for now she was glad that no one seemed to think Nawat was dangerous. She did wonder if Kyprioth had done anything to smooth the young crow's way, but if he had, Aly saw no traces of it anywhere.

Nawat also drew a good deal of attention from the castle and village girls. Whenever Aly returned for the day with her goats, she would find one or two girls lingering around the bench where Nawat worked, outside Falthin's workshop, where the fumes from the glue he used would disperse in the open air. Often one of those women was Sarai, who told Dove in Aly's hearing that she thought Nawat "adorable." For some reason that soured Aly's mood, until she realized that Nawat treated Sarai with the same friendly grace he showed to every other person in Tanair. He kept his most wicked glances and murmured jokes for Aly. She wasn't sure if this was a good thing or not, but she was pleased to get something from him that Sarai could not.

The hardest thing to remember is to keep your mouth closed. You'll be tempted to say what you know, or mention that you've met folk you've no right to meet. Keep your counsel, hold your tongue. Good listeners live longer. And keep in mind it's harder to keep your mouth buttoned on the things you know more about than those you're with.

—*From* A Handbook for
the Royal Intelligence Service,
by George Cooper,
given to Aly for her tenth birthday

7

CONVERSATIONS

Three weeks after the family's arrival at Tanair, Aly took her goats up into the rocky ground just east of the castle, nearly three miles north of the road that led to Kellaura Pass. Chenaol's nine-year-old great-niece Visda, who tended one of Tanair village's herds of sheep, led her flock to graze near Aly's. She led her dogs, who clearly thought they could herd so much better than these two-leggers.

When Sarai and Dove came with their bodyguards at midmorning, the four girls started a game of skip-rope on the bare ground next to a watering hole. Sarai was taking her turn, with Aly and Visda to spin the rope, when the crows who watched the road set up a racket. Aly dropped the rope and clambered onto a rock to hear them better. Once she could translate what they said, she slid back to the ground where the other three girls waited, staring at her.

"Lady Sarai, might I ask a favor?" she asked in her best well-trained-slave manner. Adding a trace of the attitude of one who is versed in secrets, she went on, "I may not say as yet how I know this, but a party is riding this way from the pass. It is led by a warrior in armor, and numbers twenty soldiers and five others—attendants, I believe. You are a swift rider. Will you carry word of this to His Grace, your father?"

Sarai raised her thin brows. "We have men on guard where the road enters Tanair, Aly," she pointed out.

"Three miles south of us, my lady," Aly replied. "The crows do not believe these men are hostile, but a little more warning is always useful."

"*You* speak to the crows," Sarai remarked in disbelief.

Aly smiled and bowed, now the mysterious mage. "Say rather, my lady, they speak to me." It's the truth, too, she thought, waiting for the young noblewoman to make up her mind. For once it would have been useful if I were Mother, she added ruefully. When she tells people to do things, they snap to. Of course, she isn't a slave in a hostile country.

"Has this got anything to do with Papa and the duchess's talking to you every night behind closed doors?" asked Dove.

Aly glanced at the younger girl, all thoughts of her mother gone. "Oh, my lady, you give me far too much credit," she said, meeting Dove's stern gaze with amusement. "As if the likes of them would have serious talk with the likes of me." Behind her humorous mask she mentally kicked herself. She had to remember that Dove was quick and perceptive!

Sarai beckoned to Fesgao, who waited at a slight distance with Dove's bodyguard and the horses. The raka led Sarai's mount forward with his own. She swung herself into the saddle. "You'd better keep up," she told Fesgao. With that, she kneed her mare into a trot, then a gallop. Fesgao urged his mount after Sarai, who rode as if she were a centaur and one creature with her horse.

"She's the best horsewoman I know," Dove remarked as

her guard brought her mount. "If Mother could ride like Sarai, she'd be alive now. Sarai never would have tried that jump, not without knowing what lay on the other side." She mounted and followed her sister to the castle, her guard at her side.

Aly turned to Visda. "Watch my goats for me?" she asked.

The girl nodded. "The dogs won't mind," she told Aly with a grin.

Aly raced up into the rocks, bound for the ones that afforded a clear view of the distant road. As she climbed, she realized that she needed to cut herself free of the goats. She had covered all of the ground reachable with a herd in tow. Today she'd been lucky to have Visda there when the alarm sounded. Otherwise she might have been forced to leave the goats, risking the loss of some, if not all. They couldn't afford to lose a single animal, and she needed more freedom of movement.

Panting, she approached the highest point of a giant slab of granite. Once there, she lay down until only her head rose above the stone, noting the crows scattered among the rocks and trees between her position and the road. Now that she was visible to them, they fell silent. Here came the new arrivals, clothed luarin-style in tunics and breeches, their armor and weapons glinting in the sun. Their pack animals were heavily laden, as if for a long march or a long stay. At the head of their double column rode a helmeted man in light armor. Aly sharpened her Sight to get a better look, as the Balitang men-at-arms who were posted to watch the road motioned for him to stop.

She instantly recognized the leader. Silently she wriggled back from her vantage point until she could turn over and stare at the sky. Prince Bronau. Why was he here? Had he come as the duke's friend or as a servant of the Crown? If so, what were the Crown's orders?

She hummed to herself, thinking. If Bronau had been ordered to capture or kill the duke and his family, he hadn't brought enough men. He knew how many trained soldiers the duke had, because he had seen them off on their journey north. For all he knew, the duke might have added new fighters on the way. Aly smiled. Actually, the duke had done just that, binding the six bandits to him with blood. Their families had trickled up to Tanair, solidifying the former bandits' allegiance to the duke, who now fed and housed them.

Carefully, she rolled onto her stomach and crept back to her vantage point, bringing her magical Sight to bear on the prince once more. Bronau looked to be in a good mood, joking with the roadside guards as they waved him on. The guards' messenger was already leading his horse out of the shelter of the rocks. As soon as he reached flat ground he rode off at a gallop, carrying the word of the new arrivals to the duke and duchess, not knowing that Sarai would be there before him.

Aly continued to inspect Bronau's party. The servants who rode behind the prince also looked relaxed and comfortable. If Bronau's errand was a violent one, surely his attendants and soldiers would be more wary. These soldiers looked as if the only thing on their minds was shedding their armor on this hot, sunny day.

Aly slid down the granite slab. She wouldn't know anything more until tonight, when she could collect the gossip at Tanair.

The duchess, however, had other plans. Aly and Visda were about to eat lunch when one of Lokeij's boy hostlers rode up on Winnamine's own gelding. "Her Grace asks for you to attend her, Aly," the lad told her, dismounting. "I'm to take the goats and you're to report to Her Grace in the keep. Hullo, Visda." When Aly blinked at him, caught off balance, the boy rolled his eyes and thrust the reins at her. "I know you're practically fresh-caught, but even you ought to know better than to keep the mistress waiting."

"Oh—yes, of course," Aly stammered. She mounted the gelding clumsily, so that the two watching her wouldn't mention how curiously at home Aly was on horseback, and set out, with much flailing and rein tugging, back toward the road. Only when she knew Visda and the boy couldn't see her anymore did she kick the horse into a gallop.

She slowed when she came within view of Tanair's walls but kept the gelding at a trot up to the castle, allowing herself to bounce on his back like the greenest of riders. Lokeij himself took the reins from her as she tumbled from the saddle. "You need practice," he told Aly, grinning.

"Not on your life," she gasped, as if she had never had to ride before. She lurched into the keep.

Dove waited for her at the door. "*She* wants you," she told Aly, and towed her into a small room off the main hall. Normally it was a study, but Winnamine stood there now with a basin of steaming water, a towel, soap, and a clean tunic and leggings.

"Thank you, Dovasary," she said. "Close the door behind you." Dove obeyed. Winnamine turned to Aly. "Wash up, please," she ordered. "I have just promoted you to maidservant. You'll serve the wine right now, while my lord entertains Prince Bronau, and at table tonight. Ordinarily I would do it myself, but we have no housekeeper now, which means I must make all of their sleeping arrangements."

"Could not Ulasim . . . ?" Aly inquired.

The duchess shook her head. "Ulasim is off with the

men cutting wood for our fires. How could he know we were to have company? Which means I must take charge of our servants and make room for Bronau and his train. Besides, if you are to be our advisor, now is a good time to start. I would like to know what you make of Bronau's presence. You may see things with your fresh gaze that His Grace and I would not, having been friends with the prince all our adult lives."

"The duke does not expect me to wait on them?" Aly wanted to know.

"No," Winnamine replied calmly, "but I can't arrange this any other way. He may be polite and ask you to stand where you can't hear them, but at least you'll be able to form an impression of the prince. Is he hiding anything, is he uncomfortable, is he frightened . . ." Winnamine sighed. "I wish he'd given us warning!"

"I'm honored to serve, Your Grace," Aly told her mistress smoothly. "It won't matter if His Grace asks me to stand out of earshot. I read lips."

Winnamine put her hands on her hips and looked down the three inches between her eyes and Aly's. "Well! Now there's a bit of luck! Or maybe not luck, with a god involved. You read lips. Amazing."

Aly grinned. "I thought you might feel that way about it, Your Grace," she replied.

"I am grateful for any advantage," the duchess confided. "What a mess! Let's have that tunic off, Aly." As she helped Aly to pull the dirty tunic over her head, Winnamine continued to speak, thinking aloud. "We'll give the second floor to him and his servants. My lord and I will share with Sarai and Dove. His men will have to sleep in the new guest quarters. We haven't got enough beds, but I won't quarter them on the villagers. Our people work hard enough to feed and house themselves. I wish Bronau had known what a burden he was placing on us. Chances are he didn't know how small this place is. At least you don't need a comb."

Aly soaped her hands and arms. "Why me, Your Grace?" she asked. "Why not a regular maid? You asked for me before I told you I read lips."

The duchess rubbed cream onto her hands. They were trembling. "We've tried to put a good face on it, for the servants, and the children, but Aly, we are in mortal peril. Two years ago . . ." Her voice shook.

Aly looked around the room and spied a pitcher and cups on a tray. The pitcher held water. She poured some into a cup and offered it to Winnamine. The older woman took it with both hands and drank. When she had composed herself, she said evenly, "His Majesty dreamed that his son Hanoren turned into a rat and bit him. Hanoren and all his household were nailed to crosstrees along Rajmuat harbor." Her mouth twisted bitterly. "Needless to say, shipping fell off badly that year."

Aly started to say she knew the story, but held her tongue. It was not something a country maid would have heard.

"Now my lord and I are out of royal favor," Winnamine said, returning her cup to Aly. "The king might still dream about us. And here is Bronau. His could be the breath of wind that knocks us into Rajmuat harbor."

Aly removed her leggings and pulled the clean clothes on, watching the duchess through her eyelashes. "Is this your only reason for calling on me, Your Grace?"

Winnamine twisted a handkerchief in her fingers. "Bronau is amusing, charming, and careless. He goes after what he wants. When he doesn't want it anymore, he drops it. We live on the edge of the king's suspicions, Aly, and Bronau doesn't think. The god says we must trust your insights. I mean to place you where you will get them." She got to her feet and left as Aly straightened her clothes.

Watching the duchess go, Aly glimpsed a flicker of orange the shade of Dove's gown as the door opened. She wondered how long Dove had been listening. If Dove was going to make a habit of it, she ought to learn that anyone who looked at the opening between door hinges would see a color that didn't match that of the door.

The duchess returned with the wine tray, two pitchers, and cups. "Don't kneel, just bow. Serve the prince first," she told Aly. "The pitcher with the mermaid on the grip is for Mequen. The wine in it is well watered. Fill Bronau's cup as often as you can, of course. Wine always loosens his tongue, another thing that makes him a perilous friend."

Aly nodded. Balancing it carefully, she carried the heavy tray up the stairs to the family's private chambers.

A footman let her into the duke's sitting room, now given over to the prince. Mequen and Bronau sat in chairs on either side of a table, perfectly relaxed. Aly bowed and set the tray down, ignoring the duke's questioning eyes. She poured out a cup of wine from the unmarked pitcher for the prince and one from the mermaid pitcher for the duke. Mequen accepted the cup with a slight frown. "Will Her Grace not be joining us?" he asked, obviously puzzled.

"She is finding quarters for His Highness's servants and guards," Aly said with a polite bow. "She sends her regrets."

Mequen's frown deepened. "Then why does she not ask the house—" He stopped abruptly, then sighed. "I had forgotten. We no longer have a housekeeper." To Bronau he said, "I didn't realize what a spoiled creature I had become until we had to make do with twenty-odd servants and slaves instead of over a hundred. I think you'll like this vintage,

Your Highness." To Aly he said, "Stand by the far wall, please, Aly. Out of earshot."

As she obeyed, Bronau asked, "Do your people expect us to drink ourselves under the table, sending up two pitchers?" He and Mequen touched cups and tasted their wine.

"Actually, I've been drinking the local brew, to help the villagers make a little extra coin against the winter," the duke replied easily. "It's crude stuff, but if I don't drink it after I buy it, they'll return my money. Proud people, these highlanders. I won't subject you to it. What you have is a proper wine laid down by my father."

"It has a southern taste," Bronau admitted, drinking. "You coddle your people, Mequen."

"It would be different in Rajmuat," Mequen admitted. "We're isolated here, and must depend on these folk to get us through the winter."

Aly took her place and read the men's speech on their lips. She also employed her Sight to catch any lies.

"King Oron has turned that suspicious gaze on *me* now," Bronau told his friend. "The old man gets stranger with each sunrise. He's hiding in his quarter of the palace, has been for weeks. All of his food is tested for poison. He had your old friend Athan Fajering executed for—are you ready for this?—wrong thoughts."

Mequen turned white under his summer tan. "But Athan was his chancellor for eighteen years!"

Bronau nodded. "He was also an enemy of my dear sister-in-law Imajane, and my charming brother Rubinyan. You know Rubinyan has never been that fond of me," Bronau continued. "When Oron started to watch me, I started to think that Imajane and Rubinyan might well decide to inform him that I have 'bad thoughts,' too."

Mequen sighed, shaking his head. "I wish that you and Rubinyan would reconcile. It grieves me that my two best friends are at odds. And I think you wrong your brother, suggesting that he is turning the king against you. Rubinyan is a good man," he said earnestly, almost pleading. "He is reserved, and hard to know, but he is a wise and strong ally."

Bronau shook his head. "You always think the best of people, Mequen. If he is so good, why didn't he come to see you off?"

After a few more attempts, Mequen gave up trying to get the prince to see his brother in a kinder light. "One day, mark my words, you'll change your tune about Rubinyan," he said.

"The two of them are isolating that old fool Oron," Bronau said after his fourth cup of wine. "Soon he'll see only Imajane and Rubinyan, and one day they'll come to tell the court he's dead. They also spend plenty of time with Prince Hazarin," the prince confided. "I have to hope they don't turn Oron's most likely heir against me."

"Don't be ridiculous," Mequen assured him. "Hazarin likes you. He always says the rest of court's much too grim when you're away."

"The rest of the court is terrified of Oron," Bronau replied with a laugh. "They don't dare twitch."

At last Winnamine came to say a hot bath awaited Bronau. Mequen shooed Aly out. She gathered up the wine tray and cups while he and Winnamine told Bronau they would see him at supper. Once they were outside, Winnamine put the tray on a side table and indicated that her husband and Aly should go upstairs. She led the way into the sitting room of what had once been Sarai and Dove's chambers. Neither girl was in sight.

The duke and duchess took seats as Aly checked the

door to the servants' stair. She could hear the maids preparing rooms for the prince and his servants. To be on the safe side, when she closed the door, she pulled the carpet up until it covered the space where the door didn't quite touch the stone floor, and stuffed the rag she used as a handkerchief in the keyhole. Then she covered the crack under the main door. She found a dust cloth and stuffed a corner of it into the keyhole. Then she opened the door to the older girls' bedchambers so that she would see if anyone came in that way. At last she nodded to her masters.

Mequen looked at his wife. "My dear, why send Aly to wait on us?" he wanted to know. "I know you were busy with your domestic arrangements, but surely one of the girls with experience waiting on the nobility would have served." He smiled kindly at Aly. "Though you did a creditable job."

"Aly isn't used to Bronau as we are, my dear," Winnamine explained. "She might see what would be hidden to us. And she has certain useful skills."

"Useful?" Mequen asked, raising his brows at Aly.

"I read lips, Your Grace," Aly said meekly. "And I can tell you that the prince is telling the truth about why he came."

"What? How could you possibly know that?" the startled duke demanded.

"Liars blink more when they lie, or they look away while they answer," Aly explained. She did not want anyone to know about her Sight if she could help it. Only a fool told all of her secrets. "The prince is frightened." She looked at the duke. "Did you see he was sweating when he talked about the situation at court?"

Mequen raised his eyebrows. "All of us sweat when we think of the royal court," he said drily. "I am so accustomed to it that I didn't even notice. Truly, the god blessed us when he sent you." He held Aly's gaze with his own. "But he didn't bless you, did he?"

"I am Your Grace's servant," Aly told him, wide-eyed and earnest.

"Very courtier-like," remarked the duke. "One would think you a practiced associate of kings."

Aly had to shoo him away from this line of thought. She beamed at him. "So many compliments from Your Grace tonight!" she said, allowing her lashes to flutter. "I will become conceited, and the other servants will be hurt that they have not drawn your gracious attention."

"Aly, the Players lost a star performer when you didn't elect to train as a professional fool," the duchess said with a smile.

Aly shrugged comically. "The Players' loss is Your Graces' gain," she said, then added as a deliberate afterthought, "Mine, too, of course." She looked at the duke. "Truly, Your Grace, why fidget over what use the god makes of insignificant me?"

"Because I receive better service from someone who is happy," replied Mequen. "Because you are not insignificant, however much you may jest about it. And we know so little about you, except that bright Mithros says you will guide us through great trouble. Don't blame a man for curiosity, messenger." He looked at his duchess and sighed. "Well, my dear?"

From the corner of her eye, Aly saw orange cloth in the crack between the door to the bedroom and the wall. She really would have to suggest better ways for Dove to eavesdrop.

"We can accommodate them. Barely," Winnamine replied, bringing Aly's attention back to the duke and duchess. "We're putting his men-at-arms up in the new barn. They're not at all pleased, but they have no choice.

What of our people? Shall we send them out of the great hall at mealtimes?"

Mequen shook his head. "Perhaps if Bronau sees how limited our space is, he'll rusticate somewhere else. Besides, our people earn their place in the hall through their work."

Realizing they had finished with her, Aly murmured a farewell, bowed, and went to the main door of the suite. Carefully she returned the rug to its correct position and removed the dust cloth from the keyhole.

"You'll remember to pour the wine at the head table at supper, won't you, Aly?" asked the duchess.

Aly turned and bowed. "Of course, Your Grace."

First she ought to see to her goats. When she went outside, she found the inner courtyard awash in Bronau's people, as well as anyone from Tanair who had a reasonable excuse to be present. The only quiet place was the spot near the guard barracks where Nawat worked at his bench in the sun, gluing feathers to arrow shafts. For once he wasn't encircled by admiring females. Aly hesitated, then walked across to him.

Nawat didn't even look up from the painstaking task of setting a goose feather in its bed. "Your feathers are ruffled," he said.

"Well, it's very exciting, having visitors and all," she said, looking at the new arrivals.

"You act like a flock when a snake crawls by," the crow-man pointed out. "If that is excitement, it is not the good kind. Do you wish to mob them, to drive them away?"

"I couldn't even if I wanted to," she informed him, smiling. For all his human guise, he was still very much a crow. Impulsively she asked, "Did you get a look at him? The prince?"

"The one with fox-colored hair? He came to see me

work." Nawat looked up at Aly and grinned, white teeth flashing against his tanned skin. "I did it badly."

"What do you make of him?" Aly wanted to know. "Or did you not have time to get a sense of him?"

He replied with a wing shrug, then said, "I do not need time. I know a hawk when I see one."

"A hawk?" she repeated, thinking he had recognized Bronau's hunter bird look.

"A hawk," Nawat said firmly, his eyes on his work once more. "He will drive you off your own kill and steal your nestlings. He *should* be mobbed, before he steals any of yours. Shall you and I mob him?"

Aly tugged her ear, frowning. Somehow Nawat didn't have the same view of hawks as that held by people who'd been born human. "Unlike a hawk, Bronau comes with a flock of soldiers. You and I are outnumbered."

"We could mate," Nawat suggested eagerly. "In a year our nestlings would be large enough to mob anyone we like. In two or three years we could have still more nestlings, until no hawk will venture near our territory. Shall I court you? Do you like grubs or ants better?"

Aly smiled, finding him both silly and lovable. "It takes longer for human nestlings to get big enough to mob," she explained, wondering if Aunt Daine's conversations with animals were like this. "And I'm too busy to court. I've the goats to fetch, for one."

"I will be here," Nawat said placidly, returning to his work. "In case you change your mind about mating."

Aly brought her animals in early, then spent the afternoon idling around Bronau's people. All of them were relieved to be away from the king. They spoke of the arrival of more Stormwings, and of the many noble families who had decided to summer in the country. Only those who feared that the king would consider their departure suspicious had remained at court. Prince Hazarin was the only noble who acted as he had always done, drinking and attending parties in the pleasure district night after night.

When Bronau joined the Balitangs for supper, he brought gifts for the family. For Mequen and Winnamine he had newly published sets of books, which they received with true enthusiasm. A soldier marionette went to Elsren, a gorgeous doll dressed in Yamani fashions to Petranne, and a history of Carthak to Dove.

For Sarai, Bronau produced eardrops that were clusters of tiny peach-colored moonstones the same golden tint as her cheeks, and a gold necklace with a matching pendant. Sarai was overwhelmed. She immediately removed her white pearl eardrops and donned the new ones in their place. When she fumbled with the catch on the necklace, Bronau offered to help. Sarai lifted the heavy braided coils of her hair so that he could see better. With the necklace fastened, he turned Sarai to face him as she beamed at him.

"Lovely," Bronau said with a tender smile. He took Sarai's hand and kissed it.

Aly, standing behind them on the dais, looked at the wine tray she was holding, her mind working busily. Prince Bronau had brought gifts nicely chosen to appeal to each Balitang. It might just be coincidence that his gift to the oldest, marriageable daughter of the house was the kind of token a girl would see as an indication of special affection. It might also be coincidence that his gift had given Bronau a chance to touch Sarai, and Sarai an excuse to let him.

Aly glanced at Dove. The twelve-year-old held her book open to a detailed map, but her eyes were on Bronau and her sister. Mequen and Winnamine had also seen the exchange between their oldest daughter and their friend.

A footman collected the books, doll, and marionette as kitchen servants brought out the food. Aly poured wine into the cups of everyone on the dais, then took up the water pitcher. It was customary to dilute supper wine. She used less water for the prince, duke, duchess, and Sarai, and a good bit of it for Dove, Petranne, and Elsren, then took her position behind the prince and the duchess.

The servants passed along the dais, starting with the prince and ending with Elsren, offering a loaded tray to everyone. The older diners selected the things they wanted, while the healer Rihani chose Petranne's and Elsren's meal. The offerings were a mixture of foods of the Eastern Lands, Southern Lands, and raka kitchens. Aly recognized the salad of long beans, chilies, coconut, shrimp paste, and garlic, having sampled it in the leftovers from a meal back in Rajmuat. There was a noodle salad, another favorite raka dish adopted by the luarin, this one with garlic, chilies, cashews, peanuts, and celery. There were chicken dumplings, dates stuffed with curried jackfruit, and pickled asparagus.

Looking at it all, Aly shivered. She had eaten a great deal of rice since her arrival in the Isles, to the point where she was beginning to feel a bit grainy. It was hard to trust local fare when there was always a risk that some bright bit of red or green would set her mouth afire, but the diners here, luarin and raka, ate this strange selection as easily as her own family consumed meals of apple fritters, fish pasties, and venison. The chief change to the Balitangs' diet since their arrival at Tanair was the absence of seafood, which was otherwise the backbone of Isle cooking. She was grateful for the lack. There were too many volcano-blast chilies in the seafood dishes of the Copper Isles.

During the meal Bronau relayed news of the capital. He described recent plays, performers, and books, and news from the Eastern and Southern Lands. Aly took it all in, noting that Scanra continued to attack Tortall, despite heavy losses and rumors of rebellion among Maggur's lords. The luarin free servants listened to every word, as did Sergeant Veron and some of his luarin and part-luarin men-at-arms. The raka and many of those who were part raka seemed indifferent. Bronau's people looked around at their surroundings, obviously unimpressed.

If you think we're countrified now, Aly thought evilly, wait till they bring out the dishes made with goat's milk. That should put a pickle up your noses!

Petranne and Elsren were soon squabbling, their bellies full. Their nursemaid had to gently scold them several times. Dove was intent on Bronau's conversation, but what she made of it Aly couldn't tell. Sarai, too, was listening to the prince, her lovely eyes shining in admiration. Like Dove, Winnamine and Mequen listened with polite interest but without giving away their thoughts. Aly approved. After her observation of the prince, she no more trusted him not to repeat anything the Balitangs might say than she could trust him not to repeat what other nobles had told him since the Balitangs' departure. Though their remarks were cruel, Bronau didn't seem to notice that his gossip upset his hosts. Sarai's admiring mood evaporated as she listened to what their fellow nobles had said of them. She folded her napkin into small pleats, her lips pressed tightly together. The duke and the duchess toyed with their wineglasses, their eyes glittering.

As Aly was pouring the last cup of wine for the meal, Bronau half turned to get a better look at her. "I know you," he said with a smile. "You're the little luarin slave who opened the door, the night I brought the king's news to my friends. You've risen in the world, from doorkeeper to wine pourer."

Aly bowed. "I do all manner of chores now, Your Highness," she murmured. "I would not have had this opportunity in Rajmuat."

"I'll bet it's not as exciting here as in the capital," the prince said. "If my memory's right, you had more of a Tortallan accent then. Did it rub off in the jungle? And your hair has grown more. The color is most becoming." He was teasing her, his gray eyes dancing.

Aly knew what she was expected to do. She did it, bridling and smiling at the prince. "I've learned ever so much more since I first saw Your Highness," she told him, acting the flattered female. Privately she supposed that Bronau was well enough, as men went, though he was much too old for her—he looked to be in his mid-thirties. Smile as he might and wink as he did when he straightened in his chair, Aly was unmoved. He did have nice hair, charm, and elegance, but he was lipless, shallow, and direct. He would bore her within a fortnight. Queen Thayet had once teased Aly that she would never find a man who could keep her attention for very long. Aly hoped that wasn't true. For now, she considered ways to avoid Bronau in case he invited her to share his bed.

"Sleep with him?" Chenaol asked when Aly mentioned it, once she had returned to the kitchen with the wine tray. "As I told you early on, you can say no. His Grace lets his people make their own choices."

"I thought the nobility would bid their servants to please their guests," Aly remarked as she sat down to a meal of leftovers.

"Not His Grace. If they're willing, and they're protected from getting themselves with child, they may do as they please, and His Grace will defend them," Chenaol replied.

She was greasing her favorite wide cooking pot, the one like a large bowl. "But he won't have anyone forced." The woman looked Aly full in the face. "Why do you think people are so loyal to this family?" she asked quietly. "Because *all* are people in this house—raka and luarin, slave and free. The first time Petranne slapped a slave and called her a lazy cow, the duchess spanked her, and took away her dolls for a month. Petranne said she'd heard it at a friend's house, and the duke ended the friendship. There are good luarin here, Aly-who-knows-so-much."

Aly gnawed on her lower lip, then murmured, "And of course, there are Duchess Sarugani's heirs." She knew it was a risk to say it, but with the household aflutter with the new arrivals, the raka might accidentally reveal more than they had before. Aly hoped to catch them off their guard.

"Why do you say 'heirs'?" Chenaol demanded, her voice soft. Her small brown eyes were sharp as she looked at Aly. "Under the luarin, only males inherit."

Under the luarin, Chenaol had said. Aly stuffed a rice ball into her mouth and chewed as she thought. So Chenaol knew of the old law, the law under which the females could inherit—females such as Sarugani's daughters. Aly had once heard a man-at-arms figure the population of the Isles was one white among six brown. Did that number cover the mixed-bloods? Where might they stand if the raka chose to take back their home?

She was reaching for another rice ball when a sharp knife pricked the delicate skin under her ear. She was filled with admiration. She hadn't even seen Chenaol palm the blade. "Is that the boning knife, or a chopping knife?" she asked politely. "If you press hard and cut down, I should bleed to death quickly. Of course, I'll make a mess."

"You're very calm for someone who's about to get her corpse dumped somewhere for the crows to eat," whispered Chenaol.

"Now, this simply will not do." A white, bright figure in the shape of a man appeared, seated across the table from Aly. Elsewhere in the kitchen everyone froze in place, eyes and chests unmoving. Only Aly and the cook were free. "Chenaol, my dear girl, stop that." The bright figure spoke with Kyprioth's crisp, cheery voice, accented just now with impatience. "I send help, and how do you thank her? We won't get very far if you kill a luarin who can be of use."

"Bright One, she's a royal spy," Chenaol snapped. "Too curious by half, sticking her nose in everywhere . . ."

"She is *our* spy, not the Crown's," Kyprioth informed the cook. "Imported for your purposes with not a little trouble on my part, I might add. I'll take that." The knife vanished from the cook's hand to reappear in front of the god's light-shape.

Aly glared at him. "I was handling this," she informed Kyprioth. "I didn't need you."

"Yes, but you're so careful about asking around that our wager will be done before my people realize you can help," Kyprioth said reasonably. "Chenaol, why has it taken you so long to realize that Aly is someone special? Think of all the things you can do with her to help."

Chenaol glanced at Aly, then at Kyprioth's glowing form. She held out her hand. "You and your games, Bright One. It would be so wonderful if you ever once gave a body a hint about what you had in mind. I'll take my knife back, please."

"She isn't very respectful," Aly pointed out, interested. She couldn't be angry with Chenaol. In her shoes, Aly would have killed such a nosy slave on the road to Tanair.

"Respect is hard to get when you're a trickster," the god said mournfully. "People are so often inclined to think the worst of one."

Aly propped her chin on her hand. "I can't imagine why," she retorted. "Give the knife back."

"I mean to be sure that she won't murder you when my back is turned," argued Kyprioth. To Chenaol he said, "If you kill this spy, I'm not getting you a new one."

"You should have told us," the cook repeated.

"I expected you to work it out," snapped the god. "*I* wouldn't have let a royal spy get a whiff of our girl. Really, must I do everything?" Without so much as a flicker he was gone. The knife was back in Chenaol's hands. The other servants and slaves in the kitchen began moving about again, unaware that they had been held captive for a short time.

Aly watched Chenaol for a moment before she said, "I'm glad he's not *my* god."

The cook gave her the thinnest of smiles. "As long as his eye is on you, girl, you are his. Mountains give way before that one does."

Aly shrugged. "All gods are like that. You can't reason with them." Hastily she added, "Or so I've heard." She knew it from her mother, the Goddess's own warrior, and from her Aunt Daine, a demi-goddess in her own right, who had met far more gods than any human would think healthy.

Chenaol sighed. "And so you are a spy."

Aly winced. "Please keep your voice down."

"I'll have to tell the others," Chenaol pointed out, eyeing the edge on her knife. "They feared that we'd have to kill you, when all of us like you so much. Fesgao insisted we give you a chance." She put down the knife. "At least the god didn't steal this. He's as bad as a crow for taking things. I got my cooking knives from my mother, and she from hers."

Aly rubbed the back of her neck. "Then raka inheritance is through the mother's line," she confirmed.

"Yes, of course. And the oldest child inherits. We don't care if it's a boy or girl."

Aly looked around. No one was within hearing. Most of the staff had gone back to the main hall, where Bronau's minstrel was tuning a lute. A shimmer of bells told her some of the staff had brought out their instruments. She murmured, "So under raka law, Sarai and Dove are their mother's heirs. And their mother *was* royalty, wasn't she?"

Chenaol got up and poured herself a cup of arak. She sat and propped her feet on a little stool. "The last of the house," she replied, as quiet as Aly. "You know, some of the luarin nobility have taken up the custom. The first child inherits, whatever sex it may be."

"But not the royal line," Aly reminded her.

Chenaol lifted her cup in a silent toast. "Anything can change," she said, and drank.

Aly was drifting off to sleep when she heard steps approach her in the dark main hall. She waited, a hand on her stolen knife. Feathers rustled as two shadowy figures dropped pallets on either side of her. Aly caught the drift of jasmine scent from her left, and soap mixed with aloe from her right. "You're supposed to be in your parents' room," she whispered to Dove and Sarai.

"But you're more interesting, and it's too hot upstairs," Sarai whispered.

"Can I bear the compliment?" Aly asked. "I'm not telling Lioness tales all night."

"It really is too hot up there," Dove said. "And we're not used to such close quarters. We can tell you stories, if you like. Since you're not from here."

Aly yawned as she thought quickly. "I'm too tired for a long story," she told the girls. "But I'd like to know what your mother was like."

"She came from the old raka blood, the nobility before the luarin conquest," replied Sarai, her voice dreamy in the shadows. "She was light, and color, and fun. She had a laugh like small gold bells. Every day was a holiday with her. She and the present duchess were best friends. I suppose that made it easier for Winnamine to take her place." Her voice had turned bitter.

"If she was trying to replace your mother, would she and your father have waited years before they wed?" Aly wanted to know. "I heard it was one of your aunts who made him remember he owed it to the family to remarry."

"What's *your* mother like?" asked Sarai abruptly. "You're so cool and thinking all the time—is that how your mother is?"

Aly had wondered what she would say when this question was asked. The obvious lie, that her mother was dead, felt too much like an ill-wishing to her. Her mother walked dangerous roads too often for Aly even to lie about her fate.

Instead she told a different falsehood. "I never knew her," she replied. "I'm told she is a traveling musician. Her company spent winters in town, and she'd live there with my father, who's a merchant. Only, the year after she had me, she stopped coming."

For a moment both girls were quiet. Then Sarai whispered, "Aly, I'm sorry. We never meant to pry."

Aly put a small quiver in her voice and replied bravely, "I hardly ever think of it. Da's so good to us." Softly she added, "She didn't leave because of my sisters. Only me."

"Do you *mind*?" someone growled nearby. "We have work in the morning, in case some of us have forgotten."

"Aly, forgive us," whispered Dove as she lay down on her pallet.

"I'm your slave," Aly replied. "You have the right."

Sarai murmured, "No, we don't." The sisters fell silent.

And that should be the end of *that* kind of question, Aly thought, satisfied.

Essence spells. We carry our essence everywhere, in our skin, in our hair, our nails. This means that everything we touch picks up some of ourselves. The longer the contact, the more essence is transferred. Thus, if you get clothing someone has worn when he or she has been active, or hot, or upset, that clothing will supply you with more than enough essence to work a spell. Mages favor essence spells for things such as locks and keys, because such spells can be linked to the owner alone. They are foolproof. They work if the owner touches something in a hurry, while under stress, in the cold. And there are ways to go around such spells.

—From a lecture on basic magical theory by Numair Salmalin at the Royal University at Corus, attended by the thirteen-year-old Aly

8

A SPY'S WORK

Aly rose before dawn, as usual, since the duchess had not suggested that she give up her daytime work. She emerged from the kitchen wing to find Nawat seated on the rim of the well that served the cooks. He was surrounded by crows. The birds had found seats on the well's cover, Nawat's shoulders, the ground, the kitchen garden fence, and even the archery targets set up between the barracks and the garden. All of the birds looked as pleased as any human to be up so early, with the sun just showing above the eastern horizon. They sat or stood or walked, feathers ruffled against the early morning chill, eyes half shut with sleep. They stirred as Aly moved through them. Nawat turned to look at her.

"My clan has come," he explained. "We will mob the Bronau hawk if you ask it. He is a danger to humans and their nestlings."

Aly scratched her head. What was she supposed to say to *that*? Certainly she agreed. Her wager depended on keeping the Balitang nestlings alive this summer. Bronau was one of the factors that put them at risk.

"It's not so easy among two-leggers," she explained, wondering how she could explain human politics to her feathered allies. "We can't drive him off. We'll put the nestlings in more danger if we do."

One crow made a croaking noise that sounded like a variation on the call to attack and kill.

"Then let us kill him and his flock," Nawat said brightly. "He cannot kill or steal anyone if his bones are scattered between here and the mountains."

Aly sighed. "Nawat, it's not just Bronau. These soldiers who follow him? They are not his entire flock. He has a vast flock that will come to destroy everything where he was killed, understand? His brother, his sister-in-law, the king . . ."

Nawat regarded her with puzzlement, head cocked to one side. The other crows had the same expression and tilt to their heads.

"Humans do these things differently." Aly knew she sounded feeble, but she was unsure how to explain matters so that they would make sense to them. "They aren't as consistent as crows. Rank and alliances change among humans all the time, inside the flock and outside. And if you hurt one of their kin, they'll punish whole families, even whole towns. You are here to help me, and I am here to keep the Balitang nestlings alive all summer, yes?"

Nawat smiled. "Yes, Aly."

"Then you must trust me when I say that mobbing the prince would place them in even more danger," Aly told him, now feeling weak and peculiar. She wondered if Aunt Daine ever felt this way, and if being able to speak animal languages made times like this easier for her aunt. "If we are vigilant with the nestlings, if we never let them stray from our eyes, we can hold them safe without mobbing anyone." She rubbed her forehead, which had begun to ache. "Will you tell your friends, Nawat?" she asked. "And I will explain to you about humans and royalty later."

"Yes, Aly," Nawat told her with that particularly sweet smile. It was a smile that could divert her attention from Kyprioth's wager, so she thrust all thought of it from her mind and went to collect her goats. She was leading them through the village gates when she heard the crows take flight from the castle. For a while she turned and walked backward to see the birds soar above Tanair, delighting at the sight of their iridescent blue-black feathers in the early light, and the graceful sweep of their wings. Soon they were gone, some to the trees among the eastern rocks, others to the fields that supported Tanair. She only hoped they hadn't left large, white, streaky signs of their presence for the household to find when they went outside.

Aly walked on, savoring the fresh morning air and the promise of warmth to come. The weather here was nearly perfect: warm to hot days, and cool nights. She walked among fields that showed signs of crops coming in, down roads lined with wildflowers and the occasional tree. There were worse places to spend the summer, she decided as she led the goats into the rocks about the Dimari road. With Bronau's presence to keep her alert and with the understanding that Kyprioth would not have troubled to involve Aly and the crows if he'd anticipated a peaceful summer, she knew she could pass a few interesting, pleasant months here. She *did* like a challenge.

Aly settled the goats in the rocks above the road to Dimari. Once they were happily grazing, she sat to peel the casing from her morning's cold sausage. "Kyprioth," she called teasingly. "I'll share my breakfast with you."

"Spare me." The god appeared atop a nearby boulder,

dressed as a raka with his usual scrambled collection of jewelry and sparkling ornaments. He sat casually, his arms looped around one bent knee, so the jewels in his bracelets caught the morning sun. "Sausage has no appeal for me whatever."

Aly sighed. "It's cooked, silly."

Kyprioth turned his face into the wind. "Cooked or raw, sausage is not the food of the gods. Why are we talking? My brother and sister won't stay occupied with other wars forever, you know."

Aly examined her fingernails as if she weren't interested in her next question: "Are you looking to start a war here, sir?"

Kyprioth grinned, white teeth flashing against brown skin. It was a grin that was the essence of mischief, with none of the sweetness of Nawat's smile. "A fine effort and well executed. May I remind you that you never call me 'sir'?"

Aly grimaced. Tiny slips like that betrayed an impersonation.

"Why should you care?" the god went on. "You have but one task between now and the autumn equinox: to keep the Balitang children alive. War isn't a concern for you."

Aly leaned back against a tree, her eyes on the goats rather than the god. "You see, that's what I wanted to ask you about," she explained in her friendliest manner. "It's just that I worry Chenaol will believe I am here for a bit longer than the summer. I would hate to disappoint her when I go. She might even believe that *you* might keep me here."

"Oh, no, I will do nothing of the kind," Kyprioth said. "I doubt that Chenaol takes it that way."

Aly sat up on her knees and looked at the god. "Good," she said. "A wager is sacred in the Divine Realms—anyone knows it. If you try to change the terms we've agreed to? I'll bring the matter before your fellow gods, including the two whose attention you least want to draw. The two who kicked you off your throne. Don't even think of pulling the wool over my eyes."

He vanished from his rock to reappear in front of Aly. "The thought never crossed my mind," he said, and kissed her on the forehead. "A wager's a wager." He vanished, making the air pop where he had been.

Aly shook her head, then stood and stretched. "I should feel relieved," she mused aloud. "And yet, somehow, I don't."

She dozed for a while in the sun. When she woke, it was to a crow's announcement of riders on the road south from Tanair. Aly sharpened her Sight and saw a noble riding party below her: Prince Bronau, Duke Mequen, Duchess Winnamine, Sarai, and Dove were out riding. The prince called a mocking challenge, which Sarai accepted with a whoop, nudging her horse into a gallop as the prince spurred his own mount. They thundered down the southern road, Sarai like a warrior out of legends, her hair springing from its pins. Two bodyguards followed the racers at the gallop, while Mequen, Winnamine, Dove, and their guards kept to a lively trot. They waved to Aly, who waved back, as they rode on.

Aly stretched out her leg tendons, touching her toes as she turned things over in her mind. Did Bronau think Sarai might be a bride for him? The prince was a younger son, which meant his pockets might not be very deep. Did he think Sarai had money? Through enthusiastic eavesdropping, Aly had discovered that Balitangs inherited by luarin law. Elsren would get the bulk of the duke's lands and wealth at his death. Sarai and Dove would split their inheritance from their mother, Tanair and a few other small estates. They would not be wealthy brides.

She heard footsteps, quiet but not noiseless, among the rocks to her left. Aly bent casually and picked up two of a small pile of stones she had made before her nap. Back at home she had learned to throw rocks from the village boys, until she could kill rabbits or dent heavy wood with the force of her throw.

"She rides well, our Sarai."

Ulasim stepped out from between the rocks. Aly looked him over. Today he wore homespun and moved as easily in the rough garments as her own father moved in his clothes. Aly noticed something else: the outlines of dagger sheaths against his sleeves and on his breeches where they fell over his calf-high boots. Ulasim hadn't worn blades before.

"She does ride well," Aly said. "I suppose you've talked to Chenaol."

"Of course," said Ulasim. "We are all in this together."

"This," Aly said musingly, guessing that he spoke of the conspiracy among the Balitang raka. "Tell me, did you ever want to put Sarugani on the throne?"

Ulasim shook his head. "The time wasn't right." After a moment's hesitation, he added, "And she wasn't right—more heart than head, when everyone knows the head is what matters when dealing with the luarin. It matters, too, that she had no royal blood through the luarin line, which will bring more of the part-raka to our cause. Our lady has the Rittevon blood as well as the ancient Haiming blood, and she is wiser than her mother. The people will love Sarai as queen." He fell silent for a moment, then said, "We have waited a very long time for this. We shall have only one chance—if we fail, the luarin will see to it that we cannot rise again. That is why so many came to see her. They know what is at stake. They have prayed for this chance for generations."

The head hostler Lokeij rode up on Duke Mequen's hunter. The old raka used no saddle, Aly realized, and no bridle. Her estimation of the tiny man rose several notches.

She would have shrunk from riding such a big horse with full tack, let alone with none.

Lokeij dismounted easily and set the horse among the goats to graze. Then he lay down atop a rock, apparently there just to bask in the sun. Ulasim picked up a stick and whittled on it. It seemed they were waiting. Aly put her rocks back in their pile and practiced head and handstands on the soft grass.

She had just progressed to walking on her hands when Chenaol arrived through the rocks, panting from the exercise. "I told them," she informed Aly as she collapsed beside the girl.

"I noticed," Aly said with a grin. "Who else did you tell?"

"Fesgao," replied Chenaol, fanning herself with one hand. "Veron's got him in charge of the watch today, and he dares not leave."

Somehow Aly wasn't surprised to hear that Fesgao was part of the conspiracy. She hesitated for a moment, then shrugged. Time to get my feet wet, she thought, and said, "Veron is the king's spy. He keeps his papers and coding materials in a box set on the lintel over his door. Have you someone who can watch him, and intercept any reports he might try to send out? Not Fesgao—he's too obvious."

"One of my stable boys will do well at such work," said Lokeij. "Boys are less obvious than men, and these boys are forever trailing behind the men-at-arms when I've no work for them. It will be easy."

"Should we tell His Grace?" asked Ulasim.

Aly shook her head. "The duke and the duchess do not need to know," she replied. "I will tell them when it is necessary."

Lokeij turned his head to stare at her. "They listen to

you?" he asked, plainly startled. "But they only know you as a slave."

Aly grinned. "Your friend appeared to them as Mithros and told them to listen to me," she explained. "They think I'm his messenger."

"That explains . . ." Chenaol's voice trailed off as she considered what this information did explain.

"Fesgao said that you suggested he check the forest for bandits on the way here," Ulasim remarked. "He wasn't sure if there were people abroad, having been in the city so long, but you convinced him."

Aly shrugged.

"Well!" Chenaol said, more pleased than she had been the previous night. "Things should go better, now that we have a proper spy. We're ready for anything."

"Anything but a mage," Aly pointed out, lying back and linking her hands behind her head. As clouds scuttled by, she added, "The healer Rihani is good only for healing, and only a certain amount of it, at that. A true mage, come here on King Oron's behalf, could crack us wide open. Speaking of the king . . ."

Lokeij leaned over and spat to one side.

"Satisfying, but not useful," Aly said. "If spit made a difference, you raka would have had the Isles back as soon as everyone got to know the luarin. With regard to the king, if he has one of his bad twitches, Veron and his boys won't be enough to hold off a royal assault. And you can't count on Veron. Like as not, he'll just open the Tanair gates like a good dog. Have you raka made your own provisions for warriors? Patrols of the plateau? If outsiders infiltrate this area, you should stop them before they reach Tanair."

"But why?" Ulasim wanted to know. "Surely it's enough to retreat to the castle. We're safe inside the walls."

Aly shook her head. "If they trap us in the castle, then we are well and truly *trapped*," she explained. "It would be far better for any assassins the king sends to vanish before they reach Tanair. That way, when the king asks what happened to his soldiers, His Grace can say, 'What soldiers?' without even needing to lie. What he doesn't know won't hurt him."

Lokeij whistled. "Make the king's warriors vanish if they come . . . what a deceitful turtledove you are."

Aly smiled at the sky. "Oh, don't," she replied in the tones of a flirtatious court lady. "Stop, I insist. Your flattery makes me blush."

"Have we the warriors?" asked Chenaol slowly.

Lokeij cleared his throat. When the other raka looked at him, he raised his eyebrows. They nodded. The old hostler turned his eyes on Aly. "There are some fighters up here, waiting," he explained. "In the villages. Over the last three years they have come, young men and women, nearly sixty in all, to train and to wait. The elders will be happy the time has come to put them to use. They hunt, they fight, and they flirt with their daughters and sons." He smiled. "They are also very good at riding, scouting, shooting, and building walls. They have their own mounts, and can live in the open air."

"The crows will help," said a voice from nearby. Nawat had come up soundlessly to stand near a boulder. "We will teach your fighters as we taught Aly."

Aly didn't even see Ulasim leave his place, the man was so fast. He jammed Nawat against the boulder and put a knife to his throat. Nawat twisted, an arm moving. Ulasim went down on his knees. He bent over, gasping, dead white under his coppery skin. Nawat jumped five feet in the air to the top of his boulder. Two long strides took him across the rocks; a short jump put him on a tree branch over Aly's head.

Chenaol went to Ulasim. "What did you do?" she demanded. "If you've killed him . . ."

Nawat smiled at her from his leafy refuge. "I only pecked him with my fingers. He was rude to try to cut me. I will help Aly do whatever she must. He should know that."

All three raka stared at the young fletcher. "What *are* you?" demanded Lokeij. "You aren't raka."

"Isn't he?" Aly asked lazily, watching Ulasim and Chenaol through her lowered lashes. "What is he, then? Luarin?"

Ulasim straightened with a grimace. He patted Chenaol on the shoulder, reassuring her that he wasn't stabbed, then stared at Nawat. Ignoring him, Nawat picked something off the tree trunk, eyed it, then ate it. His eyebrows shot up. He looked around, found a twig and broke it off, and used it to root in a crevice of the tree bark.

Ulasim wiped a hand over dry lips and crouched a little, holding the spot in his side where Nawat had struck him. "Not luarin," he said at last, wonder in his eyes and voice. "But not raka, either."

"Does it matter, if I give your warriors the secrets of the crows?" asked Nawat. He brought his twig close to his face. A grub squirmed on the end of it. He popped it into his mouth and thrust his twig under a new piece of bark. "We have a wager with the Bright One, too, the god of tricks," the crow-man explained as he wriggled his twig. "To help Aly, we must help the nestlings. Surely it makes no difference what I am. You humans worry about proper names too much."

Chenaol looked at Aly. "Do you vouch for him?"

"Why not ask your god?" Aly demanded in return. "The crows were his idea."

Ulasim rubbed his side. "Things were simpler in

Rajmuat," he complained. "Nawat, tonight you'll meet with Fesgao and me in the guard barracks. We must work out patrol schedules and decide how your crows will communicate with our fighters. And come down out of that tree. You're making my neck hurt, and your eating habits make my belly squirm."

Nawat jumped to the ground, then found a rock to sit on. "No more knives?" he asked Ulasim.

"No more pecking?" Ulasim retorted.

Nawat looked at Aly. "I cannot teach the raka as we taught you. We will sort that out."

"I leave it in your capable hands," Aly told him with a smile. She looked at the raka conspirators. "Any other royal spies in the household?"

"Just Hasui, and she's in the kitchen under my eye," Chenaol replied with a firm nod. "I prefer not to kill her, if it can be helped."

"No, don't," Aly said. "It'll leave you short-handed in the kitchen. For another, we can send the wrong information through Hasui and Veron to their masters. Knowing who is your spy can be quite useful." She scratched her head, reviewing all the things they had discussed. There were plenty of factors to keep in mind, and she wanted to make sure that they had covered the most important ones. She had always expected her first job as a spy to be a simple matter of watching targets and sending reports on their behavior. Da would never thrust a green spy into a political swamp like this one for her first assignment. She grinned. She would have a tale to tell him when she went home!

Ulasim was staring at her. "What?" she asked.

"Where did you learn to think this way?" the raka asked slowly. "We would have killed Hasui outright if Chenaol had not said she would be controlled in the kitchen. Killing Veron would break no one's heart. He's too fond of whipping raka to get them to move. We never would think to make the spies pass on bad information. And it never occurred to us that a castle might be a trap."

"Oh, the god fiddled with my mind," she replied wickedly. "They're fond of doing things like that. You never know what they'll get up to."

"I do not believe you," Ulasim replied, an amused glint in his dark eyes. "No god ever needs to know such tiny things. Who are your people?"

"Tortallans," Aly informed him. "Merchants. Harmless. Unless you count my mother, who was a Player. What of Prince Bronau's people?" she asked, changing the subject. "Are any of them more than they seem to be?"

The raka looked at one another and shook their heads. "They just got here," Chenaol reminded Aly.

Aly yawned. "I'll have a look around, then. Perhaps Her Grace will excuse me from pouring the wine tonight. You might want to keep a constant watch on them, too. After all, they might find the weapons hidden in the storerooms under the stable."

Lokeij cursed eloquently. "You can't know about them! I've got the stables watched all the time!"

"I didn't know until now," Aly replied easily, enjoying the joke she had just played on the old man. She ignored Lokeij's muttered curse, though she stored it in her memory as a useful one to know. "It's a central location, after all, and the raka linger there all the time."

Ulasim whistled softly. "Our friend picked well when he picked you."

Just don't get used to me, Aly thought at she smiled at him. *I don't mean to be here after the autumn equinox.*

Chenaol looked at the sun. "I'd best get back," she told

them. "Those lazy wenches will slack on the cooking if I'm not there." She set off among the rocks. Ulasim murmured quietly to Lokeij, then stood aside as the old man mounted his horse as nimbly as a boy. Aly looked around for Nawat—he was nowhere to be seen. Like any crow, he seemed to have the ability to come and go unnoticed, something that didn't involve magic, only animal craft.

At last Ulasim was alone with Aly. "Tomorrow I will send Visda to you. She and her dogs will graze her herd with yours every day after this. She will tell no one what you do once you have settled the flock. This way, should you need to leave your post, she can look after the goats as well."

Aly nodded. "Good idea. I thank you."

"Also, what are your preferred weapons?" he wanted to know. "Can you use any, O child of merchants?"

Aly raised an eyebrow at him. "You don't believe what I told you of my family. I'm hurt. Maybe even crushed." Ulasim was unmoved. She delayed by reminding him, "It's my life if I'm caught with weapons, you know that. Slave owners don't arm slaves." She wasn't sure if it was wise to let anyone know of her skill with knives.

"Then you must not be caught," Ulasim replied coolly. "Have you been to the shrine between the stable and the wall?"

Aly shook her head.

"The flagstone before the altar can be lifted. What shall we leave there for you?" He smiled thinly.

Aly nibbled her lower lip. It would be nice to have more blades than just the stolen one hidden in her bedroll. She'd always teased her father when he complained about the magic that alerted the king and queen of people carrying hidden weapons. She had liked telling him that he sounded like a child without his favorite blanket. Now she understood his feeling of vulnerability. Like Aly, he could fight hand to hand at need, but daggers were what he loved. He'd taught that love to her. "Daggers?" she asked. "Good ones, as flat as may be, with sleeve and leg sheaths? They would be a blessing."

"Merchants," Ulasim remarked drily, referring to her false background again. "Yes, of course I believe you. I must, mustn't I? You *are* Kyprioth's chosen, so the truth drips from your tongue like honey from the comb."

"Again you are suspicious," Aly told the raka, shaking her head in sorrow. "You wound me so deeply." She liked Ulasim. He was smart.

"I can see that," retorted Ulasim. "Daggers we shall provide you, under the flagstone tonight." Aly relaxed, looking at the clouds again, but the raka was not finished. "And since you are so busy watching the plotters who creep up behind us, I will assign a guard to you. Someone who won't look out of place with the goats." His voice was firm, his eyes direct as Aly sat up and groaned a protest. Ulasim said firmly, "At the very least he can run your errands."

Aly sighed. "What about a girl?" she asked, "or a woman? Less conspicuous and less likely to stir up gossip."

Ulasim stiffened. Aly made a face at him. "Sarai told me your women fought together with the men in the raka armies," she said patiently. "It seems reasonable to guess that the raka who aren't under the luarin eye continue to train their women to fight. I can understand your not wanting folk to know. This way, the luarin think the number of raka who might give them trouble is half of your actual force. But *I'm* not going to tell, and a female won't be noticed as much as a man."

"I will see to it," he said. He started to go, then turned back to face Aly. His dark eyes were puzzled. "I suppose I must trust the god's opinion of you, but you still worry me.

He is a trickster, when all is said and done."

"But I'm not," Aly assured him, the picture of earnest youth. "Why, I'm just as true and honest as dirt. And I'm even more charming than dirt."

Ulasim winced. "Thank you for describing yourself in such unforgettable terms," he said. "I see you and the god are well matched."

Aly watched him go. *Ulasim is their general,* she decided, thinking about the roles each raka played. *Lokeij is in charge of communications and storage for weapons and supplies. Fesgao must be their war leader, used to straight-forward combat. And Chenaol . . .*

She plucked a grass stem. She supposed every army needed a chief cook who was quick with her knives, but surely there was more to Chenaol than that. Did she command the women of the raka? What could she do that the men could not?

Aly's memory showed her an image of Chenaol talking to the merchants who stopped by Tanair from time to time. She was accepting boxes from them, boxes that Aly had seen open in the kitchen: knives. No one questioned a raka cook in the purchase of knives. And it would be easier to smuggle longer blades to a cook than a man-at-arms watched by a luarin superior. Aly smiled. *Chenaol was the raka armorer. That was why Ulasim has said "we" when he talked of giving me knives,* she thought. *He may plant them, but he'll get them from Chenaol.*

Truly this was a fine morning, Aly reflected as she stretched and thought. Now she had human allies and their resources. With Bronau in residence and the king's disfavor, the Balitangs' luarin and raka alike had an excuse to strengthen their defenses. Any of them who had been wait-ing for "someday" to come would know that day was nearly upon them. They would be razor-sharp, with no need for Aly to sharpen them, and, unlike the crows, they would understand that Bronau might serve as a lightning rod to draw the king's wrath.

Aly gnawed a grass stem. The raka and the crows were prepared for attack by armed fighters both from within and without. However, they still could not withstand a strong magical attack. Somehow they would have to produce a mage.

Once again Aly brought the goats in early. After they were safely penned, she waved to Nawat, who was fletching arrows near the archery butts, and entered the keep in search of the duchess. She found the lady in the small bedchamber where Petranne, Elsren, and their nursemaid slept, giving her son a bath while the maid toweled his sister dry.

Aly bowed. "Excuse me, Your Grace," she said.

Winnamine looked up at her. Her hair had escaped its severe domed style to curl around her face and neck. Her indigo linen gown was water-spotted, and she was flicking drops of water into her gleefully squealing boy's face.

"Pembery," she said to the maid, "would you get some more drying cloths? I fear both Elsren and I will need them."

The maid curtsied. "At once, Your Grace," she murmured. She wrapped Petranne in a cocoon of cloths and trotted from the room.

"Your Grace, Hasui, one of the kitchen slaves, will take my place as wine pourer tonight," Aly murmured in Kyprish. Neither Elsren nor Petranne spoke it very well, though Dove, Sarai, and their parents did. "There are some things I must do in your service. And I will need to report to you and His Grace later, once the prince has retired."

Winnamine's eyes sharpened. "You will be careful?" she asked, keeping her voice low as she, too, spoke in Kyprish.

"You will take no risks that might endanger us?" Unconsciously she grasped Elsren's hand in hers.

"Your Grace, no one will even know what I did," Aly assured her.

"Mama, why are you talking that way?" demanded Petranne from her corner by the fire. "Only raka talk that way."

"But the raka are our people, too, dear," Winnamine told her daughter. "We honor them by learning their tongue. They were here long before our ancestors came."

"But Aly isn't raka," the girl pointed out. "She's luarin."

"She honors our raka friends, too," Winnamine said, absently soaping Elsren's back.

Aly bowed and left the watery room. She had no interest in explaining the language of conquest to a four-year-old, and knowing Petranne from the journey to Tanair, she was aware that the girl would stick to the subject until the end of time if not muzzled.

She retreated to a small closet off the servants' stair and changed into the dark, long-sleeved tunic and leggings she kept hidden there. She had stolen them from the Balitang storehouse back in Rajmuat and hidden them for special occasions. She then wrapped a length of dark cloth around her face and head until only her eyes showed. By the time she finished, the household was assembling for the evening meal. Aly hid in the closet where she kept her prowler's clothing until she heard no footsteps on the servants' stair for a good space of time. Pocketing the lock picks she also kept there, she emerged carefully and peered into the main hall around the door behind the Balitangs. Hasui, cleaned up and dressed to serve at the dais, poured Bronau a cup of wine as Aly watched. Supper had begun.

Quickly Aly counted the prince's household in the hall.

Everyone was present, eating with the duke's servants. Satisfied, Aly climbed the keep stairs, past the floors where the prince, then the Balitangs, slept. When she reached the fourth floor, where Bronau's household stayed, she got to work on the servants' trunks, using her picks with care.

By the time the first course was over downstairs, she had uncovered two royal spies among the prince's servants. She didn't flatter herself that it was her skill that made the discovery so easy. Anyone who searched their baggage would have seen it. Both men carried unusual supplies of paper, as well as the general code book issued for the Isles' lower-level spies. Aly had memorized its contents over a year ago, when it had become the new general code for the Isles. Swiftly but expertly she checked each nook and cranny on the floor where the servants might have hidden more surprises.

That chore done, she padded down to the second level and used her picks to enter the prince's rooms. She searched his two menservants' belongings first. They, too, carried more than their share of writing paper as well as one book. Their volume was *The Perfect Servant,* a popular book of advice for those who worked in a higher capacity in a house or fiefdom. These men did not report to the Crown, however. One of them had already started his next report to his master. Using the faint marks in the book on service, Aly swiftly deciphered the greeting on the document: "To my lord Rubinyan."

She raised an eyebrow. So the Crown used Bronau's general servants to spy on him, while his older brother bought the services of Bronau's body servants. What kind of bad feeling existed between these two? She couldn't imagine Alan or Thom hiring anyone to spy on her. Of course, neither of them was eyeing a feeble king's throne.

She left the servants' belongings exactly as she had found them and proceeded to Bronau's private writing case.

The magic on the lock blazed in her magical Sight. The case wouldn't open if she tried the various unlocking words that she knew. There was also no keyhole in the lock, which didn't surprise her. Bronau struck her as the kind of man who was careless with keys, even important ones. He wasn't the sort to fuss with complex things, either.

Aly peered more closely at the lock, shifting her Sight to read magic. The signs on it turned dark and appeared one at a time, over and over, until she identified what each meant. The case had been locked with an essence spell, the perfect thing for a man who didn't like the bother of keys or details. Fortunately for Aly, she had studied these matters under very fine teachers. An essence spell was quite easy to break once recognized.

Aly reached for Bronau's riding gloves, which he had thrown on his bed in his rush to dress for supper. His hurried servants had left them right where a bright girl would find a use for them. Aly took a glove and turned it inside out, then pressed a leather fingertip to the lock. A line appeared through the middle of the device. The lid opened. Carefully she turned the glove right side out and replaced it in the exact spot she had found it. Her father had drilled her in such habits over the years, during exercises where he would send her out of the room, shift the things in it, then summon her back to replace everything as it had been. When she was little it was her favorite game. Now it was habit to remember the exact placement of anything she moved.

Aly knelt on the floor and raised the box's lid. The first seven letters inside were addressed to businesses: a draper, a moneylender, a cobbler, a horse coper, a jeweler, an armorer, and a bowyer. In them Bronau wrote that he was aware of the sums that were owed to them. Aly leafed through the papers and found the bills he had mentioned. Reading how much he owed to these people, she raised both eyebrows. This man spent more on shoes than Maude did to supply Pirate's Swoop with food for a month.

Aly paused to listen for outside sounds. Hearing only the faint noise from the great hall, she returned to the letters. Bronau wrote the merchants that his debts would be paid, within the year, with interest, and he swore it by Mithros. He also wrote that they would be well rewarded for their patience.

Aly arranged the letters neatly and put them aside with their bills. Prince Bronau seemed very confident he would be able to pay his creditors in full, even the moneylender. And he'd taken the risk of dragging a god's name into it. The receipts all had "fourth notice" or "fifth notice" written on them, and the dates covered the last four years.

How *did* he intend to pay? Aly wondered. None of Bronau's people had said that he'd snagged himself a very wealthy heiress. From what Aly knew, the money would not come from his brother and sister-in-law. Now he was out of favor with the king, and yet he was strangely confident. These letters were dated two days ago. Sarai was no heiress, not the kind that Bronau needed. From the notes on their bills, the prince's creditors were about to haul him before Mithros's altar, where lawyer-priests would strip Bronau of all he owned.

Aly looked at the next sheet of paper in the box. It was covered with scratch-outs and rephrasings. It seemed to be a letter to an old friend, chatting of this and that. Aly read it over twice, eyed the scratched out words, and nearly groaned aloud. The letter was in the most simple-minded code in existence, the very first code she had memorized. It was based on *The Book of Mithros*. Nearly every household in the Eastern and Southern Lands had a copy, even if the residents took some other god as the center of their belief.

"Duke Zeburon," she translated, "though you are both on the Royal Council, I have reason to know you are no friend to my brother R. We might find common ground between us, with the end in mind of ousting R. from his position."

That was as far as Bronau had written. The rest of the box held empty paper and *The Book of Mithros,* but Aly checked it all, just to be sure. There were no other signs of code or magic. Carefully she replaced everything as she had found it. After a double check of the room to make sure it looked as it had when she broke in, she left by the servants' stair, changed into her normal homespun tunic and leggings, and walked into the kitchen.

The prince has given me plenty to think about, she thought, scrounging leftovers. *As soon as the house is quiet, I'll make sure the duke and duchess are thinking, too.*

Aly was dozing by the kitchen fire as the staff began to carry the dishes out for washing. Pembery woke her with the message that Their Graces had errands for her. Aly grumbled a reply and trudged up the servants' stair once again.

The duke and duchess awaited her in the sitting room of their new quarters. To Aly's surprise and discomfort, Sarai occupied the chair next to her father.

The older Balitangs correctly read the rigid set of Aly's body. "Sarai is of age," the duke said gravely. "She will have to learn these things to survive. We have already told her of the god's message to us."

Aly pressed her lips together. "The more who know, the more you risk" was a motto she'd memorized practically in her cradle. Still, Sarai was Aly's own age. That had to be old enough to be told there were mysteries afoot. Resigned, Aly swept the room with her Sight, wondering if Mequen and Winnamine had thought the thing all the way through. As she suspected, she caught a flicker of movement in the gap between the door to the main stair and the floor. Immediately she heightened her magical ability to see color and detail and identified the eavesdropper. She crossed the room silently and yanked the door open. Dove stumbled into the room and almost fell. Aly caught her by one thin arm.

The duchess started from her chair, then settled back into it, biting her lower lip. Mequen scowled at his daughter. "Dovasary, it is the most common of all behaviors to listen at doors," he told her. "As a lady, such coarseness is beneath you."

As she covered the crack under the door with a carpet and stuffed a cloth scrap from the duchess's sewing basket into the keyhole, Aly glanced at Dove to see the effect of the duke's words. Dove looked at Aly and rolled her eyes, then went to stand before her father. "You told me curiosity was healthy," she said. "Is that confined only to books and nature? Sarai would just have told me anyway. I'd have made her."

"As if you could!" her older sister snapped.

Aly ignored their debate as she filled in the cracks under the remaining doors and plugged their keyholes as well. Just to be on the safe side, in case one of the spies who had come with Bronau had the nerve to dangle on a rope outside the window, she closed and barred the shutters. When she finished, the discussion was over. Dove wore a tiny smile of satisfaction as she pulled up a chair next to Sarai.

"Are you ready?" Aly inquired. The duke nodded. Aly said, "I searched the belongings of the prince and his servants tonight," she informed her listeners.

Mequen frowned.

"Your Grace?" Aly inquired.

"I'm not sure I approve," he replied quietly. "He is a friend, a guest in my house. He is entitled to his privacy."

Aly caught the glance traded by Sarai and Dove, one that showed exasperation over their father's unbending good manners. The duchess showed only concentration as she seemed to focus on the neat stitches she set in her sewing.

Aly thought the duke's scruples were sweet, if unrealistic. Da had always told her that noble honor hindered those who had it as much as it helped them. "Your Grace is an honorable man, and I respect that. However, I am charged with the safety of you and your family. Honor of the type you describe is a luxury." Before he could order her never to do so again, she held up a hand. "Before you speak, Your Grace, you should know that the prince already enjoys no privacy whatsoever. His attendants include Crown spies. His body servants are both in his brother's pay."

"*Rubinyan?*" whispered the duke. He gripped the arms of his chair with white-knuckled hands. "Ridiculous! He would no more spy . . . Rubinyan is as much my friend as Bronau. He is a good man. They don't get on, but it is temperament, not politics."

"Unless you are connected to the royal family and the court," Winnamine pointed out, keeping her voice low. "Then politics and temperament are never separated."

"I cannot believe it," repeated the duke. "I will not believe it."

At least he knows the difference between "cannot" and "will not," thought Aly. "Would Your Grace like proof of what I say?" she asked. Da had warned her that sometimes people refused to believe even when evidence was waved under their noses, but she thought she should offer.

Mequen shot her a startled look. "Aly, no, of course

not. You are the god's messenger. You would not lie."

I would if I thought it was for your own good, Aly thought as Winnamine patted her husband's arm.

"This might be Imajane's influence," the duchess murmured. "She has seen so many conspiracies in her own family that she would suspect them of anyone. Wouldn't you, growing up as His Majesty's daughter?"

"True, true," whispered the duke, but Aly could see his eyes. Mequen was too intelligent not to see that it was sensible for someone near the throne, like Rubinyan, to watch a powerful, charming fellow courtier, even if that courtier was his own brother. The duke also had to be thinking that if Prince Rubinyan suspected his brother, he might suspect anyone, including Mequen himself. "Why am I surprised?" he asked, and sighed. "That is the way of things at court. Everyone spies on everyone else."

Aly could see that the duke understood her. No wonder Da prefers to work with clever people, she thought. They can work out the obvious without openly speaking of it. She said, "There's more, Your Grace. I took the liberty of going through the prince's writing case."

"Aly!" cried the duke, shocked. Winnamine hurriedly put a finger over her husband's lips, to remind him to keep his voice down. The duke tightened his mouth, then leaned forward and fixed Aly with his sharp brown eyes. "Nobles do *not* read one another's mail."

"I would not know, Your Grace," replied Aly smoothly. "I *was* a servant. *Now* I am a slave. It's a matter of survival for us to know what our masters know."

"I don't believe I noticed before, but you have perfect grammar," remarked Dove. "Isn't that odd for a slave who was once a maid?"

"The god chose me for my skills at mimicry, my lady," Aly replied. That was not a lie at all, she virtuously told herself.

"I take it you found something in Prince Bronau's case, or you would not have raised the subject," Winnamine said.

Aly nodded. "His Highness is greatly in debt," she told them.

The duke batted this aside with an impatient hand. "He is always in debt. Really, Aly, if you waste your time with small follies . . ."

She named the sum she had added from the receipts, stopping the duke in midsentence. The duchess went pale. Sarai gasped.

At last the duchess said, "He'll spend the rest of his life repaying that."

"He says not, Your Grace." Aly then told them of the letters he had written but not yet sent—letters to his creditors that promised repayment within a year. She then repeated the contents of the partial letter to Duke Zeburon, offering an alliance against Rubinyan.

"Papa, whatever it is, I'm sure he can explain," Sarai said hurriedly, anxiety in her eyes. "Perhaps he believes Rubinyan doesn't trust him. Perhaps he just wants to make sure he has friends, in case Imajane ever turns the king against him. It's just more of that jockeying for power you always say goes on at court."

"And the money?" asked the duchess, inspecting her sewing.

"He must have an heiress he's courting," whispered Sarai, looking down at her lap. "Perhaps Lady Tyananne. She's come out of mourning. And the Ianjai family wants to marry into the nobility. No one will mind a merchant wife, not if she's married to someone as popular as Bronau is." A tear rolled down her cheek and spotted her gold velvet lap.

Aly, pretending not to notice that Sarai wept, asked the duchess if she had messages for her to carry. Her task was done. She had reported what she had learned, and unless they asked her opinion, they had to decide for themselves what to do with that information. She had no opinions of her own, so she wouldn't try to influence their thinking. Bronau was still a threat. She did make a mental note of the fact that if she wanted to influence Mequen at some point, she could appeal to his honor, just as she could appeal to Sarai's love of adventure and excitement.

Winnamine dismissed her. As Aly pulled the carpet back into place and removed the cloth from the main door's keyhole, she glanced back at the silent Dove. The girl was sketching the carved whorls in the arm of her chair with a finger, her brow wrinkled, deep in thought. Aly saw no distress on that small face, only calculation.

It's those who are overlooked by the folk around them you want to watch. They see more than they tell, and they think more than they talk. You want them for your friend. You don't want them asking questions about you.

—*From a letter to Aly from her father when she was nine*

9

LEARNING THE GROUND

In the morning Aly visited the shrine between the stable and the wall. There, under the promised flagstone, she discovered six knives, all of a finer make than her stolen one. *Chenaol knows how to pick a blade,* she thought admiringly as she tested them on the fraying hem of her undyed goatherd's tunic. One, as long as her middle finger in the blade and wickedly sharp, had a sheath that hung by a cord. When she put it over her head, the knife and sheath slipped between her breasts under the band she wore. All that showed above her tunic collar was the kind of cord from which might hang a religious pendant of some kind. Two perfectly flat knives fit in sheaths under her leggings so well that they barely left a mark on the cloth over them; two more flat knives and their sheaths went under the sleeves of her tunic. The most substantial she could wear in her waistband at her back or carry it with her lunch and water bottle. She put it into that bag and moved one of her leg knives up under her waistband at the middle of her back, where she could reach it in a hurry.

The raka conspirators had revealed more with this gift of weaponry than perhaps they intended her to know. They were desperate for help. They knew they were unused to the world of armies, spies, and nobles. The god's gift of Aly must have seemed like the answer to their prayers.

"It's not fair, you getting their hopes up, when you know I'll be gone in the fall," she muttered to Kyprioth as she collected her goats. The god chose not to reply. Aly shook her head. Perhaps before she left she could teach the raka the potential dangers of any move they might try against the king. She led her animals out of the castle walls.

Aly and her flock were halfway through the village when the little shepherd girl, Visda, joined her, along with her sheep and the boy who had summoned Aly to Tanair the day before. "Aunt Chenaol says we're to graze with you," the girl confided, waving to the baker as they passed. "And if you're called off sudden, me and Ekit"—she jerked a thumb at the boy, who stuck his tongue out at her—"we'll take both flocks. Well, me and Ekit and Grace and Arak," she added, naming the shaggy herd dogs. "Aunt Chenaol says you're doing important work for the One Who Is Promised, and we should help you—"

Aly halted and stopped the girl. Bending down, she drew Ekit over so that he could hear as well as she whispered, "Never repeat that, either of you, all right? Not to anyone. Even if you hear others talking about me. Not even if your friends say it. For that matter, if 'the One Who Is Promised' means who I think it does, you must *never* speak of her that way again. *Never* let on that you know more than what you need to know to herd animals, understand?"

Visda scowled. "I *know* that," she said crossly. "Great-aunt Chenaol made us promise. But you already know."

Aly sighed. "Look—the fewer times you say anything

aloud, the better your chances that no one will hear you who shouldn't. Understand? Enemies can't report what they didn't overhear. Now, what shall we talk about?"

"Sheep, goats," Visda replied brightly.

"Dogs," added Ekit.

Aly grinned at them. "Better."

With a wave to the town men who stood morning watch on the gate, they passed out of the village and onto the dusty road. Visda began to skip, Ekit to run with one of the dogs. "I love summertime!" Visda told Aly. "All the bees, and the flowers, and the sun, and no one to stop us from running!" She raced ahead gleefully, trying to catch Ekit, her bare brown feet thumping against the road. The sheep, resigned, picked up their trot, along with the goats.

Aly shook her head, smiling, then ran to catch up with the children.

Their little group settled among boulders. The goats ate grasses tucked between stones, while the sheep grazed on more level ground just below. The dogs placed themselves where they would spot a stray the moment it wandered off from its fellows. Once the animals had settled, Visda and Ekit removed hand spindles from their packs and clumps of wool combed and rolled for spinning. As Aly climbed higher into the rocks to get a more commanding view of their surroundings, the boy and the girl began the painstaking work of spinning thread, just like the children who minded flocks throughout Tortall.

Aly had finished her breakfast when she heard the thump of bare feet on the rock just behind her. Resting a hand on her leg knife, she looked back. Nawat crouched on the rock, smiling at her. "Would you like a grub?" he asked, offering a plump one. "I got it just for you."

Aly struggled to think of a diplomatic reply. "We humans

don't eat grubs." Remembering stories she'd heard from some of her father's agents, she added, "Not when we don't have to."

"But these are juicy and filling," Nawat assured her. "I saved the best of them."

Aly gulped. Her breakfast bread and cheese rolled in her belly. "Let the grub live to make more grubs," she suggested.

Nawat sighed. "It is hard to mate-feed someone who will not eat."

Aly leaned back and looked at the sky. A winged horse soared overhead, flying, it seemed, for the sheer joy of it. "We're not to the mate-feeding stage," she informed Nawat lazily. "We barely know each other."

"What if I filled my mouth pouch and spilled it for you?" Nawat asked. "Would you take food that way?"

"I would *lose* food that way. I'd throw it up," Aly retorted, amused and nauseated at the same time. "Aren't you supposed to be making arrows?"

"I am supposed to be finding goose feathers," he said comfortably, apparently unhurt by her refusal of his offer. "But my friends are getting them for me so I may see you." He reached over and ran his fingers through Aly's hair. "None of the other human females are so easy to preen."

The movement of his hand was soothing. "Are you preening other females?" Aly asked, warm in the sun.

"Only little ones, for practice," Nawat explained. "The old ones chitter—giggle—and bounce if I try. It's annoying. You don't giggle and bounce. I like that."

"You keep trying to preen the ones who giggle and bounce, and you might find yourself preening one of them for the rest of your life," Aly teased. "Their fathers and uncles and brothers will see to that."

"Humans do strange things," Nawat told her with a

sigh. "I must go soon. My brethren call that they have my feathers."

Aly strained to hear, but Nawat's ears were better than hers. She heard only goats, sheep, and Visda's humming.

"The raka did as they told you they would," Nawat continued. "Yesterday their warriors began to leave the villages here. They took horses, food, shelters. Some moved into the forest at Pohon, others into the woods and cliffs outside the village of Inti. More rove the fields. Fifteen made their camp a mile on the other side of the road, in the rocks. They will keep watch for those who come through the mountains."

Most of these were words and concepts Aly had taught the crows in their dream lessons. One was not. "How can you tell they are raka?" she asked. Perhaps he had gotten the idea that *raka* meant "human." "Am I raka?"

Nawat shook his head. "Crows know the raka," he said. "They are our people. Time long past, when the first nest had given birth to the first flocks, Sky, our goddess, laid green eggs in her nest. The Dawn Crow, her mate and our god, was very confused. They hatched to become our brothers and sisters, the raka. In time they stopped hearing the voices of Sky and the Dawn Crow, and turned to Kyprioth to serve, but they never forgot their brothers and sisters the crows."

Aly shook her head. "I had no idea. I'm glad to know the patrols are out, though."

Nawat smiled. "I knew you would want to know they do as they say. They respect tricks you will do for them."

Aly sat up to protest that she did not do tricks, but Nawat was clambering down through the rocks to the road. Crows flew in from the east, circling him. He was nearly gone from Aly's view when they began to rain feathers down on his head.

Aly leaned back on her rock to think, without success.

All her mind would produce for her was the memory of Nawat's fingers as they passed softly through her inch-long hair, and a repeating thought: "This place gets stranger every day."

Some time later she heard the distant thud of hooves. She sat up. A party trotted by on the road below, trailed by guards. Prince Bronau rode with his hosts again, or rather, with Mequen, Sarai, Dove, and their guards. They were almost gone from sight when the prince and Sarai broke into a gallop, riding hard down the strip of empty earth.

Aly propped herself on her elbows. Apparently Sarai had recovered from her unhappiness over the possibility that the prince was looking for a rich wife. It was either that or the prince had flirted enough to make her forget. Aly shook her head. She hoped Sarai wasn't too infatuated with Bronau. Aly's instincts shrieked that the prince was trouble looking for a place to happen. She did not want it to happen on her watch.

Once they were gone, Aly slid to the ground. What was the good of having knives if she was too out of shape to use them? She needed to exercise, and to keep exercising. When she found a level patch of grass, she began her stretch routine, loosening all of her muscles, a group at a time. She followed those with routines for hand-to-hand combat: punches, kicks, pivots, leg sweeps, blocks, elbow and palm strikes, tucks and rolls. She was lost in it, feeling her muscles warm up and loosen, when a crow nearby gave the call that meant "friend."

Aly looked around, wary and waiting. A tall raka woman moved out of the shadow between two large boulders. Crossing her hands, Aly gripped her wrists, ready to release the straps that secured her knives. "Good morning," she said pleasantly in Kyprish, every nerve of her body quivering despite her relaxed appearance. "I don't believe we've been introduced."

The woman leaned on the six-foot-long staff she carried. "I am Junai Dodeka, daughter of Ulasim Dodeka. I am here at my father's request, to keep you alive."

Aly inspected the newcomer. Junai was four inches taller than Aly and lean, covered with wiry muscle. Her cheekbones were sharp enough to cut with, her nose the same shape as Ulasim's. She wore her straight black hair braided and pinned tightly down. She dressed in a faded olive-green tunic and loose brown breeches. Her feet were bare.

This woman was clearly a fighter. There were knife scars on her hands and arm muscles and on her right cheekbone. Dagger sheaths made lines against the cloth of her breeches and waistband. She also wore leather and metal wrist guards and a leather band around her neck, a rough guard against a knife to the throat.

"I don't know how much a stick is going to do as a weapon," Aly remarked casually.

Junai spun the staff until it was level, then twisted the hand grip at the center. Blades twelve inches long sprang from each end of the staff, turning it into a double-ended spear.

"Well," Aly said, raising her brows. "Of course, that is a very different matter." She looked at the older woman—she was in her middle twenties, Aly guessed—and decided to try a theory she had in mind. "I don't suppose *you* know of any mages we might recruit?"

Junai took a step back. "What makes you believe there is a mage here, luarin, or that I would know of such a one?"

Aly leaned against a tree and thrust her hands into her breeches pockets. "My gracious, whyever would I think such a thing?" she asked, batting her eyes as she clasped her hands under her chin. "Well, let's see. We're attacked by bandits just on the other side of the mountains—we brought some with us, did you know? They're sweet, in a starveling way. Yet here we are, on this lovely flat plateau, with thriving farms, and raka who aren't nearly so ragged and thin as most of the ones who watched us come here. Tanair is just a fat goose ready for the plucking, yet no one speaks of bandits. Ever. No one mentions raids in the past, or patrols—your father had to be nudged into setting patrols out in the open lands, to look for royal soldiers or assassins. Back home, bandits huddle in isolated places, waiting to make their fortunes by taking them from others. Oh, wait, I forgot. There are no bandits at home where a strong mage is to be found. Did I miss anything?"

Junai stopped leaning on her spear and began to spin it, hand over hand, casually. "Father was right. You are clever. So take my advice. Don't ask about our mage. She hates luarin. She'll burn your face off if you come near her. Doubtless I would perish in your defense. There are ways to live without mages. You have the god's favor, I am told. It will serve you better than she will."

Aly rubbed her nose and looked Junai over. "So if this mage sees to the bandits, how am I to have faith in *your* ability to protect *me*? I'd think your only fighting practice would be from mock battles with people you've known all your life."

Junai bared teeth in a menacing grin. "I was a caravan guard for seven years," she informed Aly. "You want to try me?"

"No," Aly said, waving an arm in dismissal. "I'll take your word for it." She let the conversation end. Junai had told her more than she had planned to. Certainly she had not meant to agree that a mage lived on the Tanair lands, but that much she had done openly. She had also told Aly that her orders to guard Aly's life were more important than her fear of the mage. The mage was raka, probably a full-blood, if she hated luarin with such unmixed passion. And since Pohon village was notorious for its hate of luarin, chances were the mage lived there. Aly had scouting to do, then, before she approached this mage herself.

Aly went back to her exercises. The sun was almost directly overhead when the riding party returned to the castle. Aly heard the beat of their horses' hooves as she searched for a stray kid among the rocks. When she found the youngster and returned him to his mother, she discovered that one of the riders and her bodyguard had come to join her. A horse idly cropped grass where Aly had set her knife-throwing targets. A guard lingered near Visda and Ekit, talking with the children. There was no sign of Junai, but Aly guessed that the woman was around somewhere, watching.

She rounded the horse and stopped, looking at Dove. She had spread a blanket to sit on and was placing food on it. Aly had thought that if any of the Balitang girls wanted to investigate Aly after learning she represented a god, it would be Sarai, the oldest, who had one foot already in the adult world. Yet here was her younger sister, meek in a pale green riding costume with no embroideries or ornaments at hems and collar. She sat cross-legged in loose, comfortable breeches, a napkin on her lap as she gazed at the meal she had laid out. She wore her black hair in multiple long braids under a sheer head veil, the style favored by maidens in the Isles.

"I thought you might tire of bread and cheese," Dove remarked, looking up at Aly. "And *I'm* tired of Bronau mooning over my sister when he thinks the duchess isn't looking. I know Sarai's just keeping her hand in at flirting, but it makes me queasy to watch."

Aly sat on the grass beside the blanket. "Your ladyship

honors me," she said, wondering what the girl was up to.

Dove didn't look at her. "What honor? I doubt my father lied to us and you aren't really the god's messenger. If you *are* the god's messenger, don't you have a particular standing which has nothing to do with the collar on your neck? Oh, curse it, Chenaol forgot the butter." She tossed a roll to Aly. This was not the rough brown bread that Aly normally brought to her duties with the goats, but a white bread studded with dates, raisins, and bits of fig.

"Even if your father didn't lie, and he doesn't strike me as the kind of man who does, it would still look very odd if you socialized with me," Aly explained.

"I'm not socializing." Dove picked up the open book at her side. "I'm the shy little sister, seeking time to read alone with enough people close by that my bodyguard won't fret." She looked at Aly. "It was my idea."

Aly studied her companion and helped herself to a handful of olives from a small crock. She'd heard people talk of Dove. The household had decided she was the intellectual one, without the warmth, charm, or dash of her older sister. Certainly Dove liked to read, but Aly had also noticed that the girl was both curious and observant.

"There's little I can tell you," Aly said, spitting an olive pit onto the grass. "I don't know myself why the god called on me." Except that I'm to keep you alive through the summer, she added to herself.

"And if you did, you wouldn't tell us," said Dove, eyeing dried slices of mango. "Being the close-mouthed sort. Is there anything you need? Information about the family, Tanair . . . ?"

Aly shrugged. Just because Dove wanted to test her didn't mean that she couldn't test Dove back. "I could use the best maps you can find of this area," she said. "I know nothing about the layout of the ground here, and that could be very troublesome. I'd like to see the other two villages and the road down to the western sea, but for now I can manage with maps. Copies will do, if you have only one original, but they should be good copies, no mistakes."

Dove shook her head. "Papa gave Sarai and me the maps for all our mother's lands, since they are our inheritance. And the bailiff has extras. I'll get a set for you. You'd tell Papa and the duchess if we're in danger from Bronau, wouldn't you?"

Aly picked up a sausage baked in dough, country food from the Eastern Lands. She looked it over, wondering if Chenaol had spiced it in the Isles way and if she would regret taking a bite. "Do you have a reason to distrust His Highness?" she asked. She took a careful bite of sausage. It tasted just like those at home.

Dove nibbled her mango. "I don't trust anyone who feels you should like them because they love themselves so much," she said tartly. Aly snorted, spraying crumbs on the grass. "Don't laugh," Dove told her. "It's true."

"I wasn't laughing at you," Aly said when she had swallowed the rest of her mouthful and taken a drink of water. "I was laughing because you put it perfectly."

"He thinks if he smiles at you and gives you presents you won't notice he can't keep his mouth closed," grumbled Dove, appeased. "If we were in Rajmuat and the king's spies heard the way he talks, we'd all be under arrest. Does he believe there aren't any spies out here?"

"We'll just make sure they don't have the chance to report anything," Aly assured the girl. "That's the nice thing about being all tucked away like this. We can control what information comes into these lands and what information leaves them." She passed a sausage roll to Dove. "Try one of these, and tell me which members of King Oron's family are still alive."

In the days that followed, Aly settled into her expanded role among the Balitangs and the raka conspirators. Junai became a silent, constant presence from the moment Aly left the main hall in the morning until she reentered it at night. Wherever Aly spent her days, Junai was at hand, looking on as Aly tended goats, talked to Visda and occasionally Dove, and practiced her hand-to-hand combat.

The raka patrols were now visible. Aly would look up from studying the maps Dove had brought, to note distant groups of riders, mounted on nimble ponies. They skirted the farms and wound through the estate's rocky eastern border. Sometimes younger riders came with them, to practice fighting and tracking away from the gaze of the duke's and prince's men-at-arms.

Aly traded on and off with Hasui as wine pourer on the dais. Every second night she searched the rooms occupied by Bronau and his attendants for new letters. Bronau's spies wrote nothing, having no way to get correspondence out of Tanair, but the prince himself wrote every day, preparing letters that offered alliances to nobles who were not friends of his brother. Aly memorized each noble's name, knowing that Bronau would send these calls for aid as soon as the opportunity came. She wanted to know whom Bronau felt was safe to approach.

When Aly took pouring duty, Bronau always made sure to say hello to her. He also flirted constantly with Sarai in the dining hall. Fesgao and the servants said that he did so at all other times as well. Everyone saw how Sarai responded to Bronau's compliments and teasing, obviously flattered by the man's charm and attention. At night, as Aly recited what news she found worth the family's time, Sarai listened without comment. She could not keep the trouble from her face as Aly quoted Bronau's latest piece of correspondence, any more than her parents could. Only Dove showed real curiosity and appreciation of what Aly had learned.

Bronau did not neglect Mequen and Winnamine, so his dealings with Sarai caused few ripples apart from idle speculation. Aly heard the servants' and slaves' observations when she and the chief raka conspirators—Ulasim, Chenaol, Lokeij, and Fesgao—met over a late supper in the kitchen. They talked softly over drinks and snacks while most of the household listened to music in the great hall. Ulasim summed up the patrols' reports for his three comrades and Aly. Chenaol had the day's gossip and discoveries from the servants and the villagers, where her own family played a vital part in everyday business. Lokeij and his stable boys shared news from visitors to the stables, as well as Tanair's herdspeople, while Fesgao passed on the gleanings from the prince's and the Balitangs' men-at-arms. Sometimes Nawat joined them if the crows had seen anything of interest. Aly was surprised at first that the raka accepted Nawat so readily, until she overheard Chenaol tell Fesgao that their prophecy had mentioned the help of Kyprioth's crows. Between the reports from the people and the crows, Aly had as perfect a spy network as her da could have put together.

So far there was little of interest to discuss: crop news, deer and elk sightings, human movement such as the route followed by the daily riding party, and bedroom intrigues between the locals and the royal guests. Aly was confident that she would know about danger before it got very far. With so much information coming in, she felt more like Aly of Pirate's Swoop every day.

One night Aly finished her day's report to the Balitangs. She turned to go when the duchess stopped her. "Aly, can someone else take your goats tomorrow?"

Aly nodded.

"The prince wants to see our villages," explained Sarai. "Inti and Pohon. We thought you might want to come as well."

"You did want to see more of the plateau," Dove said. Normally she kept silent during these reports. Now she gave Aly a tiny smile and returned to setting out the chessboard for her nightly game with Mequen.

"I'm having the maid pack some of Rihani's potions to bring to the villages," the duchess added. "That will explain your presence. We'll have soldiers, but you can say I didn't wish to entrust the bottles and jars to a ham-handed warrior."

Aly smiled. "Thank you, Your Grace," she told the duchess. "I await your orders in the morning." Finally, she thought. A chance to ferret out the mage at Pohon!

She rose at her usual time so that she could take the goats down to Visda, then returned to the castle. Waiting in her cleanest tunic and breeches, a small cloth bag with a few necessary items slung over her shoulder, she watched the men-at-arms at their morning combat drill. There was a quiet, grim competition between the Balitangs' and Bronau's men. Neither side was at its friendliest. Blows that should have been taps hit with authority and pain. Looking around the courtyard, Aly noticed Junai in the shadows, her eyes intent on the sparring men. No doubt her guard was considering new fighting techniques.

One person Aly hadn't seen yet that day was Nawat. Perhaps he worked outside only at dawn, when things were quiet, and went back into Falthin's bowyer shop when the courtyard got busy. Aly tried to pretend she wasn't disappointed, but her illusion fell to pieces when she saw Nawat walking toward her, leading two saddled and bridled horses. He was smiling at her in a way that made her throat tighten just a little. She coughed to clear it.

"I am to ride with you," Nawat explained when he reached her. "Workers in the villages gather wood for bows and arrow shafts, and I must collect it. We will ride together and our crows will visit us."

"They'll probably frighten the horses," Aly said, accepting the reins Nawat offered. "Falthin certainly gives you plenty of time away from work."

"He says I am young only once," Nawat informed her. "He says that when I choose a mate he will help me with the bride price. Do you have a bride price? What is a bride price?"

He might as well have touched her with a branding iron. Aly jumped. Had she been someone else's daughter she might even have shrieked. As it happened, she was saved from having to answer by the arrival of the prince, the duchess, the older girls, and their guards. Lokeij himself brought out Sarai's mount, and winked at Aly and Nawat.

I suppose *he* thinks I'm interested in bride prices, too! Aly thought, indignant. She would have to explain things to Nawat, so he would know how very uninterested in such things she was. For now she had a performance to give. As far as anyone here knew, Aly had not spent much time in the saddle. To that end she dragged herself onto her shaggy chestnut mare, every inch of her the ignorant servant rider. The horse bridled, pranced, even reared twice. Aly stayed on while she pretended to be on the verge of falling off, flopping here and there as the mare worked off her early-morning fidgets. It seemed that the horse figured out that she was experienced. Once the chestnut calmed down, Aly took the basket of potions from the duchess.

As they set off, Aly and Nawat rode between the nobles and the men-at-arms. Snatches of conversation came back to Aly: talk of weather and crops, hunting and books. More than once she heard the prince tell Sarai, "When you return to the capital," as if they were on Lombyn for a holiday. Today for a change Aly watched from close quarters as the prince and Sarai had their daily gallop, their bodyguards following. The duchess, confident the pair would never be out of sight of their guards, remained with Dove and the main group of riders.

As a riding companion, Nawat was perfect. He sat his mount as if born in the saddle. Aly supposed it was because in many ways he was as much an animal as his horse. Staying close to Aly, Nawat pointed out the land's features as they rode across it. Aly memorized them all, placing them on her mental copy of the Tanair map: roads and trails, creeks, springs, farms, stands of trees and of rocks where enemies might hide, herds of animals, clumps of wild berries and fruit trees. She also saw that the raka who labored in the fields stood at attention as Sarai galloped by and bowed to the duchess. They watched Dove from the corners of their eyes. Aly hoped their restraint was due to the Tanair conspirators' warning them not to show any favor to Sarai before outsiders.

It was almost noon when they reached the village of Inti, astride the road that cut down through cliffs and waterfalls to reach the western coast of Lombyn. Inti itself was set on a mound of raised earth. To Aly it was the second most dangerous point on the Tanair lands, a less obvious route into Balitang territory. Ulasim had assured her that his people were aware of the problem. The road was watched. Inti's villagers kept messenger doves to carry word of an enemy's approach to the castle. There was also a large flock of crows in the trees around Inti and the road west. They bawled wary greetings to Aly and Nawat, then reported normal activity.

At Inti even Bronau could not ignore the rakas' behavior. The villagers stopped whatever they did to look on in silence as the headman and elders came to greet their company.

I suppose I should be grateful they don't have signs up proclaiming, Welcome to the One Who Is Promised, Aly told herself. She made a mental note to ask Ulasim and Chenaol how many noble luarin knew of the prophecy.

The raka remained silent as the duchess gave half of the contents of Aly's basket to the village midwife, then followed the village headman to his home. There the headman and the elders offered the nobles herbal tea, coconut custard, sticky rice, rice flour cakes, cassava melon slices, and banana fritters on woven grass platters. They ate seated on the headman's broad porch as the townspeople looked on.

Aly knelt just behind the duchess and Sarai, within earshot as Bronau sipped his tea and quickly set the cup down. "Murky stuff," he whispered to Sarai in Common, his eyes dancing merrily. "Do you suppose they scooped it from a swamp? Perhaps we'd best check for slugs and salamanders. They eat anything that doesn't eat them first, these wild folk."

Aly doubted that he even realized he was insulting their hosts; he was simply bent on flirting with Sarai. To her credit, she kept her eyes down as a blush mantled her golden brown cheeks. Let Bronau think the blush was maidenly confusion. Aly, seeing the girl's trembling hands, knew it for rage. She glanced at the raka elders. From the flashing eyes of three of them, she knew they understood Common as well as their own language.

I need hand signals, she thought, putting it on her mental list of things to do. In case I have to tell the family things without speaking aloud. Right now she wished she could ask Sarai to steer the prince away from his present line of chatter. She was wondering if she would have to spill tea on the man when Dove said, "Your Highness, perhaps these elders would like to hear news from Rajmuat?"

With everyone's attention now on him, Bronau was happy to perform the role of the great man for the townspeople. He patronized them, explaining the most obvious things, but at least he was no longer making fun of their hospitality. I love that girl, Aly thought, passing the banana fritters to Dove. The younger girl met her eyes. Her mouth twitched slightly in a tucked-away smile.

The visit ended with an exchange of politenesses between the duchess and the village elders. The Inti raka stood in silence as the nobles mounted up and rode on their way.

"That was odd, don't you think?" Bronau asked Winnamine as they left Inti behind. "Did you see how they stared? Surely they've seen luarin nobility before. And they weren't chattering as they always do, in that dreadful language of theirs."

"We are still a novelty here," Winnamine replied, her face and eyes serene, with no hint of any emotion but pleasant interest. "Remember, these are highlanders. They hardly ever see *anyone* new, let alone of the luarin. Really, my dear, the tea and the food were perfectly safe. We all took our share. You insulted them by not taking any."

"I would have insulted my belly even more," Bronau said with a grin. "Just because I keep pigs doesn't mean I eat their slop."

A chill rolled off the raka among their men-at-arms. Bronau had not even tried to keep his voice down.

"For our sake, Bronau, will you be gracious to them?" Winnamine asked playfully, resting a light hand on the man's sleeve. "We have to live with these people for the time being."

Bronau took her hand and kissed her fingertips. "For you I will risk it, Winna. But don't be so resigned. Once I return to the capital, I will use all my influence to bring you back to civilization." He turned to Sarai. "After all, the young men don't know what they're missing while you are here."

As they rode on, Nawat drew closer to Aly. "Raka aren't pigs," he murmured. She wondered if Falthin had told him to speak quietly, or if Nawat sensed that it was a bad idea to be overheard. "Why does he speak of them that way?" the crow-man wanted to know. "They are humans, just like he is."

"I don't think he sees them as just like him," Aly explained.

"He is foolish, then," said Nawat. "There are more raka than Bronaus."

They rode on to Pohon, on the north side of the plateau. Once again the farmers stood up from their work to watch them pass. Aly, sharpening her Sight, noted that the closer they rode to the village, the more farmers had weapons close at hand in the fields. She also noticed that the men-at-arms had closed ranks and moved up to ride two deep on either side of the column, enclosing it on three sides. They entered forested land beyond the fields, until they came to Pohon. These villagers were different from those of Inti, except for the mute attention they gave Dove and Sarai. They accepted the duchess's medicines without thanks. Their eyes were hostile when they looked at the men-at-arms, sullen as they regarded the prince, the duchess, Aly, and the luarin maid. Aly wondered if they remembered that their precious Lady was half luarin.

In the confusion of greeting the elders, Aly asked Winnamine to excuse her, implying that something she had eaten
had not set well in her belly. When the duchess looked at her
with the tiniest of frowns, Aly raised an eyebrow. Winnamine's eyes crinkled with mirth, then she gravely nodded
her permission.

Carrying her cloth bag and the empty medicine basket,
Aly slipped into the shadows along the sides of a village
house and put on the disguise she had packed into it: a beige
head scarf such as farm women wore, tied at the nape of her
neck, and a jar of brown skin tint, made of sap, that she could
wipe off quickly. She smeared it on her face, arms, hands, and
the tops of her feet where the leggings did not cover the bare
skin. At the last moment she remembered the back of her
neck, a mistake her father told her was often the death of
spies. She hoisted the empty potion basket onto one shoulder as the raka women did, and sauntered through the area
between the houses. Nearly everyone was gathered before the
headman's porch, where the nobility sat. Aly walked away
from them.

Somewhere around Pohon there was a mage. Aly hoped
it would be here, within the palisade walls. She kept her head
down as she ambled along the beaten paths that were streets
and walkways, keeping an eye open for any house that was
decorated with the colors of a raka mage: red and purple
braids, and green threads strung like spiderwebs in small
wooden circles. People might visit a mage in her house for
the treatment of their illnesses, or the mage could be elsewhere, helping a woman in labor while the midwife sat with
the dignitaries at the headman's residence. If the mage was
away, Aly's Sight would show her where the mage could be
found.

She did see magic. Its white fire gleamed everywhere, in

signs written on doors, windows, ladders, and wells, on the sides of jars and baskets, scratched in garden dirt. She didn't know what they were for; the raka used very different signs from the eastern mages. From experience Aly could guess at their meanings and file in her memory the signs that obviously were for house blessing, disease, or fire prevention.

When she reached the rear wall without Seeing even a hint of a mage, Aly chewed her lip. She had prowled all over Pohon without luck. She had to return to the duchess's party. Certainly she didn't want to get left behind. Her disguise wouldn't stand up to close inspection. The raka's hate for the luarin was a nearly solid thing. It discouraged plans to stay the night.

She turned. Three raka men and two raka women blocked her path.

"So what is it?" asked one woman, a dark, feline creature who radiated contempt. "You thought raka are so stupid they wouldn't notice a stranger prowling our village?"

"What are you nosing about for?" demanded one of the men. "Plots, weapons, treachery?"

"Or just something to steal?" asked the biggest man. "As if you luarin left us anything of worth."

Aly crossed her arms to hide her movements as she freed her wrist knives. "Actually, I'd meant to talk to you about that," she said cheerfully. "I thought I'd make a list, tell you what I need . . ." She lunged right, clearing that side of her attackers' line. They charged her and halted, clear of the two blades she now held like the expert she was, one pointed out, one pointed back. She waited, her feet well placed, her balance perfect. It was important that she be careful. Killing one of these people would create more ill will for her and the Balitangs.

The big man came at her, tossing a long knife from one

hand to the other like a market-day tough. Aly darted in, knocked the knife flying while it was between his hamlike hands, and jammed the edge of one of her blades up under his chin. His eyes flicked left. Aly snapped out a side kick that forced the man sneaking up on her to stumble away, protecting his bruised arm. On both feet again, she hooked the big man's legs and yanked his feet from under him, dumping him onto his back. She jumped and landed on his belly with both knees, knocking the wind from his lungs.

A woman threw herself on top of Aly, who rolled away. The woman hit the big man instead, slamming the breath from her own lungs. Aly jumped to her feet and waited, her eyes on one of the men and the other woman. They closed in on her, blades out.

A knife cut the air between the two advancing raka to strike the earth just ahead of them, quivering, planted in the dirt. As the man looked back to find the thrower, Junai advanced, slowly turning her weapon hand over hand. When she passed the two on the ground, she smacked the woman on a kidney with her staff, drawing a yelp of pain. Junai kicked the man in the ankle, her boot slamming a sensitive bunch of muscle. The man swore. The woman facing Aly backed away from Junai, hands raised. The third man, trying to get around her, went down face-first, Nawat on his back.

"Don't kill him," Aly told Nawat quickly, not sure what the crow-man would do. "Let him breathe." She looked at Junai. "Are you going to scold me now? I was handling things myself."

"How did you do it, back there?" Junai inquired, brows raised. "No magic, no smoke or mist, you were just gone. And I wasn't born yesterday."

The woman who held up her hands looked at Junai, then Aly. "She's *that* one? But she's luarin!"

"Don't talk to me, talk to the god," Junai replied casually. "That is, if you think you'll like the way he answers. All of you, memorize her face. Don't let this happen again." She looked at Aly and sighed. "They're getting ready to leave."

Aly tore off the head cloth and began to rub the sap off her bare skin.

"How did you leave?" Nawat wanted to know. "Even *I* lost you until I heard the village dogs bark about a fight."

Aly shrugged, finding clean spots on the cloth to take off each patch of color. "That's what I do," she told him. "That's why I'm here." She resheathed her knives, then picked up the basket she had dropped.

"Do you speak only dog, or the language of all animals?"

"All animals," Nawat replied. "Is that good?"

"It could be," Aly replied. Passing the two on the ground—the woman who lay, both hands pressed to her kidney, the man clutching his ankle—she stopped and smiled. "It was ever so lovely to meet you," she said politely. "Let's do it again. Don't let me see that cheap brawler's trick a second time," she added, nudging the man with her foot. "Any decent fighter will take you when you don't have hold of your weapon."

She tucked her disguise into her cloth bag, stowed it in her basket, which had been tossed aside in the fight, and walked back to the horses. By the time she and Nawat reached them, and Junai faded to wherever Junai kept herself, the nobles had said farewell to the Pohon elders. Only when they had ridden out of the village did Aly relax and review how she had done. Not so well, she decided. She was rusty. She had used too many flashy moves of her own. She needed to practice more.

As they turned toward home, Nawat fell back. He was on foot now, the wood and arrow shafts he had collected in the villages bundled and strapped to his horse's back.

Dove joined Aly. "Did you see how they were, in the villages?" Dove asked, keeping her voice low. "The prince wasn't even *trying* to be discreet at Inti. No wonder the raka hate us."

"Us?" Aly repeated.

Dove looked sideways at Aly. "The luarin. We stole their country, killed most of their nobles, put thousands in near slavery, and made the rest complete slaves. I'd hate us, in their place."

"But you're not the same," Aly pointed out. "You and Sarai are half raka."

"Some villagers in Pohon saw the luarin half before the raka half," retorted Dove. "I noticed, even if you didn't."

"Oh, I got a good idea of it," Aly murmured.

Sarai let out a cascade of laughter. The prince smiled. Clearly he'd said something to amuse her.

"She's half in love with him," Dove said, her eyes on the man who rode between her sister and stepmother. "They'd do more than talk if the duchess left them alone."

"Only half in love?" To Aly it seemed as if Sarai was head over heels.

"She can't forget his money problems," Dove commented. "I'm not helping. Whenever she starts to gush I mention his debts. And she's no fool. She knows she has no fortune, just some land. So why does he court her? She's forgotten all about the boy from Matebo House who made up to her in Rajmuat. It used to be I couldn't get her to shut up about him. But Bronau pours on the honey, and Sarai goes all gooey-eyed."

Aly saw it then, as clearly as if she'd read Bronau's plans in one of his hidden letters. "Dove, Prince Hazarin is next in line for the throne, isn't he? Then who's after him—Princess Imajane?"

Dove shook her head. "Female. She can't inherit under luarin law. Hazarin doesn't have children—and the way he lives, nobody expects it. His only heir is Prince Dunevon, and he's just three. He's the only child of Oron's third queen. She's dead. I suppose Oron would put Dunevon under the guardianship of Hazarin or Imajane and her husband. Or just Imajane and Rubinyan if Hazarin was king."

Aly smoothed the reins over her hand. That matched reports on the kingship of the Isles she had read at home. "And if something happened to Hazarin and Dunevon?"

"No, they're healthy enough," Dove said automatically. Then her golden cheeks paled. "Papa. Papa's next in line."

"Sarai would be a crown princess," Aly pointed out, her voice soft. "So would you, and Petranne. Elsren would be a prince." Aly hesitated, then continued, hoping she did not make a mistake with this girl. "Rubinyan married into the royal family," Aly reminded Dove. "Maybe Bronau wants to do the same."

Dove chewed her lower lip. "This is too deep for me. We need to tell the duchess. Though if she likes Bronau . . ."

So Dove, at least, now thought of her stepmother as an ally. Aly was relieved to hear it. "She likes him, but she knows he is not as careful as she would like," she told Dove. "Her Grace would listen."

"Why did he come?" Dove whispered, glaring at Bronau. "We're in trouble enough with the Crown. We don't need more of the king's attention."

"I don't believe the prince thought about that," Aly replied. "Only about what he wants."

Supper that night was over in the main hall. The

conspirators, Nawat, and Aly had just finished their night's meeting. Aly was about to leave to report to the Balitangs when Ulasim grabbed her arm.

"Just what did you think you were doing, in Pohon today?" he asked quietly. "You gave Junai the slip. You left your companions to walk through a notoriously hostile village alone, for what reason? To learn they have nothing? That under the luarin they are nothing, when once they gave birth to queens?"

Aly glanced at the hand on her arm, then looked at Ulasim and raised an eyebrow. He met her gaze, his grip still firm.

"Surely Junai told you I can take care of myself," Aly said very gently.

"Not against a group," Ulasim told Aly. "Why? The god cannot watch you always. No god can. And you are too wise to take foolish chances, Aly of the crooked eye."

"Don't call me that," Aly replied. "It hurts my feelings. And Pohon isn't so badly off, not with five arms caches that I could see on a casual walk. There is also that herd of very fine horses recently moved outside the wall. I am assuming that was so we couldn't notice how well mounted the Pohon raka are. I didn't get into any of the barns, but blaze balm has a distinctive smell."

Ulasim's eyes went wide. His hold on Aly tightened.

Aly sighed and grabbed his little finger, forcing it back against its normal curve. "Now, be nice. You might startle me into breaking your finger," she pointed out as beads of sweat formed on Ulasim's forehead. "Think how unfriendly that would be. It's not like you don't trust me, after all. I *am* the god's chosen."

Ulasim let her go. She released his finger. "I'm Tortallan, remember?" she asked. "As long as the Balitangs and I live out the summer, I don't care what the raka are up to. I'd move the blaze balm, though. Bronau's served in combat. If he smells it the Pohon folk will be in trouble with the Crown. *I* was looking for a mage."

Ulasim massaged the finger she had bent, eyeing her with respect. When she said "mage," his eyebrows shot up. "Junai said you'd been at her about that. We told you, there isn't one."

"And I took it as a nice, polite lie between allies," Aly said reasonably. "But our guest's presence makes me uneasy. The longer he stays, the more likely he'll draw attention this way, attention nobody wants. My task here is quite simple, Ulasim. *I'm to keep this family safe.* That doesn't mean dealing with a threat when it actually comes; it means preparing for them in advance. For that, I require a true mage, not a healer with a few extra spells, like Rihani. The raka have one. I need her."

Ulasim sighed, and rubbed his forehead. "She doesn't live in Pohon. And you must be patient. Junai is working on her."

Aly leaned against a nearby wall and stuffed her hands into her pockets. "*Junai* is working on her?"

"And others," mumbled Ulasim.

"Why is Junai important enough that this recluse will speak with her?" Aly pressed, knowing there was a secret here, and wanting it.

Ulasim smoothed his hand over his short, neat beard. "Because Ochobu is her grandmother. But I wouldn't count on her help, Aly. I really wouldn't. She said when she disowned me that it would take a miracle for her to even come downwind of me again."

Now Aly knew the secret. "Your *mother*?"

"Who cast me out," Ulasim explained. "My father was

dying, and she summoned me home. I didn't feel I could leave the young ladies. Mother never forgave me."

Aly straightened and dusted off her tunic. "Well, we'll just have to think of a miracle, then," she told Ulasim. "Or rather, I will. You think of what to say to her when you see her again."

Ulasim grabbed Aly's arm, gently this time. "Don't ask the god," he begged. "You don't know what he might do."

Aly smiled grimly. "Don't worry," she reassured the tall man. "I already know better than to call on gods casually. But there are miracles, and there are *miracles*. I just need to think of one."

Midsummer's Day, June 22, 462 H.E.
Trebond, in northern Tortall

It was another of those not-quite-dreams that Aly knew Kyprioth had sent. The Kyprioth dreams always felt like everyday life, except that she was a ghost and the dream ended before dawn in the Copper Isles.

This dream had a familiar background: the towers of her mother's former home, Trebond, rising on a bluff just to the west. The ghost Aly stood in a woodland clearing that was filled with creatures one expected to see in dreams. A handful of Stormwings, one of them a glass-crowned queen, perched in the trees. Beside them stood a basilisk, a seven-foot-tall lizard-like immortal with skin like beads of different shades of gray, lighter on its back, darkening to thunderhead gray on its belly. A gray pony stood beside the basilisk, thoughtfully cropping grass. On her back perched five tiny monkey-like creatures, pygmy marmosets, nibbling on raisins as they looked around. Wolves, squirrels, golden eagles, horses, ponies, and dogs lined the edges of the clearing, the squirrels and the dogs tucked behind the horses, where they kept an eye on the wolves.

Among the humans Aly recognized her foster uncle Coram, Baron of Trebond, and his wife, Aly's aunt Rispah. With them stood a tall older man with silver-blond hair and tanned skin. A peculiar creature Aly knew as Bonedancer— a kind of bat-bird skeleton—rode on his shoulder, peering this way and that, fascinated with its surroundings. As Aly watched, the skeleton took flight, soaring on bone wings with invisible feathers, to land on the pony with the marmosets. One of them politely handed the skeleton something to eat.

Present also were Onua Chamtong and Sergeant Ogun-sanwo of the Queen's Riders, the former Rider commander, Buri, and her new husband, Raoul of Goldenlake and Mal-orie's Peak. Aly saw her own mother, and Lord Wyldon of Cavall, one of the commanders of the northern armies. Lord Wyldon stood on the far side of the clearing from Alanna and eyed her much as the squirrels eyed the wolves. Aly's grandmother Eleni was at the center of the clearing, dressed as a priestess of the Great Goddess. Aly's grandfather Myles was there, too.

Near Eleni were Numair and Daine, dressed in their finest clothes. Between them they held a blanket like a ham-mock, each of them gripping two ends of it. The blanket writhed as if a score of creatures did battle for room inside it. Once a pair of hooves thrust through an opening. A moment later a snake's tail fell out of one end.

Aly's father rode into the clearing on a lathered horse and slid from the saddle. He rushed over to kiss Daine's cheek and clap Numair on the shoulder, then looked at his wife. Aly's mother eyed her husband strangely, her violet eyes cold. She jerked her chin up in some kind of challenge.

George frowned, then went to her. He leaned down and whispered something in her ear; Aly saw her mother's mouth shape the words "Not now." George straightened, puzzled. Aly, too, was puzzled. Why was her mother angry with Da?

"I'm sure they'll be here any moment," Daine told Eleni. "Ma said the Great Gods ag—" She and Numair buckled, the weight in the blanket hammock suddenly large and rounded. A moment later they could raise the hammock again. Daine smiled apologetically at Aly's grandmother, who eyed the surging blanket as if it were dangerous. "Baby river horse," Daine explained with a blush.

"I can't begin to imagine nursing her—him—it," Eleni said, fumbling.

"It's a challenge," replied Daine, determinedly cheerful as she and Numair struggled to keep the squawking contents of the blanket steady.

The air behind Eleni shimmered silver. Two people stepped through. One was a man, over six feet in height, clad only in a loincloth. His skin was green-streaked brown; from his curly brown hair sprouted a rack of antlers that would have made an elk proud. His companion was gowned all in green, with a mist-fine green veil over her hair and face.

These were Daine's parents, Aly realized in wonder. These guests were divine ones: the hunt god Weiryn, whose territory included the mountains of Galla and Scanra, where Daine had grown up, and his wife, Sarra, Daine's mother, known as the Green Lady. After she had joined Daine's father in the Divine Realms, Sarra had become a minor goddess of healing. She appeared to those who lived in and around the village where, in her mortal days, she had raised Daine and served as a midwife. Since the two were restricted to the Divine Realms after their involvement in the Immortals' War, Aly could only guess that they had gotten special permission to cross over on Midsummer's Day for the naming of their grandchild.

The gods nodded to Eleni, who curtsied deeply to them. The other humans in the clearing bowed or curtsied as well. Daine and Numair could do nothing but nod. Their child's latest shape change had sent quills shooting through the fabric of its blanket.

"Now, this will not do." The Green Lady raised her veil, revealing a pretty face crowned by blond hair. Aly could see how, as a mortal, Sarra had won the love of a god. Sweetness shone from her face and eyes and turned her voice into music. "Really, dear, you must be firm with children."

Daine's mouth curled down wryly. "It's hard to reason with a six-week-old, Ma."

"We did try," added Numair, his gaze sharp as he looked at his mother-in-law. "Every way that we could."

Sarra walked over and reached into the hammock blanket, pulling out a wolf puppy. It turned instantly into a young giraffe, then a gosling. Whatever shape it took, Sarra held it firmly. "Now see here, youngster," she informed her grandchild, "you ought to be ashamed, wearing your parents out all the time. And this kind of thing isn't good for you. You'll exhaust yourself before you're ten. Enough. Choose a shape and a sex and stick to it, right now." She listened for a moment, then shook her head. "Five years at least. Learn the limits of one body. Then, if you're good, you may try others. Now *choose.*"

A moment later she held a human baby girl in her hands. The child looked up at her with wide, solemn eyes. Sarra gave her to Daine. "She'll be good now," the goddess told her daughter. "And in the future, don't shape-shift while you're pregnant. It gives them the wrong idea."

The naming proceeded from there.

Sergeant Ogunsanwo, Onua, and Aly's mother and father served as godparents for the new child. Afterward the guests came with gifts and good wishes for the baby. Numair and Daine stood as if a boulder had been lifted from their shoulders, beaming like the happy parents they were. Aly couldn't imagine what it had been like for them, with a newborn that changed shape so often. Aly had cared for human and animal babies and had been exhausted by them even when they didn't shape-shift.

Throughout the ceremony and the party, Aly watched her parents. Alanna was stiff near her husband, though obviously happy for her friend Daine. When George touched her elbow and they wandered off under the trees, Aly followed them, worried. What had vexed her mother *this* time?

"Lass, what is it?" George asked once they were out of earshot of the others at the naming celebration. "You seem angry."

"Angry?" Alanna glared up at her husband. "How would you feel if you found out one of our children had disappeared and I was keeping it from you?"

George's shoulders slumped. "You heard."

"I should have heard it from *you*, George! Not the king! She's my only daughter, you knew she was missing—"

George rested his hands on her shoulders. "You were in combat. I want you to concentrate on staying alive. I thought for sure I'd have found her by now. I thought—"

"But you've asked?" Alanna's anger evaporated. She gripped her husband's tunic. "Sent out your whisperers, asked for a girl of her look?"

"I dare not." Aly's father's voice was soft. "I dare not, my darling. If our enemies knew she was out there—we cannot risk it. The king's been scrying for her, but it's as if she's clean vanished."

Alanna rested her forehead against George's chest. "I've been scrying, every night, every morning, any moment I can. But if she were dead, surely His Majesty or I would have seen it." She looked up. "Have you asked Alan? Twins often know if the other's in trouble. He—"

George laid a gentle finger over her lips. "I did. He only knows she's not hurt or frightened. Alanna, what of the Goddess? She's your patron."

Alanna shook her head. "I've prayed, without a whisper of a reply. Nothing. Perhaps she's busy elsewhere, I know I'm not her only supplicant—"

Aly flinched. A few tears rolled down her mother's cheeks. George gathered Alanna into his arms. Alanna dried her face on his tunic, then turned her head so that she could speak and he would hear. "I want to hunt for her myself." She cut off her husband as he drew breath to speak. "I know. I said I *want* to, I didn't say that I could. I'm noticeable. And there's still a war to fight. Maggur's like a rabid wolf, at his most dangerous when he's cornered. But then I think of our Aly—"

Aly's vivid dream faded. She woke. A castle dog sat beside her, surrounded by the shimmering glow that marked a god's presence.

You were about to try to get word to them, so they won't worry, the dog-Kyprioth said into her head. *Save your efforts. Any paper you send out of Tanair will vanish. Any courier will forget the message. Our wager is between you and me alone.*

"My mother is *worried,*" Aly whispered, not wanting to rouse the sleeping servants. "She shouldn't be thinking about me, only about the war. She could get killed if she's distracted."

The dog licked its chops. *We had a bet, Alianne of Pirate's Swoop. I won't risk interference from your parents or their patron gods.*

Assassins approach a problem differently from soldiers, you see. They can't lay siege, they can't offer an honorable fight. In their trade numbers are dangerous. An assassin's advantage lies in folk missing him when he's about. He hits hard and fast, then goes. Once you've tried to kill the first time, the target has the wind up. Failure the first time means it'll be that much harder to get close a second time.

—Told to Aly when she was eleven,
in a conversation with her father

10

ASSASSINS

Through the rest of June Aly's goat herding was often interrupted by visitors: Dove, occasionally Sarai after her morning ride, various raka. Junai never appeared, not even to eat
lunch with them, though Aly always knew where her bodyguard was. One day even the duchess came. She brought Petranne and Elsren for a picnic on the hillside, sharing their
lunch with Visda and Aly as well as her own children, and
talking about her own country upbringing.

The raka who stopped by always had questions about
Sarai and Dove. What were they like? Were they haughty?
Did they know the ways of the raka, or had their hearts been
taken by the luarin? Aly tried to build their sympathy and
liking for the girls. At the very least, if the family were attacked some night, the raka might be convinced to hide Sarai
and Dove.

Aly's supper routine was the one she had fallen into after
Bronau's arrival. One night she would pour the wine at the
head table. On the next she searched Bronau's correspondence and that of his servants. Both routines were followed

by meetings with the raka conspirators and Nawat to exchange information. Once all that was done, Aly collapsed happily onto her pallet, usually falling asleep in the middle of plans to ferret out the elusive mage.

On her nights at the head table, Aly noted that the prince got more and more restless, though he did his best to hide it from Sarai. The two of them still rode every day, with the duchess or the duke as chaperons. The rides got longer. It seemed the prince needed more and more exercise to keep from exploding. Even a game of chess with Mequen tried his patience.

A week after their trip to Pohon, Aly sat with Visda and Ekit over the last scraps of lunch. She was about to practice her combat skills some more when the calls of crows filled the air. Aly listened and translated their sounds: a peaceful caravan of some kind, probably merchants, was coming down the road from Dimari.

Turning the goats over to Visda, Aly went to get a look from the rocks above the road. She had almost reached the summit of one boulder, where she could watch without being seen, when someone clasped her ankle and yanked her down into a crack between stones. Aly twisted hard to free herself as she slid down, then jammed herself against her would-be captor's side and arm, pressing one of her daggers to his throat as she kept him from reaching one of his. The young raka who had grabbed her stared down at her with emotionless eyes. Aly looked him over. This was her first encounter with one of the raka who watched over the plateau.

She patted the man's cheek. "You would belong to the patrol, yes? Lovely to make your acquaintance. I feel so looked-after."

Cloth slithered on stone as Junai slid down to their location. "It's her," Junai explained to the raka, her voice very dry. "Don't let the silly mannerisms fool you." She looked at Aly. "Were you on your way somewhere?"

"Nice meeting you," Aly told the raka warrior, then climbed back up to the higher rock, Junai at her back. Just below the summit Aly flattened herself on the stone and belly-crawled the rest of the way, keeping her head low until she just crested the top.

It was a merchant caravan. Aly recognized most of the carts and people, who had come to Tanair twice this summer. There were faces she did not know: three full-blood male luarin, a part-raka man, and a beautiful luarin woman. The woman was a charmer, Aly thought, sent as a temptation for men. The four unfamiliar men were hard-looking fellows with their share of knife scars. Aly watched as their eyes flicked restlessly over their surroundings. They seemed more wary than alert. Though they wore only belt-knives openly, she could also see the print of hilts against their shirts and breeches. Their bulging belt purses and saddlebags were guaranteed to hold even more tools for bloody work, unless she had lost her grip on her education entirely. These were not the tougher breed of merchant who followed Lombyn's jungle and mountain roads. These were killers.

Aly did her mental trick that allowed her to see distant objects in detail. Now the unfamiliar traders were as clear to her vision as if they stood right before her. One, a luarin dressed in a buckskin tunic and breeches, drove the lead wagon with Gurhart, the chief merchant, beside him. Something about the way he held himself told Aly he was the assassins' leader. He looked to be five feet eight inches tall, with short brown hair. He was olive-skinned, dark for a luarin, with green eyes and a round scar on his left cheekbone. The remaining three male strangers, two full luarin, one a half-blood, rode as guards, their crossbows set easily on their thighs. Their tunics and breeches were unremarkable shades of brown. Two had brown hair; the part-raka had black hair. All three were lean and muscular, with swords in plain sheaths that had seen hard use.

The standout was the woman, but Aly guessed she was meant to divert attention from the men. She wore her blazing red hair coiled and pinned at the back of her head. She sat beside the driver of one of the other wagons, looking around at the scenery. Her eyes, as restless as those of the other assassins, were blue. Her dress almost matched her eyes in color. Despite the pampered smoothness of her skin, the woman had strong arms and capable hands.

Aly turned her gaze to Gurhart, who ran the caravan. He was part raka and a decent enough fellow. Over his other visits Aly had been careful to talk to him, presenting herself to him and his people as an eager young girl who desired news of the world beyond Tanair. Gurhart, flattered by her attention, had told her more than regular news. Aly knew the names of his wife and children, how much he had made the year before, and how often he'd come to Tanair before the Balitangs made it worth his trouble. From those talks Aly knew Gurhart was no more able to hide his troubles than three-year-old Elsren. She saw no discomfort on the merchant's round face now, no unease or suspicion. That didn't necessarily mean the new members of the caravan were all right, she told herself. It might just mean that Gurhart had been short of hands, and these five had shown up. She wondered how many of Gurhart's original crew of workers had vanished before he'd hired these hard folk.

Aly watched as the caravan passed, then slithered back down her rock. Only Junai waited at the bottom. The young raka had left to spread the word of the caravan's arrival.

"Dish out more stew, Mama, there's guests for supper,"

Aly told Junai. She returned to Visda and asked her to take charge of the goats, then set off toward Tanair at a trot. She had not gone far when the sound of hooves greeted her. One of Lokeij's stable boys approached on horseback. He led the mare Aly had ridden before, the chestnut called Cinnamon.

Remembering she was not supposed to ride well, Aly clumsily pulled herself into the saddle and turned Cinnamon toward the castle, with a word of thanks for the boy. The caravan overtook her at the village gate. Aly dismounted and led Cinnamon through the village with a word of greeting for those merchants she knew from their previous visits. From their responses, Aly gathered that word had reached them that the castle was full to the rafters. The merchants were unhappy at the prospect of having to find lodging in the village, but they were used to roughing it. So much the better, Aly thought as she walked through the castle's outer gate. Fewer people would spent the night inside the castle's walls, which meant fewer people for her to watch. Those five newcomers would be enough of a problem.

Lokeij awaited Aly by the stable, a look of concern on his old monkey's face, contradicted by his gaudy red sarong. He nodded toward the gate to the inner courtyard. Gurhart was there with two wagonloads of goods, talking to the duchess, Chenaol, and Ulasim.

Aly walked into the stable leading the mare. When Lokeij joined her, she said, "Assassins came with the merchants this time. You'll need to alert the others. Where's our family?"

"The ladies play chess with the prince and His Grace," Lokeij replied instantly, meaning Dove and Sarai. "The little ones are having baths in the kitchen. You saw Her Grace." He trotted out of the stable.

Aly unsaddled Cinnamon and groomed her. Her hands

trembled slightly, but that was probably just the excitement that came with a real challenge. She had done this sort of thing before, twice, with her Da when killers had gotten into a place he was guarding. The nice thing about Tanair Castle was its lack of space. It limited the ways that assassins, trained to attack in the dark while the household slept, could approach their targets.

Ulasim and Fesgao arrived together with Lokeij. Ulasim checked to make sure no one could see or hear them in the depths of the stable, then nodded to Aly. "What do you have?" he asked.

Aly leaned against the stable wall. "Five strangers are with them," she replied quietly. "They look like professional assassins to me. By now, they'll have smuggled themselves into the castle on those wagons I just saw outside the keep. Either that or they might be hiding in wait for an ally who's inside to let them in after dark." She described the probable assassins in detail adding: "I worry that there could be more hidden in the carts, and that maybe they turned some of the regular merchants to their side. Can your people search the wagons and take anyone we don't know? Just to be on the safe side."

"You speak as if we will not find them." Fesgao was the quietest of the four raka leaders, but Aly had come to value the few things he chose to say. Did he value her in the same manner? she wondered.

"These are professionals," Aly replied. "The first thing they learn is to get away from their transport, in case some bright-eyed young thing like me suspects something isn't right."

"Then how do you suggest we catch them?" asked Ulasim. He looked down at Aly, his dark eyes impossible to read. "Is it the plan we discussed? Move the family to a safe place after supper, and set our people where these murderers will attack at night?"

Aly nodded. It was a good plan, arrived at by mutual agreement among the raka conspirators, with only the occasional nudge or suggestion from her. Its success depended on the loyalty of the raka, but the Balitangs—at least their two elder daughters—had that, and none of the conspirators wanted anyone to realize their interest lay solely with the older girls.

"I'm afraid we'll have to include the prince, too. I'm *sorry*," Aly said as the three rakas' eyes blazed. "But they might be here just for him, and not care who else gets killed in the meantime. I'd as soon not risk it."

Lokeij spat on the stable floor to show his disdain for the prince. "What of the prince's servants?" he wanted to know. "We didn't account for them when we planned this."

Aly looked at Ulasim, their general, to see what he would decide. "Urge the prince's servants out to the barracks for a nighttime drink and game of dice," Ulasim said after a moment's thought. "We can guard them in there safely enough. Our extra fighters will go on the fourth floor in case the assassins try to come down from the roof." He looked at Aly. "Unless we should guard the roof now?"

Fesgao answered, "They mustn't think we know they're here, in case there are more we haven't identified. We must act normal. Usually we never go up on the roof."

"If we leave the roof and the servants' stairs open, we'll control their main line of attack. We can draw them all out right away," Aly added. "We don't want to spend the rest of the summer jumping because one got away and is waiting to finish the job."

"And we don't want any escaping to carry word to Rajmuat," said Lokeij. "If that's who sent them."

He looked at Aly, who shrugged. "We should know when we question them," she told him.

"We can do this," Ulasim said firmly. "We get our fighters in place while the family and the prince dine. Then we pick these gutless shadows up like rats in a trap, so they'll never trouble us again. The plan we have is a good one. Let's set it in motion."

The three men walked off to do their parts of the plans they had thrashed out with Chenaol and Aly over their many nighttime talks. Aly watched them go. She had faith in them, she realized. They hadn't been raised to protect themselves and those in their care as she had been, but she felt good knowing they were on her side. She wished Da had fifty like them in his service.

When Aly passed through the kitchen, Chenaol nodded to her. Her staff was busy with supper preparations. Looking around, Aly noted there were fewer knives in sight than usual. She suspected she would find them on the persons of those servants and slaves approved by the four raka conspirators. When Chenaol herself tossed Aly a roll to nibble, Aly saw the cook's tunic go flat against a cleaver-like shape tucked into the woman's waistband.

A stroll across the courtyard showed Aly a selection of raka men and women drifting into the stable. She recognized a number of off-duty men-at-arms, including the six former bandits who had been captured on the road. Others were villagers. Some were raka she had never met, part of Ulasim's extended force. Aly slipped around behind the stable and entered through a back door. Lokeij stood lookout there.

Both of them listened as Fesgao gave instructions to the new arrivals as they lounged around the horses' stalls. ". . . *quiet,* understand? Stop by the kitchen door. Chenaol has things for you to carry, to hide weapons and give you a reason for being there. Go up the stairs a few at a time before and during supper. Don't poke along, but don't rush."

"What of Veron and the men on guard duty? Shouldn't they be told?" someone asked.

"They'll be at the gates. Let them stay there in case this is only part of the attack," Fesgao replied. "We'll keep this just among us for now."

Aly nodded approval to Lokeij, who winked. The raka leaders had trained their people well. The old man followed her outside. "Too bad you don't have this organization in Rajmuat," she whispered to Lokeij.

The old man raised his thin, hard brows. "But we shall," he replied, his voice quiet. "We guarded our ladies—the girls and Sarugani—in that sinkhole for longer than you've been alive, Kyprioth's mouse. The bigger part of us went to other houses when we were exiled. Our folk recruit more people in the city even now. They know we will come again, and they mean us to have help when we do."

Aly smiled. "I don't know why the god bothered with me," she told Lokeij.

"Because you have the crooked eye, and the memory, and you can talk to the luarin," Lokeij said promptly. "We see four or five paths where you see twenty. Will you go with our family tonight?"

Aly nodded. "I won't be of any use in a fight among all those warriors," she replied. "But I'd like to have at least one assassin alive at the end, if you can manage."

Lokeij nodded. "One day you have to tell us who you were before slavery. Why it is you are so knowing, so young."

Aly shrugged. "I'm the god's chosen," she reminded him.

"True," Lokeij replied, "but the gods never build without a foundation. A crooked eye like yours takes years of work." He glanced at Aly's clothes. "Were I you, I'd clean up. You pour the wine tonight."

Aly looked down at herself. Her tunic was streaked with horse sweat. She grimaced and ran to find her spare clothes.

At supper, Aly watched everyone from her position on the dais. She couldn't tell whether the raka members of the household were excited or nervous. Their faces, ranging in color from dark ivory to coppery brown, looked just as stoic as they always had. Centuries of luarin rule had taught the native islanders iron control. The prince's servants, and the rest of the household behaved normally, chattering and eating heartily.

In the shadows by the main stair, Aly glimpsed movement, but only because she looked for it. A few raka used that route to the upper stories. Most relied on the servants' stair behind the stone veil of the wall. By the end of the meal every raka fighter who did not eat with the family was in position.

Aly saw no reason to alarm the Balitangs until they'd finished supper. They were halfway through the dessert sweets and cheeses when Aly murmured to the duke and duchess, "We must place you in the study opposite your present quarters, for your safety. If you can gather the children and the prince and go there, acting as if you are engaged in some leisure activity, I would appreciate it. No one must think there's anything out of the ordinary."

The duke gave the tiniest of nods while the duchess looked down. As Aly returned the wine to the kitchen, she heard the duchess say gaily, "I have a game we haven't played yet. My dears? Your Highness? It's one that you won't have played in quite this fashion."

I love that woman, Aly thought as she set down the pitcher. She is never at a loss.

Chenaol joined Aly. "My girls know their places. Ulasim

has men on the exits. Come down here once the fighting's done, and I'll have your supper ready."

Aly grinned at her. "You have a nice idea of what's important," she told the cook. "Try not to kill any more of them than necessary. They have to be questioned."

Chenaol drew the cleaver from her waistband as Aly walked back into the great hall. The kitchen servants were on their way to Chenaol as the tables emptied. No one was interested in music that night. Aly suspected that everyone felt tension in the air, even if they didn't know the reason for it.

Aly climbed the stairs, searching the shadows for shapes that didn't belong. By now she could have found her way through any part of the keep in pitch darkness. Tonight she saw nothing unusual. She hadn't expected to. The enemy might use the servants' stair or the fifth-floor storeroom as a hiding place from which to launch their attack, but that meant the risk of someone from the household tripping over them before it was time to strike. Aly expected the attack to come from the roof. She would use that route in the assassins' place. How many people looked up? If her instinct was right, they'd be there now, waiting for lights to go out below, knowing the shutters would be left open for cool night air to flow through the keep. Once the household seemed to be abed, the assassins would use ropes to climb down the tower's sides and swing into their prey's bedrooms.

Aly reached the third-floor landing and the family's present bedrooms. By now the enemy would know that the prince had the ducal rooms and the Balitangs occupied the third floor. Since they were obviously professionals, Aly knew they would know their targets' sleeping arrangements well before their attack. Ulasim stood by the stairway, a long dagger in each hand.

No one wanted to speak more than necessary, in case the

assassins were already inside the keep. Ulasim pointed to the floor, jerked a thumb at the ceiling, and nodded. Everything was ready on the second and fourth floors. Fesgao lounged in the shadows near the door to the family's sleeping quarters. He nodded, too: fighters were hidden inside. Aly pointed to the door of the small room by the stair that served as the children's tiny schoolroom, and raised her brows. Ulasim nodded. The family and the prince were there. Carefully Aly opened the door just enough to slip inside.

"Why is *she* here?" Bronau demanded softly.

"She is as useful in a fight as I am, Your Highness," Lokeij retorted. "We want her out of harm's way." He clutched a double-headed axe in his gnarled hands. Aly expected the old raka to fall over with its weight, but he stood easily, balanced on the balls of his feet. Behind him stood the healer Rihani, her arms around Elsren and Petranne. They stared silently at everyone. Elsren sucked his thumb.

Lokeij was not the only armed man in the room. Both the duke and the prince held drawn swords. "I don't like hiding like this," growled Bronau. "I'd rather fight them myself."

"And leave my wife and children protected only by Lokeij?" asked Mequen. "It's not as satisfying as engaging the enemy in the field, old friend, but it's important to me."

"I could defend *myself* if I had a sword," Sarai reminded the adults, her voice sharp.

Bronau smiled at her. "I would love to see you with a sword in hand," he said. It was clear he thought she would make an adorable picture rather than a combat-ready one. "With a gold hilt and gold armor to match. You could be one of the lady knights of old at the Midwinter Masquerade."

"*And* you haven't had a sword in your hand in four years," murmured Dove.

"Whose fault is that?" snapped the older girl, darting a sharp glance at her stepmother.

Aly crouched by the keyhole in the door. Outside she heard the first signs of trouble. "Hush!" she ordered as she put her ear to the opening.

"Mequen, you are indulgent of your slaves, but surely you won't let this one give orders as if she were one of us!" exclaimed Bronau, outraged.

The duchess held her finger to her lips to silence him.

Aly put an eye to the keyhole, mentally adjusted her power, and exercised her Sight to see as much of the story as she could. Fesgao was gone from his post at the bedroom door. Thumps came from the family's bedroom, and a cry from overhead. She tried to see the stairs, but the keyhole limited her field of vision to the joining of step and floor, something her Sight could not change. Just once she wished she could scry in a mirror or crystal like her mother and Uncle Numair, so she could know what was going on.

From the stairwell Aly heard a scream. Behind her someone gasped—Petranne or Elsren. Ulasim came into view at the foot of the stair, a killer's descending sword trapped between his long, crossed knives. He twisted away to free his weapons; as the assassin's sword dropped, Ulasim lunged in with a backhanded dagger swipe. Aly saw blood, enough to tell her that Ulasim had cut the assassin's throat. The assassin tumbled limply down the stairs past the raka footman. Ulasim checked to make sure his opponent was dead, then ran upstairs once more.

The fighting seemed to last forever, though Aly knew that it was her own worry and impatience that stretched the passing time. She sent up prayers to Mithros for the Balitang servants, along with frequent reminders to Kyprioth that if she was to do as he wished, he would have to keep the people who worked with her alive. Finally, the noise from the upper floors and across the hall faded. There was a long silence. Then Fesgao emerged from the family's bedchamber, his clothes slashed in two places, a bloody longsword weighing down his left arm. Behind him came the raka who had been hidden in the bedroom. Ulasim walked onto the floor from the direction of the stairs, his long, sweat-soaked hair hanging in his face. Three more Balitang fighters moved into view, carrying bodies wrapped in sheets over their shoulders. They laid them on the floor.

Ulasim said huskily, "We think we have them all."

Aly let the prince and the duke out first, then the duchess, and Sarai. She glanced at Lokeij, then nodded toward Dove, Rihani, Petranne, and Elsren. He nodded in reply, indicating he would guard them until they were certain the keep had been scoured of the enemy.

"Until we're sure," Aly told Dove. The girl sighed and took a seat. Rihani's smile was bright with gratitude. Aly closed the door on her way out, ignoring Petranne's cry of indignation.

"They came in on ropes, through the windows, Highness, Your Graces," Ulasim was telling the nobles. "They were on the roof, as we guessed they might be."

"Why didn't you take them on the roof?" demanded Bronau as he and the duke sheathed their swords. "You would have spared us some anxiety!"

"We have but one door to the roof. Only one may go through at a time, Your Highness," Fesgao said with a properly respectful bow. "They could have picked us off as they liked, and we could not be certain all of them were there. As it happens, they were not. My lads report there are still others outside." He looked at the duke and the duchess. "You appear to have been their targets. Perhaps the children, too, since they sleep here as well."

There was a clatter on the stair. Veron, with the men-at-arms who had been on guard duty, charged up, swords bared. Ulasim and Fesgao put themselves between the nobles and the men-at-arms.

"Your Grace, I heard fighting," the sergeant panted, ignoring the two raka between him and his master.

Mequen raised a hand palm out, a calming gesture. "Our servants defended us, Veron. Apparently assassins were smuggled into the keep during the day, or rather, they smuggled themselves."

"I feared it was bandits," the sergeant replied. He looked around at the bodies, then knelt and uncovered a face. "I'll have a word with my boys, letting these get through the inner gate," he promised. He looked up at the duke. "With your permission, I'd like to search the keep, top to bottom."

"Tell me something first," asked Ulasim, his face stern. "Tell me you did not know of this attempt."

Veron's jaw muscles clenched, then relaxed. When he replied, he spoke to Mequen. "No, Your Grace," he replied quietly. "I did not know of it."

Ulasim glanced at Aly, who gave the tiniest of nods. Veron was telling the truth; her Sight confirmed it, though she would tell the others that he showed none of the signs of a liar.

"What is this?" Mequen demanded, his voice sharp. "Why should Veron know assassins had come? You make it sound as if he would have helped them."

Ulasim and Fesago regarded Veron with unflinching eyes. The sergeant flushed beet-red, hesitated, then knelt, his eyes on the duke. "Your Grace, forgive me," he said, shame-faced. "Somehow these men have learned I am ordered to report your actions to the Crown. I am Your Grace's servant, but the King is also my master." After a moment Veron added, "Surely Your Grace understood that watchers would be present in your household."

"Kill the traiterous dog," Bronau snapped, gray eyes flashing. "A man should have but one master. You pay him; he should be yours alone."

Winnamine rested a gentle hand on her husband's arm. "We should not decide this now, when so much of pressing importance must be attended to right away," she murmured.

Mequen lifted her hand to his lips and kissed her fingertips before he released her. "Wise as ever, my dear," he said.

Aly nodded to Ulasim and Fesgao. They moved aside so Veron could see the duke better. Mequen told him, "Very well. Do as thorough a search as you and your men can perform."

"I trust you didn't take all of your guards off the gate," Prince Bronau said with a smile.

Veron stiffened. Really, Aly thought, for a prince he's got no tact. The duke trusts Veron to do his job properly, royal spy or no. Bronau could at least have trusted the duke's judgment.

As Veron led his men back down the stairs, Aly realized that the prince would make a dreadful husband for Sarai. Bronau would encourage Sarai to be even more headstrong than she already was, if she didn't kill him for condescending to her desire to be a warrior.

The nobles walked into the family's bedroom. Fesgao and Ulasim accompanied them. Aly took a moment to memorize the faces of the three dead men—assassins often came in families—before she went inside. There she sighed. The wide, pretty chamber was a shambles. Multicolored raka hangings, embroidered cushions, tapestry frames, pillows, comforters, bolsters, and curtains from the main bed, all were hacked and covered in goose feathers speckled with blood. Four assassins lay sprawled on the floor, weapons still in their hands.

The fifth knelt beside the door between two impassive raka. His arms, wrists, and ankles were bound, his mouth tightly gagged. Blood streamed down his face from a cut in his scalp. He was the man Aly had identified as the leader. His green eyes were stony as they met hers.

She looked at the other bodies. Here were two of the merchant's regular employees as well as two more strangers. The count of dead outside included two of those she had recognized as assassins as well as one of the merchant's people. Where was that redheaded woman? Was it possible that she wasn't an assassin but a spy, trying to root out secrets in the village at that very moment?

Sarai bent and picked up one killer's sword, easily taking its weight in her delicate hand. She held it upright. "No maker's mark on the hilt," she commented to herself. "But if this isn't royal foundry work, I don't know swords."

Bronau chuckled. "Sarai, you startle me. How would you learn that?"

Sarai lowered the blade slowly. Aly was impressed. She knew swords were heavier than they looked. It took control and strength in the wrist and arm to do what Sarai was doing.

The duke wandered over to the bed. He was idly brushing at feathers, looking around, when a heap of curtains a yard away shifted. Up came the missing woman, her teeth bared in fury, a long knife clutched in her hand.

Aly felt as if she were struggling through honey, she was so slow. Like Aly, Ulasim, Fesgao, and the prince all stood on the wrong side of the bed, closer to the door than Mequen.

The duchess gasped. Mequen scrabbled at his sword hilt.

But Sarai, the killer's weapon still in her hand, lunged across the gap. Her arm stretched out in a long, ferocious thrust that pierced the woman through. Swiftly she braced a foot against the assassin's body and freed her sword, then cut the woman's throat, just to be sure.

The sixteen-year-old looked around at the rest of them, brown eyes wide, blood on her hands, face, and clothes. "It's so messy," she murmured in surprise. Then she fainted.

Aly, trembling, went to her and knelt. Using her Sight, she confirmed the girl hadn't been wounded or poisoned. *Though it would serve me right if she had been,* Aly thought, furious with herself. *Idiot! I shouldn't have let* anyone *come back in here until I checked the room. That's* my *job, and I was too overconfident to do it!*

Feathers and cloth rustled as Winnamine joined her. She had found a pitcher of water and handkerchiefs. She wet a handkerchief, wrung it out, and began to clean her step-daughter's face. Aly soaked and wrung out other handkerchiefs and began to wipe Sarai's hands as the girl began to come around.

When Sarai opened her eyes, Winnamine gave her a tiny smile. Her mouth trembled. "Obviously halting your sword lessons was a mistake," she murmured to Sarai. "It's a crime not to encourage such an aptitude."

Sarai stared at her stepmother. "But I fainted," she whispered.

"After," said Winnamine. "You fainted *after* you'd done the important thing." She bit her lip, then continued, "We shall find you a teacher in the morning. In fact, though it may be too late, I may study swordcraft, too. And Dove . . . ?"

Sarai gulped, tried to speak, and could not. At last she cleared her throat and said, "She hates swords. She does like to shoot, if she doesn't have to shoot animals."

"Archery it is," Winnamine said. She blinked over-bright eyes, then leaned in, and kissed Sarai's cheek. "Thank you for saving his life." She took a deep breath, then rose and went to see how her husband was.

Sarai looked at Aly. "If I'd known that all it would take to start my lessons again was killing someone . . ." Her voice and humor failed. Her eyes overflowed. "Did I do the right thing?" she whispered.

Aly cleaned blood from Sarai's other hand as the other girl wept silently. "You did better than me," she replied softly. "I just stood and stared. But I wasn't needed. Sarai, balance a murderess's life against your father's. This entire household would prefer the duke to an assassin."

"There's one who disagrees," Sarai remarked as she struggled to sit up. She pointed to the last living killer. He'd made no sound as the drama had unfolded. Now he stared blankly into the air.

Aly sighed. "Will you be all right?" she asked Sarai.

A hand reached down: the duke's. Sarai took it, and let her father pull her up into his arms.

Aly stood and went to Fesgao and Ulasim. Bronau had gone out to the landing, where he inspected the dead men. "Perhaps he should be reminded that his servants are missing," Aly murmured to Ulasim, "and that if he wishes to see to their welfare, he should go to the barracks? I don't want him noticing me any more than he already has."

At a look from Ulasim, Fesgao went out into the hall. He bowed politely to the prince and spoke to him as Ulasim and Aly watched. "She was beautiful, our Saraiyu, wasn't she?" Ulasim inquired, his mouth barely moving as he whispered. "Like Gunapi the Sunrose, goddess of war and molten rock."

"She was," Aly admitted. Her eyes stung strangely. The last time she had seen so perfect a fighting move was when her mother had battled pirates at the Swoop.

"Without you, all might have been lost," Ulasim told Aly suddenly. He picked up one of her hands and pressed it to his forehead. "We owe our lives to you, and our thanks to the god for you tonight."

Aly yanked her hand from his grip, unnerved by his intensity. "Ulasim, calm down," she said, forcing amusement into her voice. "I just alerted you about some assassins, that's all."

He surveyed her from his greater height. Aly had expected him to be offended by her light brush-off. Instead he smiled. "I always forget, you are not of us. We think you are raka in your heart, but no. You are newly come. No one teaches a slave the laws that govern the Isles. Had these *sisat*"—he pointed to the still-living assassin with his dagger—"killed even one Balitang or the prince, then every raka man, woman, and child of Tanair village and castle would die. That is the luarin law governing such things."

"Oh. But these are luarin assassins, and I'd bet whatever I own that they were sent by the king," Aly pointed out. "If he sent them, surely he wouldn't enforce that law. . . ." Her voice trailed off as she registered the grimness on Ulasim's face. "Even if he sent the assassins himself?" she asked, wanting badly for it not to be true and fearing that it was.

"The idea is that if any member of the luarin nobility is killed, the nearest local raka must have helped the murderer. At the very least, the courts would say that the local raka did not die to stop the killers," added the duke. He stood behind them, one arm around Winnamine, one around Sarai. Both he and Sarai looked mournful. "It's insane, but Oron is quite mad. The law itself comes from the time of the luarin conquest. It's how they broke the spine of the raka rebellion. Some of us have laid petitions before the courts to have the Conqueror's Laws repealed, to no avail." He shook his head.

Aly stared. *That is just not right,* she thought. *To murder people who had nothing to say about it, just because they were near?* She understood why there were such laws. They were made to fit a conqueror's logic, used to keep a captive people under control. She had just never matched the law to the faces of people she knew, like the Balitang raka.

I don't want to get involved with this country, she thought as she looked at the floor. *I must go home soon, before I get so wound up in their lives and injustices that I'll never want to leave.*

The prince trotted down the stairs, two of Fesgao's weary men following. Fesgao himself walked back into the bedroom. "Aly? What do you recommend for this man?" he asked, nodding to their prisoner. "Torture?"

Startled at the suggestion, she met his eyes and realized that this was yet another test. She made a face at him. "Any amateur knows torture is chancy at best. People do still lie under torture. What you need is truthdrops."

Fesgao gave a tiny smile and went to find Rihani. Aly looked at Ulasim. "So I may look forward to these little exercises until I die, is that it?" she asked brightly. "Or will you decide I'm not some luarin brute before I am, say, fifty?"

Ulasim wiped one of his long daggers on a cloth. "Oh, more like forty, I'm sure," he replied casually. He flipped the dagger up casually, caught it by the hilt, and in the next motion cut the gag from the last assassin's mouth. "Who sent you?" he asked.

The man stared at the raka, expressionless.

"Once we have truthdrops in hand, you will speak," Ulasim pointed out. "Keep your pride and tell us now. Don't wait for magic to force you."

The man leaned forward and spat on the floor.

Fesgao returned from the room across the hall with Rihani in tow. She held a small, uncorked vial in her hand. Aly was startled by the healer's steely gaze. Normally Rihani was as fierce as pudding. "Open his mouth," Rihani ordered.

A band of green fire locked around the assassin's throat and tightened, vanishing into his flesh. The man choked. Green fire coated his mouth in Aly's Sight as his face got redder and redder. The veins bulged in his throat and forehead as he fought for air. Within a moment he was dead.

Aly bit her tongue to keep from shouting her frustration at the lost opportunity. "*This* is why we need a mage who is not just a healer," she said quietly, looking into Ulasim's face. "And I should have seen that coming." She turned and ran down the servant's stair before she gave in to the temptation to shout. It was time to get some cool air.

Sloppy! she thought as she strode outside. Sloppy not to check the room for assassins before I so much as let a Balitang set foot outside that protected room. Sloppy not to think he might have a silencing spell on him before we set it in motion. What else have I missed? There are ways to stop a silencing spell. And Sarai shouldn't have had to kill anyone!

I have to be sharper, she told herself, gently thumping her head on the keep's stone wall as a reminder. I won't get lucky a second time.

The inner and outer courtyards crawled with Bronau's and Mequen's men-at-arms. They were looking for anyone suspicious, turning the buildings upside down in their search. Three guards from the merchants' caravan lay dead at the entrance to the kitchen wing. Bronau's and the Balitang soldiers searched the bodies. Laid out in front of the barracks, awaiting proper burial, were two of the castle's own, one of the former bandits and one of the official men-at-arms. Aly murmured a prayer to the Black God for their rest in the realms of the dead, then wandered back toward the keep.

She heard voices behind the kitchen wing, where a tiny garden had been built for Tanair's ladies. A small door opened directly to the servants' halls inside the tower. Its torches cast light onto two dead merchant's guards lying on the path that led to the carefully landscaped garden. Two of Ulasim's servants stood beside them, but their attention was on the fig tree that shaded the walk.

Intrigued, Aly walked over to see what was going on. The two dead men were the first that night who had not been killed by blades. Both lay facedown, with dents between their shoulders and their heads twisted askew.

"Please come down," a Balitang hostler was saying to the tree. "You have already unnerved us enough for one night, *duan*." The title meant "honorable sir," used to a man who was not a noble. "Ulasim will wish to know what you did here."

Aly looked up. Nawat, perched easily on a branch that should not have held his weight, gazed down at her. With his dark, long-nosed face surrounded by leaves and growing figs, he looked like some wilderness god.

"*Now* what are you up to?" Aly demanded as her conscience pinched her. She should have told Nawat what was going to happen tonight so that he could have decided whether or not he wanted to be caught up in human quarrels.

"I am up to nothing," the crow-man said cheerfully. "Those two were going to mob you through that door." He pointed to the door into the keep. "I stopped them."

Aly knelt beside the dead men. Their necks were broken. The dents in their backs looked like the prints of bare feet. She glanced at his: they were bare. "How did you do it?" she asked her strange friend.

"I saw it," said another servant, one of the footmen. "We had the duty here. They was coming at us, and all of a sudden he leaps up in the dark, and hits one in the back with both feet, kicking out, like. Then he did it to the other. And then he jumped into the tree."

Aly stared up at Nawat. He must be very strong to break bone with jumping kicks from a standing position, she thought. Well, crows are very strong. "You could have been hurt," she told him. "They might have killed you."

The hostler snorted. "Not him!"

Nawat's gaze was steady as he looked down at Aly. "They were going to mob you," he repeated firmly. "I mobbed them. Only I added a hawk thing. When the hawk strikes, he breaks the head of the prey. I did that."

Aly rubbed her temples. "Thank you," she said. "Will you come down now? I think we have them all."

Nawat smiled brightly at her. "I will come down for you, Aly." He jumped down as lightly as a cat. Aly patted his cheek absently and let him come along as they patrolled the rest of the castle grounds.

It was hours before the castle's residents calmed enough to go to bed. Aly was in the kitchen, finishing a very late supper, when the duchess's maid, Pembery, found her. "His Grace wishes to see you in the ground floor study," she told Aly, and yawned. "Don't take forever. I can't go to bed until the family is settled."

Aly sighed. She would have liked to go to bed herself. Instead she found the duke in the small room where she had cleaned up the day Bronau had arrived. There was a bottle and a glass on a table by the duke's hand, but the contents of the glass were untouched. The duke himself was staring at a branch of candles, drumming his fingers on the arm of his chair.

Aly bowed. "Your Grace wished to see me?" she asked.

"Veron says the merchant Gurhart tells us that all of his people who became particular friends of the five newcomers are also among the dead," Mequen replied. "A search of their belongings has revealed gold *seratudus* and a death order under the Crown's seal."

"I'm sorry to hear that, Your Grace," Aly told him softly.

Mequen nodded. "Gurhart swears by his own blood there are no other assassins among his people," Mequen continued, his dark eyes weary as he gazed at Aly. "He says he knew nothing of the assassins' true purpose in taking work with his caravan. Some of his people had vanished, so he was forced to hire these. I think we must assume those who disappeared while they were in Dimari were killed by the assassins, so that Gurhart would be forced to take them on."

Aly nodded. It was what she had expected they would hear. Hauling goods out to the back of beyond was not a trip anyone enjoyed. The road was hard and its dangers were greater than the coastal routes. Gurhart would have leaped at the chance to replace his missing people, and assumed the vanished workers had simply decided not to go to Tanair.

The duke's voice, husky with exhaustion, hardened. "What I find interesting, god's messenger, is that you did not warn us that danger was on the way. Instead, as far as my wife or I could learn from Ulasim or Fesgao, *you* observed the newcomers with the caravan and viewed them as a danger. It argues, you see, that the god has placed you here not as his oracle, but as his warrior."

"Oh, no, Your Grace," Aly said, gleaming with innocence.

"I'd break a nail on one of those dreadful swords. I just have a memory for faces. Maybe I saw one of the assassins back in Rajmuat. Well, he'd no right to be with a Lombyn caravan, had he? Unless he was up to no good, of course. I said as much to Lokeij, who thought it worth passing along."

"And that is another thing," said the duke. "How is it that I find my chief defenders here in the keep are servants and off-duty men-at-arms, not Veron and the men on watch? It was perfectly obvious that Ulasim and Fesgao were in command here, and that they consulted you. I will have the truth now, if you please."

Behind her mask of wide-eyed harmlessness, Aly cursed. She had walked head-on into his next hard question. She thought fast. "I only noticed something odd, as I said," she lied. "And I wasn't sure of Veron, being a royal spy and all. He was carefully watched, I assure you. We made certain he sent no reports to the Crown after he reached Tanair. As for using the servants, it stands to reason that anyone Veron picks for regular night duty is probably someone loyal to him alone, willing to admit Crown servants with orders against Your Grace."

"That those men are mostly the pure-luarin men-at-arms is not a factor?" Mequen wanted to know.

Aly sighed to herself. Why couldn't this man have been stupid? Instead she replied, "Your Grace would have to inquire of Ulasim and Fesgao. Perhaps the ones with raka blood look up to Your Grace for marrying a raka the first time around."

"And producing half-raka daughters in the Rittevon royal line?" asked the duke very quietly.

Aly looked down and twiddled her thumbs. He was in possession of far too much of the whole picture for her comfort. "Your Grace's servants are devoted," she said.

Mequen scowled. "Are you incapable of giving a straight answer?" he demanded.

Aly grinned at him. "Not always, Your Grace," she replied impishly.

Mequen drummed his fingers on his leg. "We would be dead tonight were it not for you people of our household," he said at last. "Be sure I will not forget it." His gaze hardened. "*Any* of it, Aly."

She scratched her head. "You know, Your Grace, this will go so much easier for everyone if you accept the god's gifts without question," she reminded him. "Take it from me, you'll just give yourself headaches this way."

Mequen smiled. "So I will. I suppose inquiring into your origins comes under the heading of questioning the god's gifts."

Aly bowed her head meekly. "Oh, undoubtedly, Your Grace."

"Very well. You are dismissed—with my thanks."

Aly was about to open the door when she thought of something else. She faced the duke. "Your Grace also owes thanks to Lady Saraiyu," she said, not sure if she was overstepping her bounds.

"She will have her sword lessons again, if that is what concerns you," replied Mequen. "After tonight, I think your Tortallan king is wiser than we are, to allow women to take up arms. Sleep well."

A noble maiden must convey dignity and chastity without appearing to think about either one. Let common-born girls tussle in the hay with their loutish swains. The future of your family's bloodline and your future lord's bloodline should be your greatest concern. Let no man but one of your family embrace you. Let no man but your betrothed kiss any more than your fingertips; let your betrothed kiss you only on fingers, cheek, or forehead, lest he think you unchaste. And never allow yourself to be alone with a man, to safeguard the precious jewel of your reputation. No well-born maiden ever suffered from keeping her suitors at arm's length. Your chastity will make you a prize to your future husband's house and an honor to your own.

—*From* Advice to Young Noblewomen,
by Lady Fronia of Whitehall (in Maren),
given to Aly on her twelfth birthday
by her godsmother, Queen Thayet

11

MIGRATIONS

To be on the safe side, Aly suggested to Ulasim that he might want to question Gurhart, to see if he told the head footman the same story he had given to the duke. She looked on as Ulasim and Fesgao interrogated the man using truthdrops. Gurhart's answers were the same as those he'd given Mequen. It was just a safety measure, but Aly was determined not to be overconfident again. She had been virtually sure of Gurhart's innocence. He was too terrified to lie, and he should have been. Anyone but Mequen would have confiscated all Gurhart owned and demanded lives as well. Here in the Isles, the duke didn't even need to have the executions approved by a royal court, as he would in Tortall. On his own lands in the Isles, the luarin noble had the rights of a king. Bronau would have demanded everything, but with Sarai to plead with him for clemency, he gave way.

Aly also made sure to be on hand as Veron, Fesgao, and the men searched the caravan board by board. As she had expected, they had found nothing in the assassins' gear to indicate who had hired them. As professionals, they had stripped themselves of anything personal before they joined Gurhart on Lombyn.

Returning to the castle after the search, Aly was joined by old Lokeij. He looked none the worse for his late evening. He was teasing her for her yawns as they wandered into the inner courtyard. There one of the corporals put the off-duty armsmen through sword drills. Today their numbers included Sarai, paired off with Fesgao, and the duchess, who was learning the beginning drills under the corporal's instruction.

"Is she not beautiful?" asked Lokeij softly as he watched Sarai parry and disengage with catlike grace. "Like Gunapi—"

"The Sunrose, the goddess, I know," Aly interrupted, watching the girl and her partner. "If she doesn't keep her guard up, she'll be skewered by someone who knows what he's doing."

Lokeij looked up at Aly with a frown. "You know so much about it, I suppose."

Aly opened her mouth to say she knew plenty about swordplay, then closed it. Finally she said, "I watched lots of armsmen practicing. I even saw the Lioness fight."

"Who?" asked Lokeij.

Aly stared at the little man. Who had not heard of her mother? "The King's Champion of Tortall," she informed him. "The first female knight in over a century. The Lady Alanna of Pirate's Swoop and Olau."

Lokeij shrugged. "A luarin," he said dismissively. "I only pay attention to them when it's a matter of survival or of protecting my lady's girls." He rubbed a hand over his bristled chin thoughtfully. "So she's good, this Lioness?"

"She's never lost a fight as King's Champion!" Aly said, offended by Lokeij's disinterest. This was her *mother*, a lady acknowledged by all to be poetry with a sword in her hand. She looked at Sarai just as Fesgao sent the girl's sword flying into the air. "Your Sunrose has a way to go to beat Alanna the Lioness."

She walked on to the castle, feeling wistful. She'd never had to say more than her mother's name to describe her before. She was truly away from home, to say "Lioness" and not have every person within hearing turn to listen. *This* is a terrible time to find that I miss her, Aly thought, picking up her step. There's nothing I can do about it until autumn.

To shake off her mood Aly went to Chenaol and begged for chores. She was setting the dais table when Sarai walked into the great hall from outside, straggle-haired and sweat-soaked. She massaged her sword wrist wearily. Aly guessed that Sarai hadn't practiced as much as she'd meant to since her last official lesson.

She was about to call out a suggestion that Sarai wrap her arm in hot, damp towels when Bronau emerged from the study near the staircase. He halted Sarai with a touch on the shoulder and murmured in her ear. Sarai looked up into his face, startled, then glanced around with the look of someone checking for her parents. Aly knew that look very well, having often used it herself. She held perfectly still. With the afternoon's light fading, the dais was in shadow, and so was she.

Sarai nodded and whispered to the prince. Then she continued her climb up the stairs, while Bronau retreated into the study and closed the door.

It had been open before, Aly realized. The prince had been sitting in there, waiting for Sarai to return.

Once the table was set, Aly returned to the kitchen and took Chenaol aside. "Let Hasui pour," she murmured to the cook. "I have things to do."

Chenaol nodded and beckoned to Hasui. Aly left to wash up.

She ate in the shadows at the foot of the stair, her supper cheese and venison slices jammed into a cut roll. All seemed normal on the dais. Bronau, seated between Winnamine and Sarai, plied the duchess with his usual easy flow of conversation and compliments. He seemed to ignore Sarai next to him.

Sarai, too, tried to pretend interest in Dove, seated next to her, and in her food, but she wasn't good at it. A blush mantled her cheeks. She had put a jeweled chain as a band around her forehead, with a citrine droplet dangling at its center. Citrines glinted from her earlobes. Her pale yellow silk dress had a neckline properly meant for court dinners, not country ones. A gold chain with a large gold-tinted pearl drew attention to the shadow between her breasts.

Aly shook her head. If ever a girl was dressed for an assignation, it was Sarai. Aly could have taught her a thing or two about sneaking away to meet a man. Everyone in the room suspected, particularly her parents. She couldn't wait to see how the girl would get away from her family.

Getting to her feet at the end of the meal, Sarai stumbled, bumping into Bronau. He fell sideways against Winnamine as the duchess raised her wine cup to her lips. Wine spilled down the front of Winnamine's rose-colored gown.

As servants, Bronau, and Mequen scrambled to help the duchess, Sarai quietly ducked out through the servants' door behind the dais. Aly had guessed that would be her way out. She entered the passage through another door under the shadow of the stair. On this level the hall passed around the outer wall, allowing servants to bring dishes or messages to the dais without being seen by everyone in the room. The servants' stairs to the upper floors also ended here. The ground floor level had two exits, one directly into the kitchen, one to the outdoor area where Nawat had brought down the pair of would-be assassins.

To the left of the outside door lay the ladies' garden, a small green oasis with a fountain, flowers, and trees tucked between the castle and keep walls, in a spot that drew sunlight every day. Its edges were planted with pines and ferns, which made it seem like part of a forest. The plants also gave Aly cover to hide in as Sarai arranged herself on the broad lip of the fountain. With the approach of night the garden was deep in shadow. The only light came from torches on a walkway on the outer curtain wall. In these conditions Aly got so close to Sarai that she could hear the girl's dress rustle as she fidgeted. Aly settled down to wait.

The musical part of the evening's entertainment in the great hall had begun when Bronau came down the flagstone path. "Sarai, my dear." His voice was warm and soft, intimate.

Sarai's dress whispered as she got to her feet. "Your Highness, good evening."

Bronau chuckled. He kissed Sarai's hand and sat on the lip of the fountain, pulling her down beside him. "That was very clever. I'm not sure Winna will thank you, but I don't believe anyone noticed you left in all the excitement."

"You said you had something important and private to discuss," Sarai pointed out shyly.

"But I am distracted by the music of your voice, those lovely eyes, the sweet curve of your lips . . ."

Aly couldn't see, but she didn't need to. Sarai's quiet gasp, cut off abruptly, and the rustle of silk, painted a clear picture of a kiss. Oh, dear me, Aly thought, shaking her head. Making up to your host's daughter—bad prince! Now, why do you suppose he's doing it on the sly? He's not married, and her parents are his friends. He could probably get permission from His Grace to court Sarai.

"My lord prince!" Sarai was definitely flustered. "It's so improper!"

"I know. I apologize." Bronau's voice was a little hoarse. "My feelings carried me away. To watch you ride, to see you among your devoted subjects, like a true queen—none of Oron's wives were as graceful or as gracious as you. Don't look so alarmed. No one can hear us."

"But you talk something like treason, Your Highness," Sarai warned gently. "I am no queen, only the daughter of a disgraced nobleman."

"But if I asked you to be queen of my heart?"

Aly crinkled her nose with distaste. She had sighed over speeches like that one in the stories she had read and the romantic ballads she had heard. In real life they sounded tawdry. He was a prince of the realm, nearly twenty years older than Sarai. How could he talk like a minstrel performing for ladies in a bower? Did he think Sarai had no brains or honor?

"Your Highness, why have you not asked my father's permission to address me in such terms?" Sarai asked. Her voice was small but firm. "He is your friend. So is my stepmother. For that matter, you used to court Winna."

"Ah." Bronau's chuckle had an embarrassed sound. "To be honest, I hadn't meant to get so carried away, truly. But my feelings . . . The affection I had for Winna was that of practicality. She was a widow and my friend, I had found no true love, so I offered her a marriage of friendship. I thank the gods now that she preferred Mequen."

Don't fall for this dolt, Aly silently begged Sarai. I'll bet he wrote all these pretty speeches down and memorized them so he could make any maiden swoon all over him.

Unaware of his hidden critic, Bronau continued to talk. "I escaped love for years, only to be plunged into it when I thought myself immune. I need to know from your own beautiful lips: would you be averse to a union with me? You would be queen of my heart in truth, and I would put the world at your feet."

Sarai's hesitation was marked. Aly raised an eyebrow, fascinated. Back in Tortall, she herself had sighed with the feelings of kisses and strong arms, yet she was still practical. The boys who had courted her had called her cold-blooded. Now it seemed that she and Sarai had that in common: that their hearts could be racing as their heads remained cool. "Your Highness," Sarai murmured at last, "I cannot bring glory to your name. Tanair and a few estates like it are my only inheritance. You have seen how poor it is."

"I care nothing for your fortune, Sarai," Bronau said. There was enough passion in his quiet voice to almost convince Aly. "So I am an impractical fool. Certainly Rubinyan and that human Stormwing he married think so. But I would rather have a woman I loved than the plumpest heiress in the Isles. Unless . . ." His passion faded audibly, with a trained actor's precision. "The difference in our ages . . ."

"Oh, no, Highness, that's not it at all!" Sarai's emotion was not calculated. She spoke from the heart. "How could I—a man so alive as you—"

There was the movement of cloth, the catch of breath, sighs and murmurs. Aly pushed back her cuticles, then carefully cleaned under her nails, waiting for conversation to start again. Bronau would do no more than kiss Sarai, not when there was a chance a sentry would look down from the parapet and see them.

At last Bronau asked, his voice rough, "Will you marry me, enchantress? Will you let me make you queen of the world?"

Sarai was panting. Aly envied her; she liked kissing, too.

At last Sarai managed to say, "Your Highness, I am not free to choose. If my father says I may . . . He's your friend, he won't refuse us if that's what we want."

Bronau hesitated. At last he said, "I cannot ask him. Not yet. I am under suspicion, as are you. Oron might see a union between us as a threat."

"He sees everything as a threat," Sarai reminded him.

"When I am in favor at court again, I will ask Mequen for your hand—if you wish to give it." Another stifled gasp. Aly wondered if they were going to do this all night.

"I'll go back first," Bronau said. "Give me time to reach my rooms before you return. And thank you, for giving me hope."

Judging by the movement of shadows beyond her screen of ferns, Aly suspected Bronau kissed Sarai's hands, then her mouth, one last time before he left the garden. Now she also noticed that the ground under her was damp. The duchess would skin her for getting another tunic dirty.

"That wasn't very wise," a small, clear voice—Dove's—announced. "And it was *extremely* improper, letting him get you alone. People would say you aren't very well brought up."

"What do you know?" Sarai retorted, sounding like a cross sixteen-year-old, not a gently bred maiden swept away by her lover's kisses. "You're only twelve. And you're not in the least romantic."

"Good." Firm steps sounded on the earth. A rustle of cloth announced that Dove was sitting by her sister.

"Besides," Sarai added, "I *had* a chaperon. Didn't I, Aly?"

Aly giggled and stood. "How did you know?" she asked.

"I just guessed," Sarai replied. She and Dove were making sure her hair was tucked up and neatly pinned once more.

"Why did you let them do that?" Dove wanted to know, bending around Sarai to glare at Aly. "It was so shameful."

"Hmph," Sarai replied with a sniff. She tugged a lock of hair out of Dove's hold when she tossed her head. "Wait until you're my age and the blood's hot in *your* veins. He's very handsome, and charming—"

"And he's *old*," Dove interrupted. "It was disgusting."

"He's a man of the world," Sarai informed her sister, her nose in the air.

"So he's twice as likely to get you pregnant as a boy your own age who loves you and doesn't know what he's doing. That's what Chenaol says," Dove snapped.

"Dovasary Temaida Balitang!" cried Sarai, shocked. "Never say Chenaol told that to *you*!"

"No," Dove said, her chin thrust out mulishly. "She said it to one of the maids who's got one of Bronau's servants chasing her, but it means the same for you, doesn't it?"

"He never mentioned his debts," Aly pointed out, brushing a clump of moss from the front of her tunic.

Sarai drooped and sighed. "No, he didn't. And he didn't talk to Papa first. But Aly, I think he's serious about the marriage."

Aly propped her chin on her hands. "I do, too," she admitted. "And it makes me uncomfortable. I hope it makes *you* uncomfortable. Or wary, at least."

Sarai laughed. "I don't need to be wary," she said, elbowing Aly. "I have you and Dove for that."

Aly smiled evilly at Sarai, showing teeth. "But not for explaining to Their Graces where you have been since supper. You may tell them Dove and I were present, of course, but we won't be there to sweeten the discussion for you."

Sarai looked from Aly to Dove, who gave her a grin identical to Aly's. "I'm going to read in the library for a while," she told Sarai. "I'll come upstairs later."

Aly inhaled deeply. "I believe I'll enjoy the cool air for a bit," she said, her voice light. "Summer nights are *so* lovely."

"All right for you two," Sarai told them sharply. She got to her feet. "I may as well get it over with. And I'll remember this!" She flounced down the flagstone path.

"She always surprises me," Dove remarked. "She didn't try to tell you that you're a slave, so you have to go with her."

"No, she didn't, and she could have," Aly admitted. "Most *would* have."

Dove sighed. "That's Sarai for you. Just when you want to shake her until her teeth rattle, she does something like that." She stood. "I really do mean to read for a while."

"And I really do mean to sit," replied Aly. She watched the younger girl leave, her soft leather shoes making no sound on the path. Sometimes talking to Dove was nearly as good as talking to Da or Aunt Daine.

She remembered the time her mother had caught her kissing at a party for Prince Roald's engagement, and grinned. The boy had fled, not wanting to deal with Aly's mother when she seemed so displeased. "Now look what you've done," Aly had reproved Alanna when the boy was out of earshot. "It'll take me weeks to train another one to kiss like I want him to."

"Kisses are serious things," Alanna had retorted. "You talk of them as if they're party favors."

Aly had kissed her mother on the cheek. "They're serious for *you*, Mother," she'd said. "They're party favors for me."

It was worth the scolding that followed, about Aly's lack of seriousness, to see the shock on the Lioness's face, and to see her mother realize that kisses didn't *have* to be serious. Of course, when Alanna had been in her best kissing years, Aly remembered, most people had thought she was a boy. Boys were never as free with kisses among other boys.

She sighed. They had the blood of Trebond in their veins, yet she and her mother were so different. She wondered if Alanna had ever noticed that. She definitely needed Da to remind her that life could be fun.

"Was he mate feeding her?"

Aly looked up at the fringe tree across the bowl of the fountain. "Nawat," she said, resigned more than surprised. Of course he would be here.

Nawat leaped to the ground and circled the fountain to sit next to Aly. "Is that mate feeding?" he asked. "It didn't look as if he transferred food to her tongue pouch, but it is hard to tell in the dark. I've seen other humans do it, only not this close to me. They do it in shadows, as if it's a secret."

"It's kissing," Aly explained, her mind half on how she had missed his presence in the tree and half on what she was saying. "Two people touch lips. It's mating behavior, but it's not mate feeding. It's—"

Nawat turned his head sideways and pressed his lips to Aly's. His mouth was soft and warm, his breath lightly scented with spices, his smell clean, with hints of beeswax and wood oils from his work. Aly's usually distant and observing mind focused completely on the feeling of his mouth against hers. She dimly felt Nawat hesitate. Then he brushed his hand against the side of her neck and cradled the back of her head as he deepened the kiss.

Someone laughed in the distance. Aly jumped to her feet as if launched from a catapult. "Yes, you've got the idea, but you should really practice on someone else," she told him, trembling from head to toe, furious with herself because, after all, she *had* been kissed before. "Somebody who isn't so busy, or, or busy . . ."

Nawat looked up at her, smiling slightly. For the first time there was something in his gaze that was human, and very male. "You said *busy* twice," he pointed out.

"I'm very busy," Aly retorted. She stopped and caught her breath. What was the matter with her? She was no blossoming girl-child, with no experience or sense of proportion. She calmed down. "But you can see, it's not mate feeding. Still, it's very serious, Nawat. You shouldn't go around kissing just anybody."

Now she sounded like her mother. Aly turned and strode down the path, away from the crow-man. She was doing her best to pretend that she was not running away. How could she care enough about this to run from someone who became a human male through sheer curiosity, who would eventually tire of it and return to his own shape? And why did she care if he wouldn't be around one day?

The next morning the merchant caravan left for Dimari. Aly and Ulasim, along with thirty raka and part-raka, surrounded the caravan when it reached the area where the road east cut through the rocks at the edge of Tanair. Gurhart and his people obeyed orders to step away from their mounts and wagons, plainly terrified of these masked and hooded riders. As soon as the travelers were seated under guard by the road's edge, Ulasim's people began to search the wagons and horses. Following Aly's instructions of that morning, they combed through the caravan, then its people.

Aly, sweltering in her mask, followed Ulasim up and down the line of carts, horses, and people. She took care of the tricky bits herself as she taught Ulasim what she knew of caches and secret hiding places. Bronau's letters to his creditors were in Gurhart's own mailbag, as were letters from the Balitangs, their servants, and their men-at-arms. Aly glanced over these in case she had missed anything, but they were straightforward enough. Soon they found the other letters, Bronau's to his brother's enemies, and all of the reports sent out by the royal spies and Rubinyan's spies. Those were confiscated and burned. Aly would not risk word of anything unusual finding its way to Rajmuat. The merchants would tell what they had seen and could remember, but the worst piece of information they possessed was that Bronau sheltered with the Balitangs. Unless any spies in the caravan were very good and had been able to read the coded documents, they would have no other information that might alert a suspicious spymaster.

When the searchers finished, they helped the merchants to reassemble the caravan, then saw them on their way. No one would get the chance to sneak back and tell the castle's spies that they had been robbed of information.

"You scare me sometimes, little one," Ulasim remarked as he watched the caravan's dust settle in its wake.

Aly yanked off the stifling hood that had covered her face and slave collar. "You're going to make me conceited," she replied with a grin. "I'm going to blush, I know it."

"My people are not happy about Bronau's pursuit of our lady Sarai," he told her as the raka patrols returned to their day's work. "The Jimajen line is as corrupt as the king's."

"Tell them not to fret," Aly said. "Sarai's no fool."

Not long after she dozed off that night, Aly saw a glowing figure walk through the soft gray curtain between her and dreams. It was Kyprioth. Although the god appeared in her mind's eye only as a glowing figure with arms and legs, she was still sure it was him.

"Hello, there." His voice sounded in her ear, clear, friendly, and crisp. "Would you like to go for a short trip?"

"Am I going to be tired in the morning?" she demanded. "You know, I do work during the day."

"And you shall be as fresh for it as a sea breeze," Kyprioth replied. "Look."

Aly looked. There was her body, deep in slumber on her pallet. She stood on air beside the god. "Very well. What kind of trip?" she asked.

Kyprioth put a strong, surprisingly real arm around her ghost self's waist and told her, "You'll see. It's going to be instructive, trust me on that."

He bore her up through the keep's walls and into the open sky beyond. The ground, just touched with silver under the waning moon, raced underneath them, mountains, jungle lowlands, the sea. Lombyn Isle passed into the distance behind them. Below lay the Azure Sea, black in the moonlight.

"Why do we travel this way?" she inquired, feeling confused. "You show me what's going on in Tortall through dreams."

"I don't care about Tortall," replied Kyprioth. "But I do love my Isles, and I love to see them at night. You may as well appreciate the view. Tell me they are not beautiful."

"They're lovely," Aly said, and yawned. "Can I go back to bed now that I've admired them? My skin gets dry if I don't get my beauty rest."

Kyprioth didn't even bother to reply. He carried her over the eastern side of Imahyn Isle and down the long axis of Kypriang at a speed that would have made Aly dizzy if she had been in her body, instead of dreaming.

Ahead lay the lights of Rajmuat, spread over the harbor hills. The city was ablaze with light, its people milling in the streets. Kyprioth and Aly popped through the palace roof, landing inside a huge bedroom even more brightly lit than the streets. Courtiers gathered near the door, murmuring to one another. Priests of the Black God, the god of death, stood beside a great bed at the heart of the chamber, silent, waiting.

At the center of an expanse of heaped pillows, linen sheets and goose-down comforters lay an old, emaciated man with silvery hair, black eyebrows, and stubbled cheeks. Aly had seen sketches of him in Tortall: King Oron. His lips were stained black. At his side a healer lifted away a basin filled with blood and bile. She shook her head at the nobles who stood nearby.

The man who stood nearest to the old king wore a circlet crown. "Prince Hazarin," Kyprioth said to Aly.

The healer jerked around as if she'd heard. Her eyes widened as she looked in their direction. She shivered and hurried out of the room through a small side door.

Next to the prince stood a woman who also wore a circlet crown. She would be Princess Imajane, King Oron's only surviving daughter. She was beautiful in an icy, razor-sharp way. Aly looked at her for a moment, then turned her gaze to the third person there who wore the circlet, a yawning boy Elsren's age: Prince Dunevon. Imajane held the sleepy child upright.

Behind her stood a man Aly had glimpsed during her early days with the Balitangs: a tall, balding man with chill gray eyes, a thin, straight mouth, and hair that was silver on top of his head, shading to black at the ends. There was a resemblance between Rubinyan and Bronau, though Rubinyan was fifteen years older. He stood behind his wife, Imajane, his calculating eyes on the king.

The dying man struggled to sit up. As Prince Hazarin assisted him, the courtiers surged forward.

Aly was unimpressed by Oron's oldest living son. Hazarin was in his mid-forties. At six feet one inch, he towered over every other man in the room, but his commanding height was offset by his bulk. He had a round face and a belly that spilled over the cloth-of-gold raka sarong he wore in defiance of the luarin court's dress code. He combed his hair straight back from his face, which accented his soft, blobby features. A small, spade-shaped beard framed his full, pouting lips.

"His vices are the table and anything that he may smoke, drink, or breathe in," Kyprioth told her. "He has a wife who begs him for a child, but she will get none. His loins are barren from a child's disease, contracted when he was a man. He thinks Rubinyan is the wisest man on earth, except for his taste in wives. He detests his half sister, and she him. He doesn't want to be king."

"Attend, all," croaked the dying Oron as Hazarin supported him in a sitting position. "I hereby name my son Hazarin to be king after me." He glared at Hazarin. "If I were you, I'd get me an heir. I—"

"Excuse me," Kyprioth said abruptly, and vanished. The next moment Aly saw him again, this time inside Oron's body.

"A great monarch comes," Oron said, his voice suddenly full and commanding. "A sunrise of glory for the homeland, harbinger of new power and might in the councils of the Emerald Ocean, when the fields are reaped of the invading plague!"

The god left the king's body and mind as easily as he'd entered. Oron collapsed, gasping for air. The surrounding courtiers all murmured and stepped back, uncertain and afraid. Rubinyan whispered in Imajane's ear as Dunevon started to cry.

"I love deathbed prophecies," Kyprioth confided to Aly.

He'd returned to his spot beside her. "They always put the cat among the pigeons."

"I don't suppose you'd want to confide this grand plan of yours to me," Aly asked playfully. "Come on. I know you want to brag how smart you are." No one in the room seemed to be able to hear her. "Tell, Kyprioth."

The god shook his head. "You probably won't be here for it," he told her. "If you keep the children alive, you'll be on your way home in the fall. Besides, it's dangerous to say some things outright."

Aly sighed. She didn't enjoy being left in the dark.

Kyprioth patted her shoulder. "It's too serious for you anyway," he added.

"You're not letting me have fun," she retorted, pouting.

The healer returned. She shooed the courtiers to their posts by the door, walked around the king's family, and made Oron more comfortable. He grabbed her arm, struggled to tell her something, but failed. Slowly he went limp.

"The king is dead," Rubinyan said as the healer drew the sheet over the dead man's face. He turned to face Hazarin. "Long live the king!" He bowed deeply to the former prince. Imajane curtsied low. The courtiers followed them in salute to Hazarin.

Kyprioth chuckled, rubbing glowing hands together. "The first act ends," he told Aly as he put his arm around her waist. "The next begins."

"Except you won't tell me what it is," Aly said as they soared through the palace roof. "It'll be like leaving before the play's over. Why can't you just tell me how you want it to come out?"

"Because you suffer so prettily, dear," Kyprioth informed her as they leaped into the starry night.

* * *

In the morning Aly took the goats out. She was still feeling cross that she couldn't see where the god's long game might lead him, and the Isles. Rather than visit briefly with Nawat, she nodded to him as she had done the morning before, and bustled past his workbench. For a moment his smile caught and held her attention. She dragged herself away. Every time she looked at the crow-man, her lips remembered the feel of his. And she saw him so often when she was at the castle! It was too distracting. She refused to think about it. At this rate, she would become yet another girl who lingered by his bench when she was free of work. Surely she had more pride than that!

That night, in her report to the Balitangs, she told them of Oron's death and Hazarin's ascension to the throne. She assumed that the god had wanted her to pass the information along.

"That poor old man," Winnamine said. "At least he's out of his misery."

"That poor old man had hundreds murdered, Winna," Dove reminded her softly. "He's out of *our* misery, which is more important."

"But Hazarin!" exclaimed Sarai. "He's a disaster. And he can't have children. If he could, one of his mistresses would have given him some by now, even if his wife's barren."

"She isn't," Aly said. "*He* is. The god told me." She knew that she ought to feel bad about concealing the true identity of the god who really tampered with the Balitangs' lives, but she didn't. Their ignorance was healthier for Aly. She couldn't tell how they might react if they learned that Aly knew their god was not Mithros. She didn't want to find out.

The duke and the duchess now exchanged looks. "It's Dunevon, then, and a regency council, should he succeed Hazarin while still a child," Mequen remarked slowly.

"Or Imajane will get herself appointed regent," Winnamine pointed out. "Should anything happen to the king, of course. Which we pray it will not."

"Should we tell the prince King Oron is dead?" asked Dove, deliberately not looking at Sarai. "With Hazarin on the throne, Bronau is back in royal favor. He'll want to leave for Rajmuat right away." Sarai gave Dove a glare that would have peeled stone.

"Speaking of Bronau, young lady," Mequen said, turning to look at his oldest daughter. Sarai looked up at him. "You are a girl of sense and proper upbringing. This news about the king changes a few things."

"He wants to marry me," Sarai informed her parents airily. "He said so. There were enough eavesdroppers"—she glared at her sister, then at Aly—"to tell you that's the truth."

"But you need to keep things in mind now," said Winnamine. "More than the fact that he's in debt and you are no heiress."

Sarai thrust her chin out, the image of sixteen-year-old stubbornness. "What sorts of things?"

The duchess sighed. "Once Bronau courted me, remember. I learned a few things about him. He is ambitious. What can the Balitangs—disgraced, impoverished, exiled—offer an ambitious man? Seemingly nothing, except that with the king dead, your father is one step closer to the throne. Whoever marries *you* is one step closer. Bronau needs money, but in a pinch, a possible future queen might do, particularly if your father is no longer an obstacle. And he loves both of you."

Sarai shook her head. "He loves me. I *think* he does, anyway."

"Daughter, love is wonderful, but Bronau need not marry for it," the duke said gently. "Countless women at court and in Rajmuat, married and not, will happily give him all the love he requires." Without taking his eyes from Sarai he added, "He has taken the maid Pembery to his bed every night he has been here."

Sarai's eyes blazed. "I hate you!" she cried. She threw down her hoop and fled the room.

"She told me she just liked the kissing," Dove said plaintively. "I thought she was playing at being in love with him, not serious."

"No, but she is proud. It hurts her pride to think he's taken someone else into his bed when he's supposed to be pining for her," said the duchess with a sigh. "We build up pretty pictures of men, when we want to be in love. We hate to have them ruined."

Now Aly could, and did, slip away. If Bronau didn't have ways to get court news in a hurry, she would eat her pallet. He would leave them soon, which could only be to the good.

Three days later a dust-covered messenger with a guard of royal guardsmen arrived from Dimari. Word had reached the island's governor through a network of mages who communicated through scrying glasses, mirrors, and other devices. They served the Crown throughout the Isles, passing information far more quickly than normal methods carried it. The governor's message threw life at Tanair into a bustle, as everyone learned what, until now, only the Balitangs, Aly, and the raka conspirators knew. Oron was dead. Hazarin would be crowned soon, and he wanted his friend Bronau at his side. By nightfall that day the prince was ready to set out the next morning at dawn.

Hasui poured the wine while Aly waited in the shadows under the main stair. She watched Sarai as the girl picked at her food. Just as Aly had expected, Sarai left halfway through supper, making excuses to her parents and Bronau as she fled the hall. Aly moved to wait by the door that led from the servants' stair to the ladies' garden.

As the household left the main hall after the meal, Sarai, cloaked and wearing a maid's head scarf, emerged from the keep. Without a sound Aly followed her to the garden.

Bronau was already seated on the lip of the fountain, the picture of male dejection: head down, hands clasped loosely between his knees. He jumped to his feet when he saw Sarai, and crossed the ground between them in four broad strides, sweeping her up in his arms and kissing her fiercely. Sarai hesitated, then her arms went around Bronau's neck. She kissed him with the same passion he gave her.

Aly eased into a wall niche to watch. This was better than any drama that Players acted out for an audience. And this *was* a drama. Sarai played the desperate maiden, yearning for her forbidden lover. Bronau was the older, jaded man who had found his heart's desire when he ceased to look for it. By now Aly was certain that the indignation Sarai had shown her parents over their assessment of Bronau's motives came more from Sarai's belief that they thought her a child than from a broken heart.

At last the man and girl separated, though they held onto one another's hands. "I swear to you, this is temporary," Bronau said, his gray eyes intent on Sarai. "I don't know if I can bear a separation, but this is our grand chance. Hazarin is my friend. He'll recall your family from this desolation, and he'll speak for me to Mequen. Then I can court you in the proper manner, not in this hide-in-the-corner way."

"Speak to Papa now," Sarai pleaded.

Bronau shook his head. "When I have only my name and little more? Mequen would be a fool to let me have you when there are wealthier men who can offer you proper estates and all that your loveliness deserves. But if Hazarin grants me the things he has always claimed will be mine when he comes to the throne, then I won't be a second son; I'll be a wealthy man in my own right. I will dress you in pearls, then, and little else." He embraced her again.

This time when they stopped to breathe, Sarai told Bronau, "You'll find some other woman at court, I know it. One who's sophisticated, and rich. You'll forget all about an ignorant girl like me."

"You are wrong. I will not ask for your promise now, but you will see I mean what I say," Bronau told her. "Give me some token of yours, to keep near my heart."

Aly twiddled her thumbs. She tried to remember the passionate speeches that had been addressed to her. Had they been this nonsensical? Would she have swallowed them?

Perhaps when I was twelve, she thought, then grinned. Being the daughter of the Lioness and of a spymaster, she hadn't been romantic even then, well before she'd had extensive dealings with the people who made up her father's world. For a moment she saw Nawat's face in her mind's eye. He would never say such things to her, or to any girl!

She banished Nawat's face from her thoughts and watched the lovers. Bronau was tucking the citrine drop Sarai wore as a pendant into his belt pouch. There were more kisses, more avowals of undying passion. When they heard the duke in the distance, calling Bronau, Sarai fled through the rear entrance to the garden. Aly kept to the base of the keep wall as she followed the girl.

Sarai waited for her on the keep's front steps. She sat there, head propped on her hands, staring at the activity around the barracks and the torches that lit the darkness. Aly sat beside her without a word.

"I wouldn't have done it if I hadn't known you'd be there," Sarai remarked without looking at Aly. Her lips were swollen with Bronau's kisses. "Knowing you're watching helps me to keep my head. Otherwise I might well end up on the grass with my skirts around my waist, like those maids he tumbles."

"He seems very passionate," Aly said idly, running her fingers through her cap of hair.

Sarai sighed. "He kisses so much better than the boys in Rajmuat."

"*Do* you want to marry him?" Aly wanted to know.

"I'm not sure." Sarai frowned. "I daydream about it, but it is just a dream. Papa and Winnamine aren't sure of him. That has to weigh with me."

"They're his friends. They ought to know," Aly pointed out.

"Well, he's leaving tomorrow. I won't have to worry about it for a while," Sarai remarked, and sighed. "Maybe I'll see if that handsome Nawat has decided to be interested in me yet. He's only a commoner, and an odd one at that, but it might be fun, teaching him how to kiss."

Aly scowled as the other girl stood and went inside. She wasn't sure that Sarai ought to practice kissing on someone who might not realize it was just a form of amusement. Worse, what if Nawat fell in love with Sarai? Aly knew that Sarai was very much aware of her position as a noble. She would flirt and have fun, but when her father reminded her of her duty to her family, Sarai would do it. She would marry for the betterment of her family.

Aly decided Nawat had to be warned. She told herself that she didn't want that innocent heart of his broken by a noble beauty trying her wings. Aly refused to admit that she had any personal reason to warn him. It occurred to her, briefly, that she had been much like Sarai back at home, flirting with boys and men just because she was bored and liked kisses. The thought was not a comfortable one.

No one expects a woman busy at her sewing to pay attention to what's being said around her. Never mind if a man's mother and sisters showed them they heard everything while they stitched, he'll still think a woman who plies her needle saves all her brains for the work. You're a far better spy hemming sheets than if you clank with daggers.

—From a letter to Aly from her father, when she was fourteen

12

THE MAGE OF POHON

Aly rose at her usual hour the next day, but instead of immediately leaving with her goats, she waited. When Bronau's party rode out she collected her herd and followed. She had resigned herself to the fact that the men were likely taking secret communications with them. These were not merchants, who could be frightened by hooded warriors. Aly didn't worry about any report Veron might smuggle out with Bronau's company. With a new king on the throne, the royal agents throughout the Isles would await instructions from their masters before they made any reports that might offend the new government.

Aly tracked the prince and his group to the road out of Tanair, watching them until even their dust was gone. She silently wished them a dangerous voyage and death at sea, then took her goats on to graze. When Aly and the goats reached Ekit and Visda, she found that Nawat, Ulasim, and Junai waited there along with the shepherds. Ulasim was already riding a horse, while Junai held the reins for three mounts, including the mare Cinnamon.

"Did you sigh over the last of his horse's droppings?" Ulasim wanted to know, smirking. "You watched him go for long enough."

"Aly doesn't like him," Nawat pointed out. "Aly thinks he will come back and try to eat the nestlings."

Aly grinned at the crow-man and looked at the two raka. "So lovely of you to pay a call," she told them. "I wish you'd sent your messenger ahead, so I might have prepared refreshments."

"You will have your jokes," replied Ulasim. He looked like a bronze raka idol in the saddle. "Mount up. We go to Pohon. My mother has agreed to meet us—that is, you. It's going to be a long morning."

Junai revealed the thinnest scrap of a smile, the first sign of any emotion Aly had ever seen on her face. "You have no idea how long," she said.

Aly raised an eyebrow at her bodyguard. "Your grandmother's that charming, is she?"

"Come see for yourself," Ulasim said. He looked at Nawat, who was idly picking insects from a tree's bark and eating them. "Your presence will not help. I told you so back at Tanair."

Nawat bird-shrugged. "Mages do not worry me."

Aly clumsily mounted Cinnamon.

"There is no need to keep doing that," Ulasim told her wearily. "Lokeij says you can ride well."

"Then keep that to yourselves," Aly retorted. "It suits me that our associates not be aware of all my skills." To Nawat she said, "You were scarred by a mage once. Shouldn't that make you wary?"

He cracked a beetle between his teeth. "It was the Pohon mage who did it," he said. "She makes funny noises when her sheets are in the mud." He looked up at Aly. "The red ants are spicy. Would you like one?" He offered her an ant with his normal cheerful smile, but the look in his eyes was that of the human male she'd seen the night he had kissed her.

Horrified, Aly realized she was blushing. She *never* blushed. "I thank you, no," she replied, turning Cinnamon. To the two raka she said, "Let's go, then. Visda, Ekit, I'm sorry, but the goats—"

"We are ready," Visda said with a grin. "Have fun with the mage."

Aly followed Ulasim and Junai to the road. "This mage," she asked the raka, "she's decided she will join you?"

Ulasim snorted. Today he dressed as a raka in a home-spun wraparound jacket, embroidered in dark colors, and a highland raka's leggings. His long hair was tied back in a horsetail. "She has only said she will talk to you, and I wouldn't put it beyond her to change her mind. Do you know how annoying it is that you can do that?" he asked Nawat, who trotted along next to them, his bare feet scarcely making a sound on the dirt road.

"I am running." Nawat's voice was as relaxed as if he sat on his workbench, fletching arrows. "It is not as good as flying, but it is exercise."

"Yes, but—does he bother you?" Aly asked the two raka. To Nawat she explained, "I don't want to make any raka uncomfortable, you see, and maybe you would."

"We are cousins," said both Nawat and Junai. They halted and stared at one another. Both looked startled and pleased.

Finally Junai said, "Everyone knows what he was. And crows and raka are both the children of the crow god and goddess. Our legend says the first humans were hatched out of the great crow nest. We made a mistake in the egg and shed our feathers."

"Then there have been other crows who turned into people?" asked Aly. She couldn't help but think that *someone* could have mentioned that earlier.

"Rarely," said Ulasim. "But there are tales, just as there are tales of those raka who turned to crows rather than die. Do we stand here all day, or do we get on with things?" He sent his horse down the road. Aly and Junai followed, Nawat trotting along between the two women.

"Am I no longer the goatherd?" Aly wanted to know.

"Her Grace says you need to be able to move," replied Ulasim. "Our ladies wish to ride far and meet their people. Her Grace wishes to spend more time at the castle, minding the younger children and preparing the household for winter. You are to bear Saraiyu and Dovasary company, with their bodyguards, and Junai."

Aly nodded. That would work. As always, she was grateful to the duchess for seeing what was necessary. "Now, this mage is your mother?" she asked. "Junai's grandmother Ochobu?"

"She hates luarin," replied Junai as her father's face went stony. "She has agreed to talk, not to help. That will be a matter for your persuasion, unless you intend to have the god command her."

"If I were you, I would call on the god," Ulasim informed Aly dryly. "She is sworn to him. She must obey. You? We will be lucky if she does not scorch you. But you insisted on seeing her, and she is a powerful mage, powerful enough to guard this entire plateau."

Aly drew herself up in the saddle, miffed. She was the daughter of George Cooper and the Lioness, after all. It was a pretty sad thing if she had to depend on a god to step in whenever a little diplomacy would do the trick. "Have we brought presents for her? Sometimes a properly offered gift appeases even the most stubborn people."

"It would not appease her," Ulasim replied, grim-faced. "She is a cross-grained, bitter, cruel old hermit."

"She says the sweetest things of you, too," said Junai. "*I* think you are both too proud to apologize, Father." To Aly she said, "He's right about a gift, though. Grandmother would only make it explode in your hands."

"Here," said Nawat, reaching a hand to Aly. "She might like this." He passed her something hard.

Aly looked at the thing he'd given her. It was a rock, some kind of granite, bright and sparkling in the sun. "Nawat," she asked wearily, "why have you given me a stone?"

"It is sparkly," Nawat informed her gravely. "Females like sparkly things, just as crows do."

Junai made a noise that sounded very like a snort to Aly.

Aly sighed. She ought to have known that his reason didn't make sense to her in the least. "Not human females, Nawat."

"That's not exactly true," Ulasim told her in a choked voice that sounded as if he was trying not to laugh. "Rubies, emeralds, diamonds, all of those things sparkle, and human females love gems."

Aly shot the footman a look that said, *Don't confuse him!* She tucked the rock into her belt purse. "I'll explain later," she told Nawat, who watched her with worried eyes. "Thank you for trying to help me."

When they rode around the walls that encircled Pohon, Aly relaxed. She was not sure the villagers had forgotten her last visit. Instead Ulasim and Junai led her and Nawat deeper into the forest, following a narrow road. They passed into the lands behind the village, riding under tall, ancient trees alive with birds and squirrels. It was a perfect summer day, not too hot even on the open road, with gentle breezes carrying the scents of pine and leaves to Aly's nose.

At last they reached the top of a ridge that looked down into a small, cuplike hollow. At its bottom was a rough log house, hung about with charms, signs, and wind chimes. A creek raced past it, shaped with stone by human hands to form a deep pool before it reentered the trees. A line of drying clothes hung in the sunshine behind the house, a homely touch for a mage's domain. A pair of cats lounged in front of the door, watching them with eyes turned amber by the sun.

Nawat grinned. "It's washing day," he observed.

Aly frowned at him. "Leave the wash alone. You're not a crow anymore."

"No," he replied. "I am a mateless human." He sighed, trying to look forlorn.

"Stop that," Aly warned. She kneed Cinnamon down the path toward the cottage. Halting in front, she and her companions dismounted.

A tiny creature flew over to sniff Aly. She sighed in wonder. It was a miniature flying horse, a bay mare, bat-winged and perfect, its body no larger than her hand. "Where did you come from?" she asked softly.

"They nest here," replied Ulasim as other winged horses flapped around them. A piebald stallion glided over to Nawat. "The old woman puts up with any nonsense if it doesn't come from a human being," the raka continued bitterly. "Sometimes I think—"

He was interrupted by the piebald stallion. The tiny creature reared and neighed, pawing the air in fury.

"Maybe he remembers me," Nawat remarked. The stallion flew at him, hitting him in the face with his wings. "Stop it! My mother had nestlings of her own to feed!"

"You took one of their nestlings?" asked Aly, horrified.

"Several," replied Nawat, trying to shield his face. Two more winged horses flew in to attack him. "They make a very—ouch!—good meal for hungry young!"

"Why did you come if you made an enemy of the little kudarung?" Ulasim wanted to know. He and Junai backed off, leading their mounts away from the small winged creatures. "Is there *anyone* hereabouts who likes you?"

Nawat yelped as four more winged horses swooped at him from a clump of bushes, where they seemed to gather. Aly giggled as they dove at him, kicking, biting, pulling his hair and clothes, smacking him with their wings. "I thought they wouldn't remember!" he cried in answer to Ulasim. "It's been weeks, and I was a crow!"

Aly dismounted and handed her reins to Junai, then ran laughing to Nawat's rescue. "Stop that," she ordered as more of the small winged horses swarmed out of the brush. "He isn't a crow anymore." She gently tried to bat them away from Nawat. "How did you even recognize him? He's not here to take nestlings." She grabbed the piebald stallion as he tried to nip at Nawat's face. "He's quite a reformed—ow!" The tiny stallion twisted in her grip and fastened his teeth in one of her fingers, drawing blood. Aly dropped him. The stallion flew at her face. Aly squeaked and ducked.

More of the winged horses appeared in answer to their fellows' enraged calls. Half of them descended on Aly, the rest on Nawat.

"I think they believe you are a crow, too," Junai called as the still-amused Aly protected her head with her hands. The creatures bit her hands and gouged her head with hooves and teeth, battering her with their wings.

"Will you *help* us instead of gawping?" demanded Aly,

trying not to laugh. She didn't want to hurt the tiny immortals, but their assaults were painful, and she had business here. She could hardly impress Ochobu Dodeka if she was too busy fighting off winged pests with long memories.

"But it's the most amusing thing I've seen all year," Ulasim replied in a strangled voice. Speaking appeared to destroy his control; he collapsed in laughter. Junai simply watched, a tiny smile on her usually still face.

Aly flapped her open hands, trying to push the small kudarung away. Nawat covered his head with his arms. "They're clever, aren't they?" he asked Aly, wincing. "To know I'm a crow even in this shape."

"I don't care how clever they are," Aly replied. She yelped as a kudarung bit the rim of her ear. Grabbing the animal, she tried to tug it free, but it refused to let go. Not wanting to hurt it or tear her ear, she had one course of action left to her. She ran for the stream, and dove into the part that had been shaped to form a deep pool.

The water, coming from the mountains, was bone-achingly cold even on this summer day. She lunged to the surface and gasped, her teeth chattering. Water sprayed all over her as Nawat jumped in, shedding kudarung as they saw where he was bound.

Aly swam to the edge of the pool. She was about to climb out onto the land when a small flock of kudarung attacked, driving her underwater. She found Nawat there, forced under the surface as she had been to escape their tormentors. They shot up for a deep breath of air before the immortals descended. On her next trip for air, Aly looked around quickly. There, on the bank near the shallow upper stream, she saw a likely weapon. She ducked underwater and swam toward it, her head aching from the chill and the kudarungs' assault. When she came up again, the large branch was a yard away. She lunged and seized it, wading into the shallow water above the pool. There she stood, batting her persecutors away with the branch.

Nawat joined her, to huddle at her side. "They are not very forgiving," he observed.

Aly lifted a foot and shoved him back into the pool.

Above the shrill, furious calls of the kudarung she heard laughter as harsh as any crow's bawl. She turned to find its source and saw an old woman barely five feet tall. The newcomer was dressed like the highland raka women in a bright wraparound jacket and long skirt, both thickly embroidered. The fire of a magical Gift shone from beneath her skin in Aly's Sight. The old woman had a long nose, eyes like upside-down crescents framed by wrinkled flesh, and a mouth as straight as Junai's. White locks combed to either side sprang from her hairline at the center of her forehead. The rest of her short, curling hair was the color of steel shot with threads of black and white. Her laughter had a jeering quality.

"Ochobu Dodeka, is this how you treat your guests?" Aly demanded, swinging her branch at the kudarung. "We're here to talk to you. Call these things off before I hurt one!"

"I don't want to talk to *you*," the old woman replied with a grin that showed teeth. "And they aren't pets, to come and go at my command." She looked at Junai and Ulasim. "*This* is the god's messenger?" she demanded, her black eyes snapping with scorn. "If you're listening to this luarin sisat, you haven't a prayer of success. I won't go with you to die!"

Aly sighed. It was time to work. She handed the branch to Nawat, who was climbing out of the pool. When he took it, Aly went to Ochobu. The kudarung who had concentrated on swarming Aly turned to continue their attack on Nawat.

"Am I mistaken?" Aly inquired mildly, leaning her head

to clear water from one ear. "You're refusing to help us."

"If they are helped by such as you, they are beyond hope," retorted the old raka. "They would do better to take the road as roaming Players, amusing the luarin nobility."

Aly leaned her head to the other side to clear the water from that ear. In her politest tone she inquired, "So you must approve the work roster, before you will deign to help? Must the ones who risk their lives among the luarin every day bring each and every tool they choose for your inspection first?"

Ochobu scowled at Aly. "No one asked you."

Aly dug in her ear with a finger. "Your *god* asked me, Ochobu Dodeka," she replied, still polite, knowing that the old woman expected her to show rage. "And do you know what? It will be for nothing," she informed the raka with her friendliest smile. "Because as long as you and others like you find only obstacles, you can put off actually having to *do* something. You can just talk about it and dream of someday. We'll all die of old age. You raka will still have the luarin boot on your necks. After a while, *raka* won't mean 'people' any-more—it will just mean 'slave.'"

"I could blast you where you stand," Ochobu whispered, her eyes deadly.

Aly wrung out her tunic's hem. "Go on," she said cheerily. "Do your worst. Of course, the god might object." She gave Ochobu a moment to think and then another moment to act. When it was clear the raka mage was not going to kill her, Aly called, "Nawat, stop playing with the little horsies. We're going back to Tanair."

"I would gladly stop playing with them," Nawat called, swinging his branch around him to keep the kudarung at bay. "They are the ones who will not stop."

Ochobu looked over Aly's shoulder, pushing her lips in and out, as if she were thinking. Aly concentrated on wring-

ing out as much of her tunic as she could reach. Finally
Ochobu bared her teeth and whistled sharply. A handful of
kudarung flew away from the swarm. The old woman whistled twice more before the rest broke off their assault and returned to their clump of brush.

Ochobu looked at Ulasim and Junai. "Did the pesky
crow have to come?" she demanded.

Aly smiled graciously. "I like the crow."

The old woman looked at Aly, then at Nawat. "Stay
away from my drying lines," she warned.

Nawat treated her to his beaming smile. "I am a man
now. Men do not drag cloth in the mud."

The mage snorted, then looked Aly over. "Were you any
other god's messenger, I wouldn't believe you," she said drily
as Ulasim and Junai led the horses across the creek. "But our
god *would* pick a luarin."

"You choose tools for a task by their crafting, not their
look," a crow said crisply from a nearby tree. He flapped over
to land on a barrel in front of the cottage. "A smith's finest
hammer will be streaked with soot." Like the Kyprioth-crow
of Aly's first Isles dream, he wore gem-studded rings on his
talons and a gaudy jeweled necklace around his throat. He
shone in Aly's Sight.

"So you really chose this wench," Ochobu said.

Kyprioth ruffled his feathers. "Stop trying to quarrel
with me, or I will leave you to the Rajmuat luarin. Do you
think Oron was bad? He will be as nothing compared to
Hazarin, Imajane, Rubinyan, and Bronau, believe me. If
we're to change things, it must be now. The Chain's time has
come."

Aly frowned. "What's the Chain?" she asked.

Kyprioth turned a ring on one claw with his beak. It was
Ulasim who answered. "My mother and her friends," he said,

meeting the old woman's eyes with defiance. "A network of raka mages, spread throughout the Isles, waiting to take back what was theirs."

"You said it might not be so," Ochobu remarked wearily to Kyprioth. "You said we might fail."

"Every human effort has that chance," replied Kyprioth. "We gods can't change that. Besides, it would be very bad for your characters if you had things easy all the time."

"I told my children that. They didn't believe me any more than I believe you." Ochobu walked over to a bench next to her door and sat between the cats. "We wouldn't be in this state if you had turned the invaders away three hundred years back."

Kyprioth leaped off the barrel in crow form and landed on the ground as a man, in his human jewelry, jacket, and sarong. He stood before Ochobu, sparks in his dark eyes. Aly took a step back, feeling his presence as a pressure on her body and mind, like a heatless sun. Ulasim and Junai shaded their eyes as they looked on. Only Nawat seemed unconcerned. He squatted on the ground, dripping, as he ate selections from a column of ants.

"You do not think gods may be routed from their thrones, and thrust into the outer parts of the Divine Realms?" Kyprioth asked Ochobu softly. "You do not believe a god may be so battered in combat with his land-hungry brother and sister that he might need centuries to heal? Do not speak of what I should have done, Ochobu Dodeka. You were not at my side on that battlefield."

Aly wished she could go anywhere else. This was too personal for her. For the first time she felt like a true intruder in the Copper Isles. *This* was the reason he toyed with her and the Balitangs, this ancient loss. Kyprioth's playfulness had made the stakes seem small, as if he had meddled with her life for his own amusement. Now she had the truth of it, that the tide was turning in the Copper Isles. She was a pawn, the Balitang children just one more piece, on a board that stretched over miles and years.

Ochobu slid down to kneel before Kyprioth, tears streaming down her face. She had borne even more of the god's power than had Aly, Ulasim, or Junai.

Aly rested a hand on the old woman's shoulder. "Maybe she snaps at you because she's afraid," she told Kyprioth, though she didn't quite dare to look into his face. "You gods know you have centuries to turn the tables. We humans don't. We have short lives that can be made shorter with the stroke of a sword."

Burning fingers gripped her chin, forcing her to look up. Aly jerked away from the painful touch. When Kyprioth grabbed her chin a second time, it didn't hurt. Her knees quivered as she met his bottomless gaze, but somehow she managed to remain on her feet.

"Dear heart, you are wasted in Tortall," Kyprioth told her softly, his eyes showing her suns and waves that swamped islands, volcanoes, and shivering cracks in the earth. "One of us would have put a fire like yours to use sooner or later." He let Aly go and regarded Ochobu. "Old woman, let's have a cup of tea, for old times' sake."

Aly helped Ochobu to stand, but she didn't go with Kyprioth and Ulasim when they followed the woman inside. She stayed in the sun, drying out with Nawat as Junai unsaddled and groomed the horses. It took a while for her head to stop spinning from that long look into the god's eyes.

A flicker of light at the cottage's open doorway told Aly that the god had left. Ulasim and his mother remained inside for a while longer, talking. Junai and Aly practiced their combat exercises and Nawat tried to catch fish barehanded in the stream. At last Ulasim left the cottage, saddlebags hung over one shoulder. He and Junai got to work saddling their horses and the swaybacked mare that ambled out of the shelter of the trees when Ulasim left the house. Ochobu finally emerged, carrying a pack. She thrust it into Aly's hands, then walked over to the clump of brush where the tiny kudarung nested.

"Nawat, put that down," Aly told her friend, who had secured a wriggling fish. "We're leaving."

"But I just caught it," Nawat complained. "I knew I could."

"You still know you can. Let the poor fish go," Aly retorted. "With all the bugs you've eaten today, you can't possibly be hungry."

She heard a sound and turned, frowning, to see what was the matter with Junai. Her usually stoic bodyguard was actually trying not to giggle.

"If you only knew how *strange* that sounds," Ulasim remarked. "You sound like her mother." He nodded at the red-faced Junai.

Nawat sighed and released his captive back into the stream.

Aly shook her head and strapped Ochobu's pack to the back of Cinnamon's saddle. "Well, he *has* been eating a lot of bugs," she said, knowing that didn't explain anything.

Ochobu returned and mounted the swaybacked mare. Three adult kudarung flew in her wake, all of them pitch black with white stars on their muzzles. "They make good messengers for short distances," Ochobu told Aly. "And if you or the crow bothers them, you can carry your own messages."

Aly rubbed her sore ear and winced. She had bumped the deepest bite. Holding her much-smeared handkerchief to the wound, she said, "I never bothered them in the first place."

"I will not bother them if Aly says not to," added Nawat. To her he whispered, "Not until we have enough nestlings of our own to mob them back."

"We're not *going* to—" Aly began in a heated whisper, trying to deny that they would mate and have nestlings, but realized it was useless. This was just one of those ideas Nawat would have to outgrow, since words didn't seem to change his mind on the subject.

"Let's go," Ulasim ordered. "There is work to be done at home."

They rode together out of the hollow and back down the road. When they reached the fork that led to Pohon, Ochobu reined up. "Junai, ride in and let Pilia know I am gone," she ordered. "Ask her if she will keep an eye on things and feed my animals."

"I cannot," Junai replied. She pointed to Aly. "She is my charge."

The old woman glared at her granddaughter. "You think I cannot protect your luarin pry-monkey?"

"Sorry, Grandmother," Junai said quickly. She kicked her gelding into a trot and headed for Pohon.

Aly watched in awe, then turned to Ochobu. "Will you teach me how to do that?" she asked. "She never listens to me."

"I will not," said Ochobu, following Ulasim down the road. "Converse with me only when you must, luarin. I may have to treat with you, but we will not be friends."

Aly shrugged and let mother and son ride far enough ahead for them not to suspect she was eavesdropping. Ochobu might never like her, that was plain. So long as they could work together until the equinox, Aly didn't care if

Ochobu liked her or not. The old woman had every reason to hate white skins, after all. At least I don't have to share a small castle with her over the winter, she thought happily. She watched as Nawat ran into the woods a little way to examine something that had caught his eye. He would return when he felt the need.

It occurred to Aly that in her eagerness to get *any* kind of true mage to Tanair she had never asked anyone what kind of power Ochobu had. Obviously the old woman was strong, to stop bandits from preying on the villages of the plateau, and protective magic was certainly the most important thing for the Balitangs to have. Still, Aly could put Ochobu to better use if she knew the mage's strengths.

Aly let her mind drift, absorbing forest sounds: songbirds, rustling creatures, squirrel disputes, Nawat's steps among tree litter. In the distance a crow family discussed the location of a dead animal supper. An eagle's distant shriek reached her ears, and the whisper of wind in the pines. She closed her eyes, adjusted her mind to bring into play the more complex aspects of her magical Sight, then opened them.

Ochobu's Gift had been visible from the moment Aly first saw her. Gifts always appeared in her vision as a series of ripples in the air around the mage, as if he or she gave off heat. Now Aly's deeper Sight discovered more specific powers that appeared as images that glowed then faded over the round curve of Ochobu's back. She saw a mortar and pestle, a handful of plants, a storm racing over the open fields of the plateau, a charm that turned away harmful magics, a bowl of water for scrying.

"Stop that," Ochobu called over her shoulder, startling Aly out of her calm state. "It tickles."

When they got back to Tanair, Aly had a quick talk with the duchess about the morning's events. "So you're saying we have a mage now," Winnamine said when Aly was done. "And we need to make her part of the household, without raising a fuss."

Aly bowed. "Exactly, my lady."

Winnamine stared into the distance for a moment, her lips moving as she thought. At last she looked at Aly. "Rihani's never been comfortable as our sole healer. She is a wonderful herbwife, but has little experience with serious ailments. I think she'll be relieved if this Ochobu takes over, and she can be of use in making medicines. I also know my woman, Pembery, is less than delighted with looking after Elsren and Petranne during the day. Rihani may take her place, and Pembery shall wait on Sarai and me. And you, my dear, are being promoted again. It is time Dove had her own maid."

Aly grinned. "I serve at Your Grace's command," she replied, thinking that the duchess would have made a fine general, with her delicate way of rearranging her troops. From what Aly knew of the household, everyone whose job had just changed would like the new arrangement. The change for Aly herself meant that she was now free to ride anywhere that Dove might choose to go.

Once the duchess met Ochobu and explained things to Rihani and Pembery, Rihani took Ochobu to the keep's infirmary. Aly helped the footmen to move the duke's and duchess's things back to their old rooms, now that Bronau was gone. After the adult Balitangs were resettled and the older girls' rooms restored for their use, Sarai took charge of Aly's wardrobe. Dove ordered a hot bath for her new maid. "Because you should look nice, and not shed goat hair on my things," she said primly, her eyes dancing with mischief.

Aly stuck her tongue out at her young mistress and happily climbed into the tub. The main thing she had missed about home, after her family, was the luxury of a real bath. After weeks of washing in ponds or from a basin full of water, a hot bath was bliss.

Aly soaked until the water began to cool. She washed her scant inches of red-gold hair twice, scrubbed until she was crimson with cleanliness, then dried herself with a proper cloth. She noticed that she had put on some weight with the Balitangs, but the meals of leftovers, bread, and cheese had still not brought her to the weight she had at home.

"Try these," Sarai ordered, opening the dressing room door and tossing in gowns and shifts. "Can you sew?"

"I can sew," she told Sarai, thinking, Da made sure of *that*. "Of course, I require the usual tools for it."

"Use my box," Sarai offered. "Dove replaced her sewing things with ink and pens and paper. You'll need to take these clothes in—you're too big for Dove's hand-me-downs, and too bony for mine." She grinned at Aly and closed the door.

Aly spent the rest of the afternoon stitching Sarai's castoffs to fit her thinner frame. Once she had a complete outfit—a cotton shift and an amber-colored gown—she dressed and hurried downstairs in time to pour the supper wine. Afterward she joined the family in the duke and duchess's chambers, Sarai's sewing box balanced on her hip. There she sat and sewed, a perfectly natural evening's occupation for a lady's maid. Once Rihani took Elsren and Petranne up to bed, the family shifted in their seats to look at Aly.

"I thought you objected to promotion," remarked the duke. "You told us that people would notice a servant being somewhere that she shouldn't."

"I've kept my goatherd's things just in case," Aly said. "For now, acting as Lady Dove's maid will take me to the places I need to go as long as I continue to wear my collar."

There was a rap on the door. Without waiting, Ochobu came in and closed the door behind her, sealing it with a line of magical fire visible only to Aly. "To foil eavesdroppers," the old woman explained gruffly. She nodded abruptly to the Balitangs, then took a seat uninvited.

Aly sighed internally at the old woman's pride, then told the duke, "Your Grace, this is Ochobu Dodeka of Pohon village. She is the mother of Ulasim, and a true mage. Ochobu, I present His Grace Duke Mequen Balitang." Aly glared at the old woman until she bowed to the duke from her seat. "Her Grace has already made Ochobu's acquaintance," Aly continued. "Ochobu, may I also present Lady Saraiyu, and Lady Dovasary."

The old woman looked the girls over with sharp eyes. Then she bowed, but to that she added the raka gesture of respect, her arms crossed over her breasts, palms on the opposite shoulders. The girls, startled, responded with the same gesture.

To the duke Aly said, "Ochobu is sent by the god to help to protect you." She crossed her fingers behind her back, praying that no one here would mention which god was involved. She had forgotten to tell Ochobu that the Balitangs believed it was Mithros who had taken an interest in their fate.

"When Aly said she'd found a true healer and herbwife, I nearly collapsed with relief," the duchess told the duke with a smile. "Rihani is good with herbs and lesser ailments, but I've been living in fear that someone would break a leg or some great sickness would reach us. We would be in real trouble." To Ochobu she said, "You are thrice welcome among us."

"I could do no less, lady," Ochobu replied stiffly. "I served the family of the first duchess, and it is my honor to serve her daughters."

"I would like to learn from you, if it's agreeable," Winnamine said. "Unless you prefer not to have someone underfoot? I know many healers don't. Rihani will assist you, of course, but I think the more I can learn, the more useful I will be."

Aly couldn't decipher the look that Ochobu gave Winnamine. Finally the old woman said, "Most luarin do not ask. They order."

"We are not of that sort," Mequen replied, his deep voice quiet. "In this house the raka are respected, as my first wife was respected. Winnamine was also Sarugani's friend."

"We can gather herbs when we go out riding, like we did for Rihani," Sarai told Ochobu. "If we know what to look for, we will."

"Riding?" asked the duke, raising his brows. "Are you not needed here? Lessons, getting our house in order for winter . . . ?"

"We have summer chores well covered," said the duchess. "The girls feel they didn't really get to know the local people on their rides with Bronau. Everything was formal, and country matters bore him. I'd like to stay home with the little ones. I feel I've been neglecting them." When Mequen still frowned, the duchess touched his arm. "My dear, the girls will have plenty of time for lessons once winter starts. The villagers say we may be confined to the castle for days at a time. Let them ride now, while they can."

Mequen took Winnamine's hand within his. "Very well." He looked at the girls. "Behave and obey your guards, or you will be confined to the castle grounds until spring, do you understand? We are not in Rajmuat any longer. Trouble can find us here easily."

"Yes, Papa," said Dove meekly.

"Yes, Papa," echoed Sarai.

Aly glanced at Ochobu. The old mage watched the duke, her eyes and face unreadable. Still, thought Aly, she isn't cursing or spitting on the floor because he and the duchess are luarin. It's a start.

In a time of fear, the One Who Is Promised will come to the raka, bearing glory in her train and justice in her hand. She will restore the god to his proper temple and his children to her right hand. She will be twice royal, wise and beloved, a living emblem of truth to her people. She will be attended by a wise one, the cunning one, the strong one, the warrior, and the crows. She will give a home to all, and the kudarung will fly in her honor.

—*From the Kyprish Prophecy,*
written in the year 200 H.E.,
discovered in Duke Mequen's books by Aly

13

LADIES OF THE RAKA

The next morning, after Pembery and Aly helped them to dress and make up their room, Sarai and Dove took Aly to breakfast, then to the stable. They passed Nawat, seated in the sun as was his habit, carefully gluing feathers to shafts. Aly stopped for a moment, fascinated with Nawat's fine touch as he set the fletchings in glue. Sarai returned and dragged her away.

Lokeij's stable boys had already saddled Sarai's gelding, Dove's mare, and Aly's mare Cinnamon. Fesgao, two of the other men-at-arms, and Junai were already mounted, waiting for them. Aly clambered as awkwardly as she could into the saddle and made a small business of wriggling to settle herself. Their party rode through Tanair at a walk. Many of the people who were out wanted to greet the two Balitang girls personally. Aly was careful to sit her mount like a sack of flour, keeping up the pretense that she rode badly.

Once they were clear of Tanair's gate, Sarai cried, "Let's go!" and kicked her gelding into a gallop. Fesgao and one of the men-at-arms followed her, catching up before she was too far ahead. Dove did not even twitch her mare's rein for a faster gait. Aly, Junai, and the other man-at-arms stayed with her.

"I thought she just did that to show off for Bronau," Aly commented.

"No," Dove told her, and sighed heavily. "Every summer, when we go to our mountain estates on Tongkang, she gallops everywhere. She loves to ride. I think she'd do anything in the saddle if she could, including sleep."

"That talent could be useful," Aly pointed out.

"Wait till your behind starts to hurt, *then* tell me if it's useful," advised the younger girl. "I really admire Winna. All those rides with Bronau, and never once did she let on she's got saddle sores."

"She wants Sarai to like her *that* much?" Aly was surprised. She knew that the duchess wanted her stepdaughters' affection, but she hadn't guessed how far the lady might go for it.

"Well, a little," Dove admitted. "They get on well enough anymore. Mostly Winna came for Bronau." She frowned, her small dark face intent on her thoughts. "Winna likes him well enough. I mean, you could tell, she laughed at his jokes, and they talked all the time, but—Aly, she doesn't trust him. I don't think she even knows how little she trusts him. She never let them escape their bodyguards on our rides."

"Interesting," Aly said thoughtfully, sharpening her magical Sight so that she could keep an eye on Sarai and her escorts, still galloping down the road. "She doesn't think he'd dishonor Sarai, does she?"

"I don't know," Dove replied. "What I know is that Winna understands the prince as well as anybody, even better than Papa. Her not trusting him to behave honorably, that worries me. Doesn't it worry you? Because I don't think we've seen the last of His Highness, not at all."

Aly looked at the twelve-year-old. "You're very observant," she remarked.

"And cold," Dove said, her mouth pulled down in distaste. "You didn't say cold. Everyone does."

"But you're not cold," Aly replied. "You've learned to hide yourself. To hide in plain sight."

"Like you," Dove pointed out.

Aly grinned. "You have to admit, it's very useful."

Dove chuckled. When she did, her face lit with a powerful light. "Do you play chess?"

"A little," replied Aly, who could almost beat her grandfather, one of the finest players in Tortall.

"Good," Dove said cheerfully. "It's getting harder to lose so Papa doesn't realize what I'm doing. I can tell him I'm teaching you."

After their return to the castle, Aly laid out clean clothes for Dove, then went in search of their new mage. She found Ochobu in the rooms set aside for the healer and any patients at the back of the kitchen wing. The old woman was hanging up bunches of dry herbs next to those Rihani had already prepared. Shelves along one side of the infirmary, once empty but for Rihani's collection of salves, liquids, and tools, now bore a collection of medical and magical tools, substances, and books.

"What do you want?" Ochobu demanded, stretching to hang a bunch of dried mint from a beam overhead.

Aly leaned against the door frame and smiled. "I wanted to see how you were settling in. I confess, I thought you'd prefer to live in a hut behind the stable than here within luarin walls."

Ochobu glared at her. "If I say I will do a thing, I do it," she informed Aly stiffly. "I have come to safeguard the lady Sarai, and to help you win your wager. If the Balitang children survive the summer, there will be one less luarin in the Isles at least, and you are a particularly annoying one."

Aly raised her brows. "So the god told you of our bet. Does Ulasim know?"

Ochobu shook her head. "The god spoke to me in the night. He says you are only a temporary irritation. He thinks that with the summer over, the luarin rulers will have sorted out the kingship. The lady who may or may not be our promised one shall be safe for the winter." She poured juniper berries from a bowl into a mortar and began to mash them, releasing their piney scent.

The mention of the end of the wager itched Aly. Being called "a temporary irritation" was also quite annoying. "There are too many of us to kill, you know," she pointed out, thinking she was starting to talk like her father. "Too many who have been here three centuries."

"Do you think I don't know that?" demanded Ochobu, pausing in her work to scowl at Aly. "I'll have to get used to luarin, even if they aren't you."

"You will if you don't want a massacre," Aly said, holding the old woman's eyes with hers. "If you don't want to mark your return to power with killing. How much luarin blood will you discard? Half-bloods? You'd murder your own lady, then. She'd object to the murder of her luarin father and stepmother in any case. Quarter-bloods, eighth-bloods? How much do you count as being too much?"

"Stop it," growled the old woman. "The raka people are not like the first three Rittevon kings, slaughtering those who would not bend the knee to them. We are not murderers."

"That's not what I learned at my da's knee," Aly retorted. Her mental image of people executed by righteous natives was too awful for her to let Ochobu's prejudices stand without argument. "The raka used to kill all the time. Your nobles and your rather temporary queens in the years before the luarin came were so busy battling each other that you didn't have the strength to fight off an invasion. By the time you banded together, it was too late."

"I *know* that," Ochobu growled, mashing her berries with ferocity. "*All* of us who inherited this mess know."

"Is a mess what you mean to give your new queen?" Aly wanted to know. "How can she be sure her people will stand behind her? Or will you put a dagger in her back for the crime of not choosing a father the raka will approve?" Aly inspected her fingernails. They would need work if she was to continue as a maid rather than a goatherd. "Personally, I think you might do well with Sarai on the throne—"

"Silence!" Ochobu interrupted, glaring at Aly. "No names!"

Aly raised an eyebrow at her and waited.

Ochobu laid her pestle aside. "We have lived too long as tenants on lands that our foremothers owned. I know that. I know what is at stake. I can see for myself that a certain young woman is royal in two bloodlines, and that seems to fit the prophecy. But I am no lapdog, trained to roll onto my back for you or any other luarin. I am here to make up my own mind."

Aly brushed a speck from her sleeve. "Then let me tell you something I've observed. Those you call luarin here, including the ones who are part luarin, part raka—they aren't citizens of the Eastern or Southern Lands. They see themselves as Kyprians. They took your land's names for their own. They've made the Isles prosper. I think they've earned the right to stay, if they don't side with the Rittevons when the time comes."

"Is that the god speaking through you?" Ochobu demanded, her eyes flinty. "Or just you?"

Aly fought the urge to give Nawat's wing shrug for a reply. "I assume the god picked me for my opinions as well as my skills, however temporary I might be. I am an outsider. Sometimes we see more clearly than those who live inside the problem."

"I'll be better off when you leave," Ochobu complained. For the moment she sagged, the lines of her face deepening. "You've given me a headache. Go away."

Aly went.

She took lunch with the Balitang women and spent the afternoon with Sarai and Dove as they played with Elsren and Petranne. After Winnamine summoned the two older girls to their newly begun weapons training, Aly occupied herself with household mending and a quick search of Sergeant Veron's rooms, to read his latest reports to the Crown. Once she had finished, she asked Chenaol to heat water for the sisters' baths, then laid out the girls' supper dresses. Bored with nothing to do but mend clothes, Aly wandered over to the window to look out over the inner courtyard.

Below her Dove and the men-at-arms practiced archery. Aly leaned her elbows on the sill to watch and nearly yelped before she caught herself. Someone had come up with a new game.

Nawat stood against the wall, relaxed and alert. Before him two men-at-arms were preparing to shoot. Dove stood behind one archer with a handful of arrows, while the duchess held arrows for the second archer. Aly's mind told her that the duchess would hardly consent to murder just as the first man shot. The second man shot immediately after him. Then both set fresh arrows to the string and shot steadily, arrow after arrow, one at a time, until they had exhausted all the extras held by the duchess and her stepdaughter.

Nawat caught them all with grace and ease, snatching the arrows from the air as if he had all day to do so. When the archers finished, he gathered the heap of arrows at his feet and carried them back to their owners.

He's so *fast*, Aly thought in awe. *I* couldn't do it, and I'm no slouch! She sighed, wishing Da were here to see it. He'd taught her to catch daggers in midair, but this game was much more hazardous.

The game was not done. The men-at-arms repeated the experiment with javelins, then hunting and combat spears. Nawat caught them all, moving so fast Aly couldn't follow his hands. She cheered him and the men-at-arms on.

When the bell rang to remind the household it was nearly time for supper, he looked up at the applauding Aly and waved. "This is my favorite game," he called to her. "Do you want to play?"

"I wouldn't dare!" she cried, laughing, before she retreated into the room. She'd seen men catch knives before. She had seen the finest archers in the Queen's Riders draw an outline in arrows of someone positioned against a wooden fence or wall, just to show they could do it. She had never seen anything like this.

Sarai and Dove ran in. Sarai smiled at Aly. "You should have *seen* your face! Did you know he could do that?" she asked as she collapsed on her bed.

Dove unstrung her bow, shaking her head. "He's amazing," she said, coiling her bowstring.

"You know, maybe this horrible old place isn't so bad," Sarai told the ceiling. "Not if these wonderful men keep showing up."

Aly raised an eyebrow at her. "I wouldn't try kissing him," she warned. "It wouldn't be what you expect."

Sarai wrinkled her nose. "Aly!" she complained. "I found out he eats bugs! I'm not kissing a man with bug breath!"

Aly blinked. I don't remember him tasting of bugs when he kissed me, she thought. I'd better pay more attention next time.

Her mind promptly reined her up. This was highly improper. There would be no next time. Her task was looking after the Balitang children, not mooning over someone, particularly not a crow turned man.

Even if he *could* pluck arrows from the air.

The next morning Aly, still on a goatherd's hours, walked out of the keep into the dawn. The sun had just cleared the walls to light the inner courtyard and the young man who straddled a bench there. Aly stopped to watch him carefully glue pieces of feather onto the wooden shaft.

Nawat looked up at her with a smile that lit his eyes. "You are beautiful in the new light," he told her. "If I were the Dawn Crow, I would bring you the sun to hatch as our first nestling."

Aly blinked at him. Her heart felt strangely squeezed by some powerful emotion. She bit her lip to distract herself from a feeling that made her horribly unsure. "Have you been kissing anybody?" she asked without meaning to, and gasped. She had let words out of her mouth without thinking, which was not like her! Worse, they were such personal words, ones he might feel meant personal feelings she did not have! This was the kind of thing that other girls said, those girls who were not bored by all the young men who had courted them. How many handsome fellows had sighed compliments to Aly while, unconcerned, she had mentally wrestled with breaking a new code? At home she never cared about her suitors enough to worry if they kissed other girls. She scrambled to blot out what she'd said. "Not that it's any of my business, but you should understand, people have a way of kissing for fun, without it meaning anything serious, and I'd hate for you to think someone wanted you to mate-feed them just because they're kissing—" Stop babbling, her mind ordered. Aly stopped.

Nawat's smile broadened. That disturbing light in his eyes deepened. "I have kissed no one but you, Aly," he assured her, serious. "Why should I kiss anyone else?"

Aly gulped. You can continue this conversation, or you can talk about something less . . . giddy, she told herself. Less frightening. "You know I won't always be around," she said abruptly. "I don't belong here, really."

"Then I will go with you," Nawat said. "I belong with you."

He doesn't know what he's saying, Aly told herself. He doesn't know what that means.

She looked at him, arms folded, trying to keep any extra feelings from leaping out. "What are you doing?" she asked, to change the subject to anything less dangerous. Then she grimaced. He was fletching arrows, as always.

She glanced at his bench, then bent down. He was fletching, but these arrows were heavier, and the feathers he used were not bird feathers, but Stormwing. "How did you cut them up?" she wanted to know, genuinely curious. More scraps of cut-up steel feathers lay on the bench.

Nawat pointed to a long piece of what looked like black, chipped glass. "Shiny volcano rock," he told Aly. "Chip the edge until it is sharp. That cuts Stormwing feathers. They come from the heat of the place where Stormwings were born."

Aly touched the glassy blade. "Obsidian," she said. "That's its name."

"Yes," Nawat replied. "Shiny volcano rock." He set a length of steel feather into a thin groove filled with glue and held it in place.

Aly didn't see a single cut on his hands, though the feathers were lethally sharp. "Won't they be too heavy for the glue?" she asked.

"I shaped the glue. It holds Stormwing feathers," Nawat answered.

"Stormwings really are born in volcanoes?" Aly inquired, curious.

"In the beginning time, when they were first dreamed," replied Nawat, setting another piece of steel feather in its slot. "Now, if carrying an egg does not kill the mother, they are born from steel eggs." He looked at Aly and sighed, his dark eyes wistful. "The eggs are too heavy for a crow to take."

"You've already taken enough from Stormwings," Aly told him, pointing to the small pile of glinting feathers beside his bench. "You could have been killed."

"There is a trick to it," he replied, and blew lightly on his fletchings. Holding the arrow shaft before one eye, he squinted down its length. "Perfect," he declared, and set the arrow down.

"It seems like a lot of trouble and risk when goose feathers are safer to work with," Aly remarked. "What is a Stormwing-fletched arrow for, anyway?"

"They are mage killers," replied Nawat. "No matter if the mage is powerful, if he has great spells to protect him. A Stormwing arrow will cut through illusion and magic."

Aly whistled softly, impressed. "Take very good care of those, then," she told Nawat. "We might find a use for them."

"I made them for you," Nawat said, giving her that

radiant, innocent smile. "They are yours, for a day when they will help you." He offered a finished arrow shaft to her.

Aly smiled at him despite the goose bumps that rippled along her skin. "Keep them until they're needed, please," she told him. "My archery skills aren't very good."

"You could practice," Nawat pointed out.

"I'm a slave," Aly explained. "Slaves who are caught with weapons are killed."

"Then do not be a slave," he said, matter-of-factly. "Fly free."

"Not just yet," she replied. "I'll see the summer out first."

Five days later a well-guarded messenger arrived on the plateau. Crows and raka patrols encircled and held the small group until Veron and the castle guard arrived. As the Balitang men-at-arms approached, the raka guards scattered to make Veron think they were robbers and not fighters who had been assigned to keep new arrivals away from the Balitangs until they were searched.

Aly and her riding companions, out on the road west of Tanair, heard the crows' alarm. They arrived at the eastern road at the same time as Veron. Aly murmured a suggestion to Fesgao that he join in the search. If the new arrivals were royal assassins, Aly suspected Veron would take them to the Balitangs. With Fesgao involved, she knew no killers sent by the Crown would go undiscovered.

She watched as the men-at-arms questioned the strangers, looking for anything unusual. None of them lied in answer. As it turned out, their errand was a normal one. They bore thank-you gifts from Bronau, purchased in Dimari before he sailed. They also brought letters from those friends who had been writing to the exiles all along, as well as letters from those who had decided it was safe to correspond now that Hazarin might recall them to the capital.

After supper, Winnamine, Sarai, and Dove played soldiers on the floor with Elsren and Petranne. Pembery, Aly, and Rihani worked on sewing as the duke opened the letters and read them aloud to the family. Aly saw that Winnamine, normally so controlled, could not keep a tiny, sarcastic smile from her lips as people who had been silent for weeks now proclaimed their affection for the Balitangs. Sarai's toy soldiers acted fiercely as she struggled to control her anger with such fair-weather friends. The duke shook his head sadly as he read. Dove practiced that staple item of a young noblewoman's studies, a facial expression of polite interest that gave away none of her true feelings. Aly silently applauded Dove's skill. The twelve-year-old was much better at that polite control than Sarai.

For herself, Aly could only give a mental shrug as she stitched. It was human nature for people to protect themselves from a monarch's temper. That went triple for everyone who lived under the king's eye in Rajmuat.

There was news, too, from the Eastern and Southern Lands. Aly barely listened to the word from Carthak. Emperor Kaddar and his empress were still dealing with that realm's far-flung malcontents, though Kaddar's grip on his throne grew firmer with each passing year. She was far more interested in news from the Eastern Lands, though she pretended the same indifference as she had for Carthak. The Scanran war continued, but the end was in sight. There were rumors that unhappy clansmen had secretly reached out to the Tortallan monarchs, offering peace in trade for their king's head. Aly hoped that Their Majesties, ably assisted by people like her mother, would choose to hammer the Scanrans for a while longer. It would ensure that fresh Scanran attacks would not take place for at least another generation.

After the duke had read all the letters he wanted to share, he opened the trunk from Bronau. Once again there were new books for him, the duchess, and Dove. There was a wooden pull-along knight on horseback for Elsren, who abandoned his soldiers, and a new doll for Petranne, who immediately did the same.

For Sarai there was a gold necklace, its fine chain decorated with citrine drops along its length, and a matching bracelet. The older girl put them on immediately and went to the duchess's looking glass to admire them. "He remembered how much I like citrines!" she told them all.

"Huzzah for him," muttered Dove. Aly, the only one who heard, grinned.

Mequen shifted uneasily in his chair. Winnamine reached over and rested a hand on his arm. "So my old friend courts you, Sarai," the duke said, watching her with concern in his eyes. "Of course, his friends have suggested that he marry for years, but we thought . . ."

"Oh, Papa, it's not serious. He's just flirting," Sarai replied.

"That's very different from what you've said before," the duchess pointed out.

"Well, I'm sixteen, and giddy," Sarai told them mischievously. "My husband had best be faithful to me alone. Bronau isn't likely to do that. Besides, unless King Hazarin gifts him with offices or estates, he's not very wealthy." She went to kneel beside her father. "Don't fret, Papa," she said, her face turned up to his. "I'd never do anything without your approval." She looked at Winnamine, hesitated, then said, "Or yours, Winna."

Aly looked down, not wanting anyone to realize she had

seen the sudden happiness in the duchess's face. It made her feel very much an outsider. She missed her mother, prickly though she was.

The July days that followed were filled with hazy summer heat that made even the lightest cottons stick to their skins. Despite the temperatures, Aly did not give in to the urge to laze. She sewed, cleaned, and helped Sarai and Dove to amuse the younger children so that Rihani could help to put up herbal teas and medicines against the winter. At night Aly met with the raka conspirators, Ochobu, and Nawat, going over what news had come in that day from crows, people, and Ochobu's scrying bowl. They discussed fresh arrivals in the valley while the raka filled Aly in on who in the Isles might support them in times of trouble—the nature of those times left carefully undescribed—as well as who it was who might turn on them.

Each day Sarai bounced away from the breakfast table, Aly and Dove following at a sleepy distance. Outside they would find their mounts and guards waiting by the stables. Some days they had instructions: errands to run for the duchess or mushrooms, berries, and herbs to collect for Chenaol and Ochobu. Other days Nawat came with them, to collect wood for arrows or simply to keep the girls amused.

"Falthin is an easy master indeed," Sarai remarked on Nawat's third such ride with them. She looked at him side-long through her lashes and made her mare prance so that Nawat might look at her hips if he chose. Aly just shook her head, remembering that she had flirted just as much when she wasn't working for her father and grandfather. She wished that Sarai had something serious to do with her time instead of wasting it in the enticement of a man who didn't see her as a potential mate.

Not, she told herself hurriedly, that she cared if Nawat *did* look at Sarai as a potential mate.

"Falthin the bowyer tells me I am only young once, and the winters indoors are long," Nawat replied, his eyes not on Sarai's hips but on Aly's face.

Their group often carried medicines brewed by Ochobu and Rihani to the villages of Inti and Pohon. If they were not invited to take their lunch with the wealthier families, they found shady brookside places to eat their bread, cheese, and whatever else Chenaol might have packed for them. Afterward they would doze, cool their feet in the water, talk, or sew. If it wasn't too hot, they practiced hand-to-hand combat and weapons skills with Aly and Junai. Aly loved the long, slow days, filled with the buzz of crickets and the sight of blindingly white clouds scudding over the turquoise sky. Summer was as beautiful on Lombyn as at Pirate's Swoop. She barely missed the stacks of reports at home, the bustle of messengers coming and going, or her fair-weather round of visits to relatives and foster relatives.

As lazy as the time could be, Aly never forgot who her companions were. Everywhere they went, the raka turned out to look at the Balitang girls. Sarai always stopped to say hello, to learn their names, admire their children, and listen to their old people. The girls would be offered cups of the villainous Kyprian tea, which they had to accept or risk offending their hosts. Drinking it, Aly always wondered if it could be used to remove varnish from furniture.

She had hoped that the novelty of watching Sarai might wear off, but she reckoned without Sarai or the raka. Like Aly's mother, Sarai detested going home by the same route she had taken to leave it. She led them along tracks Aly would have sworn were game trails, past small farms, hunters' cabins, and mining and lumber camps on the plateau's edge.

They chatted with people Aly suspected were poachers and others she knew were smugglers. Sarai greeted women dyeing cloth and men tanning hides. Aly would not have suspected that so much of the plateau was taken up by farms, or that Sarai had a talent for locating them all.

Despite her reservations about the raka mounting a successful rebellion, Aly had to admit that Sarai showed promise. She had the same air of genuine interest in people's lives that Queen Thayet had shown when Aly had accompanied her godsmother on trips. Sarai cared for the people, and they responded. Looking at her, their faces were bright with hope. Aly could only pray that their hopes were fulfilled, for them and for Sarai.

One day they rode to Inti. When they got within view of the village, Aly, who had been using her Sight to eye the road ahead, made the girls halt. Thirty-odd people were camped on the village outskirts. As they stopped, a raka patrol melted out of the trees on the northern side of the road. Their leader rode out to meet Fesgao. The two men spoke briefly. Fesgao then brought his horse around and came back to their group.

"They are raka," he told the girls. "They have come to see the lady." His long eyes flicked up to Sarai's face, then away. To Aly he said, "It is well. They came up from the coast, and have no taint of the assassin to them."

"Then let's say hello," Sarai declared. "It's the least we can do, if they've made that horrible climb up the western road."

Aly still didn't like it, but she had no choice. Sarai had already urged her gelding forward. As they approached, the raka patrol vanished under the trees once more, while the raka in the camp gathered on either side of the road.

Watching Sarai approach the nearest of them, Aly sent a hurried call to Kyprioth for help.

"Let them see their ladies," the god replied. His voice boomed in the empty air, coming from the open sky. The raka from the camp immediately dropped to their knees. Sarai hurriedly controlled her mount and Dove's as the frightened horses began to plunge and fight the rein. The guards' mounts held steady, though white showed all the way around their eyes. Aly's Cinnamon calmly helped herself to mouthfuls of grass. "Let them greet Saraiyu and Dovasary," Kyprioth went on, "and return to speak of them in their home villages, with hope."

As Sarai dismounted, Aly directed an angry but unspoken remark to the god. *It was a* private *question. Why did you have to make such a revelation of it?!*

Because this is part of the biggest trick I have ever played, the god said for her ears alone. *Because they must be heralded with signs of divine favor. I just showed them some.*

You upset the horses, Aly retorted silently. *Show-off.*

Now you begin to understand me. The god's private voice was filled with amusement. *I knew it would happen sooner or later.*

Sarai passed her reins to Aly. She started forward, then turned to glare at Dove.

Aly nudged Cinnamon closer to the younger girl. "I'll hold your mare," she offered.

"What are we getting ourselves into?" Dove whispered. "If word of things like this gets back to the palace, we'll be cooked in front of its gates over a slow fire."

Despite her concern, she dismounted and gave her horse's reins to Aly. Fesgao and the rest of the guards were getting down from their mounts, too. Aly sighed and did the same for them. She knew better than to even ask Junai to hold the horses' reins. Junai would say, quite properly, that as a guard in an uncertain situation she had to keep her hands and her attention free.

The raka bowed low to the girls, arms crossed over their chests, palms to their shoulders. These were poor people, Aly noted, with scarcely an unpatched jacket or sarong to their names. Their numbers encompassed all ages and both sexes, from people so old they were carried in stretchers to babies still at the breast. Aly observed the crowd as the guards watched those closest to the Balitang girls, alert for assassins who might have slipped by the patrol. All went quietly. Once each raka had said hello and told Sarai a little about him- or herself, they bowed, collected their belongings, and quietly left their camp.

"They appeared overnight from the coast," said Inti's headman when they finally reached the village itself. "They haven't been any trouble, but they said they meant to stay until they saw you. I don't see what I could have done."

"Next time, send word," snapped Fesgao, his normal calm disturbed by the unexpected encounter. "We could have brought more guards with us."

On their way home, Aly dropped behind to ride next to Fesgao. Softly she asked, "Is there any way to keep such groups from coming? It attracts attention."

The man shook his head. "The raka have lived without hope for so long," he explained. "I cannot blame them for wanting to see it with their own eyes."

"If you think these girls will let you foment a rebellion in their names, you will get a rude awakening," Aly cautioned Fesgao. "They and their parents are loyal to the Crown."

"Ah, but is the Crown loyal to them?" asked the raka. "That has yet to be seen."

* * *

Fort Mastiff, Tortall, on the Scanran border

This was yet another of her dream visits to Tortall, Aly realized, coming from sleep to wakefulness in the air above a large, new, wooden fortress. It flew the flag of the realm of Tortall, a silver sword and a silver crown on a blue shield. Beneath it flew a scarlet flag with a golden cat rearing on it, the banner of the King's Champion, Alanna the Lioness.

Aly could see her famous mother below, planted solidly at the center of a ring of onlookers. She was dueling with someone. From the fighters' quilted tunics and absent helmets, Aly judged that this was a practice session, not a real fight, though both her mother and her opponent wielded live sword blades. There was a risk.

Aly drifted down, curious about who might be mad enough to take on her mother, even for practice. By the looks of things, Alanna was overmatched. Her opponent was nearly six feet tall, broad-shouldered, with muscled legs revealed by cotton breeches. Sweat-soaked brown hair, cut short at the nape of the neck and across the forehead, framed a face tanned in the sun, and brown-hazel eyes, a dreamer's eyes, with ridiculously long lashes. Those eyes were steady as they watched the Lioness's sword.

"Go, Kel!" someone yelled from the sidelines. "Youth and skill!"

"Age and treachery!" bellowed a large man on the far side of the ring. Aly knew him. Lord Raoul of Goldenlake and Malorie's Peak was one of her adoptive uncles, a big man who kept a short, brown-skinned woman in the circle of his arm even as he urged his friend Alanna on. Aly recognized the brown woman as yet another of her adoptive aunts, Buri, married to Uncle Raoul less than a year.

"Youth and skill!" cried another man Aly knew well,

Nealan of Queenscove, her mother's former squire. "Don't let that old lady cut you, Kel!"

"Whose side are you on?" Alanna demanded, her eyes flicking over to Neal. "You were *my* squire!"

Her opponent surged forward as the Lioness's attention wavered, her blade slicing the air in an overhand swing. This had to be Keladry of Mindelan, Aly realized, fascinated. Since Aly had been eight or so her mother had spoken continually of Keladry, the first girl to go for her knighthood since Alanna. For a while Aly had been jealous of the girl, thinking her mother was more interested in Kel than she was in Aly. Only in the last few years had she realized her mother simply understood Kel better than she understood Aly.

Kel bore in on her smaller foe fast, but Alanna came up and under Kel's attack, smacking the bigger woman hard in the ribs. "You've been using that pig-sticker of yours so much, you've forgotten how to wield your Griffin," Alanna taunted. "You've gotten lazy!"

Griffin, Aly thought, then remembered. Mother said Kel had named the sword Alanna had given her Griffin.

Kel lunged in again, her sword blade tangling with the Lioness's, until the two women were locked together, hilt to hilt. Now Kel brought her superior height and weight to bear, forcing the Lioness down and back. "Lazy, is it?" Keladry said, panting. "I'll give you laziness, shorty."

Alanna laughed and sprang free of the tangle, darting around to swat Keladry on the behind with the flat of her blade. "Age and treachery!" she taunted Kel.

Kel stood back and, gasping, saluted Alanna with her weapon. "I guess I need to work on my sword skill after all, Lioness," she said, accepting someone's water bottle. She nodded toward the gate. "I think we have company."

A tall gray figure—Tkaa the basilisk—strode through the gate, holding his long tail off the ground as a lady would hold the train to her gown. From crown to tail he was covered in dust that turned his beaded gray skin to gray-brown.

"Tkaa," cried Alanna, running to greet the newcomer. "Whatever brings you here?"

The basilisk bent his head so that he could whisper into her ear. Aly dropped down until she was close enough to hear him. "I bear news from your husband." Tkaa's voice was like the whisper of flutes. "He asks me to tell you that he's got real word at last, from Rajmuat. You must not worry if he disappears for a time."

Alanna seized the basilisk's paw. Aly, looking around, saw that everyone else was keeping a respectful distance from the unlikely pair.

"Aly?" whispered Alanna. "He's got word of her?"

Tkaa nodded.

Alanna turned and walked speedily back to her quarters, the men shifting out of her path. Like Aly, they knew the set look on Alanna's face meant she didn't want to talk to anyone.

"Please tell me you have good news." Lord Raoul had walked over to greet the basilisk. "Whatever it is. She's been as jumpy as a horse covered in ants all summer."

"I sorrow to hear it," said the basilisk. "I can tell you that diplomats from Scanra are in Corus to negotiate a peace treaty."

His information was greeted with a shout from the people who had followed Raoul to say hello to the newcomer. Aly's dream began to fade as men and boys ran to tell their fellows Tkaa's news.

Aly opened her eyes. She lay on her pallet in the great hall. Looking at the torch that still burned to light any late comings and goings on the main stair, she saw that it was the middle of the night, with a few more hours to go until dawn. A fresh torch set by the stairs always burned out just before sunrise.

Someone nearby snored. Aly heard a dog's claws scratch on the stone flags as their owner dreamed of hunting. Farther off she heard a rustle of mice.

She stared into the dark. Da was coming to Rajmuat, she realized. He would track her to the slave pens, then to the Balitangs' town house, then to Lombyn. It might take him weeks. He could not use his Kyprish agents. He would have to question people without seeming to question them. He would be looking for a girl with hair, not one shaved bald, but sooner or later he would find Aly and want to take her home.

She'd go, of course. She hoped he could wait till the equinox, so that her bet would be done with. And then she'd return to the safety of Pirate's Swoop. If all went as it was supposed to, Da would then let her do field work.

And what happens to the Balitangs then? she asked herself. What happens to the raka?

She wouldn't think of that. Da needed her. Mother missed her. And there were her brothers, her grandparents, and her adoptive family. She could see them once the Balitangs were safe, if she didn't go home with Da right away. There was an idea.

Back to sleep. The only result she would have from worrying about it now was daytime exhaustion from lack of a proper night's rest. Da would come when he came.

If you're to lie to a god, and sometimes it's fair useful, do it with the truth. They smell lies on two-leggers, or they see it, or whatever it is they do. But if all you're telling them is whatever part of your lie that's truthful, they'll accept it. The gods don't see what's always in our minds. Mayhap they'd go mad if they knew everything we think as we think it—I know I would. Besides, mortals were granted the right to make our own choices when we were shaped. So if a god's got no reason to be suspicious, he won't enter your mind to find that you've only spoken half the story.

—*Daine Sarrasri, daughter of the Gallan goddess The Green Lady and the hunt god Weiryn, to her fifteen-year-old adopted niece, Aly, during a discussion of the Immortals' War*

14

PIVOT

The first group of outland raka had been gone three days when another came in. They, too, would not leave until after they had seen Sarai. Five days later a third group arrived at Inti. This one was the largest yet, a regular caravan from the coast that masked its real purpose by carrying sealskins, whale oil, shell buttons, salt, beads, and dried seaweed to trade.

To support their story of coming to Inti on business, Sarai sent a villager for her father and Ulasim, who could ride to Inti and do business for the family. She told her companions they would spend the night in the village, since she had so far met only half of the caravan's members. Their group took supper with the newcomers and introduced them to Mequen and Ulasim when they arrived with their guards.

In a gesture of goodwill, Inti's headman gave up his home to the Balitangs for the night. Inside at last, Aly set the pallet they'd found for her at the foot of the large bed shared by Sarai and Dove. Exhausted by watchfulness among a crowd of unknown raka and by a secret but thorough search of their wagons and gear, Aly plunged into sleep as soon as her eyes closed.

Kyprioth awaited her in the glowing form he'd used to show her King Oron's death.

"What now?" Aly demanded crossly. "I have enough on my plate at the moment, without you dragging me all over the mortal realms."

"You will be glad to know this by the time we are done, my dear," the god informed her. "It is the pivot on which all else turns. I've yet to meet a spy who didn't want all the information he—or she—could stand."

"You could at least pretend to be sorry you bothered me," Aly grumbled as the god passed a glowing arm firmly around her waist.

"And deprive you of whining?" he asked as they shot through the roof of the house, into the open sky beyond. "I *have* noticed how careful you are not to complain to those you serve. I thought it only fair to let you berate me a little."

"That wasn't berating you," Aly said darkly, even as she savored their passage over velvety land and watched the brilliant stars overhead. "When I berate you, you'll know it." She sighed dramatically. "Not that you'll care."

"I won't," Kyprioth replied as they soared over the Azure Sea. Far below, a long, sinuous form arched up along the water, scattering it in diamond drops in the starlight. Kyprioth crooned a greeting to the whale, who called back as its tail popped free of the water, then passed into it again. "Though I know that I will prize the way you phrase yourself. I am certain that you will be more than eloquent at the art of berating."

Aly replied with a rude invitation not commonly offered to a god, startling a peal of laughter from Kyprioth. "Whatever else I may say of you, and I'm sure there will be plenty, at least you have a sense of humor," she added.

"I *am* a trickster," he replied in a modest tone.

Gods, Aly thought. They always insist on having the last word.

All too soon the journey was over. They settled into the king's bedroom in the palace at Rajmuat. The curtains over the terrace doors were drawn against the night air, cooler here above the harbor. The chamber was dark except for one small lamp by the door to the outer room and another by the door to what looked like the privy. Servants slept on pallets all around the room, ready to jump up to do the king's bidding if he needed anything in the night. On the bed King Hazarin slept alone, pouting even in his dreams. He labored to breathe, releasing the occasional snore.

"He ate richly tonight," Kyprioth observed in a tone of mild interest. "Venison in wine sauce, pork with a pineapple and honey gravy, buffalo coconut curry, sticky coconut peanut rice with currants and almonds, five different wines from the Eastern Lands . . ."

"He *always* eats like that?" Aly wanted to know, awed.

"The richer, the better," replied Kyprioth. "He insists on at least five coconut dishes at every meal, though healers keep telling him a lighter diet would be better. It's really a toss-up as to what kills him first, his heart or an apoplexy of the brain. Actually, I have a bit of a wager on with my cousin the Graveyard Hag about that."

He went quiet. Hazarin bolted upright in bed, his eyes open and staring as he fought to breathe. His plump hands went to his head. He uttered a strangled noise loud enough to wake two of the sleepers around him. As they struggled to their feet, Hazarin fell back on his pillows, eyes wide. He stared blankly upward as his hands flopped down. He gaped endlessly as the anxious servants felt his throat and his wrists.

The woman who held his wrist looked at the man who touched the big veins in Hazarin's throat. The man shook his head, then cocked his head to put his ear over Hazarin's open mouth.

The woman turned to look at the other sleepers. "Wake up, you fools!" she snapped, her voice low and cutting. "Something's happened to the king!"

Blankets flew as the sleepers roused in a panic. Within moments they had silently lit more lamps. One man thrust a blanket under the edge of the main door, to keep the light from showing outside. Aly understood what was going on. These were the acts of people who might die if anything questionable took place in the room where the king slept. They all gathered around Hazarin, some making the star-shaped sign against evil when they saw the king's face.

"He's dead," the man who had listened for the king's breath told his fellows. "I don't know why, but he is."

"We must call a healer," said a young maid. As she turned toward the door, one of the men grabbed her arm.

"Idiot!" he snapped, keeping his voice low. "What if it's poison? Who will be blamed? He was fine when he rose from supper, fine when he came to bed—"

"He mentioned a headache," interrupted the woman who'd been the first to wake.

"Not a headache bad enough to call the healer," retorted the man who had stopped the younger maid. "Now he's dead. If it's poison . . ."

"They'll say it was one of us," murmured someone else. "They always do."

None of them said another word. Silently they collected their belongings and fled through a door to the servants' stair hidden behind a tapestry. The last to leave blew out the lamps.

"They'll have gone to ground in the city by dawn," Kyprioth remarked to Aly. "And they'll escape Rajmuat by noon, if they have any sense. Stay here. I have a wager to collect from the Graveyard Hag. I told her it was folly to bet on a Rittevon king actually having a heart."

"Wait," Aly said. The god bent his glowing head down to listen. "Why don't you tell those poor people his death was natural? That they can't be blamed?"

"I could, if you want them to return and be tortured anyway. The new regents will want to make sure his death was accidental. Healers make mistakes, after all. Actually, since I'm in a good mood . . ." He touched a finger to Aly's forehead, sending a small shock through her. "Find the king's healer. Tell her this would be a good time to catch a ship for Carthak." Then he vanished.

The magic he had placed on Aly told her where to find the healer on duty. The woman slept in a nearby chamber. Aly tried to grab her by the shoulder and shake her, but her hand passed through the healer's flesh.

"Excuse me," she said.

The healer twitched.

"Excuse me," Aly said loudly into the healer's ear. The woman sat up with a yelp, passing through Aly.

The healer glanced around.

"Right here," Aly told her. "Don't I glow, or something?"

The healer gasped. "I meant no offense, Goddess—"

"I'm not a goddess," Aly interrupted. The gods hated it when someone who wasn't a god took the title. "I'm a messenger. King Hazarin just died. I think it was ap—ap . . . that thing where blood vessels in the brain explode."

"Apoplexy," muttered the healer, scrambling out of bed. "If I warned him once . . ."

"He's beyond warning now," Aly informed her. "Perhaps

this would be a good time to leave the country. Before they find him."

"I must warn his servants," protested the healer, going to her door. "We'll all be questioned, to ensure he wasn't poisoned."

"His servants are warned," Aly said flatly. The healer turned and stared at her. "They're leaving right now, and they didn't think to tell you. Grab your essentials and run."

As the woman scrambled to pack, Aly returned to the dead man's bedroom. Kyprioth was still absent, but Hazarin's ghost sat by his former body, smiling. She could tell it was the king: he looked as if someone had painted his complete portrait on sheer cloth, except that no painter would have done a picture of Hazarin in his nightgown.

"You're very cheerful for a man who's dead," Aly remarked.

The ghost looked at her. "But I'm well out of it," he explained. "All the plotting, never knowing who's a friend and who isn't, wondering if the food I eat is poisoned or if someone's buying grim spells to use against me. It's done. Are you the Black God?"

"No," Aly replied, "I'm a mortal. The god I—" She hesitated, not wanting to say it, but she had to give *some* explanation. "The god I serve brought me here, to see what happens."

Hazarin shook his head. "It's a bad business, meddling with gods," he told Aly wisely.

"I know," Aly said ruefully. "If it helps, you died a natural death. That's what my god said, anyway."

"I would have died of something," Hazarin replied. "Really, I suppose I signed my death warrant the day I made Dunevon my heir, with my sister Imajane and her husband as regents, should I die before Dunevon came of age. My spies told me this afternoon that Imajane's looking for death spells. This was a much better way to go, and probably everyone will think she had me killed anyway." He grinned at the thought.

"You don't sound upset," Aly remarked. "If *my* half sister looked to have me killed, I'd be *very* upset."

"Not at all," Hazarin replied. "We weren't raised to *like* one another. My father thought that if we did, we'd band together and get rid of him."

"It doesn't sound like a happy way to live," Aly murmured.

"Now you know why I'm glad to be out of it," Hazarin told her. "It's—" Abruptly he stood and bowed at the door. Aly glanced at it over her shoulder and turned. A tall shape, robed and hooded, made all of shadows, was standing there. "I am ready to follow you, Great One," Hazarin told the shadow that was the Black God. "This girl says she's mortal."

Though Aly couldn't really see much of the god's form in the dark room, she was convinced he looked her way. She didn't want to die with so much left unfinished. This god could take her now if he wished to do so. Trembling, Aly knelt. She felt a warm, comforting pressure on her shoulder, as if someone had squeezed it. When she looked up, Hazarin's ghost and the god were gone, leaving behind the shell of Hazarin's body.

Time passed. Kyprioth finally returned at dawn with a glowing chess set. He and Aly played until a guard, concerned by the lack of activity in the royal bedchamber, cautiously opened the door. He cried the alarm. As Kyprioth and Aly watched, people came and went. Other guards were called to search for the missing servants and healer.

At last another healer arrived, a blond, cross-looking

man. He was rumpled, as if they had dragged him from bed to see to the dead king. He was just finishing his examination when the icy princess Imajane and her husband, Rubinyan, arrived. Like the healer, they looked as if they had rushed to pull on their elegant clothes.

"Well?" demanded Imajane sharply, her blond head high. "Was it poison?"

"It was the poison of rich gravies, fatty meats, and too much cursed coconut, as he was warned time after time, Your Highness," retorted the healer. "He died of apoplexy. Don't think you can torture another answer out of me, if you please. Not only am I the head of the guild, but he was not my charge. The healer who had him in care is gone. Fled, I should imagine."

Imajane glanced at the captain of the guards. "The servants fled as well?" The captain bowed. "Find them and the healer," Imajane ordered in a crisp, elegant voice. "Search wherever you must." She looked at her husband. "My dear?"

"All things seem plain enough." Rubinyan spoke firmly in measured, deliberate tones.

Aly shook her head in pity for Hazarin. Except for Dunevon, these people were his only family, and they obviously didn't sorrow over his senseless death. "We must ensure that the servants do not gossip," Rubinyan continued. "Until we can make certain that the change of rulership is complete. Dunevon must be crowned as soon as possible. We need the Mithran High Priest. He can do it quickly now, and we can stage a ceremony with all manner of pomp later."

"Certainly Your Highnesses can and must crown the new king before all else," said the healer, drawing a sheet over Hazarin's face. "But it is well past dawn. There has been too much coming and going here. By noon the whole city will know the king is dead." He flung the terrace curtains wide and yelped, staggering back, eyes wide with terror. "Who needs servants to bugle the news?" he cried, pointing.

Imajane and Rubinyan moved forward to see what had frightened the man. Stormwings perched on the terrace rail, males and females alike, their bare, human chests streaked with filth and caked with dark fluids, their steel wings and claws gleaming in the early-morning sun. They grinned broadly, steel teeth glinting, and spread their wings, sending darts of reflected sunlight and an unspeakable smell into the room.

"Got something for us?" one of them asked. "Dead kings always mean trouble, fighting in the streets, with plenty of hate and dead bodies. A meal for us."

"Not today," Rubinyan said firmly. "Order will be preserved." He yanked the drapes shut.

"You've trouble at your backs, mortal, and you're too full of yourself to notice!" shrieked a female, her voice cutting through the heavy brocade drapes. "If I were you, I'd watch for the Trickster's choice!"

Aly looked at Kyprioth. "Do they mean me, or just the changes you're setting in motion?"

"They're Stormwings," replied Kyprioth evenly. "They're just stirring things up."

Aly raised an eyebrow. "Somehow I don't believe you."

Kyprioth shrugged. "And that hurts me," he said in a blithe tone. "You have no idea how much that hurts me."

Time passed. The Mithran High Priest and his acolytes hurried to the palace. There, in the throne room, Aly and Kyprioth looked on as the three-year-old Dunevon was prompted through a brief coronation. Aly felt bad for the little boy, who was just Elsren's age. Dunevon looked thoroughly terrified. He obeyed Imajane's orders, acting his part like a trained pony in front of as many nobles and guild leaders as his regents could find. At last he sat perched on the immense teak throne that dwarfed him, a small, pearl-bedecked crown on his dark curls. On his right, his half sister and regent, Imajane, held Dunevon's diamond-crowned scepter. On his left, his co-regent, Rubinyan, held a pillow with the bared sword of the king's justice on it.

Bronau stood in the third rank of the nobles before the dais. He was unhappy, the look in his eyes murderous as he stared first at Imajane, then his brother. This was not the laughing, charming man who had spent so many days with the Balitangs. Looking at him now, Aly saw him as a volcano on the edge of explosion. Imajane and Rubinyan saw it, too. Their eyes continually flicked to Bronau throughout the proceedings.

Once the last hymns were sung, Imajane stepped forward. "We have a new king, to ensure our safety as we take our beloved former king to his resting place," she proclaimed, her voice ringing through the stone hall. "Now must His Majesty, and his subjects, give way to the condition of mourning, in honor of our beloved Hazarin, and to cleanse our souls of sorrow."

Imajane beckoned the Black God's High Priest forward from the first rank of notables. It would be his duty to see to Hazarin's burial. As he stood before the dais and proclaimed the order of the funeral rites, Aly turned to Kyprioth. "It just occurred to me: if it's afternoon here, it's afternoon in Lombyn. I have to get back, before they bury *me*."

"They won't," Kyprioth said blithely. "Ochobu won't let them. Just enjoy the performance. How many royal funerals have you been to?"

"Why keep me dawdling?" inquired Aly at her most patient. "The Balitangs should know they have a new king, again."

"There are a few more things you should see," Kyprioth replied. "We'll just wait."

"I don't *want* to wait," Aly said firmly. "I need to get back. If something happens to any of the Balitang children while I'm kept here, our wager is finished. You can't say I lost if something happens to them when you have me a whole country away."

"Nothing will happen. The wager stands," Kyprioth told her.

"I'm *bored*," she informed him. "I bore easily. I do *not* wish to loll about here while everyone talks and eats and does whatever other silly things these luarin pests do for fun."

"There, at least, I can help you," Kyprioth said. He raised a glowing arm and wrote a sign in the air. Shadows wrapped around her.

She drifted for some time. At one point she thought she was waking up inside her own body. She heard Ochobu say firmly, "I can do nothing here."

"No more should you." Aly struggled to open her eyes: that was Nawat's voice. What was he doing in Inti, where she had gone to sleep? He had stayed at Tanair that day. "The god has her fast," the crow-man continued. "He will give her up when he is done with her." Into Aly's ear he whispered, "If he does not give you back, my flock and our kinfolk will make him suffer."

Aly struggled to reassure him, and to say his breath didn't smell of bugs in the least. In the end, the darkness in which she floated pulled her back into its depths.

Finally her awareness returned. Now she was standing in a luxurious child's room. Expensive gilded and painted toys lay on the floor. A pair of hounds barely out of puppy-hood wrestled for control of a silk table runner. Dunevon, clad all in black velvet, giggled and clapped his hands as he watched. Half-eaten marzipan fruits, candied violets, and raisins lay scattered on the rug around the boy.

Aly didn't like that. From her own experience with Elsren and Petranne, she knew it was bad to give a child so many sweets. Didn't the little king have a nursemaid, someone to look after him properly? Aly thought very little of those who dressed a little boy in expensive velvets, then left him to play on the floor. She looked around for the god, but Kyprioth was nowhere in view.

Wood creaked. A tapestry bulged. Someone pushed it aside to enter the room: Bronau. He was holding a wooden marionette in one hand.

"Uncle Bronau!" cried Dunevon, running to him. "How did you come in? Was it magic?"

"No, just a secret door," Bronau replied, catching the boy king up in one arm. "It's *our* secret now." He jiggled the marionette invitingly for the child. "I told you I would bring you a present. I wanted it to be a surprise, just between us. Is Your Majesty pleased?"

"I'm not a majesty," replied the king, pouting. For a moment he looked much like his dead half brother. "Hazarin's a majesty. I'm a highness. I keep telling them, and they keep doing it wrong."

Bronau chuckled, that rich, seductive sound he had so often lavished on Sarai. "Don't you see, Hazarin had to go away. Before he left, he made you a majesty," he explained. He looked around nervously.

Aly didn't like Bronau's manner. His charming mask often slipped, to reveal tension-bright eyes and tight jaw muscles. He was up to no good.

"Where's your cloak, Dunevon?" he asked.

The boy pointed to a clothes press. "But it's summer. I don't need a cloak in summer."

"We're going sailing," Bronau told him, offering the child his best smile. "I have a wonderful ship waiting in the harbor."

"Sailing?" asked the boy, clearly delighted. "Can we go see the howler monkeys at home and winged horses and maybe a kraken?"

Bronau crossed the room, still holding the boy. "I'd prefer to avoid the kraken, Your Majesty," he said, fumbling one-handed to open the press. "But there will be monkeys, even merpeople. Perhaps, if you're very good, a herd of winged horses. There's one on Imahyn Isle, did you know that?" He scrabbled through layers of clothes until he produced the cloak. Once the press was shut, Bronau stood Dunevon on it and put the cloak over the child's shoulders, tying it securely.

"Can't we go in the morning?" asked Dunevon. "This cloak's *hot*."

Bronau chuckled without humor. "Actually, sire, it must be now. Uncle Rubinyan and Aunt Imajane want to send me to Carthak. If I go there, I'd never see my favorite little king again. I'd rather take you sailing now." He raised Dunevon's hood and tightened it until the child's face was barely visible.

"But it's too *hot*," complained the boy, flailing under the garment's heavy folds. "I don't need a cloak. I don't want to go sailing now. Aunt Imajane promised I could have jugglers if I ate all my supper."

"Well, I have supper waiting on the boat," said Bronau, picking the boy up once more. "We'll find you jugglers even if you don't eat your supper. Dunevon, just hold still and do as you're bid!"

"I don't want to!" wailed the boy, his eyes filling with tears. "I want jugglers now, and my belly hurts!"

Bronau clapped a hand over Dunevon's mouth. "That's not all that will hurt if you don't be quiet!" he snapped.

The two dogs had stopped their play when Bronau came in. Dunevon's greeting had told them this was no stranger, but their manner changed the moment he began to cry. They barked shrilly, advancing as their young master fought Bronau's grip. Suddenly Dunevon shuddered with the effect of too many sweets on a young stomach. He vomited into the hand Bronau held over his mouth.

The man reacted just as Aly would have done: he swore and dropped Dunevon, holding his drenched hand out. "You disgusting little brat!" he cried, trying to clean himself on a tapestry. "You did that on purpose!"

Dunevon ran across the room, screaming as he wept. The door burst open, revealing a handful of guards. Beyond them Aly saw a bottle of wine and a pair of dice on the floor, explaining why they hadn't checked on their king until now.

"Halt in the king's name!" cried one of them, fighting to get clear of his fellows so he could draw his sword.

"Halt!" yelled another guard.

Bronau looked at Dunevon. The boy was out of his reach now. The guards planted themselves between him and his quarry. He started to draw his sword, reconsidered, then fled through the secret door. The guards poured after him, leaving the sick king to scream alone.

"Is he mad?" whispered Aly. "He just tried to kidnap the king!"

"Not mad, necessarily." Kyprioth's glowing form materialized beside Aly. "Hungry for power, which Imajane and Rubinyan will never give him. If he can't get it here, he will try to find it elsewhere. Those who search for him will bring power in their train, power they will bring to bear on anyone who tries to help Bronau. So, now, Aly of Tortall. We come to the days when you shall win or lose our wager—"

He stopped abruptly as two bright forms appeared before them, shining so fiercely that Aly shaded her eyes. They solidified until she could tell that they were male and female, and make out their features. The man, black-skinned and powerfully built, a crown like the rays of the sun blazing on his head, wore gold armor and carried a spear. The woman was bare-breasted in the style of the priestesses of old Ekallatum, with a bell-like skirt hanging from its bodice. The crown atop her tumble of dark, wavy locks blazed silver like the moon. Immense snakes twined around her bare arms.

"Brother, what is it that you do here?" they demanded, their attention on Kyprioth. Aly clapped her hands over her mouth to prevent herself from screaming. The divine voices and presences tore through her ghostlike body, shredding her like ancient silk.

Mithros—he could only be Mithros, Aly knew—added, "We left you the seas that cradle this place, and the seas alone." His voice rolled like horses at the stampede, hammering Aly's ears. Daggers of pain thrust into her skull as she fought to keep from fainting.

"We have been occupied with affairs on the other side of this world. Now we return to find you in the Rajmuat palace, which is no part of the sea." Aly's mother had described the Goddess's voice as the belling of hounds and the bugle of hunting horns. To Aly it was more like the shriek of triumphant eagles and the slow, whispering glide of snakes on rock. Her knees wanted to give way, *demanding* that she kneel. She would not do it. It was one thing to kneel to the Black God, who would take her in hand one day. It was another to kneel to the pair who had done the raka such a terrible wrong when they supported the luarin conquest.

Aly fought. She trembled as she summoned all of her willpower to stay upright. They were gods, but *she* was not sworn to them. She would *not* collapse in a heap.

"Should brothers and sisters suspect wrongdoing at every turn?" asked Kyprioth. "Are you so unsure—"

Aly kicked him. Later, when she was herself again, she would question her sanity, and wonder how his glowing body felt the kick from her insubstantial leg. Right now she saw only that all three brilliant heads turned their attention to her.

She followed her instincts. She smiled, bowed deeply to the Great Goddess and Mithros, and said in a tone her father would know quite well, "Begging your pardons, O Great Gods, ruler of we mortals, but I ask that you forgive my father's friend and patron." Kyprioth *had* said he'd worked with her da, after all. Remembering to speak only the truth, she continued, "At present I am deeply interested in the politics in Rajmuat—*vitally* interested, I should say. If my time here is to be well spent, I should understand how things work. These Isles have long been a factor in Tortall's politics—" She cut herself off carefully. She dared not play this too broadly, or they might suspect a rat. Humbly she continued, "What am I saying? You are the Great Gods. You know what there is to know. Forgive me, I beg—I am flustered, standing before you. You divine brother Kyprioth is my father's patron. He has been helping me to understand the Isles. Since I was stranded on Lombyn with the mortals I presently serve, Kyprioth generously gave me this chance to observe the change in kingship." There, she thought, wondering if her insubstantial face was sweaty. I spoke only the truth.

She kept her head down; the light of the gods' faces hurt her ghostly eyes in any case. Glowing fingers pressed her chin up and forced her to gaze into eyes as green as emeralds, as measureless as the Royal Forest in high summer. "I can look into your heart, Alianne of Pirate's Swoop," the Goddess said, her voice making Aly shiver. "I can see if you lie."

Aly stepped away from that hand, whose touch burned even her unreal body. Once again she bowed respectfully. "Great Mother, you know I speak the truth," she said, choosing her words with immense care. "You could see the lie on me. If you know the family I serve, you understand how important it is that they know of Hazarin's death and Bronau's treason." Not for nothing had she listened to Aunt Daine! "Forgive me, Great Mother. I don't mean to be disobliging. Your divine brother Kyprioth knows the danger to the family I serve. He brought me here to see these things at first hand."

It was hard to read the Goddess's alabaster features in the blaze of her glory. Still, Aly could have sworn the Goddess raised her brows and pursed her mouth. Aly knew that expression from her mother: Alanna looked that way when she had a suspicion that someone was not being honest with her. "Your mother is dedicated to me," she pointed out.

Aly bowed yet again. "That is true, Great Goddess, but I am too much like my father. I must follow his path, in service to the Trickster."

"You are very like your father," the Great Mother said at last, her voice shuddering through Aly. "It is the kind of prank he *would* play."

"No prank, Goddess," Aly assured her. "What I do here is entirely serious."

"Enough," said Mithros impatiently, his voice sounding in the marrow of Aly's bones. "The Teasai on the other side of the world strike their gongs in the call for war. Their women beg you, my sister, for the strength to fight their city's enemies." To Kyprioth he said, "When we made peace nearly three human centuries past, you lost your eminence here. Do not think we will take it well if you break that peace."

"Brother," Kyprioth said reproachfully as he spread his hands, the picture of glowing innocence, "surely I know when I have been beaten."

The universe around them wrenched. When Aly could see clearly again, Mithros and the Goddess had vanished.

She looked at Kyprioth. From the movement of his light-shape, she could tell he was stroking his beard in thought. She poked his glowing ribs with her ghostly elbow. "You owe me," she informed him.

"I know that," Kyprioth replied slowly. "Well, never let it be said that I do not return favor for favor. Shall I free you from our wager? Take you home and speak to your father on your behalf? Then neither of us will owe the other."

Aly pursed her lips. "How can I trust you?"

"I owe you. Even tricksters must pay what they owe."

Aly thought about it. To be home again, without this metal ring around her neck; to have Da give her the chance she yearned for—those would be fine things. The Scanran war was dragging to its end. Soon her mother would return, as would Aunt Daine and Uncle Numair and the baby. There would be hot baths and the newest fashions. As the warriors came home the capital would light up with celebrations. Aly could read books, laze about, dress like a girl of property once more. She could even speak her mind instead of manipulating people.

She smiled and shook her head, trying to imagine the butterfly self she was among the men of the court. Instead she saw Winnamine and Mequen, Sarai and Dove, Ulasim and Chenaol. Nawat would come back to Tortall with her, but Lokeij and Junai would not. And Kyprioth had hinted Bronau would bring danger to Tanair.

"No," she said at last, "a bet's a bet. You don't wiggle out of this one that easily. And if I win the bet, you pay what was wagered, *and* you still owe me."

Kyprioth sighed. "You drive a hard bargain, Aly."

Before she could ask him if he was trying to pull the wool over her eyes, he swept her up in a glowing arm and shot into the air, through the palace roof. They were on their way north again.

Something occurred to her as they rose into the air over the city. Her mother was the Goddess's chosen. Why hadn't the Goddess known she was missing? Aly knew her mother wouldn't have wasted all this time, knowing she could call on the Goddess and not doing so. Kyprioth, Aly realized. "Why hasn't the Goddess come for me?" she asked the god. "What did you do? You can't tell me that Mother hasn't been praying to her for a glimpse of my whereabouts."

"I wasn't going to deny it," replied the god. "You know I dare not let my sister find out what I'm up to. I would be *thousands* of years coming back from where she and my brother would send me. One of my friends keeps your lovely mother company. She catches your mother's prayers and keeps them for me."

"You'd better hope Mother never finds out, or you'll have worse than your sister and brother to contend with," Aly told him. "You don't want the Lioness hunting for you."

"I know that," Kyprioth said. "I assure you, I am being quite careful."

Aly said nothing more as they traveled. Instead she reviewed the various combinations of results that might come from the events she had just witnessed. Bronau had planned to ask Hazarin to recall the Balitangs. Now Hazarin was dead. How friendly would Imajane and Rubinyan be to the Balitangs?

She dared not underestimate Bronau. He was now more dangerous than ever, as a man on the run and in disgrace, possibly declared a traitor. Whatever had driven him to such a harebrained stunt? Surely he knew he couldn't escape the palace with a three-year-old, even if he did know secret passages?

Why hadn't Bronau waited? Once his brother and sister-in-law were settled in their regency, they would have been less vigilant for unrest. Bronau could have gathered and bribed followers in his own time, ensuring his ability to seize power without taking unnecessary chances. Now he would be hunted the length and breadth of the Copper Isles. The new regents would view all of his friends with suspicion. The Balitangs would be among the first to draw their attention, since they had housed Bronau only weeks before.

The raka would need more patrols at Tanair. She would have to talk to Ulasim and Fesgao about that. With Ochobu and Aly to make sure no spies were brought into their ranks, the raka could expand their unofficial army.

She hardly noticed when she popped back into her body. Her planning stopped only when true sleep washed over her.

You asked me why the king doesn't just call on the gods for help with Scanra. We mustn't get too dependent on the gods. On the day before King Jonathan's coronation, the Great Mother Goddess spoke of a crossroads in time, when not even the gods can predict how things might go. At such times they must step away and let us deal with things. It's a blessing, in a way. It evens the balance and saves us mortals from being the gods' puppets. Still, it's hard to think of it as a blessing when you're frightened, you don't know why, and all you want is for the god to tell you what the bad thing is so you can hunt it down and kill it.

—From a letter to Aly when she was fourteen, from her mother

15

WINGED MESSENGER

When Aly woke at last, her muscles screamed in protest as she tried to sit up. Her mouth tasted disgusting. Her teeth felt as if they had a thick coating of slime. She was lying on a cot in a house that had whitewashed walls.

"How long?" Her question emerged from her throat as a croak. She looked around stiffly. They had brought her back from Inti and put her in Tanair's makeshift infirmary.

Nawat, asleep on a chair by the door, was startled into wakefulness. He raced across to Aly and touched her face. "I am very angry with the god for keeping you so long," he said, his dark eyes worried.

Aly smiled at him. "It was very instructive, though," she whispered.

Nawat kissed her swiftly on the mouth, then raced out the door. When he returned, he brought Ochobu with him.

"How long was I away?" she asked the old mage.

Ochobu sat on the cot's edge and lifted one of Aly's eyelids. "Five days," she said. She checked Aly's other eye. "We carried you home on a litter. You need a bath." She rose and looked down at Aly, her old eyes as unreadable as a god's. "Is it bad, what he showed you?"

"Bad enough," Aly admitted. "I'll need to talk to Ulasim and the others right away. I don't care what they're doing. Are Their Graces about?"

"The duchess and the children help Chenaol to put up fruit and vegetables against the winter," Ochobu replied. "The duke is in the village. He oversees all the new building here."

"They can wait until tonight, I think," Aly said, rubbing her temples. "But I need Ulasim, Chenaol, Lokeij, Fesgao, and you, as soon as I'm cleaned up. We need to prepare for serious trouble."

For two weeks after Hazarin's death and Bronau's attempt to kidnap Dunevon Aly roamed. She covered Tanair's castle and village on her own, then rode all over the plateau in the company of Sarai, Dove, and their guards. It was a relief to leave the keep each day. After hearing the circumstances around Hazarin's death, Aly's news about the change in government and Bronau's rashness, Mequen and Winnamine seemed burdened, as if someone in the house had died. The adults understood that a nation with a child king was vulnerable to rebellion and trouble from its enemies. Sarai was furious that Bronau would frighten a child so badly. Dove's opinions stayed behind the younger girl's dark eyes.

Ulasim had recruited another raka patrol, but the harvest had begun, and every hand was needed to bring it in. Tanair winters were harsh. The crops had to be brought in and food laid up. Aly understood the thin line between poverty and starvation. Harvest at Pirate's Swoop was always a scramble, one in which the baron's entire family worked in the fields. Despite knowing that, Aly had to struggle to hide her impatience with the raka. Bronau was on the loose, with the regents searching for him. If she had an army to keep the Balitangs safe, she would still wonder if she had planned for everything.

Aly calculated the time it would take Bronau to reach Lombyn. It would be a week if his passage was as swift as the Balitangs' had been. To that she added a handful of days on the road, assuming he landed on the western coast, or a week if he came from Dimari. When a third week passed with no sign of the renegade prince, Aly relaxed slightly. Perhaps Bronau had been captured. Or perhaps he had decided that Tanair was the first place his enemies would look for him.

Waiting for something to happen, Aly met with the raka conspirators each night to review their arrangements and hear their news. She also visited Nawat to hear what the crows had to report. Only with Nawat could Aly enjoy the summer's calm. The nights were getting cool, but it was warm at Nawat's side. Once he finished with the news, he taught Aly the names the crows had for the stars, the different types of cloud, and the moon. The only thing that had the same name for crows as it did for humans was the constellation known as the Cat.

"My mother knew the Cat," Aly confided. "At least, that's what she told me when I was a little girl. That the star-Cat became a mortal one, and taught her things as she grew up. It was my favorite story, even if it wasn't true."

"Why should it not be true?" Nawat asked. "The Cat is a god of sorts. He makes his own decisions to help or to hinder two-leggers." He put an arm around Aly.

She leaned into his hold, not thinking, then tugged away. "Nawat!" she exclaimed. "What is that supposed to be?"

"Don't you like it?" he asked. "Fesgao does it to Tulpa the miller's daughter, and she nestles against him."

"I'm not Tulpa," Aly insisted. "Besides, I can't be distracted." She got to her feet hurriedly and thanked all the gods that she did not blush as easily as her mother did. "Nestling is *very* distracting."

"I know." Nawat got to his feet, resting his hands on her shoulders. "You are Aly, who guards us all." He bent down and kissed her slowly and sweetly. Aly clung to him because she was afraid to try to stand on knees gone to jelly. At last Nawat released her. "Good night," he said cheerfully. He walked out through the inner courtyard gate, on his way home to Falthin.

Aly remained where she was, a hand pressed to her lips, for a long time.

Realizing that if Bronau came they were as prepared as they could be, Aly threw her energies into the winter preparations at Tanair. There was plenty for everyone to do, from the duke and the duchess to the child who brought in the eggs each day. The older Balitang women and their twenty servants and slaves worked at the tasks of the season: boiling and jellying, peeling and cutting, grinding and sealing, smoking and pickling. Mequen was everywhere, helping to get the crops in, the wood cut and stored, and making sure Tanair was weatherproofed. Like the village children, Elsren and Petranne helped their families. Each night Petranne showed Aly her day's work, presenting the wads of lumpily spun wool with as much pride as if they were the finest thread. Elsren collected baskets of pine cones to use as kindling, losing half of them on the way home.

Weapons training was the only thing to continue uninterrupted. Sarai worked on more complex battle dances. These were combinations of footwork, thrusts, blocks, and chops meant to be used until she could do the sequences without thought in response to a real attack. Winnamine still labored to master the most basic battle dance, but she practiced ferociously, ignoring blisters and aching muscles. Dove's archery improved daily. She could now shoot a cluster of five arrows in a circle no wider than her stepmother's hand. All the same, Dove never got so good that Nawat couldn't catch her arrows. Aly grinned to see grizzled veterans consoling the twelve-year-old, assuring her that they, too, could not loose a shot that Nawat didn't catch.

One morning, as Aly rode out with her young mistresses and their guards, she noted clouds along the western edge of the mountains. "Let's make it quick," she advised. "We take the medicines to Pohon and back. That looks like rain to me."

"You worry too much, Aly," Sarai scoffed as she mounted up. "Those clouds are miles away."

"Aly is right," Fesgao told his mistress firmly. "To Pohon and back, no farther. Storms move fast up here. You should know this by now."

Sarai put up her nose and galloped her mount through Tanair's open village gate. Aly watched Fesgao gallop after Sarai and shook her head.

"She'll calm down," Dove told Aly as the two girls rode out of Tanair. Nawat followed them at an easy trot. Ochobu had commissioned him to gather roadside herbs for her that day. "She just doesn't know what she thinks about Bronau going so wrong. The only way she knows to deal with it is to ride hard."

Aly grinned and glanced down at Nawat. "I don't suppose you'd flirt with Sarai?" she asked the crow-man. "She thinks you're handsome. You could clean the bugs from your teeth."

"And you aren't old and stupid like Bronau," Dove added.

"I am too young for Sarai," Nawat replied soberly. "I am not even a month old. Sarai is ancient compared to me."

Aly and Dove giggled. "Oh, tell her that when I'm there to see," Dove begged. "I want to watch her face when you do."

They caught up to Sarai and Fesgao five miles outside Pohon. The other two riders had reined up at the spot where a barely used track met the road.

"Sarai, no!" cried Dove, exasperated beyond her usual calm. "Can't we, just *once*, go somewhere and return *quickly*?"

Nawat raised a finger, his eyes sharp. "Hold."

Aly held very still, listening. Why had the usually polite Nawat voiced something like an order? Then she heard it, the raucous clamor of dozens of crows in the East. She strained to hear, but many of them called different things, some of which she had never been taught. "What—" she began.

"A winged four-legger comes from the mountains that hold the morning sun," said Nawat. "She bears a fledgling two-legger on her back. They seek the stone sti—the castle."

Aly frowned. "Winged . . . a kudarung. A big one, to carry a child on her back."

"That's a royal messenger," Sarai commented, her perfect brows knit in disapproval. "Only the Rittevon line may call on winged horses as messengers. I doubt that Dunevon would think of using one unless he wanted a ride."

All three girls wheeled their mounts and raced to Tanair, their guards on their heels. Nawat was left behind to make his way on foot.

They had to slow to a trot through the village. By then Aly had already spotted the new arrivals: a boy or girl of ten, clad in shearling garments against the cold of the upper air, strapped to a large gray mare with a white mane and tail and huge, bat-like wings. Messenger and mount sailed over the girls' heads. With an adjustment to her Sight, Aly could see the winged horse badge of the Rittevon family—they would never use the raka word kudarung—on both the messenger's tunic and the chest piece of the kudarung's harness.

The pair set down within the castle's inner courtyard as the girls and their guards rode through the gate. Ochobu's three tiny kudarung darted from the kitchen to circle the gray, looking like blackbirds against a thundercloud. Dove tumbled off her horse's back and raced inside to alert the duchess. Sarai ordered Veron to find the duke. Aly slipped off Cinnamon and took the three mounts to Lokeij and his stable boys.

"You know what the luarin say, don't you?" Lokeij murmured as he watched the messenger unbuckle the straps that held her to her mare. "Deadly news rides horses that fly."

Aly sighed. "If only the Rittevons use them as messengers, I can see how people might think that."

"The custom is an old one, from the time before the kudarung were banished to the Divine Realms," Lokeij said. "Our people had all but forgotten, until they returned twelve years past. Once the kudarung came here in flocks, all sizes of them, to nest and rear their young."

Aly washed her hands in a bucket of water, the picture of idle innocence. To Lokeij she said quietly, "Someone implied to me they served the old raka monarchs freely, but that King Oron had to capture some and breed them for his service."

"It was farsighted of Oron, may we live to spit on his grave." Lokeij grinned, revealing all the gaps in his teeth. "When Sarai takes power, the people will see the kudarung come to her freely. They will see she holds the crown by right."

"Don't say that aloud, even to a friend," Aly warned. "The less it's mentioned, the less chance someone will over-hear who shouldn't."

"Cautious Aly of the crooked eye," said Lokeij with a chuckle.

"If you keep sweet-talking me so, I'll charge you before the duke of turning my poor frivolous head," Aly replied, bat-ting her eyelashes at him. "An incautious spy is soon dead. And don't start asking again who I was before I ended up here."

"You think that others don't wonder?" Lokeij asked, his eyes glittering with interest. "That Their Graces don't ask how many tiny signs and tricks a god could teach a mortal in a short time?"

"What I think doesn't matter," said Aly as she shook her hands dry. "I just live my life at the god's beck and call."

Lokeij snorted his disbelief.

Aly waved a lazy hand at him. "Now, if you'll excuse me, I'm going to snoop."

Once the duke arrived, he and Winnamine retired to their private rooms with Sarai and the messenger. They didn't ask for a servant to attend them. Aly idled in the great hall, restacking logs on the hearth, until Sarai appeared at the top of the stairs. "Aly, have Ulasim find this girl a place for the night," she called, urging the messenger down the stairs. "Papa and Mama have asked for you to bring some wine."

Aly obeyed, summoning Ulasim for the messenger and going to Chenaol for the wine. When she reached the duke's rooms with the tray, Sarai took it, then poured cups for her father and stepmother. Winnamine offered the messenger's letter to Aly. All three Balitangs looked haunted.

Aly took the letter and scanned it. The seal was the Rittevons': a winged horse triumphant, rearing on its hind legs, wings outstretched. The writing on the document was firm and elegant, though it was not in the professionally smooth hand of a scribe.

My dear Mequen and Winna,

I regret that this letter brings no good news to you. King Hazarin is dead of apoplexy. Dunevon, my lady's half brother, is now king, with Imajane and me as his regents. That would be tragic enough. Hazarin was in his prime, and no kingdom ruled by a child is stable. There is worse news, however. My brother, in madness or folly, attempted to kidnap Dunevon, to what purpose I cannot guess. He has been formally charged with high treason. Our agents seek him throughout the realm. Already we have learned that my brother is attempting to create rebellion among the outland nobility. This cannot be allowed.

I am concerned that he may seek refuge with you and your family, as he did when he incurred Oron's disfavor. For the love you bear me, will you ask him to come to Rajmuat, to answer the charges? If he comes of his own accord, I may be able to smooth things over with the king's council. Should his enemies take him, I fear for my brother's life. He has always said you and Winnamine are the coolest heads in the family. I agree. If you can persuade him to return, Imajane and I will be forever in your debt. We are reversing Oron's charges against you. Soon you will be able to return to Rajmuat. I cannot envision keeping the Midwinter Festival without my best friends there. With thanks from Imajane and from me,

Your friend Rubinyan

Aly reread the letter. *Rubinyan says he's worried,* she thought, *but he never calls Bronau by his name or implies that he cares for him. And he doesn't ask the Balitangs to come home now, when he is as good as king himself, for all* that he calls them "friends." Does he want them to serve as bait for his brother first?

She returned the letter to Mequen. *Of course His Grace will do it,* she thought, watching the duke's troubled face as he rolled the letter up into a tight scroll. *He has faith that Bronau can explain his way out of this, or that Rubinyan will save him from the gallows. But he can also tell that something is not right here.*

Mequen tapped the rolled letter against his leg. "He sent this by winged horse," he said at last. "It's a private letter from him to me, but he used royal messengers for it. Is he mad? In the reign of Hanoren the First, it was ruled that no regent may take on the prerogatives of the Crown. That includes the use of winged horses."

"He wanted the news to reach us as quickly as possible, with all the distance between us," the duchess explained. "He thought you would understand. And it does involve the attempt on Dunevon."

"I do not like it," replied Mequen. "It is most improper."

"Perhaps Aunt Imajane wished us to get the letter quickly, and she granted the use of the messengers?" asked Sarai. "She is as royal as Dunevon, even if she can't inherit."

Aly folded her hands in front of her. "Will Your Grace tell this to the household?" she asked politely. "Let them know that the prince's next visit may be . . ." She chose her words carefully. "Different," she finished.

The duke and duchess traded glances. It was Sarai who replied. "Is this the kind of thing servants should know?"

Aly looked at her. "If the prince comes and there is a fight, they'll be involved," she pointed out. "And some of the servants . . ." She stopped. Light was growing in the room, casting the family and the furnishings into high relief.

The source of it, she realized, was her.

With a mental sigh she silently asked Kyprioth, "Will you stop playing games?"

"You want them to listen, don't you?" asked the god. "Keep talking."

Aly resigned herself. I must be sure that my next task in life can be handled without gods, she told herself. To the Balitangs she said, "You have servants who will be useful if things go wrong. Ulasim, for one. Ochobu. Royal spy or not, Veron must be warned that Bronau may come armed, with soldiers on his tail." Aly went silently to the door to the servants' stair to reveal Dove, who had been listening again. Aly beckoned her inside and closed the door. "Lady Dove should have been here already, to further her instruction about the world she must live in."

"Dove, eavesdropping is a slave's trick," the duke told his younger daughter.

Dove looked down. "I'm sorry, Papa," she replied, though she was clearly not.

Aly looked at the family. She still gleamed with power lent to her by the god. "I advise you only because I want to ensure nothing happens to you. I want to keep you and your children safe, and I cannot do it alone. I am not the sort to go dashing around with a sword in each hand."

The duchess pursed her lips. "When you put it that way, of course, we must listen," she said drily. The glow that blazed from Aly faded.

"Find those you think must know and send them to us here," Mequen instructed. "We will explain."

Once she'd found Ochobu, Veron, and Ulasim, Aly left it to the duke to share the news. She wandered down to the kitchen. There Chenaol and the kitchen staff were feeding the messenger, bombarding the girl with questions. Chenaol winked when she saw Aly. The cook would get any scraps of information the messenger might have.

Aly nodded to Chenaol and went outside. Near the stable, the winged horse and Nawat stood forehead to forehead. Nawat's lips moved. Aly watched, fascinated. What *was* Nawat doing?

"They speak, as winged creatures will," Lokeij said. He had appeared at Aly's elbow. "Whatever news the kudarung has, Nawat will hear it."

Aly ran a finger under the metal ring on her neck. It bothered her more than usual tonight, having picked up bits of hay during her day's work.

"Annoying, isn't it?" Lokeij asked. "Now you feel like a raka. Even those who do not wear a metal collar have felt luarin rule chafing for nearly three centuries."

Aly raised an eyebrow at the old man. Here was another chance to make the point she had tried to impress on Ochobu: the greatest problem with the raka's and Kyprioth's plans. "I know luarin rule irks you," she replied evenly. "So let me ask this: does it bother you that blood will be shed to remove *your* collars? That the luarin who try to do their best by you, who only inherited the mess the Rittevons have made, may die to ease the collar off your necks?"

"Do you speak of our lady's family, or of Prince Bronau?" asked Lokeij. "The Jimajen house is known for its brutality to their raka. We will rejoice if Jimajen blood is shed."

Hands in his pockets, Nawat left the winged horse to the meal of oats Lokeij had supplied and sauntered over to the hostler and Aly. "She says that the winter rains will come late in the jungles," he told them. "The fishing is off. She says also that the free kudarung know the old blood is present here, on Lombyn. When the time comes, the kudarung will gather to salute the new queen."

Aly thought this over. A powerful symbol of someone's right to rule was always useful: the appearance of the Dominion Jewel had once convinced Tortallans that Jonathan was the rightful king. She nodded. "Thank her, please. We are honored that the kudarung will help us."

"It will be as it was before," Lokeij whispered, eyes bright with awe. "The rightful queen in Rajmuat, and the kudarung soaring in the skies."

"She isn't on the throne yet," Aly cautioned. "Don't let your dreams outrun your common sense." She took another look at the kudarung, who had folded her wings as she ate greedily. Still thoughtful, Aly returned to the castle, absently running a finger around her slave collar.

When Aly left the tower the following morning, she found Nawat at work outside, as usual. Crows were perched all around the inner courtyard, on every space they could find. There must have been thirty of them.

Nawat greeted her with his warm smile, the one that always got an answering smile from her. "My clan will roost here for a time, until the weather says it is the season to fly down to warmer country. They say they will be sure to empty their bowels off the sides of this nest." With a wave of his hand he indicated the castle walls.

Aly looked at the crows, then at the young man carefully attaching sharp Stormwing fletchings to a heavy arrow shaft. "Another mage killer?" she asked. For the first time she noticed that despite his deftness and assurance, he always worked slowly with the razor-edged Stormwing feathers.

"There are all kinds of mages in the world, and sometimes they run in packs," Nawat replied.

Aly nodded. Looking at the circle of crows, she asked, "Will we need so many?"

Nawat bird-shrugged. "They are my clan. If they are not needed, they will watch the game."

Aly raised an eyebrow as she turned her gaze on him. "Is this a game to you?" she asked.

Nawat looked up. His dark eyes held hers. "You are never a game to me, Aly. And hawks are never a game to crows."

"But you aren't a crow now," she pointed out softly.

"A crow may put on human shape or crow shape, but we remain crows," he replied firmly. "Hawks, too, are the same, whether they are born in human nests or hawk ones. The nestlings must always be protected. Since you have chosen to protect these, I and mine will protect you."

Aly nodded, blinking her eyes against sudden tears. She couldn't think of a thing to say in response to such a declaration of complete friendship. Instead she rested her hand on Nawat's shoulder. His warm fingers covered hers for a moment. Then he returned to his fletching, and Aly wandered out through the gate to inspect the Tanair defenses.

She walked down through the village, waving to the baker and exchanging greetings with the innkeeper's wife. Visda and Ekit raced by, surrounding Aly with goats and sheep. She grinned as they swirled out through the village gate on their way to pasture.

Except for those early risers and the sleepy-looking men-at-arms on the wall, Aly had the ground to herself as she examined the village defenses. Duke Mequen had worked on the wall along with other projects all summer. Much had been done since their arrival, shoring up what was left of the ancient stone wall and bracing the palisade just outside. More than anything Aly wished they'd been able to build the stone wall to the height of the log one. If an enemy came at them with battle fire, the palisade would burn, and the stone walls wouldn't stop anyone. Aly understood why more hadn't been done. The duke could only call on those of his men-at-arms who weren't on duty and the few villagers who didn't have crops to harvest or winter preparations of their own. It didn't make Aly feel any better. She would just have to pray that no enemies came with battle fire, or that those who did fell into the ditch in front of the palisade. If they burned the wooden barrier, the villagers would have to retreat within the castle walls and expect to lose everything outside them.

Aly trudged back up to the castle. Perhaps Ochobu could fireproof the palisade. She wanted to be certain the duke could summon the villagers inside the walls and warn the valley herders to hide with their stock. They needed ways to heat barrels of oil or water and get them onto the walls to dump on any attackers . . .

Enough, she told herself, leaning her forehead against the stone of the outer courtyard wall. They'll only let you do so much. His Grace and Veron will have plans laid to bring folk inside the castle and defend it. My job is to twiddle my thumbs and wait for something to happen. If I'm to do that, I may as well go sew winter clothes. I can only act on what information I have, as I have already done. Now it's a matter of waiting.

I *hate* waiting.

"Kyprioth," she called silently in a teasing voice. "Kyprioth, Kyprioth, Kyprioth. Don't pretend you aren't nearby. All this is too important to you. Talk to me."

"You are getting to know me a little too well," the familiar voice said wearily. "What is it?"

"Oh, don't be grumpy," she told him, still being playful.

"Isn't it a grand thing that I do know you so well? Now, tell me—something's about to happen, isn't it? The reason why you brought me here in the first place."

"Well?" demanded the god.

"What is it?" Aly wanted to know. "What's coming? I could use a hint. My working blind isn't precisely useful, you know."

"All I see is a coming together of lives and possibilities. Anything could happen."

"Just a little hint? You're a god, you must have some notion," she replied, prodding him.

"I DO NOT." Suddenly the god's voice boomed in her mind as it must boom in the minds of the Balitangs and the raka. Aly locked her knees. She would not drop to the ground, no matter how much Kyprioth sounded like a Great God to her just now. She stubbornly remained on her feet as he continued, "It is the hour of mortal choices. It is your turn to dictate the course of fate. I can do no more."

Just when she thought he was finished, that he'd made his portentous announcement and gone away, she heard him say, much more quietly, "Besides, my brother and sister have returned. Well, I knew they would. Don't betray my trick to them, Aly. Keep them thinking this is just another human squabble."

"Thanks ever so," she thought to him. "I'll do as much for you one day. And you still owe me."

When her sense of Kyprioth's presence faded, Aly sat at the base of the castle wall. She had her answer, in a manner of speaking. Things—events—were unfolding, and now the humans would have to do their part. The gods had to let the dice fall as they may.

Wonderful, Aly thought, leaning her head against the

wall. Might I have the Graveyard Hag's dice right now? Aunt Daine says they're weighted with lead, so the Hag wins every roll. I don't mind cheating at a time like this.

A shadow passed over her. Aly looked up to see the kudarung and her rider in flight, on their way back to Dimari.

Three afternoons later the crows at the pass shrieked the news that eleven armed riders were on the road to Tanair. Crows and a raka patrol followed them to the village to make sure that none of the visitors left their group unnoticed.

Nawat was working at his bench when the crows proclaimed the news. "They say that Bronau is with them," he told Aly. She helped him by holding a piece of leather flat on the bench while Nawat cut it up for laces. "The hawk is coming."

Aly nodded. "I have to let go," she warned him. Nawat sat back. Aly released the leather, then ran to report first to the duchess. Winnamine took Aly to the duke, who was reviewing the harvest totals.

"We'll let him in. Bronau can relax, and tell his side of the story. I want to hear what he has to say," he told Aly and his wife. "We owe him that. And I am sure he will do the right thing, once he's had a chance to think it over."

Aly carried word to Chenaol, and thus to Sarai and Dove, who were helping the cook to strain seeds from newly made jelly. To their credit, the girls finished their tasks before they raced to their rooms to change clothes and to move things so their parents could sleep on the third story with them. Bronau would have Winnamine's and Mequen's rooms, but the fourth floor was no longer available to his men-at-arms, as it was full of winter stores. Even Bronau would not suspect his friends did not want his soldiers living among them. Instead they would sleep in one of the new buildings, under Veron's eye.

Aly was cleaned up and wearing a dress by the time Bronau entered the great hall. Mequen and Winnamine waited there to meet him, as did Sarai. Dove had refused to greet the traitor, using words just that blunt. From her position behind Sarai, Aly watched as Bronau handed his outer coat and gloves to one of the house slaves. He approached his friends with his ready smile.

"So grim," he said teasingly. "Whatever can you have heard?" He kissed Winnamine on both cheeks and gave Mequen a man's brisk hug. He took Sarai's hand and kissed her fingers with comic elegance, his raised brows and twinkling eyes drawing a smile from her in spite of herself.

"We've heard dreadful things, my lord," she explained shyly.

"Come up to our rooms and talk," offered Mequen. "Aly, refreshments, please."

Aly curtsied and went to the kitchen. Chenaol had already assembled a tray for her. "Ten men-at-arms, Fesgao says," the cook reported in a whisper for Aly's ears alone. "They've been riding hard. If ten's all he's got, His Grace could simply kill them all and ship Bronau back to Rajmuat. Or kill Bronau and send his pickled head to the regents. It's a good way to make sure there's no more trouble."

"The duke wants to keep it friendly," Ochobu said icily. She was seated at a table, clutching a mug of tea with knobby fingers. "Whoever heard of a luarin that wasn't ready to shed the blood of others? And this is a fine time to have such qualms, when killing the Jimajen prince would simplify things."

Aly grimaced. "Things are not precisely friendly between him and the prince," she pointed out, though privately she agreed that their lives would be far easier if Bronau and his men were dead. The duke was not that kind of person, however. "His Grace says that if Bronau grovels a bit, it will be all right. He says Rubinyan would never order the death of his own brother. We're to wait and see."

"The duke's too good for this, you know," Chenaol said, glaring at Ochobu. "For that luarin snakepit they call the royal court. He always was."

"He's soft," the old mage said harshly. "And he doesn't know anything about the house of Jimajen. They will turn on him with a smile and a razor in their hands."

"Aly." Lokeij stood at the kitchen door, beckoning. Aly went to him. "Something's off," whispered the hostler. "None of these came with him before—not the men, not the horses. And he's brought no body servants. Warn the duke."

Aly nodded and took the tray from Chenaol. The change in attendants could be entirely harmless. Perhaps Bronau hadn't cared to burden himself with body servants when he was on the run. Perhaps they'd been captured. Perhaps his usual warriors had been unable to follow him when he escaped Rajmuat.

I hate *perhaps*es when lives are at stake, she thought as she climbed the stairs. And I'd as soon handle a jar of acid on a bumpy road than try to guess what folly Bronau will commit next.

Once more she poured out wine for everyone in the duke's sitting room, even Sarai. She also murmured Lokeij's news into the duke's ear as she served him. Mequen nodded and gestured for her to take her place behind the duchess. "You can speak before Aly," the duke assured Bronau. "Whom would she tell it to? The grass?"

Bronau smirked at Aly, then addressed his friends. "There was something wrong in Hazarin dying so unexpectedly.

I don't suspect my brother, of course," he said, grinning, holding up a hand to stop the protest he expected Mequen to make. "Imajane, though—she doesn't show the madness, but would you care to wager that it skipped her and got every other member of the Rittevon family?"

"Even Dunevon?" asked Winnamine with a smile, offering Bronau the pastry dish. He accepted one and wolfed it down. Aly wondered when he had eaten last.

"Oh, who knows?" asked Bronau. "He's only three, poor lad. Winna, it would break your heart, the way they keep him. No boys his own age in that tomb of a chamber, their servants in place of his . . . I'd never use a child of *my* blood so." He glanced sidelong at Sarai, who ducked her head shyly. "But Imajane is as cold as the ocean deeps. It would never occur to her that Dunevon's a child more than he is a king."

"But you tried to kidnap that king," Mequen said gently. "Bronau, Rubinyan has written to us."

"Ah," said the prince. "So that is why you regard me with such reserve today. It was a rash act, I see that now. I wasn't thinking of anything but getting the boy to safety. If they killed a reigning king, will they stop at murdering a child?"

"I cannot believe Rubinyan would be a part of either crime," Mequen replied stiffly.

Bronau hung his head. "No, no, of course not." He turned his feverish eyes on Winnamine. "Don't you find it suspicious that Hazarin's servants and healer vanished all at once? I'll wager *they* could tell some stories."

"These are all good points," said Mequen, "but until the charges against you are dismissed, you can only sow disorder with such talk." Nothing about him suggested that he knew the true fate of Hazarin's servants and healer. "You must answer to the king's council and clear your name. If the misunderstanding cannot be dismissed, Rubinyan may have to make some gesture. Send you into exile, perhaps, or imprison you at the Stronghold. But your friends will seek your pardon."

"Return and stand trial," suggested Winnamine. "You'll slip the rug out from under them. By running, you only create more doubt in people's minds. Once the council sees and hears you, and knows you felt that you did your duty by the Crown, I think you'll find more allies than you suspect."

Bronau chewed on a fingernail, the picture of a guilty child. "Do you truly think so?"

"Of course," Winnamine replied, resting a hand on his arm.

"Men on the hunt for other men, particularly a man known as a fighter, like you—such hunters do make mistakes," Mequen reminded his friend. "If you're caught, if you fight, some dreadful accident might happen. You might be killed by an overzealous armsman before you can speak to the council at all."

Aly refilled glasses as the conversation went on. Daylight faded into sunset. Mequen and Winnamine came at Bronau in close order, persuading, joking, and debating. They did all they could to sow a gentler, more thoughtful mood in their rash friend.

The turning point came when Bronau looked at Sarai. "And what of you?" he asked. "Do you think I am a criminal?"

She lowered her eyes. "My lord, how could I think you a criminal? It is your life, I fear for . . ." Her eyelashes fluttered like butterflies. "—And your future," she added in a shy whisper.

Oh, she's good, thought Aly in admiration, remembering Sarai's fury when she heard of Bronau's kidnapping attempt. She's very good. I could turn opponents to her queenship right around by just giving her time to work on them.

Mequen eyed his daughter and his friend. At last the silence created by Sarai was finally broken by the supper bell. Mequen asked, "Will it help if I go to Rajmuat with you? Rubinyan will listen to me, I think, and the two of us can talk to Imajane."

"Papa!" cried Sarai, alarmed out of her maidenly distress.

"My dear, I don't think you could return before the passes close for the winter," Winnamine said, her hands clenched in her lap.

"This is more important," Mequen explained gravely to his wife and daughter. "If only one of us goes to Rajmuat, it won't seem as if we are forcing our way back into favor. If I must wait to return until spring . . ." He shrugged.

Bronau stared at Mequen. "You would do that for me? They could arrest you."

"I don't believe Rubinyan will allow that. And yes, I will go, if it helps to ease the trouble between the two of you," replied Mequen, his gaze sober. "The realm needs you and Rubinyan both. We can't afford dissent in the family that rules the Isles, not with a child on the throne and our Carthaki friends eyeing us like a ripe plum to be picked."

"Of your goodwill, give me a day to discuss it with my people," he said, voice and body weary. "They have been with me over many hard miles. They deserve a chance to decide if they will return and share whatever happens to me."

"Of course you may have the time," Mequen said, getting to his feet. He went to Bronau, who stood and embraced him. "And you should rest before you return. You look worn to the bone."

Bronau looked at Mequen, then at Winnamine and Sarai, obviously puzzled. "It hasn't occurred to you, has it?"

he asked. "Should anything happen to Dunevon, *you* would be king. You—"

Mequen put a hand over his friend's mouth. "Please don't speak of that again," he said gently. "*Ever.* Haven't you noticed? Kingship in the Copper Isles drives people mad. I don't want it, for myself or my family. And in case you've forgotten, when I first married, the king had me swear before Mithros that I would never seek the crown. I keep my word."

Bronau hugged Mequen impulsively. "You were always better than the rest of us," he said, his voice thick. He let Mequen go and stepped back. "Now. Where may I clean up? I must tell you, I haven't had a true meal in days."

Aly took Bronau to the duke's bedchamber, where he would sleep as he had on his last visit. Once he was supplied with hot water, soap, and drying cloths, Aly returned to the family. The door was unlatched. She entered the room to find that Sarai had gone. The duke and the duchess were in each other's arms.

"I'm sorry," Aly said when they looked at her.

The duchess had been crying. She muttered an apology and went to the washstand to splash water on her face.

"It's all right," Mequen replied. With Bronau no longer in view, the duke's true feelings were easier to read. His shoulders drooped, and the lines on his face were deep with care. "We must go downstairs in a moment in any case."

Aly hesitated. What she had to say would distress him, but she needed to say it. "Forgive me, Your Grace, but should you not make him swear before the god to behave? To abide by your direction?" she asked, trying to tell him to do it without making it a direct order. She didn't think they trusted her enough to accept orders, even if she went against her training and gave them. "If he panics, there's no telling what he might do. An oath would rein him in."

Mequen sighed. "Aly, if you were noble-born, you would know that would be an intolerable insult to an honorable man like Bronau. To ask for such a vow implies I do not trust him. Do you wish to spark the very kind of outburst that got him into this mess? Leave the nobility to handle the nobility."

Aly blinked at him. Just once she wished she could speak her mind, to tell him that she, too, was noble-born, and some nobles could not be trusted as far as they could be thrown. She was sorely tempted to point out to him that Trebond blood was bluer than that of any Kyprish luarin. Instead she put such unwise answers from her mind, came about, and tried another tack. "Your Grace, he has a point. They might well imprison *you* if you returned." *I* would, she thought, but did not say aloud.

Mequen shook his head. "Rubinyan and I have been friends since boyhood. He would never do such a thing." When Aly opened her mouth again, he raised a hand to silence her. "Enough of plots and plotting. Don't you have the wine service at supper?"

Aly had been dismissed. *Never mind that I speak for the god*, she thought with a mental sigh. *Never mind that I am trying to keep him and his family from harm.* Aly turned and left the room without so much as a curtsy to her master.

16

BETRAYAL

Aly woke the next morning with the other servants, having taken forever to sleep the night before. Yawning, she rolled her pallet and stored it, then cleaned up for the day. Once presentable, she joined the line for breakfast. Chenaol was serving. When Aly reached the cook, she asked Chenaol to remind everyone to watch Bronau and his people.

"That's easy enough," Chenaol said drily, keeping her voice soft. "They amble about the courtyards like this was a friendly visit. Just look at that." She pointed to one of the kitchen slaves, who flirted busily with two of Bronau's men at the outer door. "They act like they haven't a care in the world. That's just not right, not with Princess Imajane at their tails. She's not nearly as kind as Oron—she once had a man flayed when he spat on her shadow. Any idea of what the prince means to do?"

"He's thinking," Aly murmured as Chenaol filled her bowl with porridge. "It will take him a while, since thinking isn't something that comes naturally to him."

Chenaol laughed hard and long. Aly smiled reluctantly.

"I'm glad *you're* amused," she said, and went off to eat her meal in peace.

She was almost finished when Ulasim found her. "The duchess asks for you," he told her. "Hurry—they just sent the order for the ladies' and the prince's horses to be saddled. Lokeij will have yours ready."

Aly gave her empty bowl to the slaves who washed the dishes, then climbed the stairs to the family's quarters. The duke sat writing at his sitting room desk. Aly heard the voices of Winnamine, Sarai, and Dove in the bedchamber.

"Your Grace sent for me?" she asked Mequen. He hadn't, but she wanted to gauge his mood and his thoughts.

The duke raised his head. "Bronau has asked to remain here a week, to rest his men and the horses," he said quietly. "Then he and I shall return to Rajmuat, to straighten this out. He understands that he went astray. He says Rubinyan will hearken to me more than he will to Bronau, and I fear that's true. In the meantime, he's riding today with my lady and the girls."

Aly cocked an eyebrow. "Did he swear?" she inquired. "Did he swear to behave?"

Mequen's eyes hardened. "Enough. You do not know him as I do. I will hear no more of this, understand? Things are different for nobles than for commoners. If you cannot believe that, at least pretend to do so."

The bedchamber door opened. Out came Winnamine with Dove and Sarai, all dressed for riding and carrying bows and quivers. "Aly, there you are," the duchess said. "Come—we're going to hunt with the prince. Where were you this morning? My maid helped both girls to dress, but she was not happy."

Aly shrugged. "I assumed that I was back in the great hall, since the young ladies were with Your Graces and Your

Graces' servants," she said, bowing to the duchess. "Will you forgive me?"

"Yes, of course," said Winnamine, pulling on her gloves. "It never occurred to me that you wouldn't see your place is with Dove now."

"Come *on*," urged Sarai. "Bronau's waiting."

They passed the day as they had during the prince's first visit. He galloped with Sarai, then rode with the duchess, Sarai, and Dove. Aly, the ladies' bodyguards, and Junai followed close behind. Bronau told jokes and talked about Dunevon's coronation, relating the list of those who attended and what they wore. As far as Aly could tell, Sarai and the duchess hung on every word. Dove rode silently as she listened. Above them crows swooped and cawed. From their calls Aly knew who was nearby and whether they were raka, members of the Balitang household, or strangers.

The group returned with partridges for that night's supper. Aly took the birds to Chenaol, while the Balitang women went to play with Petranne and Elsren before they went to their weapons practice. With free time to spend, Aly did the rounds of the castle. She spoke first to the girls' raka defenders, telling them of the duke's and Bronau's plans. Nawat reported that the crows had seen nothing suspicious on the plateau, which made Aly feel a little better. Her relief did not last very long. Bronau's presence itched more than a rash. She could barely sit still, not when her instincts were shrieking.

Sarai and the duchess came out in the late afternoon sun to practice sword skills with the men-at-arms, while Dove joined in the archery practice. Bronau looked on, smiling like an indulgent uncle. Dove was stringing her bow when Nawat approached. He slid a handful of arrows into the twelve-year-old's quiver. Dove's eyes went round. She gazed at Nawat in awe, one of the few times Aly could read clear feelings on the girl's face. Each of Nawat's arrows was fletched with griffin feathers. It reminded Aly once more that Nawat had been a crow for most of his life. No two-legger would have given precious griffin fletchings to a child, let alone a girl.

One of the footmen came for Aly. "His Highness and His Grace play chess," he informed her. "They wish you to serve wine."

Aly followed the man back into the castle, her mind busy. Perhaps Bronau would get caught up in the game and say something she could use to persuade the duke to let his friend return to the capital alone. Instead the two men spoke of the past. Mequen and Rubinyan had been pages and squires together. Bronau had served under Mequen's command in the royal navy, then commanded the naval escort that had carried Mequen on diplomatic missions to Carthak. The men discussed Isles politics, Carthaki history, and music. They discussed players and compositions for so long that Aly wanted to sleep where she stood. Every now and then, when Bronau said something funny or engaging, the duke would glance at Aly, as if to say, "You see? He is a good man and a good friend."

Aly kept her face pleasant and refilled the cups as they emptied. Prince Bronau had shown on too many occasions that he was reckless and unreliable. He probably was a good friend to Mequen, but that meant very little in a dangerous political world.

The chess game ended; the men went out to practice sword skills with Veron and Fesgao. Aly stowed her pallet and belongings in the room where Sarai and Dove currently slept, then went downstairs.

Nawat met her in the great hall. "My brethren have come to roost here for the night," he informed Aly. They stood aside as Elsren and Petranne clattered by, pursued by their nursemaid. "The light is going. They say all remains quiet on these lands."

Aly nodded. "My head aches, though," she told him. "If all goes well, why am I tense?"

Nawat ran his fingers gently through Aly's short hair, preening her. "That is your task," he replied simply. "Most humans think the appearance of quiet *is* quiet. They do not see that sometimes the enemy is as quiet as the serpent. Only when it has stolen all of their eggs will they know bad walks in the quiet as well as the noisy."

Aly leaned against the wall, looking up into Nawat's deep-set eyes. "I thought you were worried about hawks."

"Those as well," Nawat answered. "But a hawk I can see. While I watch the hawk, who is to say the serpent is not behind me?"

Timidly Aly reached up and ran her fingers gently through Nawat's hair over one ear, preening him in return for the first time. "I wish the duke were as wise—or as clear-sighted—as crows."

Nawat was bending down to Aly when Ulasim called from the stair, "Aly? Lady Dovasary is calling for you." Nawat made a face and kissed Aly lightly on the nose, then left the hall. Aly tried to scorch Ulasim with a glare, but the big raka only returned a polite, meaningless smile. She stuck her tongue out at him as she trotted by on her way to Dove's room.

The day had cooled rapidly, enough that Sarai and Dove both wore woolen dresses to supper. Aly and Pembery loaded the braziers in the girls' rooms with charcoal and set them alight so that they would be warm as they slept. Then they followed their mistresses downstairs.

Bronau's men-at-arms ate supper with the Balitang

household, then retired to their quarters. The family's servants and slaves played music and sang, relaxing. At last the Balitangs went upstairs. Aly helped to undress Dove, then spread her pallet near the door of the master bedroom. After she donned the shift she slept in, Aly refastened the sheaths of her knives around her ankles and arms. Her sleep would be uncomfortable, but she dared not risk a night without them. Once that was done, she talked with Dove as Sarai read. From the sitting room, they could hear the murmur of conversation between the duke, the duchess, and Bronau.

At last the girls' parents came in and went into the dressing rooms to change clothes, with the help of Pembery and the man who waited on Mequen. The servants laid out their own pallets at the foot of the master bed as the duke and duchess slid under the cool linen sheets and a light coverlet. Sarai and Dove lay on cots placed on the far side of the bed, between Winnamine and her dressing room.

Aly looked around. Something wasn't right. Mequen was about to blow out the last candle when Aly said, "Wait, please." She went into the dressing room and returned with his unsheathed sword.

"*Aly,*" Mequen said, his eyes sharp with anger. "You really go too far—"

Winnamine laid her palm against his cheek to silence him. "Humor us, my dear. Keep it close."

The duke sighed in exasperation. "Gods, save me from the nerves of women!" he snapped, flinging himself back against his pillows. Then he sighed and sat up. "Thank you, Aly. I know your concern is for our welfare."

Aly placed the sword on the table with the candle. She angled its hilt so Mequen would find it instantly if he reached out in the dark. "Good night, Your Grace," she said, and blew out the candle. Using her Sight, adjusted for the dark, she found her pallet easily.

Sleep would not come. She tried to keep still, so as not to wake the others, but her body trembled with nerves. When she slept in the great hall, she could hear everything outside and in. She also had freedom to move downstairs. This room felt like a trap.

Aly heard the whisper of cloth on cloth through the crack under the door beside her. She pressed her ear to it, straining to hear. The sitting room on the other side was closed. She had watched Sarai shut that door, putting a heavy wooden barrier between the bedchamber and the main stair. What had made that stray noise, mice? The old tower had its share, but this sound was not mouselike.

She heard a thump, then a creak. Someone was definitely opening the sitting room door. "Your Grace!" Aly whispered, scrambling to her feet. "Wake up!" She lunged for the door and braced her shoulder against it, cursing the absence of locks on the family's rooms. What could she use to barricade the entry besides her own weight? Behind her she heard people scrambling out of their blankets.

As Aly braced her shoulder against the door to keep it shut, someone pushed on it from outside. It edged open. She scrabbled for purchase on the floor with her bare feet, without success, and leaned into the door with all of her weight. It wasn't enough. The door slammed open, smashing her against the wall behind it. Pain seared through her as her back hit stone with a crack. Aly groaned and shoved the door away from her. She sank to the floor, fighting to stay conscious.

Someone in the room threw the water pitcher: Aly saw it fly through the open doorway. A man yelped outside; the pitcher shattered on something hard. Mequen shouted orders to his wife and servants. Then Bronau, clinking in a chain mail shirt over a leather tunic and breeches, walked in. He carried an unsheathed sword in his hand. Three of his soldiers, wearing mail and carrying torches, followed.

The duke's manservant, howling in rage, attacked with no better weapon than an iron candelabrum. Bronau ran him through, then thrust the dead man off his blade with a booted foot. His men spread out behind him. Mequen had grabbed the sword Aly had left for him. He now stood between Bronau and the women of his family. Winnamine placed herself in front of Sarai and Pembery, another iron candelabrum in her hand like a sword. Aly couldn't see Dove behind the bulk of the master bed.

"I didn't want this, Mequen, Winna," Bronau said, pain and regret in his voice. "Not a fight. We're all friends, aren't we?"

"Friends don't call at midnight with swords in hand," Mequen retorted.

"Swords don't have to come into play," Bronau said with his charming smile. "We can work this out. All you need do is declare your claim to the throne. Once you are crowned, you'll abdicate in favor of your oldest daughter and her husband—me. You'd like that, wouldn't you, Sarai?" he asked, his voice honey-sweet. "To be queen, clothed and jeweled as your beauty deserves. It could be a step forward for your mother's people. I know you have a sentimental attachment to them." Bronau looked from Mequen to Winnamine. "Don't make me do this," he pleaded.

"Our servants will be at your back momentarily," said the duke. "You can't believe you and ten men can take my daughter and me."

"Of course not. That is why the forty other warriors I've

recruited came onto the plateau after sundown," Bronau informed them. "I *did* notice all those idle raka warriors riding to and fro when I visited here. My lads are combat veterans, not peasants or slaves with arrows and rusty swords. Your gates are now open to my armsmen—I'm afraid we had to kill some of your guards to do that."

"We have a mage," snapped Sarai. "You won't defeat her so easily!"

Bronau smiled as if she were a clever student who had given a good answer. "I thought you might have one by now. I have three. They are keeping your old woman busy, if they haven't killed her yet. Mequen, be sensible. I don't want to kill you. You're going to be my father-in-law."

Aly got her feet under her. She leaped onto the back of the closest man-at-arms. Wrapping her right hand around his chin, she yanked his head back and dragged her left-hand knife across his throat. He choked, staggered, and toppled backward, crushing Aly under his body. She squirmed madly, trying to free herself.

"Papa!" cried Sarai as Winnamine held her back.

Mequen lunged with his sword, chopping at his old friend. Bronau parried the blow with a half-turn, pushing Mequen's blade aside. Mequen kept his sword moving in a sidelong cut that bit into the belly of Bronau's second man-at-arms. The wounded man dropped his torch. Mequen used a bare foot to sweep the soldier's feet from under him, dumping him onto it. The body smothered most of the flames as Mequen blocked another of Bronau's strikes.

Pembery shrieked and hid under the bed, begging the gods for help, as Winnamine and Sarai threw everything they could reach at the third of Bronau's soldiers. Aly cursed as she struggled to free herself of the corpse that weighed her down. The remaining man-at-arms advanced on Winnamine and Sarai, shielding his face from the rain of vases, plates, and cosmetics jars. Aly saw no sign of Dove.

"Don't kill the girl!" shouted Bronau as he hacked the bed curtains by mistake. Mequen cut a long, shallow slice down Bronau's leg, cutting through leather into flesh.

Aly got her right hand free. In it she held a knife. Clenching her teeth, she rose halfway under the dead man's weight and threw the blade. It struck the last man-at-arms on the cheekbone, opening a gash there. He glanced toward Aly with a snarl.

The moment his attention shifted to Aly, Winnamine slammed her candelabrum across his face. The armsman's nose broke with a dull crunch. Ornate metal leaves opened cuts in his eyebrows, cuts that blinded him with blood. Winnamine hit him twice more with all her strength. The soldier's knees gave way.

As he dropped, he lashed out, cutting Mequen's leg. Mequen glanced down and stabbed him through the throat. Then the duke's feet slipped in the armsman's blood. He fell across the downed man's body. As he fought to rise, Bronau ran him through.

"Papa!" Sarai shrieked. She darted past Winnamine and grabbed her father's sword. Facing Bronau, she brought it up to the ready position. "He is your *friend!*" cried Sarai.

Bronau stepped back, raising both hands, though he kept a grip on his sword. "He would be the first to tell you that when a crown's at stake, friendship becomes a luxury." He pointed to Mequen. "I've seen men survive worse. Only swear that you'll marry me and be my queen, and I'll call one of my mages to heal him."

"He lies," Aly croaked, Seeing it in Bronau.

"I know that," snapped Sarai. "His lips move, don't

they?" She lunged, her sword aimed at Bronau's heart. He stepped back, half-pivoting, as her sword cut a bright line across his mail. Sarai caught herself, pivoted, and lunged again.

Bronau seized her blade in gauntleted hands and wrenched it out of Sarai's grip, tossing it aside. As she stumbled, he shoved her onto the bed. "We can do this nicely, or not," he informed her calmly, "but you are going to lead a revolt at my side."

Aly wriggled free of the body that had pinned her. She gripped a knife in her left hand and jumped for Bronau's back, grabbing for his chin with blood-slick fingers. Her hand slipped. Instead she hooked her fingers in his nostrils and pulled, then stabbed blindly. Her dagger scraped bone, not flesh. She'd gotten his jaw by mistake.

Bronau roared and threw himself back, slamming Aly against the unforgiving stone wall. Her ribs cracked. Still she clung, raising her left hand for another slash. He wrenched the knife from her grip, breaking more of her bones, then slammed her into the wall again. Aly's vision went dark. She hung on for her life and dragged on his nose, keeping his head back.

Something thudded into Bronau. Aly couldn't see what it was. He went still, wobbling on his feet. Something else hit him. Aly groped the man's neck until her swelling fingers hit two long, slender shafts buried in his throat. She freed Bronau and shoved him forward. He dropped onto his face. Bracing herself against the wall, Aly looked across the bed. Dove stood on its far side, a bow in her hand. A few griffin-fletched arrows lay on the coverlet where she could reach them.

"Papa," whispered Sarai. She lurched off of the bed

without so much as a glance at the man who would have made her queen, and ran to her father's side. Dove dropped her bow and did the same.

Winnamine grabbed a shirt and knelt beside the girls. Carefully she laid the wadded-up shirt on Mequen's bleeding wound and pressed down with it. "Pressure slows the bleeding," she whispered.

Aly seized a goosefeather bolster from the bed and used it to beat out the small fire that had spread from the second man-at-arms's torch. She used what was left of that to light candles, then stumbled through the study and battered the door to Petranne and Elsren's rooms.

"Who is it?" asked Rihani, her voice shaking with terror. The two younger children were crying.

"Aly. The duke's cut in the belly. Come see to him."

"I don't know if I can help," Rihani protested.

"I'll find Ochobu!" snapped Aly. "Just keep his grace alive!"

She heard furniture scrape. Weeks ago Rihani had been told that, if an attack came, she was to barricade the door, to keep the younger children safe. When the door opened, and Rihani saw Aly, she nodded.

Aly didn't watch her enter the duke's bedroom. She raced down the stairs to the main hall. Her broken left arm hung by one side, limp and bluish purple. Sharp pains stabbed her right side, where she had broken ribs. She prayed they wouldn't puncture her lungs, then ignored them. Without Ochobu, Mequen would die.

Ochobu was not in the great hall. The room was in chaos as Ulasim and a few armed footmen fought nearly thirty invaders, most in leather armor covered with metal rings. This must be what's left of the men Bronau sneaked onto the plateau after dark, Aly thought bitterly. He thought he was evading raka patrols, but he hid them from the crows as well. Had they killed the raka who guarded the road to the pass? They looked like they'd had a fight of some kind, either with the raka or with Veron and his men.

"Stop!" she yelled over the noise. "Bronau is dead! Put down your arms!"

A ruffian grinned up at Aly, his face a blood-streaked mask. "If he's dead, we'll take as we like!" he shouted. "Lots of fine wenches here, and the men will be worth sommat as slaves."

"Oh, we make very bad slaves," someone announced from the main door.

For a moment there was only silence in the great hall. Everyone turned to look at the speaker. It was Nawat. He stood with a bow at the ready, an arrow on the string. Calmly he shot the man who had taunted Aly. The invader fell, in silence. Behind Nawat stood nearly thirty half-naked people, their hair and skin dotted with clumps of gleaming black feathers. Each held a crude weapon of some kind, sickles, hay rakes, cleavers, and kitchen knives.

Nawat placed another arrow on the string. "You were wrong to come here," he said, and shot a man in a chain mail shirt. With that shot the paralysis that had seized the enemy at the sight of Nawat's allies shattered. Trapped between Ulasim and his fighters and Nawat's transformed crows, Bronau's men fought for their lives, and lost them. The crow-people were fast, strong, and merciless. Ulasim and his raka battled ferociously.

Aly watched it all unfold, leaning against the wall as pain throbbed in her chest and broken arm. Only one man reached the stairs where she stood. She gazed at him with the glassy calm of shock, knowing she couldn't possibly defend herself. He collapsed with two of Nawat's arrows in his back.

When the crows and the raka finished, Aly carefully walked down to Nawat. "Ochobu," she told him. Her head was spinning. Her stomach lurched, a warning that she might throw up.

"She holds three mages at the village gate." Nawat selected three arrows with Stormwing fletchings from his quiver. "I will bring her. You sit."

Aly sat. Someone took her torch. She propped her forehead on her good hand, watching as sweat dribbled down her face to splash on the bloody stones of the floor. Here came Ulasim, bleeding from an assortment of cuts. Junai followed. She was unmarked except for a long gouge that sliced her shirt and skin from collarbone to navel. Aly mumbled, "My mother has one just like that, only it's healed."

"Shock," Ulasim said.

"This is broken," replied Junai, lifting Aly's left arm. Aly gasped as the world spun wildly. The gasp brought a stab of agony from her broken ribs.

"Is anyone alive up there?" Ulasim asked. "Our ladies?"

Aly bit her tongue to keep from fainting as Junai tied her wrist to a length of wood. "They're fine," she said when she could talk again. "It's the duke who's hurt." She looked at the open doors. Here came Nawat, supporting Ochobu. The old woman was pale under her brown skin, but no less ferocious for all that.

"Idiot luarin thought he could hold me with three mages," she grumbled as Nawat helped her over to the stair. "Is he alive to learn he can't?"

Aly shook her head and gulped. She was well into shock now, and had reached her least favorite stage of it, nausea.

Her stomach fought to cast out the remains of her supper. "He's dead. And His Grace is belly-cut."

For once Ochobu did not hesitate at the suggestion that she attend a luarin. Instead she let Ulasim help her upstairs. Junai continued to splint Aly's arm.

The great hall fell silent. Everyone cleaned weapons and wounds as they listened to the sounds from the duke's quarters. It was not long before they heard the wail of a woman whose heart was broken.

"Bronau couldn't even judge wounds right," Aly mumbled. "Saying he might still live." Tears slid over her dirty cheeks.

Ulasim walked down the stairs, gray-faced. "His Grace is dead," he told the household.

Aly rested her head back against the wall, wincing as she bumped the knot on her skull. A curse on the Jimajens and their power games, she thought bitterly. A curse on the rulers of this country, Rubinyan and Imajane, who let Bronau escape them. I *will* bring them down. And I *will* put a half-raka queen on the throne if it's the last thing I ever do.

By dawn the changed crow-people had vanished, leaving only some feathers and their abandoned weapons to show they had been there at all. The feathers were set reverently aside by those who cleaned up after the battle.

They lay their own people to rest in the castle's ancient burial ground two days later, in a ceremony that lasted from mid-morning until mid-afternoon. Raka came from all over the plateau to bury their folk and to witness the aftermath of Bronau's greed.

The tally of the dead was painful. Veron had been killed as he defended the castle gate. It no longer seemed to matter that he'd been a royal spy—in his own way he had been loyal. Old Lokeij was gone, but not before he'd cut down three of the enemy with a scythe. Visda and Ekit had lost their father and older brother, who belonged to the raka patrol that had been overwhelmed by Bronau's soldiers. Two dead crows were found in the great hall. They were as honored in their burial as if they'd been human. The slave Hasui had let the enemy in; they found her dead outside the kitchen wing. It was impossible to tell who had murdered her, though Aly suspected Chenaol. The raka cook would never forgive such a betrayal. There was Mequen's body servant to bury, five men-at-arms—three of them the bandits captured on the road from Dimari—and Mequen himself. Fesgao was alive, barely. He attended the funeral on a litter. Winnamine gave him the command of her remaining men-at-arms.

The next day they burned the enemy dead near the road to Dimari. Among them were the three mages who had kept Ochobu from the castle. Nawat collected his Stormwing-fletched arrows from them before Ochobu put the torch to the pyre. Bronau had a pyre of his own. A stony-faced Winnamine collected his ashes and placed them in a box for Rubinyan.

With the funerals over, Winnamine retreated to the family's rooms to mourn her husband. Sarai and Dove took charge of their stepmother and Petranne and Elsren. The younger children were like bewildered ghosts who kept asking for Mequen. Each time they did, Sarai's eyes overflowed with tears as she hugged them and tried to explain. Dove never wept. Watching her small, set face, Aly wished that the younger girl could weep. At least Aly had Nawat to comfort her, and to comfort. Aly could endure her sorrow, having seen battles and their aftermath before. The Balitangs had not. Nawat had not. Tanair had been a peaceful place before the arrival of Bronau, and Nawat was still young for a crow.

* * *

A week passed before the duchess left her seclusion, pale but steely-eyed. The first person she summoned to her seat in the great hall was Aly. "That comes off," she said flatly, pointing to Aly's metal slave collar. "It was pointless before. It is brutally pointless now. You are free under Kyprish law as well as in your own spirit."

Aly bowed her head. For once she didn't argue. The duchess was right. All the plateau knew what she was to the Balitangs now. There was no more advantage to her pretense of being a slave. She reported to the blacksmith. He spoke the spell formula that released the collar, then pulled it open. He even gave her ointment for the red scar at the base of Aly's neck. When it was off, she visited Nawat. He had resumed his old place in the inner courtyard, sitting at his large bench as he fletched arrows in the morning sun. He squinted up at Aly. "Your metal ring is gone," he remarked.

Aly sat gingerly on the far end of his workbench. Ochobu had fixed the breaks in her ribs and arm, to a point. She couldn't heal Aly completely and still have strength to help the many other wounded. Instead Aly had to move very carefully as her bones, secured by a wrapping around her ribs and a splint on her arm, finished mending the natural way. "Yes, the ring is gone. It didn't look good on me anyway. Your clan did a wonderful thing for us. Why didn't they stay?"

Nawat bird-shrugged. "They're about—as crows. They don't like the human shape. They would rather fly."

"Well, thank them for me," Aly told him. "Without them we would have died."

"They were just looking after the wager," Nawat said, putting his arrow aside.

"That's right, Kyprioth had a wager going with the crows, too, separate from the one he's got with me," Aly murmured. "What were the crows' stakes again? I'd forgotten, if I ever knew."

"If the crows help you to live through this changing season, we get a gift from the god," Nawat answered, plainly uninterested. "Now me, I think this form is fine. These human tools interest me." Meeting Aly's eyes, he added, "And human women aren't so bad."

Aly jumped to her feet and winced as her ribs complained. "Now, don't you start. I have too much on my mind."

"I know," said Nawat, looking down at his work. His voice was meek. "And Sarai tells me I must sneak up on you."

Aly fled.

Eight days later, the crows cried the alarm. A full company of one hundred soldiers was marching onto the plateau. When Aly reported it, Winnamine ordered the men-at-arms to the village gates. She followed with a sword at her hip, a bow and a quiver of arrows in her hands. Aly, Sarai, and Dove all raced in her wake, doing their best to keep up with the long-legged woman as they climbed to the watch post over the gate.

When she saw who now stood outside, Winnamine sighed with relief. Aly peered through an arrow slit to see a face she knew: Bronau's cold brother, Rubinyan.

"We're here for my brother," Rubinyan called. "Our mages say he came to you."

"Wait," called the duchess. To the girls she said, "Well, I can't exactly shout the news, can I? They were brothers." She went out to meet him as Sarai, Dove, Aly, and Fesgao watched. Rubinyan dismounted and went aside to talk with her. When his shoulders drooped, Winnamine motioned for the guards to open the gate.

To the relief of Tanair's inhabitants, Rubinyan let his

soldiers camp in a field nearby, not inside the walls. He entered the castle with only a body servant for an attendant. As he rode by, the girls could see he'd been weeping—for Mequen, not Bronau, Winnamine told the girls later.

He spent his first night at Tanair praying for Mequen and Bronau in the village's Mithran shrine. The following night Rubinyan took supper with the Balitang women in their sitting room. Aly was at hand as wine pourer.

"Come back to Rajmuat with me," Rubinyan said, his gray eyes kind as he looked at Winnamine, Sarai, and Dove. His elegant voice sounded warmer than it had in Aly's dreams of the palace. "Oron's order of exile was folly. Imajane and I want you to come home."

Dove and Sarai turned to Winnamine. They would let her decide.

Winnamine gave Rubinyan the weariest of smiles. "Truly, I appreciate the offer," she said. "And I wish to avail myself of it—but will it displease you if I wait until spring? I want to help our people through the winter. Petranne and Elsren would be so upset, uprooting again so soon after Mequen's . . . And, to be honest, we need time to mourn. You know how courtiers are when they feel you've passed beyond what they see as enough time to be sad. They act as if *they're* not sorry any longer, so why should you be?"

"They have no friends of the heart, or they might see how it is, to lose someone they cherish." Rubinyan grimaced. "Courtiers put friends on and off according to fashion. I have never been able to do so." His eyes glittered with unshed tears. He looked aside and hastily blotted them away with his napkin.

Winnamine clasped his arm and squeezed gently. "There. You understand. We will go in the spring, won't we, girls?"

Dove and Sarai nodded.

Covering Winnamine's hand with his, Rubinyan asked, "I may count on your return?"

"As soon as it is safe to sail," Winnamine said.

Rubinyan nodded. "Very good. Oh—I just remembered. We passed a merchant caravan on our way here. They have supplies for you."

He was right. The day after he and his men took the road back to Dimari, Gurhart returned to Tanair. Aly accompanied the young Balitangs to the village to look over the caravan's goods. They didn't notice the tall, broad-shouldered man who slid out of one of the wagons after they passed.

The newcomer walked to the castle and politely requested the honor of a private word with the head of the Balitang family. He emphasized his request with a gold coin to a man-at-arms on duty; another to Fesgao, who still searched him thoroughly for weapons; and finally one more to Ulasim. The footman found Winnamine to report the visitor and the size of the bribes the man had offered.

"Interesting," she said. "By all means, I'll see this Master Cooper—but in the great hall. Ask Ochobu to observe, please, in case he's a mage. Keep your people out of earshot, but arm them with bows in case he tries something. I don't want Aly to scold me for carelessness."

"Very wise, Your Grace." Ulasim smiled at his duchess and escorted her downstairs.

There she found the stranger, a man whose brown hair was lightly shot with gray. He had green-hazel eyes, a big nose, and a mobile, clever mouth. To her experienced eye his clothes looked as if they'd been very good once, but that was some time ago. They were worn but not patched or ragged. When he smiled, he was very charming.

"I am Duchess Winnamine Balitang, head of this

household," she greeted him from her chair on the dais. She glimpsed Ochobu in the shadows under the main stair. Three men-at-arms, each with a crossbow cocked and ready to shoot, stood by the main door. "How may I help you?"

The man bowed gracefully. "It is good of you to put it in just that way, Your Grace," he said. "I'm here as a buyer, if you'll excuse me for talkin' business to so grand a lady as yourself. I deal in slaves. I was told your house bought one I had my eye on, down in Rajmuat. I was short on funds then, but I've come about since. I'm hopin' you'll be minded to sell. She's a little thing, about five feet six, reddish blond hair, hazel eyes. Greenish, like. Fresh caught out of Tortall she was, then. I heard she was a fighter, so it may be you'll be glad to get her off your hands."

Winnamine smiled thinly and raised her hand to stop him. "This is quite distressing, since you came all this way. I must refuse you. Aly is free. I would take it very much amiss if anyone enslaved her again. She is part of our family now."

The stranger looked at her and raised an eyebrow. "For-give my plain speakin', milady, but that makes no sense. Slaves aren't family to nobles."

"Aly saved my life and those of my children recently. It was not the first time she had done so." Winnamine swal-lowed hard and added, "She was injured while trying to save my late husband. We cannot begin to pay her the debt we owe, but we made our start by removing the collar from her neck and burning her sale papers." She looked the man over. There was something familiar about him, in the raised brow, the crooked smile, and the way he seemed aware of every-thing around him, even though he spoke only to her. Sud-denly she realized what it was, and gave him her own little smile. "But you're not *really* here to buy her, are you, sir?" She beckoned to Ulasim, who waited with her guards. The raka came over, his dark eyes suspicious as he looked on their guest. "Ulasim, please have someone fetch Aly from the village," Winnamine ordered. To the newcomer she said, "Would you like tea?"

Down by the caravan, Aly was trying to guide Sarai away from a silver-hilted sword that was more useful as jewelry than as a weapon when a footman raced up to them. "Aly, there's a man looking to buy you up at the castle," he said, panting. "Her Grace sent me for you."

"Nobody's going to buy our Aly!" snapped Sarai, brown eyes ablaze. "Who is this interloper?"

Aly and Dove looked at one another and shrugged. Apparently Sarai was in one of her imperious moods. They followed her to the castle while Aly tried to puzzle through who the visitor might be. She knew that Winnamine wouldn't sell her: she was free, and Winnamine was incapable of playing such a foul trick. But, on the other hand, the duchess had considered the newcomer's request important enough to fetch Aly from the village.

Sarai stamped into the castle's great hall. "What's this nonsense about buying Aly? She's free. She can't leave us."

Winnamine sat at one of the long tables where the servants ate, drinking tea with a man in a worn brown coat. As he turned, Aly froze in shock.

Then she threw herself across the room, shrieking, "Da! Da!"

He knocked a bench over so he could stand and grab her, lifting her in strong arms, holding Aly so tight that her not-quite-healed ribs protested. Aly hugged back just as ferociously, weeping into her father's sensible wool collar. He smelled of crisp air, wood smoke, and faintly of spices, just as he always did.

When they finally let each other go, the great hall was

empty of anyone but them. The duchess had shooed her astonished children and servants away. George held Aly by the shoulders, inspecting her. "Now," he said with a frown, "what is this? Broken nose, eyebrow scar—did we raise such a savage?" His lower-class speech was gone, shed with his identity as a buyer of slaves.

"I did it on purpose, Da," Aly explained. "So nobody would buy me to pop into bed with them. How's Mother? How's the war going? Is she all right? What are Alan and Thom up to? What did Daine and Numair name the baby— the dream was over before I heard it—"

"Aly, a man can answer only one question at a time," George interrupted gently. "The war's winding down to its end at last. King Maggur's on the run—his own nobles hunt him like a deer. Your mother's to come home for a winter's rest. She's been half sick with worry for you. You'll see her, and your brothers, when you come home. Alan told us you weren't dead, but that was all he knew, and he worried. They tell me you're no longer a slave."

Aly's joy vanished, startling her. Of course he would think she was coming home now. Why did the thought of going back to the Swoop seem bad all of a sudden? What had happened to her? And if she didn't go back, how would she explain it? "Duchess Winnamine freed me, Da, but that's not why I didn't come home. I'd've done it as soon as I got here, but . . ." She fumbled for the right words. "Things are complicated."

George sat and patted the bench seat next to him. "How?" he asked.

Aly rubbed the back of her neck and sighed, then took a seat. "Oh, Da, there's a god. We had a wager, see. I was to keep the Balitang children alive till the autumn equinox, and if I did, he'd send me home and talk to you about letting me work as a spy, or bodyguard, or something. It's not equinox yet."

"A god laid you a wager?" Her father's voice was dangerously smooth. "Which god would this be?"

"Kyprioth," Aly said. "He's a local god—"

"*Kyprioth,*" her father said with disgust. "I might have known. Show yourself, you miserable piece of Stormwing dung," he said, his voice still quiet. "I know you're listening. You're vain as a cat when anyone speaks your name."

The main doors swung open. Kyprioth entered the room in a blaze of sunlight. Today he wore the guise he most favored, the leanly muscled, brown-skinned man with short salt-and-pepper hair and a close-clipped beard. He wore a cloth-of-gold wraparound jacket today and a sarong that looked as if it were woven copper. Jeweled rings gleamed on his fingers; jeweled bracelets shone on his wrists and ankles.

"There you are, George," Kyprioth said cheerily. "How are you, my good fellow? It's been ages."

Aly's father stood and crossed his arms over his chest, his eyes glittering dangerously. "You've been hiding Aly from her mother and our mage friends," he accused.

"Of course." Kyprioth took a bench from the next table and dragged it over, unmindful of the screech of wood on the flagstone floor. Once he placed it opposite Aly's bench, he reclined on it, propping his head on his hand. "I needed her. I couldn't have you trying to rescue her all the time. Not, may I add, that she has ever needed rescue."

"You steal my daughter and then you hide her from me. Is this the way you reward my service?" demanded George. "Aly's no pawn of yours, to be whisked in and out of your mad tricks."

Kyprioth eyed one of the gems on his rings, turning it this way and that in the sunlight. It was a clear stone, cut into multiple tiny flat surfaces that threw off light like miniature rainbows. "Such fatherly wrath. I would be terrified, except, well, I'm not."

"Let's end this," George said firmly. "When we declared our association done, you swore in blood that you owed me a debt, and I might call on that. Well, here it is. I want my daughter home. Pay up, Trickster."

Kyprioth gazed at Aly. "I don't really see anything fatal coming in the time between now and the equinox, not when my cousin North Wind has decided to remind mortals of his power. We're going to have an early winter—just as effective as fortress walls for keeping bad people away from the Balitangs. Aly, I absolve you of the remaining time on our wager. You have won. George, be a good boy and put her talents to use. If you don't, I'm sure I can arrange something so that it will be *necessary* for you to make use of her. She can't be a child any longer. She has moved among adults and changed the courses of their lives, you know." Kyprioth sat up. "Well, if there's nothing else . . . ?"

From the moment he'd declared an end to their wager and Aly the winner, her brain had been in an uproar. She could go home. She could see her mother again, her adoptive family, Daine and Numair's baby, her brothers, her grandparents. She could wear fashionable gowns and toy with young noblemen. If the war was near an end, there would be a fresh crop of romantic young knights and soldiers to cut a swathe through. The lure of home was like a mermaid's song that pulled her irresistibly east. Nawat had said he would go with her when it came time for her to leave.

But.

Mequen had been kind to her, kinder than most masters were to slaves or even free servants. He'd died for the blood in his veins. The throne was held by a three-year-old and the most predatory, grasping pair of humans Aly had ever seen, while royal blood flowed in the veins of Mequen's children, making them a threat to the regents.

The raka. The fire in Ulasim's eyes as he watched Sarai practice her combat dances. The silent rows of natives that had lined the way to Dimari just to see their promised queen. Lokeij, dead because he had defended his hope for the future. Junai, patient, silent, and deadly. Sarai and Dove themselves, with their passion, intelligence, and ideals, their love for the raka and their ties to the luarin.

She had made a promise to herself on the night Mequen died.

About to surprise herself and her father, Aly hesitated—and then she saw it. "*You*," she said furiously to Kyprioth.

He actually batted his eyes at her. "Yes, dear?"

George rested a hand on Aly's shoulder. "Lass, I don't like the look on your face."

Aly still spoke to Kyprioth. "You knew this would happen, curse you. You wove me into your festering, pustulant great trick. You didn't wager my summer. You bet that I wouldn't want to leave."

"Well, I didn't *wager*, actually," the god said modestly. "I hoped, that was all, with all the hope in my withered god's heart. You know, I do owe you a boon. I could repay it now, erase all memory of this place and these people and send you back to Tortall. No doubt your queen needs a lady-in-waiting who's good with lock picks. Or her daughter, who's now Empress of Carthak, might need you even more. Say the word, and I will let you go."

Aly scowled at him. "I'm going to make your life a misery," she informed him.

"I look forward to it," said Kyprioth.

George sighed. "I think it's very good of me to wait whilst the two of you talk in a code I don't know. I'll say this—I'm starting to dislike what I hear."

"Return his boon," Aly ordered the god. "You can't cheat and make him use it when I won't go along."

Kyprioth delivered himself of a broad, dramatic sigh. "Very well," he said, and looked at George. "I still owe you a boon, since I can't grant this one, not without her agreement." He looked at Aly. "This summer was just a trial run, and an easy one at that. Things will be much more difficult from here on. There will be more to lose, and more elements to keep track of."

Aly shrugged. "In for a garnet, in for a ruby," she said. "They're both the same to me. And it's not like I won't have plenty of help."

George crossed his arms over his chest. "You're staying? Why?"

Aly stood and hugged him. "You'd do the same in my place. So would Mother," she explained softly. "These are good people, Da. I want to keep them alive so Kyprioth can complete his great trick—putting a raka queen, not a luarin king, on the throne. You and Mother wanted me to do something with my life. Well, here it is. He—" She looked at Kyprioth. The god had vanished. *I'll deal with *you* later,* she thought. She looked back into her father's eyes and smiled slyly. "I'm sure Their Majesties will be interested in knowing that the raka plan to rise."

George raised his brows. "Will you spy for us here, then?" he asked drily. "Since seemingly I've no choice but to accommodate you."

Aly shook her head. "I can't, Da. The Balitangs don't know what my real family is, and I want to keep it that way.

You're a merchant to them, and Mother a Player who left us after bearing me." In response to her father's shocked look, Aly shrugged. "I wasn't about to say she was dead, that's all. For now, I remain in service to the Balitangs. They would never allow me to stay if they thought I worked for a rival kingdom. No, this will be for them, and the raka. For all those with luarin blood who might die if the revolt can't be, um, *guided* into a shape that fits old blood and new." She swallowed hard. "I think Mother will understand."

George Cooper sighed. "And so she and I get what we'd wished for, only to find we don't care for the form it's taken. We asked you to assume your place in the world, to live and work as a woman. You have done so, but it's a bitter reward for us. Your mother will understand all too well. I should have known that no daughter of hers would choose the easy road." He kissed the top of her head. "Anything for a poor traveling man to eat, then?" he asked.

Aly looked around to see if a servant was nearby, or if she'd have to go beg Chenaol for something. To her surprise, she saw that one of the double doors was open. Nawat stood there, an arrow shaft in one hand, watching her as she held another man.

"Oh, my," Aly said, releasing her father. "Um. Da, there's someone you should meet. Nawat?" She beckoned to him.

"Nawat?" George asked as the crow-man walked over to them.

"Nawat Crow, Da. He's a friend of mine." When Nawat reached her, she rested a hand on his arm. "Nawat, this is my father."

George inspected the younger man from head to toe, then looked at his daughter. Without a word he cocked one eyebrow.

She raised one of hers in reply.

* * *

George remained for three days, charming the Balitangs and talking with his daughter on long walks. At last it came time for the merchant caravan to leave, before the first snows closed the road through the pass. George went with them, waving to his daughter until he could no longer see her. Aly watched him until, even with her Sight, she could no longer see him. When he was gone from view, she wiped her eyes on her sleeve and called herself various kinds of stupid for allowing herself to be drawn into revolution.

A shadow passed over her. Instinctively she looked up. There, high overhead, a kudarung circled, riding the columns of hot air that rose from the rocky hills at the edge of the plateau. Alone it glided, chestnut wings cutting through the golden air of early fall.

"It's going to be an interesting spring," she muttered.

The air around her filled with Kyprioth's rich, merry chuckle.

CAST OF CHARACTERS

Alan of Pirate's Swoop	Alianne's sixteen-year-old twin brother, a third-year page
Alanna of Pirate's Swoop and Olau	the King's Champion, lady knight
Alianne of Pirate's Swoop	daughter of Alanna the Lioness and George, baron of Pirate's Swoop
Arak	herding dog
Athan Fajering	disgraced luarin nobleman
Bonedancer	living Archaeopteryx (dinosaur bird) skeleton
Bronau Jimajen	non-royal luarin prince of the Copper Isles
Buri (Buriram)	former commander of the Queen's Riders
Chenaol	free raka servant and head cook for the Balitangs
Cinnamon	Aly's chestnut mare

Coram Smythesson	baron of Tortall
Daine (Veralidaine)	half-goddess, called the Wildmage for her skills with animals, Aly's adoptive aunt
Darkmoon	Alanna's horse
Dilsubai Haiming	last raka queen of the Copper Isles
Dovasary (Dove)	Mequen's half-raka daughter from first marriage
Dunevon	King Oron's youngest child, son of third marriage, heir to Hazarin
Ekit	Visda's brother, Tanair herdboy, raka
Eleni of Olau	Aly's grandmother
Elsren	Mequen's second full-luarin child with Winnamine
Falthin	part-raka bowyer at Tanair
Fesgao	raka man-at-arms who protects Sarai and Dove

Gary (Gareth the Younger)	heir to fief Naxen, King Jonathan's principal advisor
George of Pirate's Swoop	Alanna's husband and Aly's father, baron and second-in-command of his realm's spies
Grace	herding dog
Graveyard Hag	trickster and primary goddess of Carthak, Kyprioth's kinswoman
Gurhart	part-raka merchant, caravan leader
Hanoren	son of King Oron's second marriage
Hasui	part-raka kitchen slave and royal spy
Hazarin	King Oron's half brother
Ianjai	wealthy raka merchant family
Imajane	King Oron's half sister
Imiary VI	second-to-last raka queen

Imrah of Legann	lord, knight-master to Prince Roald
Jafana	former luarin nursemaid to Petranne and Elsren
Jonathan of Conté	king of Tortall
Junai Dodeka	raka daughter of Ulasim, Aly's guard
Kaddar Iliniat	emperor of Carthak
Keladry of Mindelan	called Kel, lady knight
Kyprioth	trickster god
Landfall	Tortallan spy in Scanra
Lokeij	raka hostler for the Balitangs
Ludas Jimajen	second-in-command of the luarin invasion of the Copper Isles
Maggur Rathhausak	Scanran king and warlord
Maude Tanner	housekeeper and healer at Pirate's Swoop
Mequen	exiled luarin duke, head of the Balitang family

Musenda Ogunsanwo (Sarge)	training master of the Queen's Riders
Myles of Olau, baron	Aly's grandfather, head of royal intelligence service (spies)
Nawat Crow	a crow who turned himself into a man
Numair Salmalín	powerful mage, Daine's husband
Nuritin	Duke Mequen's luarin aunt
Ochobu Dodeka	raka mage and mother of Ulasim
Onua Chamtong	horsemistress to the Queen's Riders
Oron Rittevon	mentally-ill king of the Copper Isles
Pembery	part-raka, slave of the Balitang family
Petranne	Mequen's first child with Winnamine
Pilia	Pohon resident, watches Ochobu's house

Raoul of Goldenlake and Malorie's Peak	lord, Knight Commander of the King's Own, Tortallan hero, known as the Giant Killer
Rihani	raka healer
Rispah	baroness of Trebond
Rittevon of Lenman	leader of luarin invasion
Rubinyan Jimajen	luarin husband of Princess Imajane, Bronau's older brother
Saraiyu (Sarai)	Mequen's oldest daughter, half-raka, from his first marriage
Sarra	Daine's mother, now the minor goddess The Green Lady
Sarugani of Temaida	Mequen's first wife, raka, mother of Dove and Sarai, died in a tragic riding accident
Thayet of Conté	Queen of Tortall, co-ruler with her husband, King Jonathan

Thom of Pirate's Swoop	Aly's eighteen-year-old brother, a student mage
Tulpa	miller's daughter at Tanair
Tyananne	widowed luarin noblewoman
Ulasim	free raka servant and head footman to the Balitangs
Veron	luarin sergeant in command of the Balitang men-at-arms
Visda	raka niece of Chenaol, goat herder
Winnamine	exiled duchess, Mequen's second wife
Wyldon of Cavall	lord, district commander of Tortall's army in the north
Zeburon	royal council member, enemy of Rubinyan

GLOSSARY

Ambririp: harbor on northern tip of Imahyn Island.

Arak: distilled palm-sap liquor.

Azure Sea: body of water between Imahyn, Jerykun, Ikang, and Lombyn islands, known for its calm, bright blue waters.

Bay Cove: village one day's sail southeast of Pirate's Swoop.

Bazhir: collective name for the nomadic tribes of Tortall's Great Southern Desert.

Black God, the: the hooded and robed god of death, recognized as such throughout the Eastern and Southern Lands.

Carthak: slaveholding empire that includes all of the Southern Lands, ancient and powerful, a storehouse of learning, sophistication, and culture. Its university was at one time without rival for teaching.

centaur: an immortal (cannot be killed by old age or disease), half horse, half human; attitudes to mortal humans vary.

Conqueror's Laws: laws enacted by the luarin conquerors of the Copper Isles, exacting heavy penalties (seizure of lands and monies, slavery for rebel families, executions of leaders of any rebellion, mass executions where a noble luarin is killed) paid by members of the subject raka people should any harm befall their luarin masters.

Copper Isles: originally named the Kyprish Isles, once ruled by queens of the Haiming noble house, presently ruled by the Rittevon dynasty. The Isles form a slaveholding nation south and west of Tortall. The lowlands are hot, wet jungles; the highlands cold and rocky. Traditionally their ties are to Carthak rather than Tortall. Kyprish pirates often raid along the Tortallan coast. There is a strain of insanity in the Rittevon line. The Rittevons hold a grudge against Tortall (one of their princesses was killed there the day that Jonathan was crowned).

Corus: capital city of Tortall, on the banks of the River Olorun. Corus is the home of the new royal university as well as the royal palace.

Dawn Crow: male god of the crows.

Dimari: eastern harbor town on the island of Lombyn.

Divine Realms: home to the gods and to many immortals.

Dominion Jewel: magical artifact presently held by the Tortallan kings, a round purple gem that draws those under its influence to form tighter national bonds and tighter connections between the wielder of the Jewel and the land that forms the nation under its influence.

Eastern Lands: name used to refer to those lands north of the Inland Sea and east of the Emerald Ocean: Scanra, Tortall, Tyra, Tusaine, Galla, Maren, Sarain. Original home of the luarin nobility and kings of the Copper Isles.

Ekallatum: one of the most ancient kingdoms in the history of the Southern Lands, now part of the Carthaki Empire.

Emerald Ocean: body of water west of the Eastern and Southern Lands, containing the Yamani Islands and the Copper Isles, among others.

Fief Tameran: neighboring fiefdom to Pirate's Swoop.

Frasrlund: Tortallan port city at the mouth of the Vassa, straddling the border with Scanra.

Galla: country to the north and east of Tortall, famous for its mountains and forests, with an ancient royal line. Daine was born there.

Gempang: island in the Copper Isles, on the opposite side of the Long Strait from Kypriang.

Gift, the: human, academic magic, the use of which must be taught.

Gigit: a copper coin, smallest coin of the Copper Isles.

Grand Progress, the: a two-year circuit (457 H.E.–458 H.E.) of the realm of Tortall made by the monarchs King Jonathan and Queen Thayet, accompanied by their heir, Roald, and his betrothed, Princess Shinkokami, of the Yamani Islands. The Progress included tournaments; festivities; scholarly, medical, and legal research; aid for areas afflicted by nature or attack; meetings with immortal residents; and appraisal of worsening military relations with Scanra.

Great Mother Goddess: chief goddess in the pantheon of the Eastern Lands, protector of women. Her symbol is the moon.

griffin: a feathered immortal with a catlike body, wings, and a beak. Males grow to a height of six and a half to seven feet at the shoulder; females are slightly bigger. No one can tell lies in a griffin's vicinity (a range of about a hundred feet). Their young have bright orange feathers to make them more visible. If adult griffin parents sense that a human has handled their infant griffin, they will try to kill that human.

Gunapi the Sunrose: raka warrior goddess of volcanoes, war, and molten rock.

healer: a health-care professional with varying degrees of education, magic, and skill.

his realm's spies: network of a kingdom's agents, charged with gathering intelligence at home and abroad; spies in service to a particular country.

hostler: one who cares for horses: their feed, medicine, grooming, cleanliness, saddling.

Human Era (H.E.): the calendar in use in the Eastern and Southern Lands and in the Copper Isles is dated the Human Era to commemorate the years since the one in which the immortals were originally sealed into the Divine Realms, over four hundred and fifty years previous to the years covered by Protector of the Small.

hurrok: immortal shaped like a horse with leathery bat wings, claws, and fangs.

Ikang: island to the southwest of Lombyn (the northernmost island).

Imahyn: island just northwest of the Long Strait and Gempang.

Immortals War: short, vicious war fought in 452 H.E., named for the number of immortal creatures that fought, but also waged by Carthakis (rebels against the new emperor Kaddar), Copper Islanders, and Scanran raiders. These forces were defeated by the residents of the Eastern Lands, particularly Tortall, but recovery is slow.

Inti: westernmost village on Tanair estates on the island of Lombyn. Inti is astride the road leading down to the west coast of Lombyn.

Kellaura Pass: opening on the Dimari Road through the Turnshe Mountains on Lombyn, leads to Tanair and other estates.

King's Council: the monarch's private council of advisors, made up of those people he trusts the most.

King's Own: cavalry/police group answering to the king, whose members serve as royal bodyguards and as protective troops throughout the realm. Their Knight Commander is Lord Sir Raoul of Goldenlake and Malorie's Peak. The ranks are filled by younger sons of noble houses, Bazhir, and the sons of wealthy merchants. The Own is made of three companies of one hundred fighters each, in addition to the servingmen, who care for supplies and remounts. First Company, a show company, traditionally provides palace bodyguards and security for the monarchs. Under Lord Raoul, Second and Third Company were added and dedicated to active service away from the palace, helping to guard the realm.

kudarung: Kyprin (raka) term for winged horses.

Kypriang: capital island of the Copper Isles, holding the capital, Rajmuat, and its harbor. Location of the Plain of Sorrows, site of the last great defeat of the raka by the luarin.

Kyprioth: the Trickster, greatest of the trickster gods, former patron god of the Copper Isles, overthrown by his brother Mithros and his sister the Great Goddess, now relegated in the Isles to rulership over the seas that surround them. Cousin to the Carthaki goddess the Graveyard Hag.

Lombyn: northernmost island of the Copper Isles, home to the Tanair estates of Lady Saraiyu and Lady Dove Balitang, the legacy of their mother Sarugani. The location of the Turnshe Mountains, Kellaura Pass, Dimari town and harbor, and the villages of Tanair, Inti, and Pohon.

Long Strait: the narrow, tricky body of water between Kypriang and Gempang Islands.

luarin: raka (native of the Copper Isles) term for the white-skinned invaders from the Eastern Lands, now used in the Isles to indicate anyone with white skin.

mage: a wizard, male or female.

Maren: large, powerful country east of Tusaine and Tyra; the grain basket of the Eastern Lands, with plenty of farms and trade.

Mastiff: fort that serves Lord Wyldon as command post during events in *Lady Knight*.

matcher: a slavebroker who deals in matching experienced slaves with owners who will pay top price for them; some owners insist that matchers only sell slaves to buyers who will treat them well. Many are also talent spotters, operating schools at which they groom slaves for particular tasks before they are sold at a higher rate than the slave would have gotten originally. Some matchers have magical Gifts that help them to spot talent, both magical and non-magical.

Midwinter Festival: seven-day holiday centering around the longest night of the year and the sun's rebirth afterward. It is the beginning of the new year. Gifts are exchanged and feasts held.

Mithros: chief god of the Tortallan pantheon, god of war and the law. His symbol is the sun.

Plain of Sorrows: site of the biggest and last defeat of the Copper Isles' native raka people by the white, or luarin, invaders (opportunists from the Eastern Lands). The battle that broke the power of the Haiming royal line and of the great noble houses of the Copper Isles, and set the Rittevon kings on the Isles' throne.

Pohon: village on the northern border of the Tanair estates on the island of Lombyn. The raka of Pohon are notoriously inhospitable to their luarin overlords.

Port Caynn: port city that serves the Tortallan capital of Corus.

Port Legann: the southwestern port city of Tortall, ruled by Lord Imrah and his lady.

Queen's Riders: cavalry/police group that protects Tortallans who live in hard-to-reach parts of the country. They enforce the law and teach local residents to defend themselves. The basic unit is a Rider Group, with eight to nine members. Rank in a Group is simply that of commander and second-in-command; the head of the Riders is the Commander. They accept both women and men in their ranks, unlike the army, the navy, and the King's Own. Their headquarters lies between the palace and the Royal Forest.

Rajmuat: capital of the Copper Isles under both the raka and the luarin.

raka: copper/brown-skinned natives of the Copper Isles, under the lordship of the luarin arrivals from the Eastern Lands for nearly three hundred years.

Royal Forest: vast forest that blankets land south and west of Corus for several days' ride.

Scanra: country to the north of Tortall; wild, rocky, and cold, with very little land that can be farmed. Scanrans are masters of the sea and are feared anywhere there is a coastline. They also frequently raid over land. In recent years, their Great Council (formerly the Council of Ten, expanded in the disruptions following the Immortals War), made up of the heads of the clans, elected the warlord Maggur Rathhausak to be their king. The war with Tortall began in 460 H.E. (the events are covered in *Lady Knight*) and has moved into its second year, though Scanra is visibly weakening.

scry: to look into the present, future, or past using magic and, sometimes, a bowl of water, a mirror, fire, or some other device to peer into.

shape-shifter: one who can take the shape of an animal or another human. Those who shift into immortal form are unable to change back.

Sight, the: aspect of the magical Gift that gives its holders certain advantages in matters of vision. It can be erratic, showing holders only lies, illness, magic, or future importance. In its fullest form, it can allow the holder to see clearly over distance, see tiny things in sharp detail, and to detect illness, lies, godhood, magic, death, and other aspects of life.

Sky: the crow goddess, consort of the Dawn Crow.

Southern Lands: another name for the Carthaki Empire,

which has conquered all of the independent nations that once were part of the continent south of the Inland Sea.

spidren: immortal whose body is that of a furred spider four to five feet in height; its head is that of a human with sharp, silvery teeth. Spidrens can use weapons. They also use their webs as weapons and ropes. Spidren web is gray-green in color and it glows after dark. Their blood is black and burns like acid. Their favorite food is human blood.

Stormwing: immortal with a human head and chest and bird legs and wings, with steel feathers and claws. Stormwings have very sharp teeth, but use them only to add to the terror of their presence by tearing apart bodies. They live on human fear and have their own magic; their special province is the desecration of battlefield dead.

Tanair: Lombyn Isle estates that form part of the inheritance of Lady Saraiyu and Lady Dove Balitang, granted to them by their mother, Sarugani Temaida. Estates include Tanair castle and village, and the villages of Inti and Pohon.

Thak: language of old Carthak, used as a magical language in present times.

Tongkang: island to the south of Gempang, between Gempang and Malubesang Isles.

Tortall: chief kingdom in which the Alanna, Daine, and Keladry sagas take place, between the Inland Sea and Scanra. Home to Alianne of Pirate's Swoop and her family.

Trebond: birthplace of Alanna the Lioness, now held by Baron Coram and his wife, Rispah.

Turnshe Mountains: central mountains of Lombyn, stretching from the northern point of the island to the southern point. Travel in northern Lombyn is through the Kellaura Pass on the Dimari Road.

Tusaine: small country tucked between Tortall and Maren.

Tyra: merchant republic on the Inland Sea between Tortall and Maren. Tyra is mostly swamp, and its people rely on trade and banking for income. Numair Salmalín was born there.

Vassa River: river that forms a large part of the northeastern border between Scanra and Tortall.

wild magic: magic that is part of the natural world. Unlike the human Gift, it cannot be drained or done away with; it is always present.

wildmage: mage who deals in wild magic, the kind of magic that is part of nature. Daine Sarrasri is often called the Wildmage for her ability to communicate with animals, heal them, and shape-shift.

Wind: Kyprioth's cousin, a god.

Yamani Islands: island nation to the north and west of Tortall and the west of Scanra, ruled by an ancient line of emperors, whose claim to their throne comes from the goddess Yama. The country is beautiful and mountainous. Its vulnerability to pirate raids means that most Yamanis, including the women, get some training in combat arts. Keladry of Mindelan lived there for six years while her father was the Tortallan ambassador.

TAMORA PIERCE captured the imagination of readers twenty years ago with *Alanna: The First Adventure*. As of August 2003 she has written twenty-one books, including three completed quartets—The Song of the Lioness, The Immortals, and The Protector of the Small—set in the fantasy realm of Tortall. She has also written the Circle of Magic and The Circle Opens quartets. Her books have been translated into many different languages, and many are available on audio. Tamora Pierce's fast-paced, suspenseful writing and strong, believable heroines have won her much praise: *Emperor Mage* was a 1996 ALA Best Book for Young Adults, *The Realms of the Gods* was listed as an "outstanding fantasy novel" by *VOYA* in 1996, *Squire* (Protector of the Small #3) was a 2002 ALA Best Book for Young Adults, and *Lady Knight* (Protector of the Small #4) debuted at #1 on the *New York Times* bestsellers list.

An avid reader herself, Ms. Pierce graduated from the University of Pennsylvania. She has worked at a variety of jobs and has written everything from novels to radio plays. Along with writer Meg Cabot (The Princess Diaries series), she co-founded Sheroes Central, a discussion board about female heroes, remarkable women in fact, fiction, and history, books, and teen issues. She now runs Sheroes Central and Sheroes Fans with the help of her beloved Spouse-Creature and dedicated board members of all ages.

Tamora Pierce lives in New York City with her husband, Tim, a writer and Web page designer and administrator, and their four cats, two birds, and various rescued wildlife.

For more information visit:
www.tamora-pierce.com

Sheroes Central at:
www.sheroescentral.com